KP

Cavan County L
Withdrawn S

D0343890

Class No. _____ F _____   Acc No. C/135727

Author: _Evans, P_   Loc: ~~1 JUN 2003~~

LEABHARLANN
CHONDAE AN CHABHAIN

~~1 1 OCT 2008~~

1. **This book may be kept three weeks. It is to be returned on / before the last date stamped below.**
2. **A fine of 25c will be charged for every week or part of week a book is overdue.**

1 8 JUL 2003

2 6 AUG 2003

1 8 DEC 2003

2 4 FEB 2004

- 2 APR 2004

2 8 APR 2004

1 8 MAY 2004

1 0 SEP 2004

1 7 NOV 2004

3 1 AUG 2005

1 1 JAN 2006

7 - MAR 2006

- 3 APR 2009

1 MAY 2010

THE PRIDE OF PARK STREET

Also by Pamela Evans

A Barrow in the Broadway
Lamplight on the Thames
Maggie of Moss Street
Star Quality
Diamonds in Danby Walk
A Fashionable Address
Tea-Blender's Daughter
The Willow Girls
Part of the Family
Town Belles
Yesterday's Friends
Near and Dear
A Song in your Heart
The Carousel Keeps Turning
A Smile for all Seasons
Where We Belong
Close to Home
Always There

THE PRIDE OF PARK STREET

Pamela Evans

headline

Copyright © 2003 Pamela Evans

The right of Pamela Evans to be identified as the Author of
the Work has been asserted by her in accordance with the
Copyright, Designs and Patents Act 1988.

First published in 2003
by HEADLINE BOOK PUBLISHING

10 9 8 7 6 5 4 3 2 1

All rights reserved. No part of this publication may be
reproduced, stored in a retrieval system, or transmitted,
in any form or by any means without the prior written
permission of the publisher, nor be otherwise circulated
in any form of binding or cover other than that in which
it is published and without a similar condition being
imposed on the subsequent purchaser.

All characters in this publication are fictitious
and any resemblance to real persons, living or dead,
is purely coincidental.

Cataloguing in Publication Data is
available from the British Library

ISBN 0 7553 0040 8

Typeset in Times by
Letterpart Limited, Reigate, Surrey

Printed and bound in Great Britain by
Mackays of Chatham plc, Chatham, Kent

HEADLINE BOOK PUBLISHING
A division of Hodder Headline
338 Euston Road
LONDON NW1 3BH

www.headline.co.uk
www.hodderheadline.com

CAVAN COUNTY LIBRARY
ACC. No. C/135.727
CLASS No. F
INVOICE NO. 5317 Ebl
PRICE €21.16

To Martin, Julie, Simon, Hannah, Millie, Max and Samuel,
with love.

Chapter One

Stage fright usually reached epidemic proportions backstage before a show, and Jess Mollitt wasn't the only one quivering as she stood in the chorus line to the rear of the stage at the London Palladium, poised in the starting position behind the closed curtains. Adding to the tension were the television monitors visible in the wings, a daunting reminder that the show was going out live.

Stunning in sequined leotards with fishnet tights, and spangled skull-cap headdresses topped with feathers, the entire troupe had their heads turned towards the wings, eyes fixed on the commercials flashing by on the screens. Every nerve jangled; every heart lurched when the famous curtains in front of them appeared on the monitors, indicating that the show was about to start.

Trembling with a mixture of terror and excitement, but focusing her mind determinedly on the forthcoming dance routine, Jess barely noticed the punishing tightness of her costume or the choking elastic under her chin that was supplementing the sixty or so hairgrips holding her headdress in place.

Then came the desperate whisper of the girl next in line, who was a relative newcomer. 'I can't do it. I can't go on, Jess. I feel sick and my legs are about to give way. I'll ruin the line and make fools of us all.'

'No you won't. It's natural to feel nervous before a show, especially when the TV cameras are around. I'm a bag of nerves too,' she admitted through dry lips. 'But we'll be fine once we get started. I don't know how it works but it always does. Nerves keep you sharp. We need them.'

'I don't need to feel like this.'

'Fear makes our performance good; it gets the adrenalin flowing.' Jess hoped she sounded more convincing than she actually felt. 'You'll be all right, believe me.'

From the wings the countdown was progressing – six . . . five . . . four . . . Panic shot through her and her mind went blank; legs like jelly, feet cemented to the spot – total paralysis. The end of her career loomed; she'd lose the job if she messed up. There was no place in a troupe of this calibre for dancers who couldn't control their nerves. So much for her words of encouragement now.

But then the curtains swished back and somehow she went with the others, the famous Burton Girls in a straight line, arms linked and smiling as they high-kicked down the stage towards the packed auditorium, in the glare of the hot television lights.

As the applause rose and continued, fear turned to elation. It filled and lifted her; gave wings to her feet. Behind the beaming professional smile and the shining sloe-black eyes, Jess was concentrating on the steps. The nerves, the stress, the long punishing rehearsals – all were worth it. Dancing was in her blood and she loved every moment.

It was a privilege to perform on this world-famous stage; an experience she would never forget. She wanted it over, yet at the same time, wished it would never end. Into a mind fixed firmly on her feet, came a heart-warming image of her family at home, glued to the television set, watching the show. Sharing her career with them meant *so much* to her.

'There she is!' cried Libby Mollitt, leaping up from her seat and stabbing her finger at the screen excitedly, eyes fixed on her adored older sister. 'Cor, doesn't she look smashing? Isn't she just the best dancer you've ever seen?'

A roar of agreement filled the Mollitt living room, cosy and traditional, the french doors opened on to the small back garden on this warm summer evening.

'Out of the way, Libs,' requested her twin brother, Ronnie, a dark-eyed thirteen-year-old with a bean-pole figure, the long unruly limbs of adolescence, and a boyish voice alternating suddenly with bursts of Louis Armstrong. 'We can't see a thing with your fat bum stuck in front of the telly.'

'My bum isn't fat, moron,' objected Libby with typical sisterly outrage. She and Ronnie rarely agreed about anything. An exuberant girl, Libby was smaller than he, with the same dark eyes, and near-black hair, which she held back from her face with an Alice band. 'It isn't fat, is it, Mum?'

'Of course it isn't, love,' soothed her mother, rather absently because she was preoccupied with the show.

'It is from where I'm sitting.' Ronnie thought it was great fun to tease his sister.

'I wouldn't want to be as skinny as you.' Libby was a match for him and never short of an answer. 'You'll disappear down a drain hole one of these days and end up in a sewer.' She grinned, relishing her next piece of suitably cutting dialogue. 'Still, you'll be at home with all the rats down there, won't you?'

'Oh, very funny.'

'Move away from the telly and sit down, please, Libby,' came the reasonable request from Joy Mollitt, a tall, pretty woman in her middle forties with small features, dark eyes and shortish black hair peppered with grey. 'The rest of us want to see Jess just as much as you do.'

2

'That's right, Mum, you tell her,' was Ronnie's triumphant cry as Libby returned to her chair.

'Don't be smug, please, Ronnie, and stop annoying your sister.' As sibling rivalry was a natural part of family life and the twins were always at it, Joy's admonition was more of an automatic reaction than a serious rebuke. Of a placid nature anyway, she was far more interested in seeing her long-legged first-born dancing across the television screen than the twins' petty bickering, which was – as everyone knew – just an inherent part of their closeness, and they thrived on it. Eyes shining with pride, Joy's maternal empathy was such that she could feel her eldest daughter's every step, each uncertain heartbeat.

Libby threw her brother a victorious look. 'Good. Now that Mum's told you to stop aggravating me perhaps I'll get some peace at last,' she said.

'Don't bank on it.'

'For goodness' sake, pack it in, the pair of you, and let the rest of us enjoy the show,' came a stern intervention from their father, Charlie, a large, jolly man who'd been around for almost half a century. He had a cheery muddle of a face: a pug nose, lopsided mouth and warm hazel eyes – all set rather chaotically in a frame as round as the walnut clock on the mantelpiece, and topped with greying hair combed neatly into place with a side parting.

'Ronnie started it,' claimed Libby.

Her brother pushed his floppy dark hair from his face. 'That's right, blame me,' he objected.

'Of course I'll blame you, because you did start it, with your stupid remarks.'

'Enough,' boomed their father in a tone that finally silenced them. He was an amiable man but would take no nonsense.

'Sorry, Dad,' said Libby.

'Me too,' added Ronnie.

'Is Jess coming over tomorrow, Mum?' enquired Libby, turning her attention back to the screen. 'I can't wait to see her and hear all about the show.'

'Yes, she'll be over for Sunday tea as usual, I expect, if she doesn't have a rehearsal,' replied her mother, eyes fixed firmly on the television images of her daughter.

'Good, I'll look forward to that.'

'It's great having a sister on the telly,' mentioned Ronnie. 'Really impresses 'em at school.'

'Yeah,' said Libby in a rare moment of agreement. 'No one else has got anything as good as that.'

'Even though she's been on before, it still seems weird seeing her there,' observed the youngest of the Mollitt brood, ten-year-old Todd, who was a quiet, studious boy with the sweetest of temperaments; he was

3

much less gregarious than his elder siblings. He got up and squinted through his spectacles at a photograph of a dark-haired young woman in pride of place on top of the TV set, then looked back at the screen. 'It doesn't look like Jess on there. Not to me, anyway.'

'Probably because of the stage make-up,' observed Hilda Hawkins, who lived next door. 'Especially as her hair's all scraped back into that headdress thing.'

'I agree with you, young Todd. You'd never think it was the same Jess we see walking down the street around here, would you?' chipped in the stout bespectacled Ada Pickles, the Mollitts' neighbour on the other side. 'She looks just like any other young woman then. But on the telly she's like a film star.'

'She's more glamorous than some of the film stars, I reckon.' Enthused Ada's small, unassuming husband, Ted, staring at the screen approvingly. 'She's a real cracker and that's a fact. They all are. All got legs up to their—'

'We can do without the vulgarity, Ted, thank you very much,' Ada cut short her henpecked spouse. 'That's our neighbour's daughter you're talking about. So show some respect.'

Ted looked sheepishly towards the sofa where Joy and Charlie were ensconced. 'No offence meant,' he told them.

'None taken.' Charlie wasn't bothered because he knew Ted was harmless.

'Ooh, look, they're forming into a circle.' A keen dancer herself, Libby went to a local tap and ballet class like her sister before her, and her admiration of Jess bordered on hero worship. 'They're so much in time, they dance as one woman.'

'It's remarkable they way they keep in step,' added Hilda in admiration.

'I don't know how they do it,' said Libby, getting up and breaking into a tap routine.

'Plenty of rehearsal, I expect,' was her mother's answer to that.

'And talent,' Libby was keen to add.

'Of course. That goes without saying, love. But talent on its own doesn't go far,' her mother pointed out sagely. 'It has to be trained and developed, which means lots of hard work.'

'I wouldn't mind how hard I worked if I was in that troupe,' sighed Libby longingly.

'The Burton Girls are famous for their absolute precision,' said Hilda, staring at the screen. 'It's their trademark.'

Joy nodded. 'The management is determined it will stay that way too, apparently. They're very hard taskmasters, according to Jess. They'll accept nothing less than perfection and rehearsals go on until they have that from every single member of the troupe, no matter how late it gets.'

'People don't realise the work that goes into it or that there are Burton Girls working all over the world,' Hilda remarked. 'They see them on the telly and think that's the only team they have and that's all that they do.'

'Yeah, well, behind the scenes show business is a closed book for most people, isn't it?' Joy pointed out. 'We only know a bit more about the way it works because Jess is involved.'

'True,' murmured Hilda.

'They're certainly very good.' Praise indeed coming from hypercritical Ada.

'Not half,' added Ted.

'They're all only human, though, rehearsal or no rehearsal,' commented Charlie, eyes focused on the screen. 'None of them can be absolutely certain that they won't make a mistake during the actual performance, can they?'

'S'pose not,' agreed Hilda.

'Not one of them is out of step tonight, though,' Joy stated proudly.

There was a general murmur of agreement.

'Aah, they're going offstage already,' said Libby with disappointment. 'They weren't on long.'

I think Jess said that they're on stage for about three minutes on their first spot. They'll be back later in the show, love,' Joy told her, as the troupe kneeled to acknowledge the applause, then high-kicked their way off, leaving the theatre audience and viewers to enjoy the main attractions of the show. But the gathering at the Mollitts' house was far more interested in the next appearance of the chorus than the big stars who appeared on the popular *Saturday Stars Variety Show* every week.

'I think we'll have to start selling tickets at the door here on a Saturday night,' joked Charlie when the show was over and he and Joy were in the kitchen organising refreshments for their guests. 'We always seem to have a houseful.'

'Mm. I enjoy having the neighbours in and making a bit of a do of it when Jess is on, don't you?' said his sociable wife, removing a white linen cloth from a plate of sandwiches she'd made earlier. 'It's nice for them too, as none of them has got a telly. And, be honest, Charlie, we do like them to see our daughter on the box.'

'It's only natural,' he agreed, setting some glasses out on a tray and pouring stout into them for the women.

Just to have a television set in the house raised the standing of its occupants in Park Street, Hanwell in the summer of 1956. Actually to know someone who was on it was tantamount to world fame in this ordinary West London street of 1920s-built terraced houses, many of which were rented. The Mollitts had originally rented theirs but had purchased it at a lower-than-market price as sitting tenants a few years after the war.

Charlie Mollitt was a newsagent with a shop a few minutes' walk from here, in Hanwell Broadway. Several generations of Mollitts had served the community with newspapers in this area and Charlie had inherited the business from his father.

Being just a small shopkeeper didn't bestow great wealth upon him but the business did give him enough of a living to keep his family to a reasonable standard and run a modest car. The television set was a recent acquisition. Although still considered a luxury item by some people, televisions weren't quite as uncommon in ordinary households as they had been before the coronation.

'Anything I can do to help?' This was Hilda from the kitchen door. Squeezed into a navy and white spotted summer dress that pulled tight across her ample bosom, she was a middle-aged woman of more than generous proportions, with tightly permed white hair, high colour in her cheeks and shrewd blue eyes, which were magnified by her thick spectacles and seemed to protrude slightly behind them. She was known by some people locally as 'The Mouth' on account of her being a bit of a gossip.

'Yeah, there is, as it happens – you can go home,' laughed Charlie. He was always rude to Hilda, who took it in good part because she knew it was meant only in fun. They'd been neighbours for over twenty years and she was more than a match for his banter. 'That would really make my day.'

'Don't listen to him, Hilda,' tutted Joy with token disapproval, which was a recognised part of the repartee.

'I stopped doing that years ago, don't worry,' Hilda assured her friend.

'Nice to know how high my standing is around here,' was Charlie's ironic response.

'Glad to hear you're not labouring under any false illusions,' Hilda quipped.

'Oh, go home, woman, before you turn my hair as white as yours,' he kidded her. 'You spend more time in here than you do in your own place.'

'Someone's got to give your wife some support against a brute like you,' she riposted. 'And you ought to watch your manners when you're talking to me.'

'And change the habits of a lifetime?'

'Ignorant bugger.'

Charlie poured some beer into a glass for Ted Pickles and put it on the tray with the others. 'As you seem to like our house more than your own, you may as well make yourself useful and take these drinks into the other room,' he said, handing her the tray.

Throwing him a withering look, she took the tray and departed with a heavy step.

'You are awful to her, Charlie.' Joy was fun-loving, but she was sensitive to other people's feelings too. 'Maybe you shouldn't be so rude.'

'She'd think something was wrong if I started being polite to her,' he suggested. 'She knows I don't mean it.'

6

'Yeah, I know she does. But I do sometimes wonder if you take it a bit too far.'

'No chance. Hilda's known me too long to be bothered by anything I say,' he reminded her. 'It'll take more than my weird sense of humour to upset her.'

'I expect you're right.'

'She does spend more time in here than in her own place, though.'

'She's lonely, that's why.' Hilda's husband had died young, before they'd had a chance to have children, so she had no family. 'I know people say she's nosy and interfering and has a big mouth on her. She does speak her mind, and enjoys a good chinwag, it's true. But she's a good friend to me and she thinks the world of the kids too.'

'Hilda's all right,' Charlie agreed. 'I know I tease the life out of her but that's just my way. I know she's good-hearted.'

The conversation was interrupted by their offspring piling noisily into the kitchen in search of refreshments. Inspired by her sister's performance, Libby tap-danced around the kitchen, did the splits, then got up, grabbed the door handle for support, turned her toes out and bent her knees into a plié followed by some enthusiastic high-kicking.

As usual, Ronnie was less than complimentary about her dancing skills. 'Demented elephant' was the way he put it. A prompt parental intervention averted further verbal abuse and the children were told to take the sandwiches into the other room and offer them to the visitors.

'Can we get ourselves some lemonade first?' asked Ronnie.

'No, the guests come first.' His parents were united in this. 'When you've seen to them you can get something for yourselves.'

'That's just slavery.' Ronnie was at an age to think it clever to be cheeky, and queried authority almost as a matter of course, mostly to hide the fact that he wasn't quite as confident as he tried to pretend.

'Yeah,' added Libby, entering into the joke.

Todd nodded in agreement, albeit rather uncertainly. He was a peace-loving soul but liked to stay in favour with his older siblings. Being younger and outside of their special relationship, he was rather in awe of them.

'That'll be the day, when any of you lot are slaves,' their mother reminded them laughingly. 'So get on and show the neighbours what nice, polite children you can be when you try.'

'Exploitation,' giggled the vivacious Libby, swinging off behind her brothers, carrying a plate of sausage rolls, a slim graceful figure not in the least deserving of Ronnie's derogatory remarks.

'Cheeky beggars,' smiled Charlie when they'd gone.

'They're good kids, though.'

'They've certainly got more to say for themselves than I did at their age,' he commented. 'I'd have felt my father's belt if I'd spoken to him the way they speak to me.'

7

'Times have changed – in this family, anyway. I've made sure of that. I don't want my children's father to be some shadowy, frightening figure like dads used to be in the old days.' She stared mistily ahead. 'We're very lucky, you know, to have four healthy children. The least we can do is let Hilda share in some of our family life.'

Charlie nodded in agreement. 'And it makes you proud to see Jess on the box, doesn't it? Seeing her dancing her heart out still gives me a thrill.'

'Me too. It's wonderful that she's able to earn her living doing something she enjoys so much. Not many people are lucky enough to turn a hobby into a full-time job.'

'Is she over that other miserable business now, do you think?' he enquired.

'It's hard to say.' Joy's brow drew tight. 'She never mentions the man and seems to be getting on with her life cheerfully enough. But you can't tell what she's going through because Jess has too much spirit to let her true feelings show.' She looked at him. 'I don't want to bring it all back by asking.'

'Very wise.'

Lapsing into thought, he poured some more drinks while she arranged a pile of home-made cheese straws on to a plate. Carrying their offerings, they went to join the others, complete in each other's company. They'd been together a long time and brought up a family. They understood each other.

The gathering at the Mollitts was over and the neighbours were chatting in the street on their way home. The night was balmy, windows open, voices from inside drifting out over the privet hedges, the air fragrant with the scent of garden flowers. The hour wasn't late because Charlie had to get up early in the morning to sort the Sunday papers for the paper rounds, and guests respected that.

'An enjoyable evening, wasn't it?' remarked Hilda.

'Very pleasant,' agreed Ada.

'It's ever so kind of Joy and Charlie to invite us in, don't you think?' said Ted.

'Don't kid yourself about that,' put in his wife. 'Kindness doesn't come into it. They only do it to show off about their daughter being on the telly.' Ada was much more cynical and not nearly so friendly with the Mollitts as Hilda. 'And to remind us that they've got a telly and we haven't.'

'That's a dreadful thing to say.' Hilda was outraged. 'They like to share the excitement of it all with us, that's why they invite us in.'

'Huh,' snorted Ada, who had a nasty streak in her.

'Anyway, why shouldn't they be proud?' Hilda wanted to know. 'Who else do you know who's got someone in their family on the telly every Saturday night?'

8

Ada shrugged.

'Exactly,' retorted Hilda. 'Don't tell me you wouldn't be shouting about it if your daughter was in Jess's shoes because I won't believe you. She's brought a touch of glamour to this neighbourhood and I, for one, am enjoying it. She's the pride of Park Street, that girl.'

'To some people, maybe,' Ada admitted grudgingly. 'But as far as I'm concerned it just gives Joy and Charlie Mollitt another reason to feel one up. They invite us in there to watch her, and while they're at it they can remind us that they've got more than the rest of us – a telly, a car, a phone which neighbours are allowed to use, because it makes them feel big.'

'Rubbish!' exploded Hilda. 'Joy and Charlie aren't like that at all and you know it. They need a telephone because they're in business and I think it's very good of them to let us use it to save us going to the phone box on the odd occasion we need to make a call.'

'Quite right,' agreed Ted.

'You two can believe what you like; I know what I'm talking about.' Ada paused for a moment, eyes gleaming as though her next words had been an inspiration. 'As for what you said about my boasting about it if my daughter was in Jess Mollitt's position, such a thing would never arise because I wouldn't let any daughter of mine do what Jess Mollitt is doing for a living.'

The Pickleses' dull, overweight daughter, Maureen, was never likely to get the chance, thought Hilda, but said, 'Why on earth not? There's nothing wrong with being on the stage.'

'Depends what you do on the stage, dunnit?' countered Ada. 'I mean, it isn't as if she's an actress or anything.'

'She's a damned fine dancer, though.'

'It isn't real dancing.'

'Oh, really—'

'You can sneer but it isn't classy like ballet,' Ada cut in. 'It's just glorified high-kicking, an excuse to show off more than any decent girl should.'

'They only show their legs, for goodness' sake, and they do have tights on,' Hilda pointed out.

'They leave nothing to the imagination, tights or no tights,' clucked Ada. 'They didn't in the skimpy costumes they were wearing tonight, anyway, with legs showing up to their drawers and those skin-tight body things they had on emphasising every curve. Oh no, I'd prefer a child of mine to do a proper job.'

'It is a proper job.' Hilda was fiercely defensive. A gossip she may be but she was loyalty itself to her friends.

'Anyone would think she was Margot Fonteyn, to hear you speak,' snorted Ada. 'She's only a damned chorus girl.'

'There's nothing wrong with being a chorus girl.' Hilda's hackles were rising. 'Anyway, she isn't just an ordinary chorus girl. She's in one of the most famous dance troupes in the world.'

'It's still a tarty sort of a job.'

'That's where you're wrong, Ada,' Hilda stated. 'There's a strict code of conduct in the Burton Company. The dancers have to be smart, hard-working and impeccable in their private lives. Any hint of anything untoward and they're sacked. They're not even permitted to wear trousers when they're off duty. And they're certainly not allowed to be promiscuous.'

'Seems a bit odd to have such strict discipline when they send out such a different message on stage.'

'Oh, for heaven's sake.' Hilda was losing patience. 'They don't send out any message other than that that is wholesome, they just wear glamorous costumes, that's all. You must have a warped mind if you see anything wrong in that.'

'Just because you choose not to see it . . .'

'Look, there are showgirls who work in nightclubs and slink about half naked showing off their bodies for entertainment,' Hilda spelled out for her, 'and professional, trained dancers who dance their feet off to earn a living. Jess is most definitely in the latter category.'

'She's right, Ada,' ventured Ted. 'There's nothing suggestive in what the Burton Girls do. It's a family show and the dancing is easy on the eye for everybody.'

'I might have known you'd agree with her,' sniffed Ada. 'You just enjoy seeing young women flashing themselves about.'

'That isn't fair,' he objected, but not too strongly because his wife was an awesome woman and he liked a quiet life. 'I enjoy their dancing too. They're a real picture.'

'Well, I still say it isn't a respectable job.' Ada wasn't prepared to admit defeat. 'Not like working in a shop or an office.'

'Oh, that really is a stupid thing to say.' Hilda was reaching boiling point. What inflamed her even more was that Ada wasn't the only person to make derogatory comments about Jess's occupation out of earshot of the Mollitts. Some narrow-minded people around here seemed to think that being a chorus girl had more than a whiff of promiscuity about it. 'She works a damned sight harder than she would in either of those jobs.'

Ignoring Hilda's point, Ada moved her head forward and lowered her voice in a conspiratorial manner. 'Then there's the business of her living in a flat in the West End instead of at home,' she said.

'What's wrong with that, for goodness' sake?'

'It's downright brazen.'

'Now you really are being ridiculous.' Hilda was seething. 'Jess and her friend in the troupe share a tiny flat in the West End so that they're near to the Burton headquarters for rehearsals, and close to the theatres where they often work.'

'Come off it,' scorned Ada. 'We're not that far out here. She could live at home if she chose to.'

'She could do if it was absolutely necessary,' Hilda was forced to admit, 'but it wouldn't be very convenient for her, especially as she often travels home late at night, by the time a show is over and she's got changed. She'd be stranded if she missed the last tube to Ealing Broadway.'

'Heaven knows what goes on in that flat. I bet there are wild parties and all sorts.' Ada was in full flow and unstoppable; certainly in no mood to consider any opinion of Hilda's. 'Everyone knows that men flock around chorus girls. And they don't do it because they enjoy their conversation.'

'I'm sure Jess doesn't do anything her parents wouldn't approve of,' Hilda continued to defend. 'Anyway, she's twenty-three years old, quite old enough to live away from home.'

'When women leave home it's usually to get married,' Ada pointed out.

'Usually, yes,' Hilda couldn't deny. 'But Jess is a bit out of the ordinary because she has a special talent and has been given the chance to use it. Good for her, I say.'

'It's time she was married,' declared Ada. 'Our Maureen was married by the time she was nineteen.'

And four months gone with her eldest, thought Hilda, but said, 'All in good time for Jess. She's concentrating on her career for the moment.'

'She'll miss the boat altogether if she isn't careful.' Ada paused, remembering something. 'Come to think of it, she was courting a bloke a while ago, wasn't she? He used to come to the house. What happened to him, I wonder.'

'No idea.' Hilda did know but she was damned if she was going to tell Ada, who would have it all around the neighbourhood before Sunday breakfast. 'Anyway, if you disapprove so strongly of Jess why did you accept the Mollitts' hospitality?'

'Because they're neighbours and it would have been rude to refuse,' she replied. 'But I do think all this fuss about Jess being on the telly is overdone.'

'You seemed keen enough when you were drinking their beer and eating their food,' Hilda pointed out.

'Well, you've got to be sociable, haven't you? If they want to flash their telly and their daughter about, who am I to spoil it for them?'

'You're a two-faced cow, Ada Pickles,' accused Hilda. 'Joy and Charlie would be very hurt if they knew what you said about them behind their backs.'

'And you're not two-faced, I suppose.' The claws were really out now. 'You never talk about people, do you? Oh no, not much. They don't call you The Mouth for nothing. Everyone knows you've a gob the size of Wembley Stadium.'

11

'All right, so I enjoy a gossip with the best of 'em, but I don't say things about people I care about that I wouldn't say to their faces,' Hilda informed her brusquely. 'And the Mollitts are good friends of mine so keep your trap shut about them when I'm around in future.'

'Now then, you two, calm down,' urged Ted worriedly. 'Don't let's have a falling out.'

'I've no intention of falling out with anyone.' This wasn't the first time Hilda and Ada had had words. They'd disagreed about many things over the years and Hilda wasn't about to lose sleep over it. 'But I will do if I hear any more malicious talk about the way in which Jess Mollitt earns her living, or criticism of her parents for offering us their hospitality.' She turned and opened her gate. 'And now I'll say good night to you both.'

She marched purposefully up the path to her front door without looking back.

'She's always been very thick with the Mollitts,' muttered Ada as she and Ted walked towards their own house. She didn't have any women friends and was jealous of Hilda's friendship with Joy. 'I don't know what she thinks she'll get out of it.'

'I don't think she wants anything out of it,' he suggested. 'She seems to be genuinely fond of them.'

'She's just an interfering old bag and a gossipmonger,' declared Ada.

Ted couldn't help thinking that his wife herself had just excelled in that department. But he just said meekly, 'Yes, dear.'

Jess and her friend and flatmate, Babs Tripp, limped home barefoot from the Palladium through the West End backstreets, carrying their shoes because their feet were too blistered and swollen to get them on after being in ill-fitting Burton shoes for several hours. Now they were dressed in 'civvies', all traces of stage make-up removed, no one would guess that they were the same glamorous creatures who'd dazzled television viewers earlier this evening. Beneath the stage glitz they were just hard-working dancers, the long shapely legs that were essential to qualify as a Burton Girl hidden beneath their ordinary summer dresses.

'Ooh, my feet,' wailed Jess, who was tall and slim with dark, shoulder-length hair, an olive skin and a dusting of freckles. She wasn't beautiful exactly, but she was very appealing with her big dark eyes, lovely smile and fabulous legs. 'They're going straight into a bowl of warm water when we get in and staying there for a good long time.'

'I feel as though I've been crippled for life,' complained Babs, a blue-eyed blonde with a mass of curly hair. She was five foot six, the minimum height for a Burton dancer, and slim, as required by the company.

'My feet feel that way too, but we'll be fine after a soak and a good night's sleep,' Jess tried to cheer her. 'And we're nearly home now, thank God.'

12

It had been a long and exhausting day for the Burton Company's Palladium team. They'd been at the theatre since early this morning. When they weren't rehearsing they were sitting in the stalls watching the stars rehearse while waiting for their turn to go on stage, nerves stretched to breaking point from the strain of working with people who were often difficult but revered by everyone involved in the production, while the dancers were left in no doubt as to their low rating in the showbiz pecking order. The dance routines had been learned and practised to perfection during the week, and they'd had the costume fittings. Today the entire show had been rehearsed ready for the television performance in the evening.

'Just look at us, though, Jess,' said Babs. 'We're so worn out we can hardly walk and we can't even get our shoes on because our feet are rubbed raw. Why do we do it?'

'Because we're hoofers and we love it.'

'I sometimes wonder if it's all worth it.'

'It is to me,' was the immediate response of Jess, who'd been with the Burton Company for six years. Although she'd attended a local dance class for most of her childhood, a career as a dancer had seemed like an impossible dream for a girl without a stage-school background. So when she'd left school she'd got a job in an office and attended an adult dance class as a hobby, keeping her interest in show business alive by reading *The Stage*. When she'd seen an audition for dancers for the Burton Company advertised she'd taken her courage in her hands, and had been ecstatic when she'd got the job that had changed her life. 'And don't tell me you don't get a thrill when you're on stage because I won't believe you.'

'I do, of course, but we go through a lot of pain and stress for just a few minutes of satisfaction.'

'It's more than just satisfaction, though, isn't it, when you're on stage and doing it right?' Jess pointed out. 'It's utterly exhilarating and like nothing else on earth. To me it's the most fantastic feeling in the world.'

'Yeah, yeah, I know how dedicated you are.' Babs didn't sound quite so keen.

'Anyway, what else would we do to pay the rent?' Jess asked her. 'Dancing is what we do, what we're good at. So we have to put up with the sore feet and exhaustion.'

'I enjoy the dancing and the glamour and the companionship every bit as much as you do. It's the outdated Burton rules that drive me nuts.' Babs had been with the troupe a bit longer than Jess and was one of the more rebellious members. Most of the girls were submissive to the company's regime, which demanded total obedience and encouraged them to think as a group rather than as individuals, a bit like the army. 'Yes ma'am, no ma'am, three bags full ma'am. Don't you dare have a thought of your own. Just think Burton. And don't answer back.'

'That's just something we have to put up with—'

'For the honour of being a Burton Girl.'

'Exactly.'

'It's time there were changes and one of these days I'm going to put a few people straight.'

'Be careful, Babs,' warned Jess. 'Decent jobs for dancers are few and far between, and at least the company provides us with regular work of a high standard. They pay us a decent wage and offer us the chance to travel. It isn't easy to get into the West End musicals because of the strong competition. Making your point is all very well but it only falls on deaf ears at Burtons. You don't want to lose your job and find yourself working in some second-rate chorus line. Or not dancing at all and working in a shop or something. We'll be over the hill soon enough in this game so make the most of it while you can.'

Babs grinned. 'With a bit of luck I'll have a husband to support me by the time I'm too old to dance for my living, so I won't have to go to work at all,' she said.

Jess pondered on this. 'I think I'll always want to be involved in dance in some way or other, whatever else I'm doing and whatever my age. I don't think I could bear not to have it in my life at all.' She paused. 'But getting back to your attitude towards the Burton rules, don't forget that there are a million young hopefuls out there just longing for the chance to replace any one of us. So promise me you won't get too stroppy and put yourself out of work.'

'Don't worry about me,' Babs assured her. 'I'm a bit of a rebel but I know which side my bread is buttered, even if it does sometimes leave a sour taste in my mouth. I can hold my tongue when it suits me.'

Jess did worry about Babs, who had already broken the Burton rules by having an affair with a comedian – years older than her – with whom she'd been in a show during a summer season in Blackpool and whom she'd worked with on other shows since. Romantic relationships between Burton Girls and artistes were strictly forbidden by the management because they considered them to be disruptive. In fact, they discouraged show business romances of any kind.

'Anyway, we've got a day off tomorrow so you can forget all about rules and regulations,' Jess reminded her.

'Ooh, yeah, what a lovely thought,' was Babs' response. 'I shall stay in bed until lunchtime.'

'I shall have a lie-in too.'

'You going to see the family tomorrow?'

'Yeah, I'll go over to Hanwell in the afternoon,' Jess told her. 'You seeing Dickie?'

'I hope so.' The romance Babs had broken the rules for was still going strong. 'He said he'll be over at some point during the day. We'll probably go to the pictures or something, then back to his place.'

14

'Nice.'

Everyone knew that Dickie French was conceited, insincere and a womaniser. But Babs was besotted with him. Two years older than Jess, Babs was warm-hearted, sociable and always the life and soul of the party, a popular member of the troupe. But she wasn't quite as tough as she tried to make out, and Jess had a strong suspicion that the relationship with Dickie would end in tears. But advice wasn't welcome. Babs simply wouldn't hear a word against him.

'It'll be more than just nice,' Babs amended, smiling in gleeful anticipation of tomorrow. 'It'll be fantastic. I know I sound like some soppy teenager but I love to be with him. I'm still as crazy about him as I was at the beginning.'

'I know.'

Sensing her lack of enthusiasm, Babs paused, looking at her, swinging her shoes by the straps. 'Look, I know he's got a reputation as a bit of a lad with the women but that's all changed since he's been seeing me. He won't stray now that he's found the right woman.'

Jess had serious doubts but just said, 'No, of course he won't, Babs.'

The night was warm, the West End traffic rumbling in the distance. It was quieter in these side streets than around the theatre, which had been crammed with people and traffic. The girls were able to talk privately in lowered voices. 'Anyway, enough about me. Isn't it time you had a man in your life again? It's quite a while since you finished with Jack.'

'I'm not desperate.'

'There's no need to live like a nun just because some piece of scum let you down.'

'I'm not deliberately avoiding another love affair,' Jess explained. 'I just haven't met anyone I want to get involved with. Naturally I'm a bit wary after Jack, though. I don't want to go through all that agony again.'

'Not all men are like him.'

'Of course not. But chorus girls do seem to attract the worst sort,' Jess pointed out. 'The sort of bloke who wants a bit of glamour on his arm but not as a permanent feature in his life.'

'Being on the stage is an aphrodisiac to some men, I must admit,' Babs agreed. 'We have more than our share of lechers.'

'You're telling me.'

'Jack was just absent-minded,' said Babs lightly. 'He forgot to tell you he was married.'

'If only it had been that simple.'

'Sorry, I shouldn't have made a joke of it,' Babs apologised. 'Just trying to stop you eating your heart out.'

'I'm not eating my heart out exactly, but it isn't easy to get over something like that.'

'I know, kid.'

Jess had had a few boyfriends over the years but never anyone she'd loved like Jack. She'd met him in a Corner House one morning when she was having elevenses with a group of friends from the troupe. A sales manager for an insurance company, he'd been studying some business papers over coffee. Their attraction had been instant and after some meaningful eye contact he'd sent a note over asking for a date. The girls had teased Jess about agreeing so easily but she'd been far too drawn to him to refuse.

He'd become even keener on her after discovering that she was a Burton Girl. Even though her fame was oddly anonymous in that it came only as part of a group, it had excited him. She'd soon become infatuated with him and for months had lived at an intense emotional level, losing interest in everything else; her work, her friends, even her family had paled into insignificance against the brilliance of his presence in her life. She'd been in a constant state of longing and torment, wanting only to be with him and believing him totally when he'd told her that he loved her.

When he'd said he had something important to tell her, she'd been thrilled; had anticipated a marriage proposal. Instead she'd listened with a sinking heart while he'd told her that he wouldn't be seeing her again because his wife now suspected that he was having an affair and it was becoming difficult at home. His wife! That was the last thing Jess had expected.

She'd been stunned, absolutely devastated. He'd been unremorseful; had claimed he'd never promised her anything in the way of a future. In retrospect she could see that she'd been naïve. It should have been obvious to her that she was just his bit on the side because she never went to his home or saw much of him at weekends. They say that love is blind and it certainly had been for her, though it was hardly surprising because Jack had been more than just good-looking. He'd been charming and tender, and wonderfully entertaining company. He'd even conned her family into believing that he was just an ordinary boyfriend with honourable intentions. Being reminded of it again now, she was shocked by the ease with which her pain could be resurrected. It was as strong as ever.

'For the moment I'm more interested in being chosen for a stint of work in Paris with the troupe than finding a man,' Jess told Babs now, keen to cast out painful memories.

'Really?'

'Mm. A spell in France after the Palladium run is just what I need to help get Jack out of my system for good and all.'

'I heard that the company are looking for a replacement for the Paris show,' replied Babs. 'Someone's leaving unexpectedly, apparently.'

'I'd love to take her place,' Jess confided, 'not only to help me forget Jack but because I've never worked in Paris and I think it would be exciting.'

'It's the dream posting for every Burton Girl. Everyone wants to do it at least once,' said Babs. 'But I wouldn't want to do it again, not now.

Because I don't want to leave Dickie. Paris is good fun and a real eye-opener. A lot different from here. Blatant lesbianism among the dancers and nudity on stage are par for the course over there.' She laughed at Jess's look of horror. 'But, don't worry, kid, the Burton beady eye is sharper than ever when you're abroad. You won't get a chance to indulge in either.'

'Thank God for that,' giggled Jess, adding more seriously, 'Anyway, they haven't offered me the job yet and as there are plenty of girls after it, I don't suppose they will.'

Babs was thoughtful. 'Trouble is, there isn't anything you can do to improve your chances,' she pointed out. 'If you ask the management for the job, they'll see to it that you don't get it. You have to wait until you're asked, just to keep you in your place. They call the tune and they like to make sure we always remember that. All you can do is wait and hope.'

'And if they offer you the job and you refuse because of Dickie, they'll never offer you anything interesting again.'

'Exactly. It's all part of their "obedience to the management is everything" regime that I was talking about just now,' said Babs. 'They treat us like a bunch of kids.'

'I suppose they think they're doing what's best for us, and they do pay us quite well.' Jess always defended the company because she felt blessed to be a part of it, whatever the drawbacks. 'And the younger ones need the protection.'

'That would probably be the company's explanation for their ridiculous rules.' Babs paused, remembering. 'When I was in Paris the French dancers couldn't believe it when all of us Burton Girls were marched back to the lodgings after the show; they were all going out on the town to have fun.' Her eyes gleamed at the memory. 'Mind you, some of us managed to find a way to slip out later.'

'I'll bet you did.'

'Travel certainly broadens the mind, even though the company tries to make sure it doesn't broaden their girls' minds too much,' grinned Babs.

'It's the experience of working in Paris that I'm so keen on,' said Jess as they approached their tiny basement flat. 'I really hope they choose me.'

'It's just the luck of the draw, kid,' Babs sighed, leading the way down the small flight of stone steps. 'The sparks will fly if they ask me. I'm not leaving Dickie for six months. Not likely.'

'That lessens the competition a bit for me, anyway.'

'I'll miss you like mad if you go,' Babs told her. 'But because you're so keen I'll be keeping my fingers crossed for you.'

'Thanks.'

As they went inside and closed the door behind them, Jess realised just how much getting the Paris job would mean to her at this stage in her life. With the bitter taste of heartbreak and humiliation refusing to go away, a challenge like that was just what she needed.

Chapter Two

'So, what did you think of the show then, Mum?' asked Jess.

'Show?' Joy narrowed her eyes, looking puzzled. 'What show would that be, dear?'

Jess shot her a curious look. 'Last night. *Saturday Stars Variety Show*, of course.'

Joy's hand flew to her mouth. 'Oh damn! It was last night, wasn't it?' She bit her lip, looking extremely sheepish. 'I'm so sorry, love, but I'm afraid we missed it. We forgot all about it and watched something on the other side.'

'What!' Jess eyed her with a mixture of disbelief and disappointment because their support meant so much to her. 'Oh, Mum, you didn't.'

Her mother burst out laughing. 'Of course we didn't, you daft ha'p'orth. As if we'd miss seeing you on the telly,' she chuckled, wiping tears of laughter from her eyes. 'Oh, Jess, your face was a picture. I really had you going there for a minute.'

Up went Jess's eyes and she tutted but couldn't help grinning. 'Honestly, you lot really are the end,' she chided because the whole family was giggling, obviously in on the joke. 'I don't think you've got a serious bone between you.'

'Don't blame them,' said Joy, leaning over and patting the arm of her elder daughter, who was sitting beside her on the sofa. 'It's all down to me and my childish sense of humour. I just can't resist teasing you. The last thing we would ever do is miss a show that you're in. You must know that.'

'I do. But just for a second there . . .'

'Not only would we not miss it, we make sure the neighbours don't miss it either,' was her father's hearty contribution. 'It's party time in this house when you're on.'

'That's nice.'

'Anyway, to answer your question,' began Joy, 'the show was well up to standard and it was an excellent performance from the chorus again this week. Not one of you put a foot wrong.'

'We wouldn't dare.' Jess gave a wry grin. 'The management would have us shot if we went wrong on national television.'

'Lovely costumes, you were wearing,' Libby mentioned. 'What colour were they?'

'Yellow and gold for the first number and we were in red later on,' she told her. 'It's a pity the television viewers only get to see them in black and white.'

'Yeah, it is,' agreed Libby. 'I bet they were gorgeous.'

'They looked lovely but were hell to wear because they were so tight; they really cut into you,' she said. 'And it's very hot working under the TV lights, which doesn't help.'

'I'd give anything to be in that chorus line with you,' sighed Libby. 'I wouldn't care if the costumes half killed me.'

'I was just the same about going on the stage at your age so I know just how you feel. But your chance will come, little sister,' encouraged Jess. 'Don't be so impatient.'

'I can't help it,' the young girl confessed. 'It all seems so wonderful, I want to be a part of it.'

'It's hard work but, yeah, it is wonderful and I love every minute,' Jess confirmed. 'But you've a long time to wait before you can even think about trying to get in so enjoy your dancing for its own sake for the moment.'

Another wistful sigh. 'Yeah, yeah, all right . . .'

'Did you go to your dance class this week?' enquired Jess.

'Course I did. I wouldn't miss that for anything,' Libby replied. 'Can I show you some of the new steps we're working on?'

'Sure.' Jess took a keen interest in her sister's dancing and had been paying for her lessons ever since she'd been earning a decent wage. It was one way she could put something back into the family; one less thing for her parents to take care of. 'Later on, when I've caught up with all the rest of the family news, you can give me a demonstration, eh?'

'Try stopping me.'

'Let me know when you're gonna start and I'll go out,' chortled Ronnie. 'It isn't safe in this house when Libby starts flinging herself about. You get one of her high kicks in your face and you could be damaged for life.'

'Enough of that, Ronnie,' warned his mother. 'You know what we've told you about teasing your sister.'

'You can cope, can't you, Libs?' smiled Jess, giving her sister a friendly wink. She knew – as they all did – that the twins would brave molten lava for each other if necessary.

'With that twit, no problem.'

It was Sunday afternoon and the family was relaxing in the living room; Jess hadn't long arrived. As always when she was here she was imbued with a profound sense of belonging that warmed and strengthened her and which she experienced nowhere else. This house and these people were her anchor. No matter how exciting the highs of her job, or bleak the misery of a broken heart, the love in this house was always there, a gift and a comfort. Were there irritations? Of course, as in any family. Did she feel restricted? Sometimes, which was natural for any adult. She had long passed the stage where she could live comfortably under the parental roof on a permanent basis. But this family meant everything to her and she visited them often from choice rather than a sense of duty.

'So what have you all been up to this week?' she asked with genuine interest.

Her mother said it had been just an ordinary sort of a week for her, housekeeping and helping Dad in the shop. Libby chattered about her dance class, Ronnie told her he was saving up for new football boots from the money he earned from his paper round.

'What about you, kiddo?' enquired Jess, smiling at her younger brother, who was the only academic in the family. 'How are things at school?'

'All right, thanks.' Of a plumper build than his siblings, Todd had a thatch of light brown hair, serious hazel eyes and a paler complexion than the other Mollitt children, who had inherited their dark looks from their mother. The paternal genes were stronger in Todd. He had the same chubby round face as his father and his spectacles made it look even rounder.

'It's been more than just all right, Jess, because he came top of his class in arithmetic and English in the end-of-term tests for the third time running,' Joy was proud to announce.

'Wow,' smiled Jess.

'He'll get a place at the gram next year if he carries on like this,' Joy went on.

'You will too,' praised Jess, looking at Todd with a smile of approval. 'Well done.'

'He would get good marks, wouldn't he? I mean, he even does sums and reads books after school when he doesn't have to,' said Ronnie with a mixture of incredulity and disapproval. 'Can you imagine anyone actually wanting to do that?'

'Sure I can,' replied Jess. 'If you're good at something, you usually want to do more of it because you enjoy it, whatever it is. Football, in your case.'

'Football, yeah. But no one likes school work,' declared Ronnie, shaking his head. 'Seems weird to me.'

'Well, it would to a thick-head like you, wouldn't it?' was Libby's playful response.

'There's nothing wrong with enjoying school work,' defended Todd nervously.

'Of course there isn't,' supported his mother.

'Each to their own,' added Jess, looking at Ronnie. 'And Todd's the brains of the family.'

'That's why he'll be the first one to go to a grammar school,' put in Libby good-heartedly.

'I wouldn't go to the gram if you paid me,' announced Ronnie, who was a pupil at the local boys' secondary modern, where his sole ambition was to maintain his position in the school soccer team. 'Grammar-school kids have to do homework and they're all drippy little swots.' He paused before adding the most meaningful judgement of all. 'They're rubbish at football. None of them can kick a ball to save their life.'

'I expect some of them can,' Libby disagreed. 'You're just jealous because Todd's cleverer than you.'

'Ooh, hark at little Miss Brainbox,' jeered Ronnie. 'Anyone would think you got a place at the gram.'

'I didn't want to go there,' she informed him. 'I'm going to be a dancer when I leave school and you don't need a grammar-school education for that.'

'You each have your own gifts,' intervened their placatory mother. 'Ronnie's good at football, Libby at dancing and Todd's good at his lessons.'

'I'm really proud of you for doing so well, Todd.' Being so much older than the others, Jess often felt more like a parent than a sister. 'And so are the others, aren't you, kids?'

'Yeah. It'll be good telling people I've got a brother at the gram,' said Libby.

'My mates'll probably think he's a right little sissy but I suppose it'll be all right,' conceded Ronnie.

Libby stood up. 'Well, I'm just popping over to see Margie,' she announced, referring to her friend who lived in the next street. 'All right, Mum?'

Joy nodded. 'Tea will be ready in about half an hour, though,' she informed her. 'Don't be late.'

'OK.' Libby looked at Jess. 'I'll show you my new dance steps when I get back.'

'Smashing.'

Ronnie also left the house to rejoin his pals, who were kicking a ball about in the street; he'd only come in because he'd seen Jess arrive. Todd put his nose in a book. Jess was soothed by the normality of everything. Nothing ever changed around here.

'How's your week been, Jess?' asked her mother. 'Anything exciting to report?'

Jess was about to mention the possibility of the Paris job but changed her mind for fear of tempting fate. The time to tell them was if and when she was actually chosen. 'No. Nothing all that special,' she said.

'Your job is exciting in itself, though, isn't it?' Joy remarked. 'Dressing up all glamorous and being on the telly and that. I know it's hard work but being on stage must be a thrill.'

'Very much so.'

'You're still enjoying it then?'

'Love it.'

Her father stretched and yawned, then got up and wandered over to the open french doors. 'Well, that's enough sitting about for me. I must get on and do some work in the garden. It isn't very big but it'll turn into a small forest if I leave it to nature.'

'When you come in, use the kitchen door,' his wife requested. 'I don't want you treading mud in here on your shoes.'

'As if I'd dare,' he grinned, and went out into the sunshine.

'It's far too nice for a boy of your age to be stuck indoors,' Joy said to Todd. 'You ought to be outside too, young man.'

'In a minute,' he said predictably, and carried on reading.

'It's just the sort of day for a picnic,' remarked Jess, idly looking out on to the sun-drenched garden.

'What a lovely thought,' agreed Joy. 'A day out at Runnymede would have been just the job today.'

'Yeah,' sighed Jess wistfully.

'We should all go one Sunday soon,' her mother suggested. 'Perhaps we can talk your dad into taking us in the car next week if it's a nice day.'

Jess looked doubtful. 'Ooh, I'm not sure that Dad will fancy that much,' she said because her father was a home-loving man. He opened the shop for a couple of hours in the morning on a Sunday and liked to be at home for the rest of the day. 'He enjoys pottering about here on a Sunday, doesn't he?'

'Mm, that's true,' Joy confirmed. 'But it won't hurt him to change his routine for once. No point in having a car if you don't use it for pleasure. A family outing will do him good and I can be very persuasive when it comes to your father.'

'You can twist him around your little finger, you mean.' Jess enjoyed the way her parents were together, Mum getting her own way with a little gentle persuasion and Dad pretending to mind. Mum could be wonderfully eloquent when she wanted to win him over. Their obvious devotion was at the centre of family stability.

'I know how to handle him, that's all.' Joy grinned. 'I point out the positive aspects of an idea in such a way that he's suggesting it to me by the time I've finished.' She shot her daughter a look. 'But if I can talk him into it, will you be able to make it?'

'If we aren't called in for a special rehearsal or anything, yeah, I'd like that.'

'All the family together on a picnic,' enthused Joy, eyes sparkling with enthusiasm. 'I'll be just like the old days when you were all little.'

'It'll be lovely,' responded Jess.

'I'll get to work on your father later on,' said Joy.

'OK, everybody, let's have that again from the beginning,' instructed Elsie Tucker, who was taking the rehearsal. A tall, busty redhead, she had once danced in the Burton line, and now, in her late thirties, she worked for the company as a coach-cum-supervisor. She had a gift for choreography and was brilliant at making her ideas come to life on the stage. But she was a perfectionist and didn't give up until she'd squeezed the very best out of every dancer. Although they feared her and called her a slave driver behind her back, they all respected her ability. 'We're not leaving here until we've got it right, even if we have to stay here all night.'

As they'd been rehearsing all morning and it was now only mid-afternoon, this was a gloomy prospect and there were groans from every corner of the room.

'That's what I like to hear, bags of enthusiasm,' Elsie said with irony. 'Now come on, you lot, let's have some real spirit here. I want it right this time. Come on now, legs up and kicking high . . . in a straight line, please. No, no, no, not like that, you're all over the place.'

'Like her chest,' Babs whispered to Jess, who couldn't quite stifle a giggle.

'Perhaps you'd like to share the joke with the rest of us, Jess,' suggested Elsie tartly, stopping the rehearsal and throwing her a withering look.

'It was my fault,' muttered Babs, 'I made some daft comment to her. It was stupid.'

'At my expense, no doubt,' accused the older woman. 'It doesn't worry me in the least. My back is broad – it damn well has to be in this job – but we are supposed to work as a team and not hold up rehearsal by making fun of each other.'

'Sorry,' said Babs.

'You know the rules of the company,' lectured Elsie. 'A Burton Girl is a team player – she is not a solo artist. We're here to work, not play about.'

'Babs was just saying that she thought her bum looked fat in the mirrors,' fibbed Jess, to spare the feelings of the other woman, whose enormous bosom never seemed to be properly tethered. 'She didn't mean any harm.'

'Oh.' Apparently accepting Jess's explanation and none too pleased about it, Elsie waved a hand towards the walls, which had ceiling-to-floor mirrors. 'Those mirrors are put there for you to see your mistakes and help you to correct them; their purpose is not for you to admire yourselves,' she warned the entire troupe briskly. 'Now let's get on or we really will be here all damned night.'

The rehearsal resumed in more of a subdued mood; no one wanted to upset Elsie and hold up the session again. Everyone was dressed in the official practice outfit of white blouse, black satin pants and white ankle socks with black tap shoes. Jess received conspiratorial glances from several of the others. There was strong bonding between the dancers; always a 'them and us' feeling between them against the management.

24

When they finally got the routine to a standard acceptable to Elsie, and the rehearsal ended, Elsie informed Jess that Miss Molly wanted to see her in the office and she was to go right away. Her heart sunk. She was obviously in for a rollicking from the boss for laughing at Elsie, who must have gone to the office and reported her during one of the breaks. To anyone outside of this establishment, Jess's fears might seem ludicrous but she had known dancers to be hauled over the coals or even lose their jobs for the most minor insubordination during rehearsal.

Surely she wouldn't get sacked merely for giggling during working hours. If she did get the push for such a trivial reason she would never defend the strict Burton regime against Babs again, she thought worriedly, as she hurried up the stairs to the office.

The Burton Company had been started in the early part of the century by a businessman called Billy Burton. After his death his wife had taken over the business and when she'd eventually died their daughter, Molly, had stepped in, supported by a large management team, though Molly usually dealt with the girls personally in matters of administration or discipline. Her manner was very direct but she wasn't difficult to get on with as long as the dancers obeyed the rules. Those who didn't were shown little mercy. She was a great one for tradition and wanted things to stay as they had been in her father's day.

A middle-aged woman with mouse-brown hair worn in a bun and large spectacles, she was known to everyone in the company as Miss Molly, though she was in fact married. She was sitting at her desk when Jess went in and waved a hand towards the chair opposite.

'So,' she began, looking up from some papers and peering at Jess over the top of her glasses, 'do you want to go or not?'

'Go?' Jess was baffled. 'Go where?'

'Paris, of course.'

'What!'

'Don't sound so surprised, my dear. You must have known there was a vacancy coming up there,' she said. 'It has been made generally known.'

'I did know, of course, but I didn't dare to hope.'

'Well, do you want the job or not?' Miss Molly's tone was as casual as if she'd just asked her to go out and post a letter.

'I'll say I want it,' breathed Jess, her eyes shining. 'I want it all right.'

'Good, that's settled then,' said the other woman, as though she'd just solved some minor administrative detail rather than changed someone's life. 'You'll be leaving immediately after the Palladium run in three weeks' time and you'll be away for a minimum of six months, possibly a bit longer. Please make sure that you're packed and ready to go and that your passport is in order. We don't want any last-minute hold-ups.'

'Try stopping me.' Jess leaped to her feet excitedly. 'Thank you, Miss Molly. Oh, thank you.'

'I've offered you a job, not a million pounds, dear,' she pointed out, but she was smiling.

The job meant much more to Jess than money ever could. 'It's such a thrill,' she told her employer.

'Good. I'm glad you're pleased. Now off you go and get changed,' Miss Molly said, her mind already moving on to other things. 'You'll be given full details in the next week or so – travel arrangements, accommodation and so on.'

Jess tore down the stairs to the rehearsal room to find Babs, who'd said she'd wait for her.

'Well,' said her friend, who'd changed into a summer dress and was doing up her sandals, 'did you get ten strokes of the cane or a threat of the sack?'

'Neither,' grinned Jess, high-kicking slowly and singing the tune of the 'Marseillaise'.

'You got the Paris job!' squealed Babs, genuinely delighted for her.

'I leave next month.'

'Fantastic,' cried her friend, hugging her and dancing her around in a jubilant polka.

Most of the other dancers had already left but the few remaining stragglers offered hearty congratulations. If any of them had wanted the Paris job they showed no sign of jealousy towards Jess. She was a popular member of the troupe and everyone knew that she'd waited a long time for this.

Nestling at the foot of Egham Hill – on the site where King John had sealed the Magna Carta in 1215 – Runnymede riverside meadows were crowded with day-trippers on this fine Sunday afternoon. Sunshine bathed this verdant splendour and put splinters of gold on to the rippling surface of the Thames. The air was filled with the laughter and shouts of people at leisure; swimming, paddling, playing ball games on the grass.

The Mollitt family had managed to find a convenient spot in the expanse of grassland between the café and the changing rooms. The children had swum several times but now the whole family was sitting on the grass having a picnic.

'Anyone want another sandwich?' invited Joy. 'There's plenty left. Cheese or egg and tomato.'

'What else have we got?' asked Ronnie, whose skinny body was bare but for his navy-blue swimming trunks, his skin paper white.

'Nothing else, dear. Just cheese or egg and tomato,' she informed him.

'He isn't after sandwiches because he's got his eye on the more interesting stuff like the crisps and Mars bars you've got hidden at the bottom of the bag, Mum,' suggested Libby, slender and childlike, with just a hint of incipient womanhood visible beneath her red swimsuit.

'All of that is for afterwards, when you've finished the sandwiches,' Joy informed them.

'No more sandwiches for me, thanks,' said Ronnie.

'Nor me,' put in Todd.

'Can we have some crisps, please, Mum?' Ronnie persisted.

'Oh, go on, then.' Joy was much more malleable when she was out for the day.

Ronnie foraged in the bag, handing his siblings a bag of crisps each.

'Who's coming in swimming with me?' asked Libby, opening the blue twist of waxed paper, sprinkling salt on her crisps and shaking the bag.

'I am,' said Ronnie.

'Me too,' added Todd, munching a crisp.

'You coming in, Jess?' enquired Libby. 'You haven't been in yet today.'

'You bet I am. I couldn't come to Runnymede for the day and not go in swimming, could I?' replied Jess, who was wearing a fashionable black nylon swimsuit with a blue and white checked blouse covering her shoulders.

'I'll race the lot of you to the other side,' Ronnie announced. Swimming to the opposite bank from Runnymede meadows was a challenge most youngsters aspired to when they came here.

'You won't beat me,' stated Libby.

'Don't make me laugh,' was Ronnie's predictable reaction. 'You can't even swim to the other side, let alone beat me.'

'I can, too.'

'You didn't do it earlier.'

'That doesn't mean I can't do it,' Libby pointed out. 'I wasn't in the mood earlier but I have done it before.'

'I'm going to swim across this afternoon,' announced Todd.

'No you're not,' warned his mother sternly. 'You're not even to try. Understand?'

'Why not?'

'Because you're not a strong enough swimmer yet to get out of your depth in the river,' asserted Joy, looking at him darkly. 'I mean it, son. You're not to go that far out. It's dangerous unless you're a really good swimmer.'

'We'll look after him, Mum, don't worry,' Jess assured her.

'None of you is to go in the water until your food has been properly digested anyway,' lectured their mother. 'It can be dangerous to swim straight after food.'

'We could have a game with the ball while we're waiting,' suggested Libby.

'Nah. I think I'll sunbathe.' Ronnie put his arms forward and studied them. 'I'm getting tanned already.'

Libby roared with laughter. 'Don't kid yourself. Compared to you milk looks brown.'

27

'You're not exactly glowing with colour yourself.'

'Never said I was.'

'Change the record you two, for goodness' sake,' admonished their mother.

'Sorry, Mum' Libby turned to Jess. 'Will you catch my legs if I do some handstands later?'

'Course I will.'

'I can do good back bends now too.'

'I'll have a look later.'

'You're not to do any of it until your food has gone down,' her mother repeated. 'Just try to sit still for a few minutes, girl. You're like a ruddy squib.'

'Sitting around's boring.'

'You'll have to lie still and sunbathe if you want to get brown,' said Ronnie, now prostrate on the grass.

'Not necessarily. You can catch the sun moving around.' Bored with the subject, Libby asked Jess, 'So you're going to Paris then?'

'Yeah, isn't it exciting?'

'I'll say it is. Wait till I tell Margie. She'll be green with envy. No one else at school has a sister living in France.' She frowned. 'I'll miss seeing you every week, though.'

'We all will.' Joy couldn't hide a plaintive note. 'But it's a wonderful opportunity and we're all delighted for you.'

'Not half,' added Charlie.

'Six months will soon pass and I'll write lots of letters,' promised Jess.

'You'd better, or I'll want to know why,' warned her mother in a jovial manner.

Convivial chatter continued for a while longer, then the younger children went to the café armed with their pocket money. Joy packed what was left of the picnic away and Charlie lay down on the grass and closed his eyes.

Sitting there quietly, warmed by the sun, Jess was aware of a deep sense of contentment she hadn't felt in a long time – since before she'd met Jack, anyway. She had so much: an exciting new job to look forward to, good friends and a dear family encouraging her every step of the way. At that moment she thought she must be the luckiest woman alive.

'Beat you to the other side, Jess,' Ronnie challenged his sister.

'You can try,' grinned Jess, entering into the spirit of competition. 'But you'll be up against strong opposition.'

'Nothing I can't handle.'

'We'll see about that.'

'I want to be in the race too,' cried Libby. 'I know I won't beat Jess but I'd like to join in.'

'OK. Just turn back if you feel you can't manage it before you get too

28

far out of your depth,' advised Jess, who was always very protective towards her younger siblings.

'That's what I'll do too,' announced Todd.

She turned to him sharply. 'No, not you, Todd. You'd better stay this side of the river as Mum doesn't want you going out too far.'

'Oh, all right.' He was disappointed but it wasn't in his nature to whinge. 'I'll be the starter.'

'Good idea,' approved Jess.

They were all in the shallow waters not too far from the bank in the crowded part of the river. The three older Mollitts stood in line while Todd did the countdown. 'On your marks, get set . . . go.'

They were off, skimming through the water with barely a splash. Having an occupation that provided her with a great deal of exercise, Jess was in good physical shape, and a strong swimmer. She felt wonderfully free, like a child again, because swimming in this stretch of the river had been such a memorable part of her childhood. Runnymede had always been a Mollitt favourite for a day out – that and Southend. She reached the other bank well ahead of the others and was sitting on the grass in the shade of a weeping willow tree when they arrived, panting and breathless, Ronnie just ahead of Libby.

'I told you you were up against an awesome opponent, didn't I?' Jess joshed.

'You've got longer legs than us,' puffed Ronnie.

'Exactly, and if you hadn't been so cocky I'd have let you start ahead of me,' she laughed.

'Now she tells me.'

'Don't worry. I'll give you a start when we swim back.'

'Let's have a good long breather before we go back,' suggested Libby, flopping down on the grass and lying flat with her eyes closed. 'I need to recover.'

'Suits me,' agreed Jess, waving to Todd, who was watching them from the opposite bank.

Feeling the need to stretch her legs, Joy left Charlie dozing in the sun and mooched barefoot to the river bank and walked along to a quieter part where the water was deep enough to dangle her toes from the grassy bank. She sat down on the edge, pulled up the skirt of her bright blue and white striped summer dress and let her feet drop into the cool water. Lovely!

Shading her eyes from the sun, she scoured the crowded part of the river for her children, glad that they were all good swimmers. They were sensible and wouldn't take risks. They'd all learned to swim with the school at Ealing Baths. She'd often thought how nice it must be to be able to swim, but no such facility had been available to her as a child and she certainly had more to do with her time than to bother about learning now.

It wasn't easy to pick her children out with so many bathers in the river. Ah, there they were, the three older ones sunning themselves on the opposite bank. But where was Todd? Panic flashed instinctively through her but was short-lived because she spotted his brown head bobbing up and down this side of the river. She swung her legs contentedly, feeling that all was well with the world.

Todd was bored with his own company in the shallow waters, and hoped the others would come back soon and they could play some sort of a game. Swimming about on your own got tedious after a while and he was beginning to feel chilly. An idea to amuse himself came into his mind. He'd practise going underwater like he'd been doing at the swimming baths recently. It might not work so well in the river but he'd give it a try and see how long he could stay under. That would impress the others when they came back. He took a deep breath, bent his knees and went under.

Joy was thinking how much Hilda would have enjoyed this day out. She loved to visit Runnymede. The two of them sometimes brought the kids on the train in the summer holidays on a weekday when Charlie was at the shop. But with the whole family on board there wasn't room for another passenger in the car. Perhaps Hilda might like to come with them one Sunday when Jess was away in Paris. There would be room for her then.

The thought reminded Joy of Jess's departure. How much she would miss her eldest, born nine months almost to the day after they were married; a first-night baby, she and Charlie had privately agreed. They had often chuckled about 'hitting the jackpot' right away, especially as they'd had to wait so long to increase their family. Charlie always likened it to the old joke about London buses. None for ages then two at the same time with another following up in the rear.

In a mood of happy reflection, Joy couldn't think of one thing she wanted to change in her life. She had four lovely children, a devoted husband, and a family business that gave them a decent living and also provided her with a part-time job and an interest outside of the home but didn't interfere with her family commitments. Home and family were paramount to Joy, and Charlie respected that. If one of the kids was ill or needed her for any reason at all, she didn't go into the shop and there was no argument about it.

Now, with the primal instinct of a mother to check on her young, her glance darted along the river, settling on her three older children, who were still on the opposite bank but standing up and looking towards the river as though they were about to swim back. And Todd was on this side of the river. Good. All was well.

In the next instant she was struck with terror when Todd's head disappeared beneath the water; just vanished completely. Her heart

30

hammering against her ribs, holding her breath, she stared hard, waiting for him to emerge. It didn't happen. Her child was under the water. 'God Almighty, he's drowning,' she muttered, jumping off the bank into the river and wading towards the place she'd last seen Todd, hampered greatly by her skirt clinging to her legs.

'Help, someone,' she gasped. 'Help, please. For God's sake somebody help me, my boy is drowning.'

But she was too far away for her words to be heard above the clamour of enjoyment filling the air. 'Help, help,' she repeated again and again, tears running down her cheeks, her maternal instinct carrying her into deeper waters with no thought for her own safety, her eyes fixed firmly on the spot where Todd had disappeared so that she didn't see him reappear in a different place.

A stab of pain pierced her foot as she trod on something sharp on the riverbed and she stumbled, losing her balance and falling backwards and landing on her bottom, head submerged. Being a nonswimmer she panicked, scrambling to get up but unable to, feeling as though she was choking. Eventually managing to find her feet, she stood up, gasping for breath.

But she was still so unsteady on her feet she was staggering on the uneven riverbed, which felt soft and spongy and seemed to be moving beneath her. Suddenly she was out of her depth and couldn't find the bottom at all. Gasping and paralysed with fear, she felt the water rise swiftly . . . past her chest, her shoulders, her chin . . .

Fighting a losing battle against the force of the river and still calling out Todd's name, her head finally slipped beneath the water. This time it didn't come up.

Unaware of anything untoward on the other bank, Jess gave her young siblings a good few yards start before she struck out in the homeward stretch. She still managed to end the race victoriously but nobody took much notice because they were all more interested in what was going on further along the bank where a crowd had gathered.

'What's going on up there?' Jess asked Todd, craning her neck and peering along the bank.

'Someone's drowned, I think,' Todd informed her shakily.

'God, how awful,' said Jess. 'Is it a child who got out of their depth?'

'I heard someone say it's a woman,' Todd told them. 'An old man saw someone in trouble from the bank and raised the alarm. A man went in to try to save her.'

'Blimey,' gasped Ronnie.

'Terrible,' added his twin.

'They've got her out of the water and are trying to revive her, so I heard, but you can't see anything because of the crowds,' he explained.

'Everybody started rushing up there. I thought I'd better wait here for you in case you wondered where I was.'

'You did right,' Jess assured him. 'I'll go along there and see if I can do anything to help.'

'Yeah, come on, let's go,' said Todd, making to go after her.

Turning suddenly, Jess put a restraining hand on his arm as, through the crowds, she caught a terrifying glimpse of someone lying on the grass at the centre of the activity; someone in a blue and white striped dress. 'No, you three go and get dried or you'll get cold,' she instructed, frozen with fear and trying not to show it. 'Too many people crowding around will only cause problems.'

'OK,' said Libby, and the three of them wandered off towards their parents.

It can't possibly be Mum, Jess reasoned with herself, as she tore along the grassy bank with her heart pounding, nerves raw with terror. She never goes in the water. Not even to paddle. Anyway, she isn't the only woman wearing a blue and white striped dress here today; they're very popular at the moment.

But when she managed to push her way to the front of the crowd, her heart almost stopped. It was her mother and she was lying ominously still on the grass, face blue, hair and dress sodden and clinging to her. There was a man on his knees beside her.

'Keep back,' said someone as Jess pushed through.

'She's my mother,' she sobbed, kneeling down on the grass beside her. 'Oh, no, Mum, no, please no.' Her voice rose almost to a scream. 'Somebody do something, for God's sake. Please.'

'I've done what I can but I'm afraid it's no use,' said the man on his knees.

'I'll do something myself then,' she told him, becoming hysterical. 'I'm not letting her go. So please tell me, what can I do to bring her round?'

'I do have some first-aid training,' the man explained. 'I've done everything you're supposed to do in these circumstances but there was no response.'

'Oh God.'

'She must have inhaled too much water,' he suggested to the stricken young woman. 'She was underwater for too long. I'm so very sorry.'

'There must be something we can do,' wept Jess, cradling her mother in her arms. 'Mum, come on, please. Stop messing about.' Tears were running down her face. 'Please, Mum, don't do this, please. You can come through. You can't leave us.'

'I really am very sorry, love,' said the man kindly, adding in a rather pointless attempt at reassurance as he stood up with a sad, defeated air, 'The ambulance should be here at any minute. Someone's gone to the café to phone from there.'

'Jess,' said a frightened young voice, and Jess turned to see Libby standing there with her horrified brothers, all dripping wet, with towels draped around their shoulders, ashen-faced and eyes wide with fear at the scene in front of them.

'Can you go and tell Dad to come, please, kids, then get yourselves dried and dressed before you catch cold? Wait by our picnic spot until I come for you,' she said in a gentle but commanding tone, holding her dead mother in her arms, her body heaving as she sobbed. Despite her own agony, her instinct was to try to protect her siblings from this tragedy, even though she knew that no one could.

That night the four Mollitt children sat close together on the sofa, Jess in the middle with her arms around Libby and Todd. Ronnie was next to Libby holding her hand. There were no wisecracks or insults being traded tonight. Everyone had been weeping intermittently, except Ronnie, who had struggled against it because he was trying to be grown up and manly. Now exhausted, they were all pale and quiet.

Their father was upstairs in his bedroom with the door shut, refusing food but drinking lots of tea. Since the heart-rending scene on the river bank when he'd at first denied that his wife was dead, he'd hardly said a word. After the ambulance had taken her body away, he'd driven his children home in shocked silence, then gone to the mortuary, refusing Jess's offers to go with him for moral support. When he'd got back he'd gone straight to his bedroom and had been there ever since. There had been a dreadful pallor about him, Jess had noticed, and he'd been strange and distant towards them. Not like their father at all.

'Let me get you something to eat, kids.' Hilda had been here since they'd got back. She'd been the first person they'd turned to.

'They say they don't want anything,' Jess told her thickly. 'I've tried everything I know to tempt them.'

'I meant all of you. You need something as well, Jess.' Hilda was very shaken by the death of her closest friend but was trying to stay in control for the sake of the family, especially as Charlie seemed to have deserted them. 'I know it's hard but you must try to keep your strength up. It's what your mother would expect of all of you.'

'Mum isn't here, is she?' said Ronnie gruffly, his pale face suffused with red blotches, eyes tired and shadowed. 'So how can she expect anything?'

'All right, Ronnie. There's no need to be rude to Hilda,' reproached Jess. 'She's only trying to help.'

'Sorry, Hilda.'

'That's all right, son,' she said sadly. We're all feeling a bit edgy at the moment.'

'How could it have happened, Hilda?' Jess asked, shaking her head in disbelief. 'I mean, Mum never goes in the water. So how could she have

33

drowned?' She clasped her head as though in pain. 'It just doesn't make sense.'

'No, it doesn't. But she was fully dressed so she must have gone paddling and lost her balance or something,' was the only explanation Hilda could come up with. 'You were told that the man on the bank who raised the alarm only arrived as she went under. No one saw her actually go in the water, did they? We'll probably never know how it came about so there's no point in fretting about it. It won't change anything, anyway.'

'I suppose you're right.' She went to get up but Libby said, 'Don't go, Jess. I need to feel you near to me.'

'We all do,' agreed her very subdued twin.

'You stay there, Jess,' urged Hilda, almost choking with grief but soldiering on as best as she could. 'I'll go and see what there is in the larder and make you all something to eat. It doesn't matter if you can't manage more than a mouthful.'

Jess didn't protest because she knew that Hilda's heart was breaking and she needed to feel that she was doing something useful to help them because that was her way of coping with her own feelings. Jess held her siblings ever tighter and wished her father hadn't shut himself away from them when they needed him so badly.

'What a terrible thing, Jess,' said Miss Molly the next day on the telephone when Jess called her to let her know what had happened.

'Yes, it's awful.'

'I really am so very sorry, my dear.'

'Thank you,' muttered Jess, biting back the tears. 'I thought I ought to let you know what's happened so that you won't expect me at rehearsal today.'

'Of course you can't come in to rehearsal. We wouldn't expect you to at a time like this,' Miss Molly said in an understanding manner. 'You take as much time off as you need.'

'Being realistic, I don't suppose I'll be able to come back to work until after the funeral,' Jess went on to say, though she didn't actually feel capable of coherent thought. 'I hope this doesn't make things too difficult for you. But the children need me here. And my father, of course.'

'How is your father?'

'Pretty bad. It's knocked him sideways.'

'I'm sure it must have done,' Miss Molly said with a sympathetic tut. 'You look after him and don't worry about a thing as far as we're concerned here. We'll manage.'

'I'll be back at work just as soon as I can,' Jess told her. 'It shouldn't be longer than a week or two.'

'Come back when you're ready, my dear. You'll get no pressure from us.'

Jess was still too deeply immersed in her own grief to consider

34

seriously such practicalities as how she was going to pay her rent if she wasn't working, and who was going to look after her siblings when she did return to her flat and go back to work.

'I appreciate that.'

'We'll see you whenever you feel able to come back, then,' said Miss Molly, as though wanting to bring the conversation to an end. 'Meanwhile don't worry about anything as far as your job is concerned. It'll be here for you when you're ready to come back to work.' A crackly silence echoed down the line while she thought about something. 'I shall have to replace you in the Palladium team, though the current run is nearly over anyway.'

'I realise that,' Jess said numbly. 'Thank you for being so understanding about my having time off.'

'Not at all. If there's anything at all we can do to help, don't hesitate to get in touch.'

'That's very kind of you, Miss Molly.' Jess felt unreal and could hear her own voice in the distance as though it belonged to someone else. 'I'll bear it in mind.'

'Good.'

'I'll keep you posted.'

As she put the receiver back on its cradle, she was conscious of some horrible knot of anxiety above and beyond her personal sadness, nagging away at the back of her mind. But she was still too grief-stricken to work out what was causing it.

Chapter Three

Umbrellas were out in force in the cemetery when they buried Joy Mollitt. Soft summer rain fell with gentle persistence and a light mist hung over everything – the dark clothes, the mossy gravestones, the vicar's expressionless face as he uttered the burial service in a low solemn voice. The Mollitts were a well-known local family, and Joy had been a popular member of the community, so there was a high turnout of friends, neighbours and customers, distant relatives adding to the numbers.

Jess and her siblings stood close together by the grave, Libby clutching her sister's hand, the boys next to Libby beside their father, lips tight, heads bowed slightly. On Jess's other side stood Hilda, who had been a tower of strength to Jess this past week as she'd struggled to cope with her own personal grief as well as comfort her siblings, and attend to the grim practicalities her father should have seen to, including registering the death and organising the funeral. He'd sunk so deeply into a trough he seemed unable to face up to his responsibilities.

She could forgive him for not pulling his weight with the practical tasks – he was in a state of trauma and not thinking straight – but she hated him for failing to give comfort to his younger children, who had effectively lost their father along with their mother. At a time when they needed him more than ever before, he wasn't there for them. Rather than bringing them closer together, their mother's death had ripped their family apart.

The change in Charlie was incredible. The man normally so warm-hearted and outgoing had become cool and withdrawn. He didn't smile, barely talked; he even looked different. He was permanently whey-faced and the greying process in his hair seemed to have accelerated to such an extent that he was almost white around the hairline. Having eaten hardly a thing for a week, he had an emaciated look about him too.

But now the current ordeal was nearing its end and Jess felt Libby's hand tighten on hers as the coffin was lowered into the ground. Through a blur she saw people weeping all around her and could feel her own tears falling. Struggling to be brave as usual, Ronnie was holding back his own emotions and comforting his twin sister while Jess held Todd, who was crying silently. Dabbing her eyes and sniffing quietly, Hilda stood in dignified silence for a few moments before taking Jess's arm in a supportive manner. Ashen-faced and tear-stained, Charlie stared ahead of him, looking oddly vacant and making no effort to encourage or soothe his poor bereaved children.

When the formalities finally ended, the relieved mourners headed out of the cemetery in a sad procession, talking in low voices and barely noticing the rain.

'Don't have any more to drink now, please, Dad,' Jess begged her father later that afternoon when he staggered into the kitchen where she was waiting for the kettle to boil for tea for the guests, and poured himself another whisky.

'Why not?'

'Because it won't help.' Normally a moderate drinker whose usual intake was a quick one in the pub after work, he'd been drinking steadily since they'd got back from the cemetery. As a consequence, his behaviour had been bawdy and embarrassing. He's been talking too much and too loudly, and telling inappropriate jokes, much to the mortification of his children.

'It already has,' he told her in a boozy, argumentative tone. 'It's got me through the worst ordeal of my life.'

'But you've got through the funeral so you don't need to go on drinking now, do you?' she pointed out as he took a long swig and stood swaying by the kitchen door.

He looked lost suddenly, as though all the aggression had ebbed away. 'It helps to deaden the pain,' he said in a strangled voice, his eyes filling with tears. 'I just can't bear it, Jess.'

'Oh, Dad, I know how much you must be suffering,' she told him, her tone softening with sympathy. 'But drinking your way through it is only going to make things worse. You know how bad-tempered it makes you after a while.'

As though to illustrate her point, his inebriation entered the belligerent stage. 'Since when did my daughter have the right to tell me what I should and shouldn't do?' he demanded aggressively. 'Answer me that.'

'Since you started giving me cause,' she came back at him. 'God knows, Dad, I understand how terrible it must be for you, but the rest of us are all hurting too and we need your support. It isn't so bad for me because I'm an adult – I'll get through it somehow – but the others are just kids and they've lost their mum. They need to feel that the two of us are there for them at this terrible time.'

'I'm here, aren't I?' he pointed out in a slurred but angry tone. 'Anyone would think I'd cleared off and deserted my family or something to hear you talk.'

'You have, in a manner of speaking.'

'I'm doing what I can under the circumstances.' He looked helpless again, his behaviour extremely volatile. 'Even though I've wanted to stay in bed with the covers over my head every morning, I've been going to the shop every day to keep things ticking over to put food on the table. Even today when we've closed as a mark of respect to your mother, I still got up at five to do the papers for the rounds.'

'You won't be able to get up to do them in the morning if you carry on drinking like this.'

'So what if I can't?' he argued, his mood changing yet again. 'It won't hurt people to go without their morning paper for once.'

This wasn't her father speaking. In the whole of her life she had never known him not to care about his business. It had always been such a joy to him. His eyelids were drooping and his skin shining with sweat. She ran a distracted hand through her hair, her face looking paper white against her dark hair and the black fitted suit she'd bought for the occasion. She wanted to weep with pity for him but sympathy wasn't what was needed at this moment. 'Look, Dad, I realise that your pain must be unbearable and I know you miss Mum more than any of us could possibly imagine but please don't get any more drunk than you are already, not at her funeral. Don't let her – and yourself – down.'

But he was too far gone to listen to reason. 'Surely a man's entitled to a few drinks at a time like this.' He was stumbling over his words now.

'A few drinks, certainly.' Jess was imbued with both pity and exasperation. 'But you've already had a skinful and if you have any more you'll make a complete fool of yourself.'

He blinked a couple of times, then peered at her as though through impaired vision and leaned back against the wall. 'I'm sorry, Jess,' he muttered, his words barely comprehensible. 'So sorry.'

'Yes, I know you are, Dad.' She knew he meant it and it pierced her heart to see him lose his dignity this way.

'I don't know how to carry on without her.'

'I don't know how to either but we have to keep going,' she said thickly. 'You and I have to be strong for the others. I need you so much.'

'Yeah, yeah,' he muttered, lids drooping.

She watched in horror as he slid slowly down the wall and sat on the floor with his eyes closed and head slumped forward on to his chest.

At that moment, Ronnie came into the room. 'Oh, so he's passed out, has he? I guessed it was only a matter of time.' His eyes were simmering with rage. 'Drunk at his own wife's funeral. How disgusting is that?'

'He's just heartbroken, that's all.'

'He's drunk.'

'Yeah, that too.'

'It's bad enough that Mum died and we had to have this awful funeral,' grumbled Ronnie. 'He didn't have to make things worse by making a complete idiot of himself and showing us up. You'd think he'd show some respect for our mother.'

Jess chewed her lip, more concerned with dealing with the situation than criticising it. 'I think you'd better go and get Hilda,' she said. 'She'll help us to get him upstairs to bed without anyone noticing.'

'Everyone knows he's stinking drunk anyway, so there's no point in trying to hide it,' Ronnie said in disgust before heading off to find their neighbour.

'Oh my Lord,' said Hilda, sailing on to the scene and taking in the situation. 'I knew he was knocking it back but I didn't realise he was quite so plastered. Let's get him upstairs sharpish. We'll make his apologies to the guests afterwards, tell 'em it's all been a bit too much for him and he's gone for a lie-down.'

'He's let our mother down and made a laughing stock of the family,' declared Ronnie. Taking his role of the elder son rather too seriously, and terrified of seeming to be lacking in strength somehow, he was being surly and difficult. 'He ought to be thoroughly ashamed of himself.'

Jess was prepared to make allowances for Ronnie because she knew that he was devastated by the loss of his mother and distressed by the change in their father. But Hilda rounded on the boy in defence of Charlie.

'Pity for your father is what you should be feeling, young man, not shame,' she rebuked. 'Your dad's a broken man, that's why he's behaving the way he is. He's never put a foot wrong before. He's always been a damned fine father to all of you. He's worked hard to give you a decent life.'

'He's let us down today, though,' the boy mumbled. 'And he's been no help to anyone since . . . since it happened.'

'All right, perhaps he's not coping with his loss as well as he might be, just at the moment, but that doesn't make him a bad person,' she lectured. 'He and your mum had been together a long time and it might take a while for him to come to terms with her not being around. It's still very early days and we're all going to have to be patient with him.' She paused for breath. 'Now help me and your sister get him upstairs to bed, please.'

Ronnie didn't argue, and the three of them hauled Charlie to his feet, dragged him upstairs and laid him on the bed. He didn't protest, just mumbled incoherently. Eager to escape the possibility of having to help undress his 'disgraceful' father, Ronnie hurried from the room, muttering something about going to find his siblings.

'What a way to carry on at his wife's funeral, eh?' Hilda said to Jess as the two women removed his shoes. 'I shall tell him what I think of him in no uncertain terms tomorrow.'

Jess shot her a look. 'But you've just given Ronnie a trouncing for criticising him.'

'That's right,' Hilda confirmed. 'The boy needed reminding of a few facts. What I said is true: your dad has been a good father and has always done his best for you until now. But that doesn't mean he can get away with this sort of behaviour without a rollicking from someone.'

'I've already given him a bit of a ticking off,' Jess told her.

'He needs someone from outside the family to have a few strong words,' Hilda opined. 'Someone older.'

'It's good of you to take the trouble, Hilda.'

'It's no bother at all, love.' She was astounded at the suggestion that it might be. 'Your mum and I were friends for a long time. What sort of friend would I be if I didn't look out for her family now that she's not here to do it herself?'

Jess was enormously warmed and comforted by her. No one could have stopped today from being anything other than hellish, but Hilda had made it bearable with her endless supply of moral support as well as practical help with the organisation and catering. Nothing was too much trouble. Jess had never really considered her own feelings for Hilda until now. She'd always just been Hilda from next door, always around, 'a nosy old bat' Dad had sometimes called her in a jokey sort of way. Jess remembered what good pals her mother and Hilda had been. It hadn't been unusual to see Hilda helping Mum prepare the vegetables or peg the washing out when she'd called in for a chat. Sometimes of an evening they'd shut themselves in the front room and play piano duets for the sheer fun of it, both having been brought up in an age when piano lessons for children were a matter of course in many ordinary families. But this past week Jess had realised Hilda's true value. She was much more than just a neighbour with an interfering streak. She was a gem, a true friend to them all. It was no wonder Mum had been so fond of her.

'Thanks, anyway,' Jess said. Then: 'I've just thought of something I mustn't forget to do.'

'What's that?'

'Set my alarm clock for five o'clock in the morning,' she told her. 'His nibs here isn't going to be in any fit state to get up and do the papers. And someone's got to do it.'

Hilda sighed worriedly. 'Good old Jess. Everything falls to you.'

'It's only natural, now that Mum's not here,' Jess pointed out as they covered her father with the eiderdown. 'And now I'd better go down and finish making that tea.'

'I might have known you'd stick your big nose in,' objected Charlie the following evening.

Spotting him in his back garden smoking a cigarette, Hilda had nipped in through a gap in the fence to make her feelings known while the children weren't around.

'If I get drunk it's my business. It's got nothing to do with you.'

'Somebody has to look out for that family of yours,' was her answer.

'Yeah, and that somebody is me,' he told her glumly, as angry with himself as he was with her for reminding him of his shame. 'It's my job to do that and I'm doing it.'

'Really? I can't say I've noticed it.'

'The kids aren't babies; they don't need me to wipe their noses for them,' he pointed out irritably.

'They don't need you to shut yourself off from them either.'

'I haven't.'

'It looks that way to me . . . and to them.'

'They're old enough to bear with me on this.'

'They're also old enough to feel the death of their mother deeply,' Hilda informed him gravely. 'They're breaking their hearts over it and you're not helping them one little bit.'

'Oh, give us a break, you nosy old cow,' he exploded. 'I came out here for a quiet smoke. The last thing I need after a long day is you bending my ear.'

'Long day, my foot,' she retorted. 'Jess got up and did the papers for you and looked after the shop until you managed to get your arse out of bed around the middle of the day.'

At least he had the grace to look sheepish, she noticed. 'All right, that shouldn't have happened,' he admitted.

'You'll have to pull yourself together when she goes back to work at Burtons. She won't be around here for ever, you know,' she reminded him. 'She'll be wanting to go home to her flat soon.'

'I know that.'

'Have you got any idea what it was like for those children, your being paralytic at the funeral yesterday?'

Expecting a furious retaliation, she was surprised when, after a pause, he said mildly, 'Look, I already feel bad enough about it, I really don't need you to rub it in.'

She didn't enjoy interfering but neither did she feel able to stand by and let a family she cared about fall apart. 'I know you're having a really rotten time, Charlie,' she said less harshly. 'But so are the kids, and they're relying on you.'

'Oh, for God's sake, woman,' he snapped. 'Do you think I don't know what my responsibilities are?'

Realising that she had gone as far as she dare, Hilda lowered her eyes. 'I was out of order. Sorry, Charlie.' She was uncharacteristically subdued.

He raked his fingers through his hair anxiously. He wasn't used to seeing Hilda looking so sombre and he felt a stab of guilt, realising that she had suffered a painful loss too. 'Look, I know how fond you were of Joy, and this can't be easy for you either,' he told her. 'But I have to deal with this in my own way.'

'I understand,' she nodded. 'If there's anything I can do, just let me know.'

'Thanks.' He drew on his cigarette, looking at her. 'But to be quite honest, I think the biggest favour you can do for me is to leave me alone to get on with it.'

'Sure, I'll leave you alone,' she assented. 'But I won't stand by and see those children suffer if there's anything I can do to help. As long as they need me I'll be there for them, whether you like it or not.'

Without waiting for a reply, she turned and went back into her own garden the way she had come, along a well-trodden path between the two properties.

Charlie stayed outside for a while longer, smoking, then went inside, a thin dejected figure, a mere shadow of the man he'd once been.

Jess was sitting on a bench in a quiet corner of Churchfields recreation ground, staring ponderously into space. It was a sunny Sunday afternoon so there were plenty of people about in this twenty-two acres of parkland, the entrance of which was just across the road from the end of Park Street.

In the two weeks since the funeral, she'd had a dismally sad and exhausting time coping with her traumatised siblings, the housekeeping, which had somehow become her responsibility, the shop and her increasingly morose father, who was absent from his place of work far too often.

She'd come here for a break from the house where her father was sleeping off a lunchtime session at the pub. The twins were out with their respective friends. Todd and Hilda had come with Jess but had walked on to nearby Brent Lodge Park – the Bunny Park, as it was usually known – because Todd liked the little zoo there, especially the peacocks, who'd been delighting visitors by fanning out their beautifully patterned tail feathers in a colourful display ever since Jess could remember.

Desperate for a few minutes alone to clear her mind, Jess had told Hilda and Todd that she would catch them up; had suggested that they all have a cup of tea and a bun in the park cafeteria later. A distant rumble grew into a deafening roar as the express train to Paddington thundered across the Wharncliffe viaduct with its eight magnificent arches, hidden from view in places by the lush foliage of the many old trees that lined the banks of the River Brent beneath it. It was said that Queen Victoria and Prince Albert had used this line and the queen had been so impressed with the view across Churchfields that she'd given instructions for her train to stop briefly on the viaduct whenever she passed this way.

Having spent so much of her childhood here, Jess knew every footpath, every blade of grass. Childish games had been played here, picnics eaten, adolescent problems thrashed out with girl friends, boys fancied, dreams dreamed and plans made. Then she'd grown up and left home and visits had been rarer. But she still loved to come here, and felt especially drawn to it when she was distressed or worried about anything.

Now she was imbued with a plethora of emotions: ineffable grief for the loss of her mother, compassion for her siblings, and frustration tinged

43

with sorrow for her poor distressed father, who was beginning to spend more time at the pub than he did at home. There was something else on her mind too, something she was ashamed to admit because it seemed so selfish. But she couldn't stop the thoughts and feelings coming. As much as she fought against it, she longed for the personal freedom she had taken for granted just a few weeks ago.

She'd put off thinking about the problem; had hoped that somehow it would resolve itself. But it wasn't going to, that was now obvious to her. With a sigh of resignation, she came to the decision she had been avoiding making and her eyes swam with tears. But there was no choice for her. She knew what she had to do and wouldn't shirk it, no matter how much it hurt. Admonishing herself for self-centred feelings of resentment, she swallowed hard and headed for Brent Lodge Park to meet Todd and Hilda.

'Oh, Jess, I'm so sorry you can't go. I know how much the Paris job meant to you,' said Babs sympathetically. It was a few days later and she and Jess had met for coffee and a chat in a milk bar in Leicester Square. Jess was in the West End, having been to the Burton Company office to see Miss Molly to tell her her decision in person, and collect some pay that was owing to her.

'I'm sick about it but there's nothing I can do,' she explained glumly. 'I just don't have a choice.'

'You must be absolutely gutted.'

'I'll say I am. But it's just one of those things,' Jess told her. 'It is only a job, when all is said and done.'

'The Paris job is more than that to you,' corrected Babs. 'It's a chance that might never come your way again.'

Jess stirred her coffee, looking idly into the cup. 'I know but I can't go and that's all there is to it.' Her eyes were sore and shadowed from lots of bad nights. 'There's no point in my dwelling on it; that won't change anything.'

'It's a damned shame,' Babs commiserated. 'Is there no way at all that you could—'

'None at all,' Jess cut in. 'I can't be away for six months, not with things how they are at home.'

'But the kids aren't babies,' Babs pointed out. 'And your dad will be there.'

'They're old enough to fend for themselves up to a point but I couldn't desert them.' She was adamant. 'It's too soon. They're too upset, too emotionally vulnerable and too young. And having the long school holidays to think about Mum not being there isn't helping. Dad's too grief-stricken to be much help to anyone, poor thing.'

'Oh, Jess, that is a shame.'

'It isn't only the family who's suffering, it's his business too,' Jess went

44

on. 'He's not paying proper attention to it so I'm having to help out in the shop as well as look after things at home. Mum used to work in the shop in the afternoons and he's done nothing about replacing her. The morning assistant can't always stay on for the whole day so I have to step in then as well as get up and do the morning papers more often than I'd like.'

'Strictly speaking, it isn't your responsibility, though,' suggested Babs.

'It's the family livelihood so I can't just ignore the situation and leave it to my father to sort out, can I?' Jess pointed out. 'He's missing more often than he's there anyway, so I have to be on hand at all odd times.'

The other woman sipped her coffee slowly, looking thoughtful. 'You will be coming back to work at Burtons eventually, though, won't you?' she queried.

'God, yes, and the sooner the better, as far as I'm concerned but I can't say when it'll be. I'll have to wait until Dad's more on top of things.' She fiddled with a strand of hair anxiously, looking at her friend with apprehension. 'And that brings me to the other bit of bad news. When I do come back to work, I think I'll probably have to live at home so that I'm on hand for the kids. So you'd better start looking for another flatmate because I know you can't afford the rent on your own. Sorry.'

'Don't worry about me.' Babs looked even more concerned now on her friend's behalf. 'Living at home won't be so convenient for you, will it? Having to travel out to the suburbs after a show?'

'No, but I'll do it if necessary for the sake of the family,' Jess told her. 'It'll just mean I'll spend more time commuting into the West End, that's all. And I'll have to make sure I don't miss the last train.'

'What about if you're put into a show outside of London?' wondered Babs. 'You could get sent anywhere so you won't be around for the kids then.'

'I'm hoping that the management will give me the London jobs while I'm still needed at home,' she said. 'I know we're supposed to go where we're sent without complaint, but under the special circumstances they might co-operate. I know they like to call the tune but they're not completely heartless, and there are several Burton teams working in West End revues and other shows.'

'Mm, there is that.'

'Anyway, I'll have to cross that bridge when I come to it. I'm taking it one day at a time for the moment.'

Babs emitted a worried sigh, fearing that her friend might lose more than just the job in Paris. 'You've just lost your mum, Jess. Be careful you don't lose your career as well by staying away too long,' she advised her. 'You'll soon get out of practice and out of shape, and the company won't keep your job open for ever. As you've pointed out to me many times in the past, there are plenty of young hopefuls out there only too eager to fill our shoes.'

'Don't rub it in.'

'Sorry, kid. Just making sure you know what's at risk here,' Babs explained. 'You'll just have to make arrangements for the kids while you're working, and try to stay on at the flat if you possibly can. Once they're back at school after the holidays, with something else to think about, they'll soon pick up. And your father can't expect you to give up your career as a dancer to step into your mother's shoes. That wouldn't be fair.'

'He doesn't expect that of me.' Jess was fiercely defensive. 'He just isn't himself at the moment. And the fact of the matter is, he has himself and three children to support from the shop. If he lets the business slip so badly that he loses it, what will happen to them then? What I earn as a dancer only just keeps me. It wouldn't keep a family. So you can see that I have to make sure things run properly.'

'Yeah, I suppose so,' Babs admitted. 'But from what I know of your dad, he isn't the type to stand by and let his daughter miss the chance of a lifetime on his account. Yet that's what's happening. Things are getting out of control.'

'Normally he wouldn't let it happen, but he's still in shock,' Jess was at pains to explain. 'The poor man is in a world of his own.'

'I'm really sorry for him,' Babs said. 'But all of this is so tough on you.'

'It's tough on us all. The kids are at a sensitive age, especially Ronnie and Libby. Adolescence is difficult enough at the best of times, but having to cope with the death of your mother as well . . .'

'I understand all of that and I sympathise with the rest of the family,' Babs said, 'but you're my friend so you're my prime concern, naturally. You're a born dancer. It's what you should be doing, not standing behind a counter selling newspapers.'

'I know exactly what's at stake as far as my career is concerned,' Jess told her.

'As long as you do.'

'How could I not? But it's out of my hands.'

'It just seems so unfair.' Babs' big blue eyes softened. 'Look, I won't start looking for a new flatmate just yet because it might not come to that,' she suggested kindly. 'You might think of some way around it. Look on the bright side, eh? I bet everything will be all right in no time and you and me will be in the flat talking until all hours, as usual.'

'But I'm not earning at the moment so I can't pay next month's rent,' Jess pointed out to her. 'I don't want you to be out of pocket.'

'And I don't want a new flatmate,' Babs made clear. 'I can manage for a short time.'

'I can't let you do that, Babs.'

'Yes, you can, because I'm offering and I'm your friend.'

Realising that it would be ungracious to protest further, Jess said, 'Thanks, kid. I owe you one.'

46

'Anything else I can do to help, promise me you'll give me a shout?'

'I promise.'

They chatted for a while longer, then Babs said she had to go. 'I'm due at rehearsal in ten minutes and I've a feeling it's going to be a long one today,' she said, making a face. 'Not one of us could get it right yesterday. Elsie was in a right mood.'

'I can imagine.' A pang of regret ached inside Jess. 'I wish I was coming with you,' she sighed. 'I miss the dancing . . . and the troupe, more than you could possibly imagine.'

'I bet you don't miss the sore feet, though,' Babs grinned in an attempt to lift the mood.

'That's the one thing I can do without,' confessed Jess, managing a watery smile. 'That and the costumes that squeeze the very breath out of you.'

'Don't remind me.'

Smiling, they left the milk bar together. Babs walked back to the rehearsal studio and Jess headed for Oxford Circus underground station through the summer crowds, a tall, willowy figure in a white blouse and full floral skirt. The traffic was almost at a standstill and she could hear Elvis Presley's hit record 'Blue Suede Shoes' on a car radio through the open window. Outside the station there was a newsstand with a headline about British and French troops sailing for the Suez Canal because of the crisis out there. Suddenly she felt very insignificant in the scheme of things. A career as a chorus girl seemed unimportant compared to this serious problem in the wider world and the possible loss of life if it wasn't resolved.

But despite the indisputable comparison, she continued to be plagued by an overpowering sense of loneliness all the way to Ealing Broadway on the tube. She missed the fun and camaraderie of the troupe as well as the dancing. She loved her father and her siblings dearly but she felt isolated without the company of her friends. She needed her life outside the family. Oh well, she told herself, it can't be helped, and it might not be for much longer.

She was still in a wistful state of mind when she got home. But when she got in and saw the state of the place, her gloom turned to fury. The breakfast things were unwashed in the sink, none of the beds was made, her siblings' clothes were littering the bedrooms, and comics and crumpled magazines lay around in the living room along with dirty cups and biscuit crumbs.

Being a surrogate mum was one thing. Being a slave to her sister and brothers was quite another and it was time she did something about it. Ronnie had been left in charge with instructions to go next door if there were any problems. She had an ongoing arrangement with Hilda that she would be on hand for them when Jess was out since she couldn't be here every second of the time. Their father's shop was only just round the corner from here if she was needed, anyway.

She rounded them up in the long narrow kitchen, Ronnie from the street, Libby from the garden and Todd from the living room where he was reading a book, apparently oblivious to the mess and unaware of the rising storm. They all clattered in and sat down at the wooden table with Jess standing at the head.

'What's all this about then?' demanded Ronnie sulkily. 'Why have I been called in like some little kid? I was in the middle of doing something with my mates.'

'Isn't that just too bad?' Jess was trembling with rage.

'I wanted to finish my chapter,' added Todd, further fuelling her anger.

'Tough,' she replied.

Libby remained silent, eyeing her sister with caution.

'I've called you in because it's time we made a few changes around here.'

'Huh. Haven't we had enough of those just lately?' complained Ronnie, seemingly unaware of the fact that Jess was seething. 'We don't need you to create more.'

'You three are the most selfish people I've ever set eyes on,' she blasted at them. 'You never think of anyone but yourselves. You're incredible!'

Now she had their full attention. They all stared at her in silence, looking worried.

'But I'm about to put a stop to that because you are all going to start pulling your weight around here.'

They remained silent.

Jess waved her hand towards the sink full of dirty dishes and looked back at them. 'I suppose you're expecting me to do that, aren't you?'

'Hadn't thought about it,' shrugged Ronnie.

Libby looked much more sheepish. She hated to be in trouble with her beloved sister. 'I suppose we should have done it,' she said, biting her lip. 'I just didn't give it a thought.'

'That's the trouble – you don't think, any of you.' Jess was blazing mad. 'You're so used to Mum doing everything for you, you expect me to do the same. Well, it isn't on, do you understand? I'm your sister, not your mother or your maid, and I've more than enough to do without having to clear up after you.'

Silence echoed around them.

'Boys don't do housework,' announced Ronnie at last.

'They do in this house, mate,' was Jess's reply to that. 'When I'm in charge they do, anyway.'

'I suppose this has come about because you just did everything, you seemed to take over from Mum,' suggested Todd, pale with worry because he didn't like being on bad terms with anyone. 'We didn't realise—'

'More fool me for taking over and letting you get away with murder,' roared Jess. 'I did it automatically because you're just kids. But you're all old enough to do your share and that's what's going to happen from now on. You are not going to leave everything to me in future. Is that clear?'

'What future?' said Ronnie miserably. 'You're going away to Paris soon so you won't be here anyway.'

'I'm not going to Paris.' They hadn't been told yet because she'd wanted to wait until she'd made it official at the Burton office.

Six eyes widened in surprise. 'You're not going?' said Libby with obvious relief.

'No.'

'What . . . definitely not?'

'Not at all?' added Todd.

'That's right,' Jess confirmed. 'That's why I went into the Burton office this morning – to tell them that I won't be going.'

'But I thought it was all arranged,' said Ronnie.

'It was, but it's all unarranged now.' She was so disappointed, her tone was snappy.

'All right, there's no need to bite my head off,' objected Ronnie. 'Go to Paris if it means that much to you.'

His thoughtless assumption that she had a choice in the matter exacerbated her regret, frustration magnified by the sight of the dirty dishes and the thought of the contents of the laundry basket needing to be dealt with before she went to work at the shop because she hadn't had time to do it before she went out this morning. Suddenly the disappointment was too much and all she wanted was to escape from the trap she was in.

'I wish to God I could go,' she shouted, eyes bright with angry tears.

'Don't stay on our account,' shrugged Ronnie. 'We're old enough to look after ourselves.'

'Don't be so ridiculous,' Jess barked. 'You'd realise, if you took the trouble to think about it, that I can't go, that I don't have a choice in the matter. But from now on you're all going to do your bit to help around here. I'll run the household but you're all to do your part. You'll each make your own bed every morning and take turns with the washing-up and all other minor household chores. And you can start by clearing up the mess you've made while I was out.'

And with that she stormed upstairs to her bedroom and slammed the door behind her. She was shaking with anger but compunction was already on its heels. Had she perhaps been a bit too hard on them, making them feel guilty because she couldn't go to Paris because of them? It wasn't their fault they'd lost their mother while still at an age to need a substitute. Neither could they be blamed for an indulgent mother who'd looked after them so well they'd grown up to believe that everything happened by magic.

To add to her shame she couldn't stop crying. All the emotion she'd held back since her mother's death because she'd wanted to stay strong for the others now culminated in a great outpouring of grief. Her body was heaving with sobs. And all the while she was hating herself for what seemed like a display of self-pity.

There were noises downstairs: the clatter of dishes from the kitchen and the whine of the vacuum cleaner. Jess's immediate impulse was to go down and tell them it didn't matter, that she would do it. But she knew that wouldn't do anyone any good in the long run. The Mollitt children needed to pull together if they were going to get through this bereavement without a serious falling-out.

She sat on the edge of her bed, staring at Libby's unmade one and forced herself not to make it. Exhausted suddenly, she lay down and closed her eyes, wishing life could be back as it had been a few weeks ago.

After a while everything seemed to go quiet downstairs. Then there was a tap on her door and the trio came in, looking extremely shamefaced.

'We've cleaned up,' Ronnie said, 'and we're gonna make beans on toast for lunch. One slice or two?'

'One, please.'

'Are you going to help Dad in the shop this afternoon?' Libby enquired.

Jess nodded.

'We'll do the dishes after you've gone,' offered Todd.

'And get the tea if you tell us what we're supposed to do,' Libby was keen to add.

'I said you're to help out,' Jess said thickly. 'I didn't say you had to do everything.'

'We're ever so sorry you can't go to Paris,' Libby went on with a quiver in her voice. 'But thanks for not going. We don't know what we'd do without you.'

'She's right,' added Todd.

'It isn't that we can't look after ourselves, or anything.' Ronnie was still pretending to be tough. 'I'm almost a man and Dad's around . . . well, some of the time, anyway. But we'd sort of miss you if we didn't see you at all for six months now that Mum isn't here. When you go back to your flat you won't be actually living here but at least we'll see you on Sundays and know that you're not far away if there's an emergency.'

Jess's face crumpled. 'Come here, you little monsters,' she choked out, standing up and going towards them with her arms open wide and tears streaming down her cheeks.

As they stood in a huddle in the middle of the room, hugging each other, the Paris job no longer seemed to matter.

50

Chapter Four

The first action of dancers when they reached the wings after a show – hot and sticky and out of breath – was always to unzip each other. Nobody could wait until they got to the dressing room to loosen their costumes.

'Phew, thank God for that,' puffed Babs as a girl called Jean undid the top of Babs' skin-tight, white satin bodice over which she wore a floaty, multilayered chiffon skirt in a beautiful shade of rose pink. This flimsy addition completely transformed the look of the costume by adding glamour and elegance, especially as a white picture hat with trailing pink ribbons completed the outfit. 'It's like having concrete corsets on. I was sweltering hot under those light too.'

'I thought I was going to melt as well,' confessed Jean, removing her own hat as Babs loosened her bodice for her. 'Still, the costumes look good so it's worth a bit of suffering, I suppose.'

'They're the prettiest outfits we've had in a long time,' agreed Babs as they headed for the dressing room with the rest of the troupe. 'All that lovely chiffon makes you feel so feminine, doesn't it?'

'Mm. I really enjoyed that last number,' said Jean.

'Me too. "Cherry Pink and Apple Blossom White" is a good tune to work to.'

In the communal dressing room there was a clamour of female voices; dancers in various states of undress were swarming around the mirrors or queuing for the washbasins, everyone talking at once.

A voice from the door rose above the others and produced instant silence.

'Well done, girls,' complimented Molly. 'It was an excellent perform- ance tonight.'

'Thank you, Miss Molly,' they chorused like a class of primary schoolchildren.

'Have a nice restful Sunday and recharge your batteries ready for work next week,' she advised. 'No late nights, now. I want you fresh and full of energy for rehearsals on Monday morning.'

There was a polite murmur of assent before the dancers continued getting changed.

The older woman didn't leave; she walked over to where Babs and

51

Jean were creaming off their make-up and idly chatting. 'You need to get your hair cut,' she stated without preamble to Jean, who had a glorious mane of auburn hair.

'Oh? Really?' Jean was clearly disconcerted, holding a piece of cotton wool in one hand and touching her hair nervously with the other. 'But it isn't long since I had it cut. I didn't think it needed doing again just yet.'

'It's longer than our acceptable length,' declared Molly in a loud and categorical manner, causing a tense silence to creep through the room. 'I was walking behind you on the way up here from the wings and couldn't help noticing it.'

'I honestly don't think—' began Jean.

'You need at least two inches off the length,' interrupted Molly, leaning forward and tugging disapprovingly at Jean's locks. 'And I'd like you to get it done before the next show, please.'

'I think it looks lovely as it is,' put in the outspoken Babs. 'And it isn't as if it gets in the way of her headdress or anything.'

Molly's lethal stare was enough to send even the hardiest soul into a state of nervous debility. 'Did I ask for your opinion?' she asked fiercely.

'No, but—'

'In that case, keep it to yourself.'

'But it's so damned petty, making girls have their hair cut unnecessarily,' pointed out the indomitable Babs.

'Leave it, Babs,' urged Jean worriedly. 'I'll get it cut. It doesn't matter.'

'But it does matter,' persisted Babs, meeting Molly's eyes in a challenge. 'It's downright ridiculous, this insistence on the part of the management that girls get their hair cut for no sensible purpose. I mean, what possible difference can an inch or two of hair make to her performance? She's hardly going to trip over it, is she?'

'You know the rules,' Molly reminded her in an uncompromising tone. 'Burton Girls do not have long hair. You all have a clause to this effect written into your contract.'

The rule about compulsory hair length was the one most detested by all Burton Girls. It had even been known for dancers to hide their own hair under a wig of shorter hair.

'Jean's hair isn't long, though, is it?' Babs was at pains to remind her.

Molly emitted a sigh of seething irritation. 'As I've just said, it's longer than we allow our dancers to have it,' she answered through gritted teeth.

'The hair length rule is completely unnecessary,' muttered Babs under her breath.

'The management doesn't think so, and that's what counts around here.' Molly gave Babs a hard look. 'You've been with us for long enough to know how things work in this company.'

'Yes, but that doesn't mean I have to agree with it.' Babs couldn't bring herself to give up.

'Perhaps I should remind you that no one is forced to join this

52

company or to stay with us if they're not happy with the way we do things,' came Molly's forceful reply. 'I'm sure there are plenty of jobs around with far fewer rules and regulations, jobs where you can wear your hair at whatever length you please.' She gave Babs a dark look. 'As I'm sure you already know, we're not short of people wanting to dance in our line. Every day of the week we are inundated with enquiries. No dancer is indispensable.'

There was a deathly hush. All eyes were on this altercation, the warning felt by everyone.

Babs met Molly's steady gaze. She was tempted to take up the cudgels and fight this one out to the end and to hell with the consequences. But she couldn't afford to be out of work at the moment. When Dickie made an honest woman of her and she wasn't reliant on this job, that was the time to stand up for her principles. She loathed herself for this feeble attitude but facts had to be faced. Anyway, it wasn't the company in general she had a quarrel with, just the way they clung on to outdated rules, no matter how senseless. And she did enjoy being a Burton Girl – maybe not so unconditionally as Jess did, but for the most part she liked it.

'Yes, I'm fully aware of that, Miss Molly.' Her manner was polite but firm. Even in defeat, it wasn't in her nature to grovel.

'I'm very glad to hear it,' said Molly, and marched from the room, calling out a general good night at the door.

The relief in the room was tangible.

'You'll push the management too far one of these days, Babs,' someone warned her. This wasn't the first time Babs had stuck her neck out on someone else's behalf.

'That's what I'm afraid of too,' added Jean, removing the last of her make-up and throwing the cotton wool in the bin. 'I know you were sticking up for me, and I really do appreciate it, but the hair length issue isn't worth losing your job over. I don't mind getting it trimmed. And Molly is right, it is written into the contract.'

'You've got to look after yourself, Babs,' said one of the other dancers. 'I mean, let's face it, to all of us in this room, dancing in the Burton Company is a precious thing and we put up with the daft rules because we love what we do. So it isn't worth getting yourself into trouble for any of us. We don't want to lose you.'

'Let's hope Jess comes back to work soon,' Jean put in. 'She always seemed to be a calming influence on you.'

'You're one of the best, though, Babs,' called out another colleague, raising a rousing cheer of agreement.

'I doubt if Molly thinks so,' grinned Babs. 'They've probably got me down in their files as a disruptive influence, to be dispensed with at the earliest opportunity if I step out of line too often.'

'You're not only a good dancer, but useful to them because you're very

53

quick to pick up the routines,' pointed out one of the others, 'so they won't get rid of you unless you push them too far.'

'Not until they're ready to replace me, anyway,' replied the realistic Babs, slipping into her dress and running a comb through her hair.

People were leaving in groups. Feeling a sudden pang at the thought of going home to the empty flat, she asked if anyone fancied a drink or a coffee before they went their separate ways. But they were all anxious to catch their trains and buses.

Oh, come back soon, Jess, she thought. I miss you.

When Jess got up on the penultimate day of the school holidays, she could have no idea that a series of minor events would bring her to a major decision by the time she went to sleep that night.

It was a still, cloudy Monday morning and she was doing the family wash; boiling the whites in the copper as her mother had done before her and washing the rest in the sink with soap flakes, scrubbing stubborn marks on a wooden board, before rinsing each garment and putting it through the mangle in the back garden.

There was a conflicting atmosphere in the house. While Todd anticipated with relish the return to school, the twins were positively doom-laden about it.

'Will my school clothes be ready for Wednesday, Jess?' enquired Todd brightly as Jess pegged some washing on the line, hoping for a breeze that would speed up the drying process since there was no sign of the sun.

'Yeah, course they will.'

'Mum always used to have everything ready for us,' he said, seeking further reassurance.

'And so will I,' she promised.

'Change for our dinner money?'

'Consider it done.'

'We always have a bath and a hair wash the night before going back.' He liked everything to be just so.

Jess looked down at this serious young boy, who was ten going on thirty-five. 'Don't worry, Todd, I'll make sure that there's plenty of hot water and that all your school clothes are washed and ironed. Everything will be just the same as when Mum was here.'

He smiled, his plump little face lighting up under his thatch of straight hair that fell into an untidy fringe at the front. 'I usually go to the barber's too, the day before we go back,' he reminded her. 'The one near Dad's shop.'

'Then we'll make sure you do this time too,' she assured him. 'I'll give you the money and you can go tomorrow.'

'Thanks.'

Pegging out the last item, she picked up the empty bowl, pausing and looking at her brother, who was dressed in short grey trousers with long

54

grey socks and a pullover that his mother had knitted, over a checked shirt. 'I must say your attitude is a bit different from that of your brother and sister,' she told him with a wry grin. 'I expect they're hoping I'll forget that school starts again on Wednesday and they can somehow get out of going.'

He grinned. 'They'd love that. School isn't exactly their favourite thing,' he observed.

'But it is yours?'

'I wouldn't go so far as to say that,' he told her. 'But the summer holidays get a bit boring after a while, so I'll be glad to go back, especially as I'm going into the top class.'

'Looking forward to bossing all the little kids about, eh?' She was teasing; it wasn't in Todd's nature to do any such thing.

Already thinking of something else, he didn't respond to her joshing but said in a solemn tone, 'I'll have to work hard because we've got the eleven-plus exam towards the end of term.'

'From what I've heard, you'll sail through it.'

'You can't be sure; no one can,' was his sage response. 'But I'll do my best.'

'I'll do what I can to help,' she told him. 'If you want me to test you on anything, you only have to ask.'

'Thanks, Jess,' he smiled.

She ruffled his hair in a gesture of affection. For the first time, the seriousness of his educational aspirations registered fully with something of a jolt, especially in terms of the back-up support he would need at home. She realised also that the domestic routine would change dramatically come Wednesday. With the holidays over there would be disciplines to be upheld. Because there had been no school since she'd been running the household, they'd muddled through. But a proper routine must be established with the start of the new term. In pensive mood, she went back inside.

While Jess was slicing cold meat from yesterday's lamb joint to go with mashed potato for lunch, Libby burst in the kitchen door and rushed straight up to the bedroom without saying a word.

'She's sobbing her heart out up there,' Ronnie informed Jess a few minutes later. 'And she won't tell me what's wrong.'

'Oh dear, what now?' Jess frowned at him. 'Have you two been quarrelling again? Have you upset her?'

'No, I haven't.' He was most indignant. 'Why does everyone automatically assume it's my fault when anything goes wrong in this family?'

'Because you're such a stirrer,' she replied. 'As you and Libby are always getting at each other, it's natural I'd think you had something to do with it.'

'Oh, come on, Jess. Can you imagine Libby bursting into tears over anything I said?'

'No, not really,' she was forced to admit.

'There you are then,' Ronnie said. 'Anyway, crying is what girls do, isn't it? They don't seem to need a particular reason.'

Jess tutted worriedly. She had to be at the shop before Dad's assistant went off duty and she was already running late with lunch. It was probably something and nothing with Libby but she'd better go and see what was the matter. Turning the gas down under the potatoes, she hurried upstairs.

'What's up?' she asked Libby, who was standing by the window looking pale and tearful.

'Nothin'.'

'It doesn't look like nothing to me.'

She shrugged.

'Come on, love,' coaxed Jess. 'You're obviously upset, so tell your big sister all about it.'

The young girl wiped her eyes with a handkerchief and blew her nose. 'I suppose you'll have to know anyway,' she said thickly. 'It's happened.'

'What's happened?'

'I've started,' she blurted out.

'Oh, oh, I see,' said her sister, slipping a friendly arm round her shoulder. 'You've got your first period. Well, that's nothing to be too upset about. It happens to all us girls.' She paused, giving her a quizzical look. 'You knew it would happen sometime soon, didn't you? Mum had talked to you about it?'

'Of course I knew about it,' Libby informed her, managing to sound lofty despite her distress. 'And I didn't need Mum to tell me. We talk about it all the time at school and a lot of my friends have already started.'

'Why so upset then?'

'I'm not sure. Must be because I feel weird now that it's actually happened,' she explained in a small, childish voice. 'Sick and funny, and I've got a tummy ache.'

'Aah, you poor thing,' sympathised Jess. 'But it'll soon pass and I'll give you something for the pain if it bothers you too much. But first let's get you fixed up with the necessary.' She went over to the wardrobe and reached for a packet on a shelf at the top. 'Then we'll have a bit of a chat.'

'I wish Mum was here.' Libby was still weepy. 'I miss her ever so much. I think I always will.'

'Me too,' added Jess, hugging her sister's thin trembling body. 'And I expect we always will even though we'll get used to it eventually. But we've got each other. Just us two women in a house full of men. We have to stick together and not let them rule the roost.'

'Yeah, I suppose so,' said Libby, seeming calmed and comforted by her sister.

At the times when Jess went to help her father in the shop, she left Ronnie in charge at home, with the usual back-up support available from Hilda if he needed it. The arrangement was that he didn't go off anywhere until she got home.

So when she popped out to the cake shop that afternoon to get some buns for tea and spotted him sitting on the clock tower steps with some rough-looking youths, she wasn't pleased.

'What are you doing here?' she demanded, going over to him.

He gave her a withering look and acted out a performance for the benefit of his pals. 'Having a bath,' he replied sarcastically. 'What does it look like?'

'Don't use that tone with me,' she responded angrily. 'You know perfectly well what I mean. You're supposed to be at home with your sister and brother.'

'Nursemaid, eh?' scoffed one of the others, a dark-haired boy with an exaggerated quiff in the style of Elvis Presley. 'I wouldn't put up with that when I'm on my school holidays. Not likely!'

'Nor me,' said his ginger-headed companion.

'Do you mind? This has nothing to do with you so stay out of it.' Jess glared at the boys, then switched her attention back to her brother. 'Home, Ronnie – *now*!'

'I'm staying here.'

She stared at him. 'We have an agreement, remember?' she pointed out.

'What right does she have to tell you what to do?' queried the dark boy. 'She ain't your mum.'

Fired up and showing off, Ronnie met Jess's eyes and blurted out, 'A good point. Why should I have to stay at home?'

'You know why. Because I have to help Dad in the shop and the others aren't quite old enough to be at home on their own for any length of time.'

'Libby's the same age as me,' he was quick to remind her. 'Anyway, they'll be all right. They've got Hilda next door and you and Dad are only round the corner at the shop.'

'That isn't the point. We've lost our mother and we all have to do our bit to help the family,' she told him. 'We made this arrangement and you can't just break it because you feel like doing something else. It just isn't on, Ronnie.'

Flushed with embarrassment, he avoided looking at his friends. 'Oh, all right then, I suppose I'll have to go,' he grumbled. 'But I don't like having to stay around the house and I'm not gonna keep on doing it indefinitely.'

'You'll go straight home now, though, won't you?' She needed confirmation.

'I don't have a choice, do I?' he complained, and swaggered off, his neck scarlet with humiliation.

Jess didn't know which worried her most: the fact that he had reneged on their agreement or the sort of company he was keeping these days.

When she got back to the shop, she instantly perceived that all was not well. Apparently her father's assistant, Eileen, had called in to tell him that she'd decided to resign from the job with immediate effect. He didn't try to hide her reasons or make excuses for himself; he simply explained that Eileen said he was a changed man since his wife had died, and he'd become too bad-tempered and difficult to work with. She'd called to tell him in person because she wanted to collect what money was owing to her.

He looked so forlorn, Jess didn't have the heart to admonish him for bringing about the situation.

'Oh, Dad,' she sighed, shaking her head. 'What am I going to do with you?'

That night Jess lay awake staring at the dappled pattern on the ceiling from the streetlights shining through the net curtains, then through a gap in the curtains. Listening to Libby's even breathing in the other bed, Jess mulled over the predicament she found herself in. For weeks she'd been pushing the reality of her return to work at Burtons to the back of her mind. There were so many problems associated with it, she hadn't wanted to face up to it, in particular to the possibility that she couldn't return at all. Having to lose the Paris job had been disappointing enough; the prospect of giving up the job altogether was crippling.

But the events of today had forced the matter to the front of her mind. Even if the company were to give her London bookings and she was able to live at home, she would still be working long unsocial hours doing an exhausting job that took a huge amount of energy and commitment. How could she encourage Todd with his education if she either wasn't here or was too tired to be of help to him. And Ronnie needed watching; he could get into real trouble if he continued to hang out with those awful boys. Then there was Libby, whose childhood had ended today but she wasn't yet mature enough to deal with all the physical and emotional changes that were happening to her. She needed a woman to turn to.

Then there was Dad, who had amazed them all by being weak in the face of adversity. He was a different man and an infuriating one at that. But he needed her – at the shop as well as at home. It had always been assumed that Ronnie would eventually go into the family business but that was in the future and Dad needed someone now.

How could she maintain the stable family environment her mother had

58

worked so hard to create if she wasn't there for much of the time? Similarly, how could she give the necessary commitment to the Burton Girls if she was always preoccupied with the worry of her family responsibilities? Hilda had already agreed to be on hand when Jess returned to work, but it was Jess the family needed now that their mother wasn't here.

Bitterly disappointed by the decision she now knew she must make, she turned over on to her side and tried to go to sleep.

'The cavalry's here. Thank God for that,' said an impatient customer at the end of the queue when Jess arrived at the crowded shop the next morning and slipped behind the counter. 'Good to see you, Jess. Perhaps we'll stand a chance of getting served today now that you're here.'

Stopping only to put her bag down, Jess got to work on the queue, treating everyone to a friendly greeting.

Mollitts Newsagents was situated in the centre of Hanwell Broadway, between an ironmonger's and a drapery store. Built in the early part of the century, it had rooms behind the shop that were used as an office, a staff room and a stockroom. There was a flat over the top with a separate street entrance, which was rented out on a permanent basis.

Counters ran down two sides of the shop, one of which was used for newspapers. Comics and magazines were on display in a rack the length of the third wall, and the shop window and door filled most of the front. Charlie also sold cigarettes and tobacco, sweets, pop, greetings cards and other sundry items. At Christmas time he carried a small selection of toys.

The shop had a particular scent ingrained into the walls: a heady mixture of pear drops, Tizer, chocolate, liquorice, tobacco and newsprint. This morning, however, Jess was far too preoccupied to notice it.

When the morning rush of work-bound customers was over, she made some coffee and called her father into the staff room at the back, which was basically furnished with a small table and chairs and a couple of easy chairs.

'While we're having this, I'd like a chat,' she said, as they sat down at the table.

'I'm listening,' he said dully.

'I expect you've been wondering when I would be going back to work and home to the flat.'

Fear flashed briefly in Charlie's eyes. 'I guessed you'd be wanting to go back soon,' he said.

'I'm not going back to Burtons,' she informed him. 'I finally decided last night.'

He shot her a look. 'You mean you're not going back there at all?'

'That's right.'

'Why?'

59

'I should have thought the reason was obvious. Because you and the kids need me, of course.'

'We can manage,' he told her, but she guessed that he was forcing the words out. 'The kids go back to school tomorrow and I can pay someone to help out at home. Hilda or Ada might do it. The twins are almost grown up anyway.'

'Nearly but not quite,' she disagreed. 'They're at a sensitive age and Ronnie needs someone to keep a close eye on him. He seems to have got in with some very dodgy boys.'

'I'll watch him, don't worry.'

The way her father was at present, he couldn't be trusted with his own behaviour, let alone that of his rebellious son. But Jess didn't want to hurt him by saying so. 'If the two of us are on hand it'll be safer,' she said. 'Those new mates of his look like right little villains.'

'Look, it's ever so good of you to offer but I can't let you give up your dancing career,' he told her wearily. 'I'll make sure the kids are looked after and I'll advertise for someone to help me run the shop. Don't you worry your head.'

She was sorely tempted to take him at his word but he wasn't in a fit state to make promises. 'I don't think it'll be the best thing for any of you, Dad. Hilda's wonderful with the kids but they need to know that I'm around too.' She paused warily. 'And to be perfectly honest, in the mood you're in at the moment you're likely to upset any assistant you employ in the shop and they'll go the same way as Eileen. Whereas you won't get rid of me that easily. If you upset me, you'll soon know about it, I can promise you that.'

Lowering his eyes, Charlie sipped his coffee. 'I'll just have to change my ways, won't I?' he said, his eyes resting sheepishly on her over the rim of the cup.

If only it was that simple none of this would be necessary. But his grief was still too raw; he wasn't in control. He seemed perfectly normal now but that could have changed dramatically by the time the pubs closed tonight. She wouldn't have a minute's peace of mind if she returned to her career. 'I think it will be best if I stay,' she told him.

'But it'll break your heart to give up your dancing career,' he pointed out. 'You love that job.'

'I'd be lying if I said otherwise. But I've had a good run and enjoyed every moment.' She forced a cheerful note to hide the extent of her regret. 'But other things are more important now.'

'And it would be dishonest of me to pretend that your decision won't solve a lot of problems for me, especially knowing that you'll be around for the kids,' he confessed, looking guilty but extremely relieved. 'Having someone I know I can trust working with me in the shop will be a load off my mind too.'

She looked at him gravely. 'There's something we have to sort out about that before we go any further, though,' she began.

'Oh?'

'If I'm going to be working here on a permanent basis, I'd want it to be a proper job with definite hours and a wage, rather than how it is now with my coming in at odd times to help out and taking what cash I need from what you give me for the housekeeping,' she told him. 'I don't want a fortune, just reasonable pay. I can't not have any money of my own for personal use.'

'Of course not,' he agreed wholeheartedly. 'It will be a proper job now that I don't have another assistant to pay.'

'About the hours,' Jess went on. 'Naturally I'd like to be at home when the others get in from school. I don't think either of us want them to become latchkey kids.'

'Not likely,' he agreed. 'So we'll make sure your hours fit in with them.'

'OK then, it's official. I'm your new assistant in the family business. You'll have to watch yourself now that I'm going to be around.' She made a joke of it because it was breaking her heart. 'I won't put up with too much of your bad temper. And if I catch you upsetting a customer, you're dead.'

'God help me.'

A bell rang in the room, indicating that someone had come into the shop, Jess went to attend to him or her.

'Ooh, I am honoured,' said a young man of about her age who worked as a builder and who Jess had known vaguely all her life. 'This must be my lucky day, having a Burton Girl serve me with my morning paper. Wait till I tell the lads.' He grinned. 'O' course, it'd be even better if you were wearing one of those snazzy little costumes you have on on the telly.'

'Saucy,' she grinned, handing him his newspaper and taking his money.

'This is a bit of a change for you, though, isn't it?' he said more seriously. 'It must seem a bit dull being behind the counter after being on the telly and that.'

'It's different, that's all,' she replied. 'But someone's got to sell you your morning paper.'

'Yeah, and I'd sooner it was you than your dad any day of the week,' he joked, grinning towards Charlie, who appeared by Jess's side. 'You're a lot better-looking than he is.'

She smiled and he left whistling. He was right. Having an ordinary job was certainly going to take some getting used to after the different kind of life she'd had as a Burton Girl. But it had to be done, so she'd get on and do it and look happy about it.

It had long been Charlie's habit to call in to the Red Bear in the Broadway after he'd finished at the shop, for a quick pint and a chat with

61

the other shopkeepers. When Joy was alive, he'd never stayed longer than half an hour or so because he'd always been eager to get home. Since her death he tended to linger because he dreaded going home; he hated being in the house when she wasn't there. Alcohol took the edge off the pain, but when the effect wore off the guilt was unbearable because he knew he should be at home with the family; he was also aware of the fact that he was drinking too much.

Now he stood at the bar smoking and drinking alone, the traders he'd been in company with earlier having left some time ago. He was thinking back on the conversation he'd had with Jess that morning and the sacrifice she was making because of the family, without so much as a word of complaint. He should have refused her offer to stay at home; he should have, somehow, forced her to go back to her career. But he'd been that relieved he'd seized the opportunity with both hands.

It had been on his mind all day. If he loathed himself for being unable to drag himself out of the pit he was in to comfort his children, he hated himself even more for allowing his grown-up daughter to give up so much for the sake of the family. But the truth was, she could give the younger children something he couldn't: the presence in their lives of a woman who loved them. That was an undeniable fact. But was he just making excuses for himself? Would he have found another way around the problem if he hadn't been so enfeebled by his bereavement?

He remembered how proud Joy had been of Jess, and how they'd both loved to see her dancing on the television. The pride he'd felt then was nothing compared to the admiration he had for her now; for her infinite capacity to make the best of things and for her selfless insistence that she give up a job she loved to look after her siblings and help him to run his shop. He hadn't told her about his feelings; he'd wanted to, but the words never came, somehow. He'd never been one for sentimental speeches.

In reflective mood, he could see that everything had changed the day Joy died. There were occasional bursts of anger but most of the time he was just plain miserable and locked into a world of his own. Everything seemed to be out of focus and he was unable to communicate properly with his loved ones. Although full of self-castigation for failing in his duty to his family, he felt powerless to change anything.

Guilt and grief rose to unbearable proportions, feeding off each other and aching inside him like a physical pain. He ordered another pint, then changed it to a large whisky because it was a quicker route to oblivion.

Several whiskies later, a man appeared at the bar beside Charlie and they got talking with the ease that men in pubs do. When it transpired that the man was also a widower, it seemed like a special bond to the inebriated Charlie.

'I didn't know it was possible to feel this lonely,' he muttered drunkenly.

'Don't talk to me about loneliness,' said the man, who had introduced himself as Don Day. 'I've become an expert since my wife died.'

As confused as he was, Charlie was able to discern that the man was not in an age group normally associated with widowhood. He appeared to be in his mid-thirties, a staid-looking fellow, thin-faced with sharp features and brown wavy hair slicked flat to his head with Brylcreem. He was tall and smartly dressed in a suit. 'Your wife must have been a bit young when you lost her,' Charlie suggested.

'Just turned thirty,' Don informed him. 'She was killed in a car accident.'

'My wife died in an accident an' all,' muttered Charlie morosely. 'She drowned.'

'Sorry to hear that, mate,' consoled Don. 'It's a terrible thing when you lose your other half.'

'You're telling me.'

'You feel so alone, don't you?' said Don. 'You can't know what it feels like unless you've been through it.'

Charlie nodded. 'Thank God I've got children. They're everything to me, even if I'm not much use to them at the moment,' he added in slurred tones. 'They're all good kids. My elder daughter's been a saint since her mother died – there's no other word for it. A lovely girl. A dancer, you know. On the telly and everything. She's given it all up now for the family.'

'Get away.'

'It's true.' Charlie swigged his drink. 'You got any kids?'

'No.'

'Shame . . . It must be even worse without them. You got any other family?'

Don seemed to need to think about this. 'A brother,' he said at last.

'Oh good,' said Charlie. 'At least you've got someone.'

'No I haven't. We don't get on.' Don's voice became bitter. 'I hate the sight of him, to tell you the truth.'

'That's rotten luck.'

'You can't choose your relatives, can you?'

'No.' They lapsed into a morbid silence until Charlie gave Don a bleary look and said, 'I haven't seen you in here before. Do you live around here?'

'Just moved in.'

'Near the Broadway?'

'I've just taken over as manager of Dean's Stores,' Don explained, referring to a large grocery shop in Hanwell Broadway on the opposite side of the street to Mollitts. 'I'm living in the flat over the top. It goes with the job.'

'That's handy for you.'

'Very handy,' Don confirmed. 'What about you? Is this your local?'

'Not half. I'm your neighbour, in a manner of speaking,' drawled Charlie, his voice slow and laboured. 'I've got a shop here in the Broadway. Mollitts Newsagents, that's my business.'

'Oh, that's a coincidence. I've been meaning to pop in to arrange to have the paper delivered. I'll call in tomorrow and do it. Or can I arrange it now?'

'You'd better come in to the shop, mate, in case I don't remember to put you down in the book.'

'Sure.'

Charlie squinted at his watch through the alcoholic haze. 'Well. I'd better be going,' he said, before draining his glass. 'My daughter will have a meal ready for me.' He turned away from the bar and swayed, a drunken smile on his face. 'Whoops, my legs seem to have gone a bit queer.'

'Here, hang on to me,' suggested Don, who'd had only a couple of pints so was still in pretty good shape.

'Thanks, mate.'

With Don supporting Charlie, the two men left the pub together.

'Here you are, Charlie, home safe and sound,' said Don Day. 'You'll be all right now, won't you?'

'Course I will,' Charlie replied boozily. 'You're a good bloke. Do you know that?'

'Yeah, yeah,' said Don to humour him. 'Have you got your key or shall I knock at the door?'

Charlie swayed. 'I've got my key somewhere but I don't know where, mate. Better knock at the door.'

Don did as he was asked and found himself staring into the amazing eyes of a tall, dark young woman with the most brilliant smile he'd ever seen. It faded when the state of Charlie registered.

'I thought I'd better see he got home safely,' Don explained. 'He's a bit the worse for wear.'

'Oh, Dad,' she burst out, fixing him with a glare.

'I've only had a couple, love,' he stuttered.

'And the rest.'

'Do you need any help?' Don asked as Charlie staggered over the threshold and disappeared inside.

'No, it's all right, we can manage, thanks.'

Two boys and a girl appeared at her side. 'Dad's drunk again, then,' said the elder boy disapprovingly. 'Nothing new there.'

'All right, Ronnie,' admonished the young woman, flushing with embarrassment. 'There's no need to broadcast it to the whole neighbourhood.'

'I was only saying—'

'Well don't,' she cut in. She looked at her siblings, 'You three go back inside and make sure Dad doesn't fall over and hurt himself. I'll be in in a minute . . .'

'I'm Don Day,' said the stranger as the others disappeared. 'I've just moved into the area.'

'Oh, really.' She tried to sound interested but it wasn't easy, given the circumstances. 'I'm Jess Mollitt.'

'I guessed you must be,' he told her. 'Your dad's been saying nice things about you.'

'Has he now?' She wished he would go.

He nodded. 'I've just taken over as the manager of Dean's Stores.'

'Oh, good. I hope you like it here.' Why didn't he just leave and put an end to the small talk? She couldn't care less who he was or what he did for a living.

'I'm sure I will.'

She would have been much happier if he'd turned out to be some stranger who was just passing through and would never be seen around here again, given the embarrassing state of her father. 'Dad doesn't normally get . . .' she began. 'I mean . . . well, it's just that he's still grieving for our mother.' An explanation of some sort seemed imperative for the sake of the family reputation.

Don gave her an understanding nod. 'Yes, he's been telling me about your sad loss. I'm so sorry to hear about your mother.'

'Thank you. It was a blow to us all,' she responded politely. 'I'm afraid Dad's been drowning his sorrows a bit too effectively just lately. One pint is about his limit in the usual run. I realise it might not seem like that to see him now.'

'Well, we all have a bit too much now and then.' He paused, looking at her kindly. 'But you've no need to worry as far as I'm concerned. No one will hear about this from me.'

'Thank you.' Of course, everyone in the pub would have seen the condition of her father but at least the man had had the decency to offer to keep shtoom, and she warmed to him for it; she noticed that he was tall and thin and had small grey eyes, but little else about him registered, as she had more important things on her mind. 'I appreciate that.'

'It's all right.'

Remembering her manners but keeping her fingers crossed for a negative response, she asked, 'Would you like to come in for a coffee or something?'

'Thanks for asking but I'd better be getting off home,' he replied. 'It's time I had my supper.'

'See you around, then,' she said, relieved to get away at last. 'And thanks for bringing Dad home.'

'No trouble at all.'

'Night then.'

'Night.'

As she closed the door behind him, she felt bleak at the thought of the sort of future that lay ahead of her. Is this all she had to look forward to – long boring days working behind a shop counter and helping her drunken father up to bed every night?

Chapter Five

Jess came out of Ealing Broadway tube station and walked briskly down Station Approach to the Uxbridge Road to catch the 607 trolley bus to Hanwell, shivering and pulling her coat collar up around her ears against the penetrating November chill. It was late Sunday afternoon, and already dusk on this grey day, a smoky mist catching in the back of her throat.

She was on her way home from the West End where she'd been visiting Babs, who now had a new flatmate, a dancer from Burtons called Pat. The conversation between the three of them had centred around Burtons: the latest dance routines, the laughs, the rows, the gossip. Whilst enjoying all the news up to a point, it didn't have quite the same impact for Jess now that she wasn't a part of it.

Babs and Pat were currently working at the Victoria Palace and would be together in pantomime at Golders Green for the Christmas run. Babs was especially delighted about the latter because Dickie was playing Buttons in the same show. Jess reflected wistfully on the fact that this was the first year since she'd joined Burtons that she herself wouldn't be in pantomime. She'd played London and the provinces and had loved every moment.

There was a long queue at the bus stop and – judging by the amount of foot shifting and impatient peering into the distance – the crowd were already feeling the effects of the Sunday bus service. The town was shrouded in the unmistakable quietness of a winter Sunday afternoon, she observed, with almost everything closed at this time of day. About the only sign of life she could see from here was around the Palladium cinema where people were going in and out, some lingering outside looking at the advertising posters.

It was more than two months since Jess had made her momentous decision to stay at home and she still believed she'd done the right thing. But her new role was a demanding one, both physically and emotionally. Being a constant source of succour to her grieving siblings and her father, running the home and working full time at the shop, very often single-handed, was very draining even for someone as resilient as Jess. Her dad hadn't relinquished his responsibilities altogether but he had become even more unreliable; surprising for a man who had once been so dependable.

Some days he really seemed to make an effort, even though he never quite managed to shake off the air of gloom that had become so much a part of him. Then he'd be polite to the customers and more sociable at home, albeit that his conversation was so obviously forced and his voice either sad or devoid of expression. Other days he'd disappear to the pub at lunchtime and return in belligerent mood, upsetting everyone in sight, especially the customers. His subsequent remorse seemed genuine but didn't prevent a repeat performance. Mercifully, most of his drinking was done in the evening and, as yet, didn't happen every night.

It wasn't easy to stay patient with his self-obsession and irritability, and Jess didn't always manage it. But one belief remained constant and helped her to cope: she knew in her heart that no matter how selfish he sometimes seemed, he did actually love his family, and one day would prove it to them as he had in the past.

There was gossip, of course, though she didn't believe Don Day had broken his word; something about him inspired trust in her even though she hardly knew him. Anyway, people could see for themselves the state her father was in when he'd had a liquid lunch. She seemed to spend her whole life apologising to customers for his drunken behaviour.

None of this upset her nearly as much as the loss of dance in her life. Working in the shop wasn't a job she would have chosen, but since it had been forced on her she tackled it with a willing heart, determined – despite her father's efforts to the contrary – to maintain Mollitts popularity. She did actually enjoy some aspects, especially the sociability and community atmosphere. She could even take getting up at the crack of dawn to sort the papers because her father was too hungover, and tolerate having no life of her own and a double helping of hormonal mood swings from the twins. It had given her pleasure to be on hand to encourage Todd when he'd sat his eleven-plus exam recently too. There was immense satisfaction in filling a need. But not being involved with dance in any way at all was like being only half alive.

The trolley bus came into sight and whirred to a halt. She found a seat downstairs and stared idly out of the window. Behind her was a woman whose two talkative little girls were in the seat behind their mother, their high-pitched voices drifting in Jess's direction. The children, who Jess presumed to be sisters, were discussing their hopes for Christmas presents. Apparently beyond the age of illusion, they were mercenary in their demands.

'I want a pair of roller skates,' said one.

'I want a bike for my main present,' added the other.

'I want new tap shoes too,' declared the first speaker. 'Mine are too small.'

'You don't need tap shoes now that you've stopped going to classes,' pointed out her sister. 'That's just a waste of a present.'

'No it isn't 'cause I'll be going to classes again soon. I only stopped because the teacher stopped doing it and the class finished,' the child reminded her. 'I'll be starting again when Mum finds me another class to go to, won't I, Mum?' There was a pause. 'Mum – you have remembered to look out for a dance class for me, haven't you?'

'I've asked a few people but no one knows of one,' the mother replied absently.

'Oh, Mu-um,' said the child in a tone of admonition. 'You said you'd find one.'

'And I will, in due course,' she assured her. 'I'll have a look in the local paper this week. You sometimes see that sort of thing advertised in there.'

'I hope we can find one because I really enjoy dancing and I think I was getting to be quite good.'

'Anyway, I want doll's house furniture as well as a bike for Christmas.' Her sister was obviously bored with the subject. 'And a new skipping rope in my stocking.'

'Want, want, want, that's all I can hear from you two,' came a sudden explosion from their mother.

A silence.

'We were only saying—' began one child warily.

'I heard what you were saying, me and the rest of the bus, I should imagine,' their mother cut in. 'You sound like a couple of greedy little brats, demanding this, that and the other. You'll get what comes at Christmas and be grateful for it.'

'We are grateful,' came a childish voice.

'We were just saying what we wanted because it's fun talking about it,' put in the other supportively. 'We know we won't get everything.'

'I'm very glad to hear it,' was the adult's response.

The conversation continued along similar lines but Jess drifted off into her own thoughts. By the time she got off the bus at Hanwell Broadway, she knew exactly how she was going to bring dancing back into her life.

'I'm going to start a dance class,' she announced excitedly to the family over tea that same day.

'Cor, that'll be good,' enthused Libby.

'I think so too,' said Jess.

'Having a sister who's a dance teacher doesn't carry quite the same glamour as having one who's in the Burton Girls, but it's almost as exciting,' Libby effused. 'Can I come to your class instead of the one I already go to?'

'No. That wouldn't be a good idea because your teacher is more qualified than I am and she can take you to a higher level,' explained Jess, who had already worked out how she was going to proceed. 'My class will be basic tap and ballet. No exams, no pressure. I'm aiming to cater for youngsters who want to learn the basics and dance for fun.' She paused for a moment, thinking. 'But although I won't be putting people forward for exams I will want them to do it right,'

'I bet you will,' grinned Libby. 'I wish I could come to it.'

'You can come along and help with the little ones if you want to be involved,' suggested Jess. 'I'm going to do tots to teens in three different sessions.'

'OK, I'll do that then.'

'I think I'll join,' laughed Ronnie in waggish mood.

His siblings found this hilarious. 'Imagine you in a ballet dress,' joshed Libby. 'You'd look like something out of the chamber of horrors.'

'And you're Little Miss Ballet Beautiful of Nineteen Fifty-Six, I suppose,' riposted Ronnie.

'She probably would be if there was such a competition,' supported Jess. 'She looks lovely in her dance clothes.'

'Don't tell her that, for goodness' sake,' wailed Ronnie. 'We don't want her head to get any bigger.'

This earned him a playful slap on the arm from his sister.

'Where is the class going to be held?' Todd enquired, helping himself to another fish paste sandwich.

'A good question,' Jess replied. 'I shall have to find a hall for hire before I can go any further.'

Her father was looking worried because he had grown to rely on her at the shop and wasn't sure if this new venture was going to be a full-time job. 'It's a nice idea, Jess, but I don't see how . . . I mean with the shop and everything.'

'Don't panic, Dad. I'm not going to desert you,' she assured him. 'But if I can get this organised I will be asking for Saturday mornings off. I shall have to have the class on a Saturday morning when children aren't at school. The little ones are too tired after school and some of the older ones have homework.' She shot him a questioning look. 'But that'll be all right, won't it? You can manage without me for a few hours then.'

'Well, yeah, I suppose so.' He was still rather doubtful because he felt so vulnerable and tended to worry much more than he used to about every little thing. 'But won't it be a bit complicated, setting up something like that? Aren't there regulations? Are you allowed to just set up a dance class?'

She nodded. 'I am because I've got certificates up to the required standard for the stuff I'll be doing,' she told him.

'It still seems like a big commitment,' he said.

'It'll be a serious commitment, certainly, but it will only be once a week for about three hours. I'll need three hours to fit in the different age groups,' she pointed out. 'All I need is the use of a hall, a piano and someone to play it.'

'I'll ask around among the traders to see if anyone knows of a hall you can use,' he said, more amenable to the idea now that he knew he wasn't going to lose his second in command.

'It'll have to be cheap, though,' Jess mentioned. 'I'm not going to charge much for the lessons – just enough to cover my costs, the hire of the hall and the pianist. Later on, when I'm established, I'd like to provide tap and ballet shoes for children to borrow free of charge – if their parents can't afford to buy them. Just have a few pairs available in case they're needed.'

'It isn't a commercial enterprise, then?' he remarked.

'Oh, no, nothing like that.' She was very definite. 'I have a full-time job so I don't need to make money from this. It'll just be a hobby. I want to teach children to dance for pleasure, maybe give them the chance to perform in a show every now and again, just for the thrill of it. If they like it and want to go further, they can move on to another teacher. My only reason for doing this is as a way of using my training and staying involved. And I've already got someone in mind as a pianist,' she added with a half-smile. Just thinking about her new project made her feel better about everything.

'Dancing classes,' said Hilda, when Jess called in to see her later that same evening to tell her the news. 'Now *that* is a good idea. Something like that is just what you need to bring that old sparkle back to your eyes.'

'My thoughts exactly,' she enthused. 'I'm dead excited about it. It'll be lovely to be involved in dance again.'

'I bet.'

'Mind you, just because I can dance doesn't necessarily mean that I'll be any good as a teacher,' Jess pointed out. 'Teaching is a special skill.'

'Mm, that's true. But your enthusiasm will carry you through, I should think.'

'Time will tell,' Jess said cheerfully. 'Anyway, my first move is to find a hall.'

Hilda nodded.

'And the second is to find a pianist to play for the lessons,' she added. 'Which is where you come in.'

'Ooh, I'm not sure I know anyone who could do that,' Hilda frowned. 'I know people who can knock out a tune but you'll need someone who can play properly for that job.'

'I had you in mind, actually,' Jess explained brightly. 'I was wondering if you might help me out on this one.'

'Me? Play for a dance class?'

'That's the plan, yeah.'

Hilda was flattered but rather overwhelmed and lacking in confidence. 'Oh, I don't know about that, dear,' she said, looking worried. 'I only play for my own pleasure. I'm not a professional.'

'You'd be perfect.' Jess had no doubts at all. 'And don't start saying that you're not good enough because I've heard you play and I know different.'

The older woman's face was wreathed in smiles. 'Well, if you really

71

think I'd be up to the job, I'd be delighted to give it a try.'

'One thing perhaps I ought to mention, though.' Jess's manner became serious. 'I won't be able to pay you much because I don't want to charge a lot for the lessons. I'd like them to be accessible to as many kids as possible.'

'Money is the last thing on my mind,' Hilda was quick to point out. 'Being involved will be enough payment for me, dear. I'll want nothing more than that.'

'That's kind of you,' Jess approved. 'But don't sell yourself short. It will be a job of work. The pianist is entitled to be paid.'

'So is the teacher, but I bet you won't make a penny out of it,' Hilda suggested.

Since Jess couldn't deny it, she just grinned.

'Good, now that that's settled, let's go into the front room and have a look through my sheet music,' suggested Hilda excitedly. 'See if I've got anything suitable for a class of aspiring hoofers.'

'Lead the way,' smiled Jess.

Hilda was standing in the queue in the butcher's a few days later when someone tapped her on the shoulder and she turned to see Ada Pickles. After a brief neighbourly exchange, Ada lowered her voice into gossip mode.

'Seen much of the Mollitts lately?' she enquired.

'Yeah, of course I have,' Hilda replied. 'I see them all the time, you know that.'

'How the mighty fall, eh?' Ada moved her head closer to Hilda's and spoke in a confidential manner. 'Shocking, the way that Charlie's carrying on, innit?' she continued with relish. 'Nothing short of a bloody disgrace.'

'What are you talking about, Ada?' Hilda was defensive as ever.

'Don't pretend you don't know.'

'Exactly what is he supposed to be doing that's so terrible?' Hilda asked innocently.

'If you don't know, you must be the only one around here who doesn't,' Ada informed her with a knowledgeable air. 'He's in the pub more often than he's out of it, from what I've heard.'

'I'm sure that's an exaggeration.'

'It isn't you know, it's God's honest truth,' Ada insisted. 'Everybody's talking about it. Don't tell me you haven't heard what people are saying about him.'

'People don't usually come to me with gossip about the Mollitts because it's generally known that I'm a close family friend,' Hilda said pointedly.

'He must have lost a lot of custom over it at the shop.' Ada didn't take the hint. 'People stay away in case he's been boozing and doesn't have a civil tongue in his head.'

72

'I admit he drinks more than he used to when Joy was alive.' Hilda was extremely concerned about what she was hearing, even though she was at pains not to show it. 'The poor man's broken-hearted, that's why. It's perfectly understandable.'

'When did drink ever help anyone?' Ada was having a whale of a time and wouldn't be stopped. This was an even juicier class of gossip than Jess Mollitt being on the stage.

'I'm sure he knows it isn't a permanent solution and is just a temporary relief,' was her curt response. 'Anyway, it isn't as if he's drunk every day of the week or anything. He just has a few too many now and again when he's feeling low.'

'Often enough to get himself a reputation.' Ada was relentless. 'It's terrible for poor Jess, having to cover up for him and apologise to the customers he's insulted. What with that and looking after the kids, it isn't much of a life for her, is it?'

'She seems to be coping admirably to me,' said Hilda through gritted teeth.

'Even so, he shouldn't have made her give up her stage career to take her mother's place. She loved that job, and she was good at it too.'

'He didn't make her give it up,' Hilda was swift to deny, her voice rising. 'As far as I know, it was her decision. What else could she do, anyway? The younger children needed someone close to them around. They aren't quite old enough to look after themselves yet. And Charlie's not been himself since he lost Joy.'

'It's all very well for you to make excuses for him and say he's not himself,' Ada ranted on, 'but it's time that man pulled himself together. You can't wallow in self-pity when you've got a young family relying on you.'

Although Hilda wouldn't dream of admitting it to Ada, she had had similar thoughts herself from time to time. Hilda had lost her husband. She knew all about the agony of bereavement but somehow she'd soldiered on. Charlie should do the same. However, her criticism was tempered by the thought that each person's capacity to cope with adversity varied, and if Charlie had been able to pull himself together he would have done so.

Her thoughts shifted to something else Ada had said and she found herself lingering on the contrary nature of her comments. 'Hang on a minute, Ada. It isn't so long ago you were telling me that Jess's stage work was disgusting and not a fit job for a decent girl and she should stop doing it. Now that she has given it up you think that's wrong.'

Ada was enjoying herself far too much to let a minor detail like the truth deter her. 'I stand by what I said then about her stage work but I don't think it's right for her to have to give up her own life and come home and be a dogsbody to the rest of the family, regardless of what she was doing for a living.'

'Well, she did give it up and I think we all have to admire her for it . . .'

'Oh, yeah,' Ada was quick to put in. 'You won't hear a word from me against Jess.'

Not much, thought Hilda. If Jess hadn't come home to step into the breach, Ada would have had a field day about her as well as Charlie.

'If you're worried about what people are saying, Ada, you've no need because the Mollitts are a very well-liked and respected family in this neighbourhood and their reputation is strong enough to withstand a bit of gossip. Charlie has always been a very popular man and that won't change because of—'

'He might have been popular once—' came Ada's interruption.

'Still is in my opinion,' Hilda cut in. 'Anyone worth bothering about will realise that he's basically a good man and this is just a temporary lapse.'

'Don't make me laugh,' scoffed Ada. 'People have short memories when it comes to this sort of thing. A good reputation is worth bugger all when someone falls from grace. I tell you, Hilda, that family is heading for the gutter fast, the way Charlie Mollitt is carrying on.'

'Don't be so melodramatic, for goodness' sake,' Hilda bluffed, careful to hide her anxiety from this spiteful gossipmonger. 'They'll get through this bad patch, you just watch them.'

The butcher's cheery voice booming through the shop brought the conversation to an instant conclusion. 'Right, ladies, let's be having yer,' he called out. 'Who's next?'

Having a private conversation with Charlie wasn't the easiest thing for Hilda to organise. When he was at home, one or all of the children were usually there, and Jess was with him at the shop for most of the day.

She did usually leave at around four o'clock to be home in time for the children, however, so Hilda waited until then and went to the shop, which was full of people. She pretended to be browsing through the magazines while waiting until the place emptied, then went up to the counter.

'Wotcha, Hilda,' Charlie greeted, and she was glad not to smell alcohol on his breath. 'You come for the *Evening News*?'

'No, I've come for a few quiet words.'

His brow furrowed. 'Nothing wrong at home, is there?' he asked in a worried tone.

'No – not yet.'

'Meaning?'

'Look, Charlie, I know life isn't easy for you at the moment, having to cope without Joy,' she began. 'I know how devoted the two of you were. But you're getting yourself talked about because of the amount of boozing you're doing. And that is going to hurt the kids, which will give you plenty of trouble at home.'

'Oh no, not another lecture.'

'Use your head, man,' she implored him. 'It isn't only your family who'll be affected by the bad reputation you seem intent on making for yourself. It's your business too. People avoid going into shops where the proprietor is known for being rude to his customers because he's been on the booze. You're not the only newsagent in the area, remember.'

'I am the nearest one for the people who use my shop, though, and it's quite a step to the next one,' he pointed out. 'Anyway, if people have nothing better to do than stand about gossiping, I feel sorry for them. While they're talking about me, they're leaving some other poor sod alone.'

Hilda chewed her lip. 'That sort of attitude will do no good at all,' she warned him.

'Surely you're not suggesting that I live my life to suit the neighbour-hood gossips.'

'Of course not.'

'What are you suggesting then?'

She mulled this over for a moment. 'It isn't my place to tell you what to do,' she made clear. 'I just thought a friendly warning about the general feeling about you around here wouldn't go amiss.'

'Haven't I told you before to keep your nose out of my business?' he snapped.

'Oh, yes, you've done that all right. And haven't I told you that I won't stand by and watch those kids suffer?' she returned sharply. 'I don't want to come around here, reading the riot act but—'

'Don't do it then,' was his answer to that.

'Whether you believe it or not, Charlie Mollitt, I do actually care about that family of yours, and when people start repeating gossip to me about you, I feel obliged to say something because I don't want the kids hearing about it and being upset.' Her voice was quivering with emotion. He had the power to hurt her, despite her bold front. 'How do you think they'll feel to know that their dad's the talk of the neighbourhood?'

'Do you think I get up in the morning with the intention of hurting my children or my business?' he barked, temper flaring. 'Of course I don't. It just happens sometimes. I'm just a man, not a paragon. Anyone would think I was a hopeless drunk the way you're carrying on.'

'You will be if you carry on as you are. You're not the man I knew when Joy was alive, not the same man at all,' Hilda persisted because she believed he needed plain-speaking. 'In fact, I didn't think it was possible for anyone to change so much.'

'Yeah, yeah,' he sighed impatiently. 'So I've changed. I can't help that.'

'Of course you can help it.'

'You're the expert, are you?'

'No.' She was shaking inside, partly with rage but also from the trauma of being at war with this man she'd known for so long. 'I've been a friend of the family for a great many years, Charlie,' she continued. 'I don't

75

want to see it fall apart because you can't get a grip.' She sucked in her breath. 'That's it. Now I've said what I came to say, I'll go.' She marched to the door and opened it.

'Oh, Hilda,' he called out.

Turning, she said, 'Yeah?'

He looked contrite. 'Er . . . thanks for offering to play the piano for this dancing class Jess is planning,' he said, and she knew him well enough to know that this was his way of apologising and confirming what she knew already in her heart – that he did care about his family, despite all the evidence to the contrary. He didn't trust himself to make any promises about the drinking but he did want to make his peace with her. 'It's good of you and I appreciate it.'

Hilda's expression softened. 'Thanks aren't necessary because I'm more than happy to do it.'

Charlie shrugged and looked uneasy, as though he didn't know what to say next. 'She's a great girl and I'm proud of her,' he said at last.

'Me too.'

'See you then.'

'Yeah. See you.'

As she left, a flurry of customers came into the shop and it pleased her to see that he hadn't driven them all away. There was hope for him yet.

The availability of a hall wasn't something Jess had ever given much thought to until she tried to find one to hire for a few hours on a Saturday morning. There were several about in the area – church halls, scout huts, community halls and large rooms over shops that were sometimes used for communal activities. But they were either out of her price range or already in use at the time she needed to hire. Her father had asked around but had had no luck.

She'd deemed it courteous to mention her plans to Libby's dance teacher, who took a class in a church hall near the Broadway on a Saturday morning and also on a Friday night for older children. She told Jess that her classes were fully subscribed so she welcomed the fact that someone else was starting up, and suggested various establishments that Jess might try for hall hire, but they too were all either too expensive or not available on Saturday mornings.

'It looks as though I'll have to have my dancing school out of the area,' she mentioned to the family one night over their evening meal. 'Which is disappointing because I so much wanted it to be a local thing. But if I can't get a hall around here, I'll just have to look further afield.'

'Have it here,' suggested Ronnie jokingly. 'There's a piano in the front room.'

'I'm hoping to have more than one or two pupils,' responded Jess. 'That's about all that room will comfortably hold with the sort of movements we'll be doing.'

'You won't have to abandon the idea altogether, will you?' said Libby worriedly.

'Not on your life,' replied Jess with her usual indomitable spirit. 'I shall just keep looking until I do find somewhere, though I would like to begin after Christmas when the new school term starts, if possible.' She grinned at Ronnie, teasing him. 'And if all else fails I shall take up your suggestion and hold my classes in the front room. Even if I have to take the kids two at a time, I won't give the idea up.'

'Leave it with me,' put in her father unexpectedly. 'I might be able to sort something out.'

'Really?' Jess was puzzled. 'I thought you'd asked around and had no joy.'

'I have but I've just had another idea.'

'Come on then, tell us what it is,' she urged.

He tapped his nose. 'Wait and see,' he told her mysteriously. 'All will be revealed when I've got something definite to tell you.'

For the first time since before their mother's death, the Mollitt children were given a glimpse of the happy family atmosphere they had once taken for granted. Life had been so rich and sweet then; it had never occurred to any of them that it might change.

Jess and her father usually ate their lunch in the staff room at the back of the shop. Jess would go to the baker's during the morning and get some fresh rolls or meat pasties and they would take their break in shifts so that they could keep the shop open.

This routine was upset the next day when Charlie departed to the pub, leaving Jess with a sinking heart knowing she was likely to spend the entire afternoon administering black coffee and placating indignant customers. She was pleasantly surprised, therefore, when he came back ten minutes later with a smile on his face.

'Put the closed sign up, Jess,' he announced. 'We're going out for ten minutes.'

She shot him a look. 'We never close the shop at lunchtime,' she reminded him.

'We are today so get your coat, girl.' He was already at the door, turning the sign over.

Intrigued, she did as he said and they walked along the Broadway, stopping at the Red Bear on the corner.

'Oh, no,' she tutted in disappointment. 'You've dragged me out just for this. Getting blotto at lunchtime might be your idea of a good time but it certainly isn't mine. We've shut the shop just to come to the pub. This really isn't on, Dad.'

'Don't be so quick to jump to conclusions,' he replied, leading her past the door of the bar, round the corner and through a wooden gate into a yard at the back of the pub.

'What's going on?' she wanted to know.

'Follow me and you'll find out.'

He led her through a door and up some stairs in the back hall of the pub.

'The landlord gave me the key so that we could come and have a look,' he explained as he unlocked a door and took her into a hall with a wooden floor and a small stage, tables and chairs stacked around the edge and a piano in the corner. It was dusty and thick with the smell of stale beer but nothing a broom and duster and a few open windows wouldn't cure. 'Well . . . will it do for the Jess Mollitt Dance School?'

'Oh, Dad, it's absolutely perfect, particularly as the back stairs mean the children won't have to go through the pub,' she smiled, hugging him, then moving back and giving him an enquiring look. 'But how come?'

'I hadn't even given this place a thought as a possibility but while we were talking yesterday, I suddenly remembered that they have a functions room,' he explained. 'I had a suspicion it might not already be hired out on a Saturday morning because it's mostly used for evening dos. So I decided to come along and have a word with the landlord and he said it would be fine.'

'Thanks so much.' Her expression darkened. 'How much is it going to cost, though? As I've already said, I can't afford to pay much.'

'Ten bob for the three hours, including the use of the piano,' he informed her. 'The landlord wanted twelve and six but I told him that was daylight robbery.'

'You're all right, do you know that?' she said, her eyes moist with tears because he'd done so much more than just found her suitable premises for her dance school. He'd renewed her faith in him and warmed her heart. 'Thanks ever so much.'

'All right, love, there's no need to make a big thing of it,' was his modest reaction, which gave her a glimpse of the man he'd once been.

'And there was me thinking you'd gone on the booze again,' she mentioned.

'I do have my better moments,' he smiled.

'You've certainly had one this time.'

'Let's go and see the landlord and get it made definite, shall we?' Jess suggested. 'There's no point in my starting the lessons this side of Christmas so I'll get it arranged for the beginning of the school term in January.'

'Good idea.'

After they'd spoken to the landlord and made a firm arrangement, Jess and her father walked back to the shop together. She wasn't naïve enough to believe that this was a significant turning point and he would revert to his old self permanently. But she was now absolutely certain that no matter how many times he might blot his copybook in the future, he hadn't lost his basic goodness or love for his children.

It was just turned six o'clock in the morning, two weeks before Christmas. Wearing her outdoor coat and woollen mitts because the shop was bitterly cold at this hour before the paraffin heater had had time to take effect, Jess was marking up the papers for the rounds because her father had been out on the binge last night and wasn't in a fit state to get up. As Christmas approached – the first without his wife – he'd become increasingly depressed, and resorted to his usual therapy. It worried Jess to the point of desperation at times but all she could do was carry on because he wouldn't listen to reason when he was in this sort of mood.

The shop wasn't yet open so a tap on the door startled her. It was still dark outside and she had the blind down so couldn't see who was there; it was too early for the paper boys.

'Don,' she said in surprise, opening the door to the manager of Dean's Stores, ushering him inside and closing the door against the rush of cold air. 'What on earth are you doing out at this unearthly hour?'

'I was up early and saw your light,' he explained. 'Thought I'd come over for my paper to save you delivering it, so that I can read it before we open for business. I hope you don't mind.'

'Of course I don't,' Jess assured him. 'It's one less for the boy to deliver.'

'I don't get much of a chance to read the paper during the day at this time of the year,' he explained further. 'It gets a bit too hectic and I always seem to work through my lunch hour.'

'I can imagine,' she said, glancing at the list to remind herself which paper he had and taking a *Daily Mail* off the top of the pile and handing it to him.

'You too, I expect,' he observed casually, glancing around at the seasonal goods on offer: Christmas annuals and decorations, crackers and balloons. They even had a small selection of soft toys and games. 'It's like Santa's grotto in here.'

'It pays us to carry a good few additional lines at Christmastime,' she informed him. 'And yeah, things do get pretty busy for us, though not, I suspect, as mad as they are for you in the grocery trade. People go crazy at Christmas, stocking up with food as though there's going to be a famine or something. We all do it and swear we won't next year.'

He smiled. 'We hardly sell a biscuit during January, though,' he informed her. 'I reckon some of them are still working their way through their Christmas tins at Easter.'

'I think that's a bit far-fetched,' she said with a knowing smile. 'But I know what you mean. Our confectionery sales are right down for ages after the holiday.'

After a brief silence Don asked, 'Are you letting your dad have a lie-in this morning?'

She gave him a wry look. 'I don't have much choice and I expect you can guess why.' There was no need to hide the truth from Don, who was now a regular at the Red Bear and a pal of her father's.

'Oh dear, like that is it?' he said, raising his eyes and tutting. 'I saw him in the pub last night when I called in for a quick one after work. I didn't stay long but he looked set for a session when I left.'

'He only used to call in for a quick one when Mum was alive.' She made a face. 'It's the first Christmas without her.'

'It won't be easy.'

'Not for any of us,' she agreed. 'He's obviously finding it difficult already.'

He gave her an understanding nod.

'Dad tells me you're a widower too,' she mentioned in a conversational manner.

'That's right.'

'Been on your own long?'

'Over two years.'

'I suppose it must get easier with time.'

'Slowly. But Christmas is still hellish for me.'

'Do you have a family?'

'A brother.'

'Oh, that's good,' she said warmly. 'At least you have someone to spend Christmas with then.'

His expression hardened to such an extent that his whole face was transformed; his eyes turned to ice, his thin features became twisted with hatred, mouth turned down at the corners. 'Not likely,' he ground out, as though the mere suggestion was repugnant to him. 'I wouldn't want to spend one minute with my brother, let alone Christmas Day.'

'That seems a pity.'

'Not to me.' His tone was gruff. 'I don't go along with the theory about blood being thicker than water.'

As there was obviously a problem between Don and his brother that went deep with him, Jess considered it wise just to nod politely and change the subject.

'Actually, I was planning on coming to see you some time soon,' she informed him, taking a colourful poster from under the counter and handing it to him. 'I wanted to ask if you could put this up in your shop for me.'

'Certainly.' He looked at the home-made poster. 'A dance class, eh?'

'That's right.'

'Good for you.'

'Well, it seems a shame to waste my training. And I really do miss dancing a lot. It won't be the same as being out there on stage, of course, but at least I'll be involved and it'll give me a chance to put something back into the community.'

'A nice idea.'

80

'I think so.' Jess glanced towards the poster, which was coloured brightly with crayons. 'My brother Todd made that for me. He's done several for me to display around the neighbourhood. He's a sweet kid.'

'Which one is Todd?' asked Don with polite interest. He'd heard about the Mollitt children from Charlie, and seen them around.

'The youngest, the one with specs.'

'I know. He's been here with your dad on the odd occasion when I've called in,' he explained.

'They're all always in and out of here,' she said. 'That's the beauty of living just around the corner.'

'Indeed.'

Jess looked at her watch, shivering, her cheeks red from the cold. 'Anyway, I'd better finish getting these papers marked up for the rounds. The boys will be here soon. And that includes my other brother, who does a round for pocket money. He'll have something to say if I don't have his papers ready for him when he arrives.'

'Yes, yes, of course. I mustn't hold you up,' Don said, seeming worried that he might have kept her for too long. 'I'll put your poster up. And I hope it'll bring you plenty of interest – I'm sure it will.'

'Thanks.'

He left and she returned to the job in hand, working from a list and marking the papers with the street and house number. She found herself thinking about Don Day and what a nice sort of a bloke he seemed to be, so quietly spoken and with such a gentle manner. Until he mentioned his brother that is; then he showed a darker side altogether. I wonder what all that was about, she thought idly, going to the shop door and letting in the first of the paper boys.

Don sat in his kitchen drinking coffee and reading the paper. Or rather staring unseeing at the print and thinking about Jess Mollitt. He thought she was lovely, with her dark hair and velvety eyes. Even when her face was pinched with cold she looked attractive. She was far too young for him, of course; there must be at least twelve years between them.

From what he could gather, she didn't have an easy life. Charlie was a decent enough bloke but he was going through hell over the death of his wife and Jess was taking the brunt. That elder boy was going to give the family big trouble in the not-too-distant future, if Don wasn't very much mistaken. He'd seen him around the town several times with a couple of delinquents in the making. Don had had cause to have a few sharp words with them the other day in the shopping centre at West Ealing when they'd been making a nuisance of themselves, pushing and shouting and emitting a string of bad language, with intent to shock, he suspected.

He hadn't said anything to Charlie about it yet because it was probably only youthful exuberance that would pass, and the poor man had enough of a problem just getting through the day, without adding to his burden unnecessarily. Obviously if Don had cause to reprimand the boy again, he'd feel morally obliged to mention it to Charlie. It was only right and proper that he should. Don prided himself on his strong sense of decency; he always strived to be correct and fair in all things. The boy had recently lost his mother so deserved a chance. But after that, if he stepped out of line he had to be taken in hand.

The lad was obviously in thrall to the yobs he'd taken up with. Anyone could see he was trying to impress those guttersnipes who probably had parents who'd never bothered to teach them the difference between right and wrong, whereas the Mollitt boy was being given a decent upbringing.

Parental influence didn't always count for much in later life, though, he pondered; his brother being a case in point. The two of them shared the same stable background, and had nothing in common whatsoever, since integrity wasn't something that featured in his brother's life at all.

Feeling tension flare from this train of thought, he made a determined effort to put his brother out of his mind and thanked God that he wouldn't have to set eyes on him ever again. Now that their parents were dead, there was no reason to as far as he was concerned. All ties had been cut.

Casting out bitter thoughts, he turned his mind to pleasanter things. He put the newspaper down and picked up the poster announcing the opening of the Jess Mollitt Dance School. Warmed by the memory of her, he couldn't help wishing he was a few years younger. It was obvious from the way she looked after the family that she was practical and caring. Someone like that would be ideal for him.

Chapter Six

Jess knew that Christmas wouldn't be easy for any of them that year with her mother's absence casting a shadow over everything. But she was hoping to make the occasion bearable – if nothing else – with a little help from Hilda.

Joy's strong presence in the house – especially at this time of the year – made it an uphill struggle with very little family interest being shown in the celebrations. But Jess and Hilda persevered with their efforts to make the day special because they thought it would boost family morale and was what Joy would have wanted. They made sure there were presents under the tree, Christmas dinner the way Joy had always cooked it, and games in the afternoon, which had always been a Mollitt family tradition.

Libby and Todd seemed to appreciate the spirit the two women were trying to create. But their efforts were wasted on Ronnie, whose rampant adolescence was playing havoc with his personality, causing him to distance himself from any kind of 'family fun' on the grounds that he was too old for such mindless juvenile activities. Christmas crackers were for retards, board games too boring even to be considered, and the suggestion of charades was enough to send him stamping upstairs to his bedroom in a strop because none of them realised that he wasn't 'some little kid' any more.

Charlie wasn't much help either. He found the whole thing too hard to take without his beloved wife and worked his way steadily through the bottles on the sideboard and had to be helped up to bed at eight o'clock, much to the disapproval of Hilda, who made no secret of her opinion.

'Surely on Christmas Day you could have made an effort, Charlie Mollitt. You're just a selfish . . .'

But with a large proportion of the off-licence stock inside him, her words fell on deaf ears.

So, with all things considered, Jess was thoroughly glad to see the back of the holiday. With that out of the way she could now focus her mind on her dance class. Having put posters up in every available public place – shops, pubs, cafés, the library and doctor's waiting room – and placed a small advertisement in the local paper, she was so optimistic about a good attendance, she wondered if the hall would be big enough. Did she have the ability to pass her dancing skills on to others, though? That was the question that kept her awake at night.

The Jess Mollitt Dance School officially opened at nine o'clock on the first Saturday morning in January. She and Hilda, with Libby – who was happy to be a general dogsbody – were there early, buoyant with hope and expectation. The floor was swept spotless, the piano polished until it shone and the music set out on the stand. They all had their eyes on the door, eagerly waiting to greet a stream of hopefuls for the first class – the under sevens – which would be divided equally between ballet and tap.

Just after nine o'clock a woman with a cute little girl of about five came in, the mother clearly surprised to find that they were the only takers. As Jess faced up to the fact that there were not going to be any more pupils for this class, she had to make a decision. Did she cancel the lesson altogether because of lack of support or go ahead with just this one pupil, whose name was Beth?

'OK, Hilda, let's have some music,' she said in a rousing tone. 'Humoresque to start with, please, when we're ready. Beth, can you put your ballet pumps on, love. Libby will help you to change your shoes, then we'll get the lesson underway with a few warm-up exercises. Thanks, Libs. Ready, Beth? Good girl. OK. Now sit on the floor with your legs stretched out in front of you and your arms out to the side with your fingertips touching the floor. Like me. That's right. Libby is doing it with you . . . lovely.' Both sisters were sitting on the floor now, Libby next to Beth, Jess on the stage. 'That's the way . . . Now point your toes then pull them back to face the ceiling. Watch me,' she said demonstrating the exercise. 'And again – point and pull back, point and back, point and back. That's very good. Well done! Now we'll do something similar with our hands, shall we? Would you like that?'

The child nodded.

One pupil or a full class, it made no difference to Jess once she got started. Enthusiasm flowed from her in a natural tide and she could have gone on for hours. Beth seemed to enjoy herself too and her mother, who had waited for her on a chair at the side of the room, said they would come again next week.

Only one child turned up for the second class, but both teacher and pupil had a wonderful time, none the less. Attendance for the final session – the over elevens – hit rock bottom: nobody came at all.

'What are you going to do?' asked Libby, biting her lip.

'With the best will in the world I can't take a class of none, can I?' Jess grinned.

'I mean in the future,' explained Libby. 'Will you cancel the whole thing as there aren't enough people to make up the classes?'

'Of course not.' Jess was astonished at such a suggestion.

'What will you do to get more people then?' the young girl wondered.

'Carry on as I am, for the time being, anyway,' was Jess's positive response. 'Leave the posters up and put the ad in the *Gazette* again and hope the parents of the two pupils who did turn up were impressed enough to tell their friends to come along. This might sound a bit overambitious, given this morning's fiasco, but I'm hoping, eventually, to build the numbers on reputation. Once people know I do a decent job, word will soon get round.'

'In the meantime you have to get people here to see what you can do, and enough of them to cover your expenses,' came a wise reminder from Hilda as she gathered her music ready to put into her bag.

'I shall have to stand the cost of it myself for a while,' said Jess without hesitation. 'Obviously, I can't afford to do that in the long term so I'll just have to live in hope that things pick up over the next few weeks. I'm not giving up. Not likely!'

Hilda looked at her. Jess was looking smart and professional, wearing black pedal pushers and a loose white top, her hair tied back. Someone else might have been defeated under the circumstances but not Jess; her eyes were shining and there was a glow about her. This was the effect dancing had always had on her. It gave her new life, somehow. 'The poor turnout didn't stop you enjoying yourself then,' Hilda remarked.

'I loved every moment,' Jess confirmed. 'It feels so good to be involved in dance again.' She put her head at an angle, smiling thoughtfully. 'I know there wasn't enough of a class for me to make a proper judgement but I think I might have what it takes to teach. Working with those kids gave me a real buzz.'

'Anyone can see that you're a natural,' praised her friend.

'Thanks.' She looked at Libby with a gleam in her eye. 'We've got some time left on the hire of the hall and a pianist on hand. We've both got our tap shoes on. So, if Hilda is willing to play for us, how about it, kid? Let's have some fun.'

'Ooh, yeah.'

The rhythmic tap and click to the tune of 'Happy Feet' filled the hall. The sisters danced together for the sheer joy of it, and the pianist was having a good time too.

'I'm in trouble with the company again,' Babs told Jess over lunch in the Salad Bowl restaurant in Lyons Corner House at the junction of Oxford Street and Tottenham Court Road. They had got together today because it had been Babs' birthday recently, her twenty-sixth. The shop closed on a Wednesday afternoon – Jess's father opened for an hour or so late afternoon because of the evening papers, but managed alone – so Jess was able to get away. This meant that she and Babs were able to meet on a fairly regular basis.

'Oh no,' sighed Jess, forking some potato salad. 'What have you been up to this time?'

'Nothing I haven't been doing for the past two years.' She gave her a wry grin. 'The only difference is, the company have found out about it now.'

'Dickie?'

'Exactly.'

'I must admit, I was concerned when you said you were working together again in pantomime, knowing how dead set they are against their dancers getting romantically involved with performers on the same show,' Jess confessed. 'They were bound to find out in the end.'

'I suppose I've always known that, but it isn't easy to be careful when you adore someone and want to be with them,' she told her. 'Anyway, it isn't as though I've committed a crime.'

'No, but you broke the rules and it counts as the same thing in the Burton Company's book.'

'All right. Don't rub it in.'

'Sorry, but I'm worried about you.'

'Don't be. I'm one of life's natural survivors.'

Jess gave her a questioning look. 'In as much as you haven't said so, I take it they didn't give you the sack.'

'Worse. I'm being put in a show up north – Liverpool. So I won't see Dickie for three months.'

'Oh dear,' tutted Jess sympathetically. 'Still, absence makes the heart grow fonder, so they say.'

'Dickie and I don't need partings to boost our feelings.' Babs made a face. 'God, the thought of Liverpool gives me the horrors. Being miles away from him and working in some provincial theatre that probably has disgusting dressing rooms . . .'

'Some of them do leave a lot to be desired in the way of facilities,' Jess couldn't deny. 'But at least they didn't fire you, that's the main thing. They have been known to when dancers break the rules.'

'They usually give you a few warnings before they do anything as drastic as that, though,' Babs reminded her. 'I know I complain about their infuriating rules but the company isn't so bad really. Anyway, I'm good at the job and I can pick up new steps quicker than anyone else in the troupe. They know they can rely on me so they'll hang on to me while I'm still useful to them.'

'You'll have to be careful in future, though,' Jess warned her. 'They'll only take so much.'

She sliced a hard-boiled egg and some lettuce, then looked up thoughtfully. 'As I'm going to be hundreds of miles away from Dickie, I'll have no choice but to behave, will I?'

'I meant when you come back,' Jess explained. 'You're not going to be away for ever.'

'Three months is a lifetime in terms of Dickie and me.' She stared at her plate, seeming lost in thought for a moment, then looked up and switched her attention to Jess. 'Anyway, that's enough about my troubles. How have things been with you?'

'All right, thanks.'

'The dance classes?'

'Smashing.' Jess chased some grated cheese around her plate with a piece of beetroot on her fork. 'Oh, Babs, I so enjoy it,' she said, looking up.

'I knew you would. Has there been any improvement in the attendance?' She nodded.

'Oh, well done. Are you covering your expenses yet?'

'Er, not exactly,' Jess was forced to admit. 'But the numbers are growing. I only had two pupils on my first Saturday . . .'

'How many have you got now?'

'Twelve.'

'At each class?'

'Oh, come on, Babs,' Jess said with a rueful grin. 'Things don't move that fast. Twelve altogether.'

'It's a big improvement,' Babs encouraged. 'But I suppose you're still not breaking even.'

'No, but at least I'm getting something towards the costs now. The hall is my only large overhead. I'm keeping a small ad in the local paper but I'll cancel that once my classes get fully subscribed.'

'So it's actually costing you money to give the lessons,' Babs spelled out for her because she was a very down-to-earth person – except, of course, when it came to Dickie.

'At the moment, yes,' nodded Jess. 'But I'm sure it'll change next term.'

Babs gave her an affectionate grin. 'You'll keep it going even if it doesn't, won't you?'

'Is it that obvious?'

'Very. You're positively blooming,' Babs said. 'And good luck to you, I say.'

'It's made me feel like Jess again,' she tried to explain. 'I was beginning to feel as though I was losing my own identity, being at the beck and call of the family and standing behind a counter all day. But now that I'm doing something I really love, even for only a few hours a week, it's given me a new lease of life. I enjoy working out the routines and planning the lessons as well as the actual teaching. It's the best thing that's happened to me in ages.'

With a smile in her eyes Babs said, 'All you need now is a man in your life.'

'You're joking,' Jess laughed. 'How would I fit a man into my life between working at the shop and dealing with the trials and tribulations of family life? Anyway, I never go anywhere to meet men now.' She paused thoughtfully. 'Come to think of it, my social life came to an end the day Mum died.'

'You know what they say about all work and no play,' Babs reminded her.

87

'I do. But there isn't much I can do about it at the moment, is there?'

'I suppose not. Anyway, kid, I won't be seeing you for a while as I'm being banished to the wilds of the north.' She paused, remembering something. 'I've got someone to take my place at the flat, by the way; someone from the troupe.'

'Anyone I know?'

'No. She's only just joined the company. A young girl by the name of Rose. Her living at the flat is just a short-term arrangement, to cover my share of the rent as I'll have to pay for lodgings in Liverpool.'

'I'll miss you.'

'Likewise.'

'Will Dickie be working in London all the time you're away?' Jess enquired casually.

'He's bound to be doing some out-of-town gigs; he's always got a few of those booked,' Babs replied. 'But I expect he'll be in London for most of the time. I know he's got a few club bookings in and around London.'

'He'll be lost without you, won't he?'

'He'd better be or I'll want to know the reason why.' Babs was laughing, confident of the love of her man. 'Anyway, it isn't the other side of the world. If I get too desperate I can always hop on the London train on my day off.'

Jess smiled. Her friend's bubbly personality was always a tonic. 'Just think of the reunion you'll have when you do get together,' she said lightly.

Babs roared with laughter. 'You'll hear the reverberations all over London.'

'Oh, Babs,' Jess admonished, laughing.

Her friend's mood became more serious. 'Listen, kid, I hope things go well for you while I'm out of town, with your dance school and everything. By the time I get back, your classes will probably be oversubscribed and you'll have a waiting list.'

'Ooh, I wish,' smiled Jess.

She enjoyed Babs' company immensely, and still missed sharing the flat with her. Although she never allowed herself to dwell on it, from time to time she still felt an ache of disappointment at having had her career in the Burton Girls cut short.

But when – a month or so after that meeting with Babs – the Mollitts received the wonderful news that Todd had earned a place at grammar school, the sacrifice seemed worthwhile. While she wouldn't dream of taking any credit for his achievement, Jess was very glad she'd been around to encourage him at the time of the exam.

Libby proved to be a valuable assistant to Jess in the dance school. As well as helping with practical tasks like sweeping the floor and taking the register and the class fees, she helped and encouraged the smaller pupils, assisting them with their dance shoes and going through the movements with them. She took a keen interest in the future of the school too.

'The numbers are really picking up now,' she remarked at the end of classes one day at the beginning of their second term.

'Yeah, twenty-two in total now,' said Jess, casting her eye over the register.

'That's what word of mouth does for a true professional,' opined Hilda. 'You said you wanted to build a reputation and it's happening. It wouldn't be if you weren't doing a good job. People don't come twice if they're not getting their money's worth, and they certainly don't make recommendations.'

'Are we taking enough to cover the overheads yet?' asked Libby, whose enjoyment in the project came mostly from working with the sister she admired so much.

'Just about.'

'Terrific,' whooped the girl.

'I reckon we've got another dance teacher in the making here, don't you, Hilda?' said Jess jokingly as she bagged the takings and put them with the register into her bag.

'No, not me,' Libby was swift to deny. 'I love helping you with the classes but I don't want to teach dancing as a job. When I leave school I want to be out there on stage doing it.'

'Stagestruck, just like your sister was,' said Hilda.

'Yep. I'm going to get into the Burton Girls when I leave school.' She spoke with total confidence.

'You've a while to go before you need even think about that,' Jess pointed out. 'Let's see how you feel nearer to the time.'

'I won't change my mind.' Her expression became steely, dark eyes meeting her sister's. 'It's what I've always wanted to do. You know that.'

'You've often talked about it,' admitted Jess. 'I wasn't sure how serious you were.'

'Dead serious.'

'There are other, more secure jobs, you know,' Jess heard herself say, remembering the sore feet, the exhaustion and the late hours. 'Jobs that are much less physically demanding.'

'Cor, you've changed your tune,' reacted Libby, surprised at her sister's attitude. 'I thought being a Burton Girl was the be-all and end-all to you.'

'And it was,' confirmed Jess. 'I'm just pointing out that the actual job is different from the idea people outside the business have of what being a dancer is really like. It's very hard work and long, unsociable hours and the Burton Company is riddled with petty rules for its dancers.'

'But to be a dancer was all you ever wanted,' Libby pointed out, her voice rising. 'And you've always encouraged me to dance; even paid for my lessons.'

'You're right on both counts. Dancing is a wonderful thing and I've always been delighted that you've share my love of it,' Jess told her. 'But my position in the family has changed since Mum died. I feel more responsible for you now.'

'What difference does that make?' the girl demanded heatedly. 'Being a Burton Girl was a dream come true for you, so why can't it be the same for me?'

Jess wasn't sure what was causing her attitude, and could only put it down to her changed role, which made her more protective towards her sister.

'I didn't go into it as soon as I left school,' she pointed out. 'I was seventeen when I joined. I did an ordinary job first.'

'You would have gone into it sooner if you'd had the chance, though, wouldn't you?'

In all honesty, she couldn't deny it. 'Yes, I think I probably would have,' she confessed.

'So you've no right to try to put me off,' pronounced Libby. 'They take girls straight out of school, don't they?'

'If they're good enough, yes. But I think it's too soon for anyone to go into Burtons, unless, of course, she's been in showbusiness as a child and is from that sort of background.'

'I don't see why.'

'I've told you, Libby. The work can be gruelling, and if you go into it straight from school with no other work experience, it could be very traumatic for you.'

'I don't care how hard I work.' She was adamant. 'It's my dream, like it was yours.'

'I *was* only a chorus girl, Libby,' she reminded her. 'I wasn't in the Royal Ballet Company.'

'You weren't just any old chorus girl, though, were you?' Libby's voice rose impatiently. 'Anyway, even if you were, joining Burtons is what I want to do and I won't change my mind, *that's definite*. I don't know why you've gone anti all of a sudden. Anyone would think there was something wrong with being a Burton Girl.'

'I think Jess is just trying to make sure you realise that it isn't all glamour, dear,' came Hilda's diplomatic contribution.

'Exactly. Thank you, Hilda.' Jess closed her bag with an air of finality. 'Anyway, it's all a very long time into the future and right now we need to get out of here or we'll be over our time.'

As they made their way down the stairs and out into the spring sunshine, Jess felt uneasy about the strength of Libby's ambition. She reminded herself that her sister wasn't even fourteen yet and would probably change her mind a dozen times before she left school, so there was no point in worrying about it. But in her heart she knew that Libby's mind was made up; Jess had been there herself and knew that nothing on earth would have stopped her aiming for her dream. If it was what Libby wanted then Jess wanted it for her too, and would do everything she could to help. But not straight from the classroom at the tender age of fifteen.

Libby wasn't the only member of the Mollitt family with a burning ambition, Jess realised the next day over Sunday lunch when the subject of Todd's autumn entry into the grammar school came up in conversation. He wanted academic success with the same ardour that Libby wanted to go on the stage. Having been top of his class so often at his junior school, he wanted to do the same thing at the gram but knew he was up against tougher competition.

'Everyone there will be above average,' he pointed out, 'or they wouldn't have got a place. They'll probably all be miles cleverer than me. I hope I'm not bottom of the class.'

'I'm sure you'll hold your own,' Jess reassured him.

'Course you will,' added Libby.

'Anyway, coming top of the class isn't everything,' Jess felt she should mention. 'As long as you do your best with the work and enjoy the school life, that's the important thing. From what I've heard you won't have any trouble keeping up.'

'I dunno what all the fuss is about,' Ronnie put in disagreeably. 'It's only a bloomin' school.'

Always somewhat in awe of his older brother, a beetroot flush crept up Todd's neck and suffused his face. But he managed to find the courage to defend himself. 'It isn't just any old school. The standard will be high. I'll be learning new things.'

'Oh, yeah, like what?'

'Foreign languages, for one thing.'

'What good will that do you since you're never likely to get the chance to use them?' scoffed Ronnie.

'I might when I'm grown up,' said the red-faced Todd. 'If I get good qualifications, I might get the chance to travel. Anyway, knowing foreign languages will be fun.'

'If that's your idea of fun you must have something wrong with your head, mate.' Ronnie always felt angry lately and didn't seem able to control it or stop venting it on the family. Spots had broken out all over his face and he felt ugly and inferior to his mates, who were all better-looking than he and ultraconfident. He'd started noticing girls in a new way too, and was having feelings he only half understood. Then there was the awful blushing that happened at the slightest thing and made him feel such an idiot. 'You can stuff your poxy grammar school full of toffee-nosed sissies in poncy blazers.'

'Just because you're in a bad mood, there's no need to have a go at Todd,' defended Libby.

'Yes. Don't spoil things for your brother,' admonished Jess sternly. 'You're getting to be really nasty lately, Ronnie. I don't know what's the

91

matter with you. You're always so bad-tempered.'

'It's always me,' he retaliated, simmering with umbrage. 'No one else in this house ever does anything wrong.' He threw a glare at his siblings. 'You're all saints – I don't think.'

'Oh, for goodness' sake, stop sniping and eat your food, and that goes for all of you.' Jess looked towards their father with the intention of drawing him into the conversation as he seemed to have lapsed into one of his silent, preoccupied moods again. 'You'll back me up on that one, won't you, Dad?'

Startled out of his reverie, he said, 'What's that?'

'Can you tell these children of yours to eat their dinner and stop picking on each other?'

'Huh. When did they ever take any notice of anything I say?' he said in a feeble attempt at humour.

When you were a participating member of this family and not just a shadowy figure in the background, was the answer to that, Jess thought, realising just how seriously parental her own role towards her siblings had become since the death of their mother. It wasn't something she had sought and at times it was a burden. But she was stuck with it, for the next few years anyway, and she felt duty-bound to do her very best for them.

No one seemed to know how to reply to the father who had once been at the centre of the family but was now usually distant and uncommunicative. His jokey comment fell flat and an uncomfortable silence settled over the room.

'Any more potatoes anyone?' asked Jess, to ease an awkward moment.

Dean's Stores closed for an hour at lunchtime and Don Day either had a snack upstairs in his flat or went to the pub for a cheese roll and a pint if he fancied some company. Sometimes, if the weather was particularly fine, he would take a stroll in Churchfields after he'd eaten his lunch, to stretch his legs and help his digestion.

Such was the case one glorious spring day, the air fragrant with may blossom, the sun's golden light bathing this luxuriant expanse of parkland with the abundant trees in pale new leaf, the spire of St Mary's church presiding over everything with quiet dignity. There was a tangible sense of tranquillity here, away from the traffic noise of the town. It was almost like being in the country rather than a busy London suburb. Being a school day, the peace wasn't shattered by the shrieks and shouts of children at play either; just a few under fives with their mothers heading for the playground down the grassy slope towards the viaduct. It occurred to him that strangers passing through the town on the busy Uxbridge Road would probably be unaware of the leafy haven so close by.

Having a few minutes to spare, he sat on a bench, enjoying the gentle warmth of the sun on his face. The quiet was interrupted by a train roaring across the viaduct, and visible to him because the trees were not yet fully in leaf. In relaxed mood he felt reassured that he had made the right decision in moving to this area, which had been unknown territory to him until the day he'd come for the job interview at Dean's Stores. He'd barely even heard of the place until then.

Originally from North London, Don had found solace among strangers, away from the painful memories of the past. It was agonisingly lonely at times but that was something he'd had to endure ever since he'd lost Sheila, and he knew would be with him wherever he lived.

The son of a railway worker, Don had been in the grocery trade all his working life. He'd started as a delivery boy and worked up to manager status in a busy grocery store in Tottenham. He'd been happy enough there until the death of his wife. Then he couldn't get away from the place quick enough. So when he'd seen the job as manager of Dean's Stores advertised in the *Grocer* magazine, he'd grasped the chance of escape, especially as accommodation was available with the position. He'd needed to get away from reminders of the past and the brother he hated with a passion. Here he could be certain that he wouldn't run into him in the street or the pub.

He and brother, Bruce, had proved to have such different values, it hardly seemed possible that they had once been so close. Bruce was ruthless and self-seeking; he took what he wanted from life, regardless of other people's feelings. An ache rose inside Don as he remembered that they'd been such good mates before the rift, closer than most brothers. Having once been so fond of Bruce made the whole miserable business even harder to bear.

Still, Don reckoned he had a lot to be thankful for. He had a job he enjoyed with a comfortable flat provided, and he earned enough to live to a reasonable standard. An hour in the pub now and then was about the extent of his social life but he probably wouldn't have had more than that if he'd stayed in Tottenham. When you lost your partner, your social life went too. When you lost your brother's friendship, it was a double blow.

Don knew that he had a reputation for being too strait-laced; a bit of an old woman, some people said. He didn't care what they thought; he was scrupulous in his attitude to life and proud of it. He couldn't bear lies or deceit or bad behaviour of any sort. He gave a wry grin, remembering how his brother used to tease him about his dour personality and was always telling him not to take life so seriously. But then Bruce had a much more relaxed attitude to life altogether. Live and let live was his motto. 'We're all only human' he'd say, no matter how badly people around him behaved. He could always see the lighter side of life, whereas Don had never had much of a sense of humour. But somehow they'd got along and been good for each other. Until it had all come to a dramatic end . . .

His reverie was interrupted by three boys walking along the path, jostling and pushing and shouting at each other in a light-hearted way. Changing course, they made their way across the grass and stopped under a tree where they grouped into a huddle with their backs to him. Sudden clouds of smoke left Don in no doubt as to what they were up to. They were a reasonable distance from him so he couldn't be certain of their ages but could tell that they should be in the classroom now, not in the park getting up to mischief.

A glance at his watch confirmed that the school dinner break would be over by now. He told himself it was none of his business. If they wanted to ruin their education and health by playing truant and smoking cigarettes, it was up to them. But the need to put them back on the straight and narrow was so strong, he felt compelled to go over and say something. It wasn't in his nature to let it go.

He got up and made his way over to them, a tall, severe-looking figure, traditionally dressed in a blazer and grey flannels. As he drew nearer, he realised that it was the Mollitt boy and his mates, thus confirming his earlier suspicions that that boy was on the slippery slope, and needed taking in hand.

'Why aren't you at school?' he demanded of them.

'Blimey. It's that geezer from Dean's Stores,' said a boy with dark hair greased into a high quiff at the front. 'Why don't you get back to your bacon slicer, mister?'

'You should be at school.'

'We've got the afternoon off,' said a lad with ginger hair styled in a ludicrous imitation of his loud-mouthed mate.

'Teachers' meeting,' added the dark boy with the sort of grin that made it obvious he was lying.

'I don't believe you,' said Don.

'You can believe what you like, mate,' the youngster responded arrogantly. 'It's none of your business anyway. So bugger off and leave us alone.'

Don was undeterred. 'You ought to be grateful for the chance of education,' he lectured. 'You should be at school trying to make something of yourselves, not hanging around here wasting your time and smoking.'

'We've told you, we've got the afternoon off,' insisted Ginger. 'It's got nothing to do with you.'

The Mollitt boy – who was blushing furiously – hadn't said a word up until now, Don noticed. Probably because he knew Don was a pal of his father's.

'Perhaps we'd better be going, lads,' suggested Ronnie, looking worried.

'You ain't scared of him, are yer?' challenged the dark boy.

'Course not.'

'Seems like it to me.'

'He's only a bleedin' grocer,' added Ginger. 'He can't do nothing to us.'

'He knows my dad.'

'So what?' said his friend. 'You ain't scared of your old man, are yer?'

'Don't talk daft,' denied Ronnie with bravado. 'But parks are for kids. Let's go and find some action somewhere.'

'Yeah,' agreed the others, and they turned and sauntered off, exuding arrogance from every pore.

Don stayed where he was for a while, mulling the incident over before making his way back to the shop, still thinking about it. He had a decision to make.

Jess was serving in the shop; she was waiting for her father to come back from the bank where he'd gone to get some change. She was absolutely seething.

'I've been on the phone to the wholesaler because our delivery of confectionery and cigarettes didn't arrive and I was told that we haven't placed an order with them this week,' she informed him when he finally got back and was emptying the change into the till.

'That's funny.'

'I don't find it in the least bit funny,' she retorted. 'You were supposed to look after it and you haven't.'

At least he had the grace to look sheepish, she noticed. 'I thought I had,' he mumbled.

'Well, you haven't and it just isn't good enough, Dad,' she rebuked. 'We're losing business over this sort of thing. People will go elsewhere if we don't have stock to offer them.'

He put his hand to his head, looking puzzled. 'How could I have forgotten a thing like that?' he muttered almost to himself.

Probably because you're either too busy feeling sorry for yourself or trying to cheer yourself up in the pub, she thought, but wasn't cruel enough to say so. 'I don't know, but this sort of thing keeps on happening lately. If you want to hand the ordering of stock over to me, then say so and I'll do it willingly, but one of us needs to be responsible.'

'I'll do it.'

'I'd sooner do it myself and know it was done, if you're going to be this unreliable.'

'All right, all right, I'll be more careful in future,' Charlie said, his voice rising.

'Can I rely on that?'

'Look, I've said I'll take care of it and I will,' he said gruffly. 'I don't want you giving me earache about it for the rest of the day.'

It was a tricky situation. This was his shop and she respected his position here. But he was continually putting the family livelihood at risk with his careless attitude towards the business, so naturally she was

95

worried. She had to watch him every step of the way and the strain was beginning to tell on her. It would be easier to run the place on her own and know it was being done properly than have errors of this type happening repeatedly.

But he would never give up the reigns, and neither did she want him to. He needed this shop. Without some sort of responsibility he'd sink even deeper into the trough.

Taking a deep breath to calm herself, she said, 'You'll have to go to the wholesalers and collect some stuff for us right away because we're low on everything. I've managed to persuade them to make up the order and have it ready for us but they can't deliver because this isn't their day to cover this area. You'll have to go to pick it up in the car.'

Charlie didn't look pleased. 'Can't we manage with what we've got until they can deliver?' he suggested. 'I don't fancy the idea of going over to Brentford.'

'No we can't. And I can't go as I don't drive, can I?' Jess pointed out. 'We need the stuff because we're completely out of our bestselling lines like Mars Bars and Frys Chocolate Cream. The kiddies' section is almost empty too.'

Tension drew tight between them. The day had got off to a bad start for Jess, with her father being too hungover to do the papers this morning. Then one of the paper boys hadn't turned up so she'd had to do his round herself. And now this. Fortunately Dad hadn't had a lunchtime session in the pub so could drive the car.

'And that's going to make a big difference to our profits, I suppose,' he said sarcastically.

'That isn't the point,' Dad,' she responded sharply. 'Small problems lead to bigger ones. If people can't get certain small items from us too often they'll go somewhere else for everything – papers, magazines, ciggies. We're supposed to be offering a service here all the time, not just when you happen to feel like it. We'll have no business left if you don't get a grip.'

'Oh, for God's sake, I made a minor mistake, that's all.' He was shouting now. 'There's no need to carry on as though I've killed someone.'

At that moment the shop door opened and Don Day walked in. Forcing her features into an attempt at a smile, Jess said, 'Hello there. What can we do for you?'

He didn't reply; just shifted from foot to foot. 'It's a bit awkward actually . . .' He looked most uncomfortable.

'Well, I've got to go out to the wholesalers to pick up some stock so I can't stop to chat, mate,' announced Charlie irritably, lifting the counter flap and heading for the door. 'Jess will deal with it for you, whatever it is.'

'I think you ought to hear what I have to say, Charlie,' Don informed him gravely. 'It won't take long.'

Puzzled, Jess and her father looked at him, waiting for him to continue.

'I wasn't sure if I should say anything or not—'

'Oh, spit it out, man, for Pete's sake,' said Charlie impatiently. 'We've got a shop to run here.'

'It's that boy of yours,' Don blurted out. 'The elder one.'

'Ronnie,' said Jess, feeling the icy grip of foreboding clutching at her heart.

'Has something happened to him?' Charlie was clearly alarmed.

'It can't have done, Dad,' she muttered almost to herself. 'He's safe at school.'

'That's where you're wrong,' Don informed them, looking from one to the other. 'He isn't at school.'

'He is,' argued Jess.

Don shook his head. 'I've just seen him in the park,' he told them.

'You can't have done,' frowned Charlie.

'Sorry, mate, but he was there as large as life with some other boys. Right little villains the others looked too.' His little grey eyes darted from one to the other anxiously. 'They told me they'd got the afternoon off but I guessed they were lying.'

Charlie's face was like thunder. 'The little sod,' he bellowed. 'I'll knock the living daylights out of him.'

'Dad . . . don't talk like that.' Her father had never 'knocked the living daylights' out of anyone in his life and Jess doubted if he was about to start now. But there were fireworks ahead, that much she was sure of.

'Sorry to be the bearer of bad news,' Don apologised uncertainly. 'I just . . . well, I thought you would want to know.'

Both Charlie and Jess were far too preoccupied with their own thoughts to reply.

'I mean, that sort of thing can lead to serious trouble, can't it? Boys of that age playing truant get into all sorts of mischief,' Don went on, clearly trying to justify his actions in telling them. 'You never know what they might get up to.' He made a face. 'I hope I did the right thing in telling you.' Receiving no reply, he cleared his throat before dropping the final bombshell. 'Actually . . . they were smoking cigarettes too.'

Jess was having a terrible day and about the last thing she needed was some interfering do-gooder bringing more trouble. 'We need to know these things, of course,' she assured him curtly. 'And don't worry, we're not about to shoot the messenger.' The build-up of tension throughout the day made her manner hostile almost without her realising it as she added with icy politeness and an air of finality, 'Thank you for letting us know.'

'No trouble at all,' Don said, turning quickly and heading for the door. Doing the right thing could sometimes leave you with the most sour taste in your mouth, he thought gloomily, as he headed off down the street.

'So this is what you've come down to, is it?' boomed Charlie who started on Ronnie as soon as he got home from the shop. 'Bunking off school and hanging about the town all day like some bloody yob, getting yourself talked about and giving the family a bad name. Not to mention missing your lessons.'

'I wasn't out all day,' came Ronnie's sullen defence. 'We came out at dinner time.'

They were standing facing each other in the living room. Jess had sent the other two upstairs but thought she'd better stay herself as mediator.

'Came out at dinner time?' her father roared. 'What are they running there, a school or a holiday camp where people can come and go as they please?'

'The older children are allowed to go out at dinner time if they have permission, Dad,' Jess explained. 'Some of them go home to dinner so they can't keep the gates locked during that time.'

'I suppose not.' He looked at his son with disdain. 'They probably think, mistakenly, that lads of your age are old enough to be trusted to go out and come back for the afternoon lessons.'

'I only bunked off school for an afternoon,' Ronnie pointed out with blatant arrogance. 'The fuss you're making anyone would think I'd robbed a bank or something.'

'That's enough of your lip.'

'Well . . . it was only a bit of fun.'

'It isn't on, Ronnie,' Charlie lectured. 'Apart from the fact that it's wrong, it won't do you any good to miss lessons. You need to get as much as you can from your education, for your own sake, for the future.'

'School's boring.'

'Oh, so it's boring, is it?' boomed his father. 'Well, it isn't meant to be like the Saturday morning pictures.'

'Calm down, Dad,' intervened Jess, who had already given Ronnie a trouncing when she got home from work and had received the same lofty attitude and lack of remorse as her father was getting. 'Don't give yourself a heart attack over it. So he bunked off school for the afternoon, it isn't the crime of the century.'

'Don't stick up for him,' her father rebuked. 'It's a very serious matter.'

'I know that and I've told him so.'

Charlie turned his attention back to his son. 'Do you want to be as thick as a plank when you leave school? Is that what you're aiming for? Is it?'

Ronnie's dark eyes were hot with resentment as they rested on his father; two scarlet stains on his cheeks indicated to Jess that he was more upset than he was pretending to be. But he remained infuriatingly silent.

'Well, is it?' his father asked again.

'Leave it, Dad.' Jess could see that this was serving no useful purpose. They both needed time to calm down before this went any further.

The boy shrugged. 'I'm not bothered either way, if I'm thick or otherwise,' he told his father sulkily.

'What sort of an attitude is that for a young boy to have?' demanded Charlie.

'Dunno. I'm just telling you how I feel.'

'Oh, I see,' Charlie ground out. 'You're not bothered about leaving school with a bad report because you think you can come into the family business and do just as you please because you're the son of the family?'

'No . . .'

'Well, Jess has given up her dancing career to help me run the business and I don't know if—'

'I can easily get another job when the time comes if Ronnie wants to work with you, Dad,' Jess interrupted. 'My working at the shop was never meant to be permanent.'

'You can stick your lousy job,' said Ronnie, fierce, angry tears rushing into his eyes. 'I don't want to work in a rotten paper shop when I leave school and I never have done.'

'Oh? And what do you have in mind then?' Charlie asked through gritted teeth. 'Brain surgery perhaps? Or nuclear science?'

Narrowing his eyes venomously on his father, Ronnie said, 'I don't know what I'll do but it'll be something a bloomin' sight more interesting than working in a paper shop.'

'In that case, you'd better pay attention to your school work, boy,' growled his father. 'Your options will be limited if you don't.'

Ronnie stared at Charlie, his contempt filling the room. 'What do you care, anyway?'

'We wouldn't be having this conversation if I didn't care.'

'That's just a load of rubbish. This is just an excuse to have another go at me,' accused Ronnie, his voice quivering with emotion now.

'And what's that supposed to mean?' Charlie was ashen-faced and trembling with anger.

'You couldn't give a damn about any of us now that Mum isn't here,' the boy stated. 'You probably never did but we didn't notice it because Mum cared enough for both of you.'

Seeing her father wince, Jess turned on her brother, even though she could understand why he was feeling this way. 'There's no call for that sort of talk, Ronnie,' she admonished sharply. 'Now apologise to Dad – tell him you don't mean it.'

'But I do mean it,' he made clear in a thick voice. 'All he cares about is himself and his own feelings. Always feeling sorry for himself and getting drunk and showing us up. He doesn't care that we miss Mum too.'

And leaving his sister and father reeling with shock, he marched from the room and thundered up the stairs, the slam of his bedroom door echoing through the house.

Charlie emitted a deep, shuddering sigh, rage turning to hopeless despair.

Jess patted his arm in a comforting gesture. 'Leave him to me, Dad. I'll give him a few minutes to calm down, then and I'll go up and have a few words with him,' she said, her heart aching at the pain in his eyes.

Chapter Seven

'I'm not ganging up with Dad against you, Ronnie,' Jess tried to convince him. 'I wouldn't do that.'

'Oh, not much.' He was sitting on his bed hugging his knees, dark hair rumpled, eyes red and swollen. He'd obviously been sobbing his heart out but Jess pretended to be unaware of this so as not to embarrass him. 'Do you think I'm deaf or something? I was there, I heard what was said.'

'I couldn't stand back and say nothing, could I, since I seem to be the peacemaker around here? And I did try to be fair,' she told him. 'If anything, I took your side. I pointed out to Dad that you hadn't committed the crime of the century, remember?'

'You told me to apologise to him, though.'

'When you made that accusation, I had to.'

'I don't see why.'

'Because he's your father and you shouldn't have said those awful things to him,' she admonished. 'Neither should you have bunked off school. It might not be a criminal offence, but it's still wrong.'

'OK, so I shouldn't have come out of school,' he admitted defiantly, and with little sign of contrition. 'But what I said about Dad was the truth. He doesn't give a toss about any of us.'

Perched on the edge of Todd's bed – he having made a diplomatic exit – Jess brushed a tired hand over her brow. She was exhausted from the constant struggle to keep the peace in this shattered family. 'I know it seems like that at times, but I really believe he does care about us.'

'Don't kid yourself, Jess,' Ronnie said in a scornful tone. 'You've seen what he's like.'

She nodded. 'He isn't the man he was, I admit that, and I don't like his behaviour any more than you do. But I honestly don't think it has anything to do with his feelings for us,' was her truthful opinion.

'Rubbish!'

'You can scoff all you like, Ronnie. But I'm a lot older than you so I can see him as a man as well as a father, and I know that us kids are everything to him. He beats himself up every day because he knows he's failing us.'

'He's right about that, anyway,' he snorted.

'All right, so he is a bit distant a lot of the time,' she was forced to admit. 'But the man we used to know is still in there somewhere, and one day he'll be his old self again. I'm convinced of it.'

'You must be living in a dream world then,' scorned Ronnie. 'If he gave two hoots about us he wouldn't always be getting drunk and coming home in a bad mood. I mean, what interest does he take in anyone except himself? None. Half the time he doesn't even bother to talk – except to have a go at me, of course.'

'He does sometimes perk up and show an interest in his family,' Jess reminded him. 'Like when he found somewhere for me to have my dance classes, for instance.'

'Oh, yeah, once in a blue moon he puts himself out,' he agreed. 'But blink and you'd miss it.'

'Look, I know it's hard to take, and I find the change in him as difficult as you do – more so, probably, because I work with him too – but he seems to have got himself locked into a depression and doesn't seem able to see beyond his own grief. Frankly, I think it's out of his control,' she said, pondering on the matter as she spoke. 'None of us realised just how close he and Mum were. He's like a lost soul without her.'

'We're all lost without her. But we can't get drunk to forget about it, can we?'

'No, we can't.' She gave him a studied look. 'So you try to forget by hanging out with those dreadful boys you've been going around with lately,' she suggested, taking this opportunity to raise the worrying subject.

'I enjoy being with them. It's got nothing to do with Mum dying, or Dad being a pain in the bum,' he protested with rather too much vigour. 'And there's nothing wrong with them. Nifty and Shifter are a really good laugh.'

'What happened to your other mates?' she enquired evenly. 'The ones with proper names.'

'They're all geeks – zombies the lot of them,' Ronnie declared disapprovingly. 'And Nifty and Shifter *have* got proper names. They just prefer to use nicknames because they're not so boring.'

'The boys you used to go around with seemed nice enough to me,' Jess said, realising that she sounded like someone's mother.

'I was just a kid when I hung out with them. Nifty and Shifter are much more fun,' he declared. 'Nothing scares them; they'll do anything for a laugh.'

'And they think it's funny to bunk off school and smoke cigarettes in the park, I suppose?'

He shrugged. 'So what if they do? At least they're game for a bit of excitement. Anyway, next year I'll be fifteen and out working and paying my way. I'll be able to do what I like then without getting a load of grief from you and Dad.'

'But now you're only rising fourteen and being kept by Dad, so you'll do as you're told.'

'You're not my mother, you know,' came his curt reminder.

'No. But I am your older sister and that does give me some seniority around here,' she asserted. 'And I still say you should apologise to Dad for what you said.'

'What's the point when I meant every word?'

'He's your dad and he deserves some respect, whatever your true feelings, that's the point,' she spelled out for him firmly. 'Bear in mind that he always did right by us all until Mum died. He was a great dad when she was around.'

'S'pose so.'

'Another reason you should apologise is because I want you to,' she went on to say. 'It'll clear the air and make the atmosphere more comfortable for the rest of us. This house is like a bloomin' battlefield at the moment.'

'But I believe what I said was true so it wouldn't be a truthful apology,' he pointed out.

'I realise that. But in this case a bit of play-acting won't do any harm.' She looked at him persuasively. 'Do it for my sake, eh, Ron?' Leaning across, she put her hand on his arm, feeling the bone beneath the sleeve of his shirt because he was so skinny. 'Look, I didn't ask for the job of looking after you all. And I certainly don't want to spend my whole life trying to patch up family quarrels. So give us a break, and say sorry to Dad so that we can have a bit of peace around here.'

He mulled it over for what seemed like ages to Jess. 'Oh, all right then,' he agreed with reluctance. 'But I'm only doing it for you. Not for him.'

'It's better than not doing it at all.'

Ronnie looked thoughtful, remembering something. 'And as for that geezer from Dean's Stores,' he began with a look of disdain, 'doesn't he have anything better to do than go around poking his nose into other people's business? What a creep, eh? Fancy running straight to Dad and snitching on me.' He puffed out his lips and shook his head slowly to emphasise his disgust. 'I guessed he would, though. I could tell by the look in those beady little eyes of his when he was laying the law down in the park. He just couldn't wait to drop me in it.'

'I'm sure he meant well,' said Jess, hoping to pacify her brother. 'He did it for your own good because he doesn't want you to get into more trouble.'

'No. He did it because he's a nosy old git,' was Ronnie's interpretation.

Jess was reminded of her own hostile reaction to Don when he'd broken the news. She wondered if perhaps she'd been unnecessarily sharp with him because she'd been so overburdened with problems at the time. She hoped not, because he seemed like a decent man and had been acting in the family's best interests.

'You're not being fair.'

'Neither was he, the slimy sod.'

'That's enough, Ronnie,' she scolded.

The door opened and Todd stood cautiously in the doorway. 'Can I come in now, please?' he asked. 'I want to get something.'

'Yeah, come on in,' replied Jess. 'We've just about finished,'

'I hate the rows in the house,' he mumbled, getting a book from his bedside table.

'Don't we all?' Jess stood up, looking at Ronnie. 'But Ronnie is going to put things right now, aren't you?'

'Yeah, in a minute.'

'Promise?'

He emitted an eloquent sigh. 'I said I would didn't I?' he said through gritted teeth.

'Good boy.' She walked to the door and turned, adding, 'But no more bunking off school. No matter how hard those mates of yours pile on the pressure.'

Ronnie shrugged in reply and Jess didn't ask him to make a promise because she suspected it would be a false one. Ronnie was a very troubled boy, she thought, as she made her way downstairs. Mulling it over, she began to wonder if perhaps the cause might not be just one single element but a combination of things: rising hormones, the lingering trauma of his mother's death and its dramatic effect on their family life, in particular their father's personality change, and the influence of Ronnie's unsavoury new friends to which he was particularly susceptible at this vulnerable time.

Heaven knew where it would all end but she had a horrible suspicion that their problems with Ronnie had only just begun.

Having had a restless night worrying about it, Jess wasn't on top form the next morning at the shop, even though her father had got up and done the papers. Her heart sank when Don Day came in. She hoped he wasn't going to be all holier-than-thou about the events of yesterday because she really wasn't in the mood.

'I was wondering, Jess,' he began, having exchanged greetings with herself and her father, 'if you'd like to join me for a spot of lunch.' He winked at Charlie who was standing beside her, and made an attempt at humour. 'I would ask you to come too, mate, but your daughter's a lot better-looking, and I know you can't both come because you keep the shop open over the lunch hour.' He looked from one to the other. 'It's by way of a peace offering. I feel bad about making trouble for you yesterday.'

'It's Ronnie who made the trouble, not you,' Charlie assured him. 'I'd have done the same thing if I'd found myself in a similar position.'

'Dad's right,' added Jess, warmed by his attitude, 'and a peace offering really isn't necessary.'

His gaze lingered on her. 'Perhaps we could go anyway,' he suggested. 'Nothing special, just a bite at the café round the corner . . . or we could go to Lyons in West Ealing, if you'd rather and take my car to save time.'

Jess felt awkward. The last thing she wanted was lunch with a comparative stranger. 'It's very kind of you to suggest it but I don't usually have a proper lunch hour,' she explained, hoping he wouldn't persist. 'I just grab something here.'

'It's high time you had a change,' put in her father, annoyingly. 'So say yes to the man.'

'I don't think so—'

'Oh. Well, if you'd rather not,' Don cut in, clearing his throat and looking embarrassed. 'It was just an idea.'

He seemed so downhearted that much against her better judgement she heard herself saying, 'Dad's right. I could do with a change. I'd like to come, and thanks for asking.'

Brightening considerably, Don said he'd call for her at one o'clock, and left with a spring in his step.

'Now what have I let myself in for?' she muttered gloomily to her father. 'You should have helped me to get out of it instead of encouraging him.'

'I didn't because I think it will do you good to get away from here at lunchtime for a break,' he replied, thereby confirming her belief in him. 'Don's a good bloke.'

'As a drinking pal for you maybe . . .'

'It's only a bite to eat out, Jess, to ease the man's conscience, nothing more.'

'Yeah, I suppose so.' But she found the whole thing a bit of a nuisance.

Much to Jess's utter amazement, she was enjoying herself. Don had driven them the short distance to West Ealing in his old black Austin and they went to Lyons where they both had braised steak and two veg with strawberry ice cream to follow. It was so refreshing to have some adult conversation with someone outside the family.

'I suppose my name is mud with Ronnie,' speculated Don, over coffee.

She gave him a wry grin, observing rather a stern face with serious grey eyes, thin pale lips and an aquiline nose. He wasn't actually bad-looking, but he was very staid and not at all sexy; his straight brown hair was plastered to his head with Brylcreem and he had exceptionally long fingers, she noticed as he held his coffee cup. 'Well . . . I don't think you'll be on his Christmas Card list, put it that way,' she informed him.

'I think I can live with that,' he told her. 'But I hated the idea that I'd upset you.' He made a face. 'And I really thought I had, the way you were with me yesterday.'

'I was feeling a bit miffed but it wasn't you who caused it, not really. You just happened to be the person who gave me one problem too many,' she explained. 'It was one damned thing after another yesterday. Then when you came in to tell us about Ronnie, I just wanted to scream.' She sipped her coffee. 'Sorry if I was a bit offhand.'

'That's all right,' Don assured her. 'As long as we're still friends.'

'Course we are.'

'Good.' He looked at her. 'So, how are things at home now? Calmer after the storm?'

'Just a bit. But it was very fraught last night. Ronnie made things worse by giving Dad some lip when he took him to task about bunking off school. Eventually Ronnie apologised, under pressure from me, but he's still confined to the house after school for a fortnight so he isn't best pleased about that.'

'And it's all my fault for grassing on him.'

'He probably sees it that way.' She sighed. 'That boy is angry with the whole world at the moment. If it isn't one row it's another in our house, what with the twins' marching hormones and Dad still grieving for Mum. Todd's the only even-tempered one, and I suppose that'll change once he hits his teens.'

'You must miss your life as a dancer.'

'Phew, not half,' she readily admitted. 'This time last year all I had to worry about was stage fright and sore feet.' She stared mistily ahead, remembering. 'It was a different world.'

'It's a shame you had to give it up.'

'Yeah. I wouldn't have it any other way, though,' she put him straight, immediately on the defensive at the first sign of sympathy. 'I love all the family to bits and I want to be there for them. And running my dance school fills a need. It brings dance into my life and keeps me happy.'

'It still seems a pity . . .'

She threw him a look, wanting to make sure he understood the situation for good and all. 'Look, I didn't want to give up my stage life to come home but I'm very glad that I did,' she stated forcefully.

'That's all right then,' he said quickly, obviously taking the hint. 'So how's the dance school going?'

'Pretty good. I've got enough pupils to cover my expenses now.' She gave a wry grin. 'Mind you, I get the hall at a very reasonable price. That's about the only good thing to come out of Dad's drinking habits. I suspect the pub landlord wanted to keep him sweet as he's such a good customer.'

'It's an ill wind then.'

Jess nodded. 'I absolutely adore running my classes,' she went on to say, becoming animated at the thought. 'It's the highlight of my week, my way of relaxing.'

'Teaching kids to dance, relaxing . . .?'

'Yeah, it really is for me. It gives me such a kick to see the kids improving and enjoying themselves. And, of course, it stops me from losing my dancing skills because I demonstrate the steps and work out the routines.'

'That's really good.' Don finished his coffee. 'So what else do you do in your leisure time?'

'Nothing much,' she confessed with a rueful grin. 'I always seem to be either working or doing some chore at home.'

'I don't have a social life either.' He stared at the table for a moment, then looked up. 'Perhaps we could go out one evening, to the cinema or something?'

Jess was caught off guard. She really had thought this lunch would be just a one-off; hadn't even considered him as dating material. He was nice enough in his way but not her type at all. He was years older than she for a start; must be in his mid-thirties at least, and seemed older than that in his ways. Oh dear, this really was difficult with him being a pal of Dad's. 'It's very kind of you to ask but I'm usually busy in the evenings.' She felt terrible and the only excuse she could think of was going to sound so lame. 'It's late by the time I've cleared up after the evening meal and everything.'

'You might enjoy an evening out,' he persisted, 'and it will certainly do me good to have some company for a change.' He paused for a moment, then met her eyes. 'Just a night out. No strings.'

Still fearing there might be more to it, she said, 'I don't think so, Don, but thanks anyway.'

'As you wish.' There was an awkward silence. 'Sorry if I embarrassed you.'

'You didn't,' she fibbed. 'It was nice of you to ask.'

'It was just a thought.' He effected a swift change of subject. 'I saw that dance troupe you used to be in on television the other day. They were very good.'

'The best,' she said proudly.

'I must have seen them when you were in it because I've often seen them before on the box but I didn't know you then so I wouldn't have been looking out for you.'

'It's hard to pick us out when we're in costume, anyway,' she told him.

'I'm sure I wouldn't have had a problem if I'd known you then.' He spoke in a complimentary manner.

She smiled graciously and they chatted for a while longer, until they realised the time and made a hasty departure back to work.

'Thank you so much for lunch, Don,' Jess said when he pulled up outside Mollitts. 'It's been lovely. A really nice break.'

'I enjoyed it too.'

He went round to open her car door for her, a real old-fashioned gent. It was nice. Much to her surprise she found herself reconsidering his invitation. True, he was different from the men she had been out with in the past. They had all been stylish, charismatic types, attracted to the glamour of her profession. And all any one of them had ever given her had been sexual pressure or a broken heart, she thought, remembering Jack in particular. What did it matter if Don didn't set her heart fluttering? He was good company, and he'd made it clear the invitation wasn't a date, as such – just two people keeping each other company because neither of them had much of a social life.

'If that offer of an evening out is still on, I think I'd like to come after all.'

'Wonderful,' he beamed. 'How about Saturday night?'

'That would be lovely.'

'I'll look forward to it then.'

'Me too.'

'I'll be in touch about the details before then.'

'All right.' She'd almost forgotten how good it felt to have an outing to look forward to.

'You're going out tonight with that slimy creep from Dean's Stores?' was Ronnie's disapproving response on Saturday evening when Jess mentioned it to him. 'Ugh, Jess, how could you?'

'Quite easily, as it happens, because he's a nice bloke,' she defended, unwrapping a package of fish and chips that Ronnie had just collected on Jess's instructions for the family's tea. 'Just because he did the decent thing and told Dad and me what you were getting up to doesn't make him a bad person.'

'Surely you can do better than him, though. I mean . . . he's so, well . . . awful.'

'I'm not thinking of spending the rest of my life with him,' she pointed out. 'We're just going out together for a night because neither of us gets out much.'

'You must like him or you wouldn't have agreed to go,' he challenged.

'I do like him,' she didn't hesitate to admit. 'There's nothing wrong with him at all.'

'He's years older than you, for a start,' he reminded her. 'And he's goofy-looking.'

'I realise that at the great age of fourteen you're an expert on the right sort of man for me,' she responded with irony. 'But who I choose to go out with is none of your business.'

'That drip, though . . .'

She gave his hand a gentle slap as it appropriated some chips from the paper while she was serving them on to the plates. The mood between them was one of affectionate joviality, which they were still sometimes able to achieve in this family, she was pleased to observe. 'So make yourself useful and go and tell the others that tea will be on the table in two minutes.'

As Ronnie made to leave, Libby bounded into the kitchen and made a beeline for the chips.

'You'll never guess who Jess is going out with tonight, Libs?' said Ronnie.

'Who?'

'The manager of Dean's Stores,' he announced disapprovingly.

'She never is,' gasped Libby, taking a chip.

'I reckon she must want her head examined, don't you?' observed Ronnie.

Libby looked at her sister, chewing a chip slowly and considering the matter. 'He is a bit ancient, Jess,' was her opinion.

'Anyone over twenty-one is ancient to you lot,' Jess pointed out. 'Including me.'

'True,' grinned Libby. 'But he's even older.'

'He isn't that old, for heaven's sake.'

'He looks a bit decrepit to me,' said Libby. 'Seems a bit of a drip.'

'That's what I think.' Ronnie was glad of the support.

'Look, when I want your approval, I'll let you know,' Jess told them both; she wasn't in the least offended because this sort of thing was par for the course in families. 'But in the meantime take these plates into the other room, please.'

Todd appeared. 'When will tea be ready?' he enquired eagerly. 'I'm starving.'

'Jess is going out on a date tonight,' announced Libby, ignoring his question.

'Is she? Who with?' he asked, and was told by Ronnie.

'Blimey,' was Todd's reaction. 'He's a bit of an old bloke, isn't he? I thought he was a friend of Dad's.'

'He's Jess's boyfriend as well now,' joshed Ronnie.

'How many more times must I tell you that it isn't like that?' insisted Jess.

'That's what you think,' laughed Libby. 'I bet he has other ideas.'

'If he isn't past it,' grinned Ronnie.

'There is that,' giggled Libby.

'Look, the only thing that need matter to you three about it is the fact that you'll be doing the dishes tonight with no help from me,' she told them.

Her father appeared at the kitchen door. 'Are you all ready to go out on your date with Don?' he asked, in one of his better moods.

'Don't you start as well,' she tutted but she was smiling. 'I'm having enough trouble with this lot.'

They went to see Doris Day in *The Pajama Game* at the Forum in Ealing Broadway. Don let Jess choose the film.

'It was exactly what I needed,' she told him afterwards, over a gin and orange in the Red Lion across the Green from the Ealing Studios; the walls here were decorated with signed photographs of famous film stars

109

who had worked there before the BBC took the studios over last year. 'A good musical with plenty of colour. It took me right out of myself.'

'I'm glad you enjoyed it.'

'Did you?'

'Yeah, it was all right.' He didn't seem to have quite the same enthusiasm.

'Would you rather see a good mystery or a war film than a musical?' she wondered.

'I suppose so. But it was fine, really.'

'You can choose next time,' she said impulsively, realising too late that she was being presumptuous.

He didn't seem to notice and just said, 'The film didn't really matter to me. The company is the important thing.'

'I agree.'

'You're looking very nice,' he remarked, running an approving eye over her pale green linen suit, which she was wearing with a white blouse and high heels.

'Thank you,' Jess said graciously. 'So do you.' Don was smart but a tad too traditional for her taste in the sort of clothes her father might wear: a tweed sports jacket and grey trousers. 'It's ages since I've been out on an evening like this. It's nice to have something to dress up for outside work.'

'Indeed.'

'It must have been a heck of a wrench for you, moving to a new area and not knowing anyone,' she mentioned conversationally.

'No, not really,' he replied.

'Surely you must have missed having people you know around you.'

'I was glad to get away. There's nothing for me in my home town any more.'

Being a person with a genuine interest in people, Jess tried to draw him out of himself. 'I gather from what you've said that you don't get on with your brother,' she dared to mention.

'That's right.'

'Seems a pity.'

'These things happen.'

'I suppose they do but I can't imagine a time when I would seriously fall out with any of my siblings,' she confided. 'We have our ups and downs and plenty of them. I could cheerfully strangle Ronnie at times just lately. But basically we're sound.'

'You're lucky.'

'I think so. I'm so much older than the others, I'm more like a mother than a sister, especially since Mum died,' she chatted. 'But I'm hoping that as they grow up the gap will lessen.'

'I'm sure it will.'

'Is there much of an age gap between you and your brother?' she wondered.

'Five years,' he replied. 'He's thirty.'

'Is that too much of an age gap to be pals?'

'It wasn't for us. In fact, we used to be really good friends at one time but not any more.' His thin lips were set in a grim line. 'That has nothing to do with the age gap.'

She was intrigued. 'Is he married?' she asked.

'Not as far as I know.'

'It's even sadder that you don't get along then,' she remarked. 'As you're both bachelors, you could have been company for each other if things were different.'

'Maybe.'

'Is he like you, in his ways?'

'God, no.' He was emphatic.

'You make it sound as though that would be a fate worse than death.'

'It would be, believe me,' he was quick to confirm. 'I think I'd shoot myself if I had his character.'

She sipped her drink thoughtfully. 'What's wrong with him exactly?' she ventured.

'He's flashy, full of his own importance and completely selfish,' he reeled off. 'He doesn't give a damn about anyone but himself. Whoever came up with the expression "I'm all right Jack" must have had him in mind.'

'He definitely doesn't take after you then,' Jess commented. 'I don't know you very well but you don't seem like that at all.'

'Tell me if ever I show signs of it and I'll do myself in.'

'Oh, Don,' she frowned, worried by the viciousness of his attitude. 'Don't talk like that. I'm sure you don't really mean it.'

'I do, believe me,' he stated. 'My brother is enough to make anyone speak in extremes.'

'You might feel differently later on as you get older and mellow a little,' she suggested.

'I won't.' He was adamant. 'As far as I'm concerned he's no brother of mine.'

'Nobody is that bad, surely.'

'He is.' His eyes were full of hate and he was becoming angrier with every word he uttered. 'You'll just have to take my word for it.'

'Hey, calm down,' she urged gently, leaning over and putting a steadying hand on his arm. 'You're getting yourself into a right old state.'

'Sorry. Just the thought of him screws me up.'

'I can see that.'

'Sorry, I hope I'm not spoiling your evening.'

'Not at all,' she assured him. 'But I do think you should take it easier on yourself.'

'I shouldn't let that brother of mine get to me, I know.'

Jess suspected that, although Don was enraged by his brother, he

111

needed to talk about him to let off steam, even though it was obvious he didn't want to give details of the rift. Maybe she should further encourage him to talk rather than let this thing fester away inside him. So she asked, 'What does he do for a living?'

'He's got some tinpot business,' he told her with fierce disapproval. 'Buys and sell things – clothes mostly: cheap tatty stuff that he sells for more than it's worth, probably. Works on the markets.'

'That's a decent enough way to earn a living, surely.'

'I'm not saying it isn't,' he told her. 'But it isn't steady employment, is it?'

'It can be,' she pointed out. 'Most market traders wouldn't want to earn their living any other way.'

'I realise that, but they're genuine market people, salt of the earth and all that. My brother is just a barrow boy,' he told her, his voice rising again. 'He likes to call himself an entrepreneur but what he actually is, is a spiv.'

'Are you saying that he's dishonest in his dealings?'

'It wouldn't surprise me.'

'You don't know for sure then?'

'I know that he's unscrupulous in his general attitude to life so I presume it extends to his work,' he said dismissively. 'The man's rotten to the core.'

'I see.' She looked at him, noting the grim line of his mouth, the rigid set of his shoulders. 'You're a man of very high standards, aren't you, Don?'

'Yes, I like to think so.'

'And you expect other people to come up to those standards?'

'I don't like lies and deceit,' he confirmed.

'Neither do I,' she said, thinking of Jack. 'But we're all only human and not everyone can live to such high standards. It takes all sorts . . . and there's no point getting upset about it.'

Don looked at her gravely. 'I am what I am, Jess,' he stated, finishing his beer. 'All my life people have been telling me that I take life too seriously, that I should be more relaxed about things. But it just isn't in me. I can't help what I am.'

'Of course you can't.'

'Anyway, I don't want to be different,' he said. 'I value my principles.'

'No one can criticise you for that,' she said. 'I'm sure you're a very good man.'

'Good enough for you to go out with me again tomorrow?' he asked, seeming to relax a little. 'Or have I put you off by going on endlessly about my brother?'

'No. I encouraged you to talk about him.'

'Am I too serious for you?'

He was actually, but she rather liked him anyway. 'Don't be silly,' she said lightly.

'In that case, how about a run out somewhere tomorrow afternoon if the weather's nice?'

Tomorrow was too soon for Jess. She didn't want to be suffocated by him or to rush things, especially after her last love affair. Fortunately she had a genuine excuse. 'I can't make it tomorrow, I'm afraid,' she told him.

'Oh, I see.' he looked disappointed.

'I'm going to the West End to the flat I used to share with a friend of mine when I was in the troupe,' she explained. 'There's something I need to collect from there.'

He brightened at this. 'What about tomorrow night then?' he suggested hopefully.

'I'm not sure what time I'll be back.' Now she was fibbing. 'I might get talking to the girls, catching up with all the news and gossip. You know how it is?'

'Next Saturday night then?'

That seemed to be a reasonable gap so she said, 'Yes, OK, Don. That would be lovely.'

'Good.' He gave her a beaming smile and looked different altogether, younger and more handsome. 'Would you like another drink?'

'Not for me, thanks.'

'Let's go then, shall we?' he said, and took her arm and guided her courteously through the crowds and out of the pub.

Jess wasn't swept off her feet by him, or even mildly excited, but she did quite enjoy being with him. When he relaxed a little he was good company.

The reason for Jess's visit to the flat was to collect a photograph album containing pictures of herself and Babs, many of them in costume with the rest of the troupe. Jess hadn't taken it with her when she'd moved out because she owned it jointly with Babs and they'd agreed it should stay in her safekeeping. But now Jess needed it to show to her class. Being keen young dancers, most of her pupils were fascinated by her time as a Burton Girl.

'I know Babs won't mind my borrowing it for a while. I'll bring it back when I've finished with it,' she explained to the girl who was taking Babs' place at the flat temporarily.

'That's fine,' agreed Rose politely.

'Thanks for letting me rummage about in her wardrobe looking for it,' Jess went on chattily, having given Rose some background details when she'd introduced herself. 'We always kept it on the top shelf there so I knew where to look.'

'That's all right,' said Rose, a lissom eighteen-year-old with a peachy complexion, a mane of golden hair and big blue eyes. She was wearing blue pedal pushers with a loose shirt, and looked fantastic. 'Do you think it will inspire your pupils with ambition to try for a place in the troupe?'

'I don't know about them,' Jess replied with a wry grin, 'but seeing the photos again will probably make my kid sister even keener. She's dead set on joining as soon as she's old enough.'

'I was like that,' Rose mentioned, speaking rapidly. 'I auditioned a few times before I actually got in, though. It's hard work but I love every minute. I wouldn't change it for anything.'

'It was like that for me too.'

'Leaving must have been hard then.'

'It was.'

'Shame.' She didn't sound interested.

They were standing in the hall by the front door, having drifted in that direction as soon as Jess had got what she came for. 'Is Pat not at home today then?' she enquired just to be sociable.

'No. She's gone to meet some of the other girls. I think they're going to the cinema.'

'I was lucky to catch one of you at home, wasn't I?' Jess remarked. 'I just had to take a chance on someone being in as you're not on the phone.'

The young woman nodded.

'I'll be on my way then,' said Jess.

There was a heavy pause, then Rose asked politely, 'Would you like to stay for a cup of tea?'

Sensing from her general attitude that Rose was hoping most ardently for a negative response, Jess obliged her by saying, 'It's nice of you to offer but I'd better be getting back now.'

'OK.'

'Give my love to the girls I know in the troupe.'

'Will do.'

'Bye now.'

'Bye.'

Jess was imbued with nostalgia as she hurried down the stone stairs. Visiting the flat had brought back memories of the fun she and Babs had had there: cooking supper at midnight and heart-to-heart talks into the small hours; experimenting with the new exciting foreign foods that had come on to the market, often with disastrous results. It all seemed positively Bohemian compared to the conventional life she now led in Park Street.

Deeply immersed in memories, she almost collided with someone coming in the street door, a tall, immaculate man with black hair and a thin moustache. He was wearing a navy jacket and a cravat.

'Dickie,' she said, surprised to see him here.

'Hi there, Jess,' he greeted, his eyes widening momentarily. 'Haven't seen you for ages. How's life treating you outside of the business?'

'Not so bad, thanks.'

'You're managing to survive without the buzz of being on stage then?'

'You have to, don't you? I miss it, though.'

'You're bound to,' he responded with mateyness she suspected was false. 'Once you get bitten with the showbiz bug, it's the very devil to shift.'

She nodded.

He ran an approving eye over her. 'You're looking good, anyway,' he complimented. 'Still as lovely as ever.'

Having just left the gorgeous Rose, Jess felt about as glamorous as a working charwoman. 'And you're still full of flannel,' she said, forcing a grin.

'I really mean it,' he said smoothly. 'You look great.'

She hated the way he turned on the charm when it suited him but said, 'You don't look so bad yourself.'

'I do my best,' he told her. 'We have to make a special effort in our business, don't we?'

'Still getting plenty of work?' she asked, just to be polite.

'I manage to stay off the dole.'

'Good.' There was a strained silence. 'What are you doing here anyway?' she enquired casually.

There was the briefest hiatus. 'I've just popped over to collect a few things for Babs,' he explained after a moment. 'Some items of clothing she's decided she can't live without.'

'You're going to Liverpool then?'

'That's right,' he confirmed. 'Just for a few days. I'll take her stuff with me.'

'When is she due back in London, do you know?' Jess asked.

'Another couple of months, I think.'

'I've missed her.'

'Me too.'

'Well . . . give her my love when you see her.'

'Will do.'

'See you around, Dickie.' She was anxious to get away; she'd never liked him.

'Cheers, Jess.'

Seeing him there had left her with a sense of foreboding she couldn't shake off as she walked to Oxford Circus tube station. It was still bothering her as she elbowed her way through the weekend crowds around the station and walked towards the ticket office.

115

Chapter Eight

Summer came and with it the school holidays and the first anniversary of Joy Mollitt's death. It seemed hardly possible to Jess that a whole year had passed since then, though, paradoxically, sometimes it felt like a lifetime since she'd last seen her mother. She could remember being convinced at the time of the tragedy that she couldn't get through one day let alone a whole year without her. But somehow the time had gone by.

The family marked the occasion by going together to the cemetery to put flowers on her grave and spend some time in quiet contemplation. Jess always felt spiritually uplifted when she visited the grave, even though it made her cry. The others seemed to feel better for it on this occasion too, but Charlie let the side down afterwards by finding solace in his usual way, much to Ronnie's disgust.

Looking after them all was second nature to Jess now. They drove her nuts at times but she'd learned to take it in her stride. Her dance school continued to be a joyful release. The classes had been so well attended during the second term, she was considering the idea of giving the pupils some stage experience by putting on a show towards the end of the year. She could now afford to supply shoes for pupils to borrow too. Dancing for pleasure continued to be her theme and she strived to inject into her pupils something of the team spirit she'd experienced as a Burton Girl.

Her outings with Don were regular now. He'd become a good friend. Well, more than a friend really. They'd slipped into a courtship of sorts, though nothing too serious or demanding, just a growing affection and acknowledgement of their mutual need for adult company. Don's precise nature meant that their meetings ran to a set pattern: they saw each other at weekends with an occasional midweek outing. Mostly they went to a cinema or a pub but sometimes – on a Saturday night – they visited one of the new, reasonably priced restaurants in the West End. It was nice having someone to go out with, though Don could be a bit heavy going. But he was steady and reliable and she knew he would never hurt her in the way Jack had.

While her father was delighted that they'd teamed up, her siblings were less enthusiastic. Libby and Todd made an effort to be friendly when he called at the house and were always very polite but couldn't quite hide their lack of approval. Ronnie made his dislike of Don blatantly obvious.

The first time he came to Sunday tea proved to be an occasion of toe-curling embarrassment for them all.

'What's he doing here?' demanded Ronnie when he came to the table to find Don sitting next to Jess.

A shocked silence fell on the room.

'What does it look like?' replied Jess at last, cheeks burning so hard they were throbbing. 'Now sit down and eat your tea and don't be so damned rude.'

'I'm not sitting at the same table as him.'

'You'll have to go hungry then, won't you,' she informed him furiously, 'because Don is staying.'

'Oh, so I have no say in what goes on in this house. That's very nice, that is.'

'If you want a friend to come to tea they'll be made welcome by all of us—' she began.

'My mates wouldn't be seen dead going out to tea,' he scorned. 'Too poncy for them.'

Jess couldn't imagine anyone inviting those new pals of his to their home but just said, 'Don is a friend of mine so I'd appreciate some manners from you, please. Anyone would think you'd been dragged up in the gutter the way you're behaving, showing us all up.'

Poor Don looked as though he wanted to evaporate, she noticed miserably.

'I think it'll be easier if I go,' he suggested, making as though to rise.

'You stay where you are.' Jess felt terrible. 'Ronnie is ignorant and I'm thoroughly ashamed of him. He's the one who should leave, not you.'

'I really think it might be better, you know—'

'You're not going anywhere,' she insisted, putting a hand on Don's arm. 'You stay there and have your tea.'

'Creep,' muttered Ronnie, fixing Don with a malicious stare.

'That's enough, Ronnie,' bellowed his father, while Todd fixed his eyes on his plate and Libby got a fit of nervous giggles and sat there quivering, with her head bowed.

'He's a nosy, interfering grass.'

'That's it, you young savage,' roared Charlie, standing up and towering over his son. 'Leave this table at once and don't come back until you're ready to apologise to Don.'

Ronnie didn't move; just say there simmering with umbrage.

'Do what you're told, boy. Get out of here and go to your room.' Charlie paused for breath, his whole body trembling. 'And don't you *dare* leave this house.'

'I wouldn't stay at this table if you paid me,' declared Ronnie, incandescent with rage as he rose from his chair, pushing it back noisily. 'And don't think I'll apologise to him because I won't. *Not ever.*' He paused, moving his angry gaze around the table. 'You never take my side

118

about anything and I'm sick of the lot of you.'

The silence was piercing as he marched from the room, muttering furiously under his breath.

'Sorry about that, Don,' apologised Charlie, hot with embarrassment. 'He's at a difficult age.'

'Don't worry about it,' said Don politely, though naturally he didn't look happy.

'I'll go up and give him a trouncing later on,' added Charlie. 'Best to let him stew for a while.'

'Meanwhile, let's get on with our tea, shall we?' suggested Jess in a brave attempt at normality. 'Don, are you going to have some ham and salad?'

'Please.'

The meal progressed against a backdrop of strained conversation and awkward silences. Nobody ate much. As well as being completely humiliated, Jess was at her wits' end about her brother. He was getting worse. And she doubted if anything her father had to say to him later on would make any difference to his behaviour, the mood he was in at the moment. He just got nastier and more out of control with every day that passed.

Hilda came dashing into the shop one Wednesday just as Jess and her father were about to close for half day.

'I'm glad I caught you,' she said, breathless and flushed from hurrying. 'I want some magazines to take to a friend who isn't very well.' She went over to the magazine display, browsed briefly then gathered a selection of women's reading. 'These'll do.' She looked at the chocolate bars. 'I'll take a Frys Chocolate Cream for her too.' She stared at them longingly. 'Oh, go on then, make that two – one for myself.'

'You devil,' teased Jess, taking her money and handing her her change.

In a chatty mood, Hilda looked into the street through the shop window. 'I see that the builders are busy in that empty shop across the road,' she observed.

'They started the other day,' said Jess, 'and they're really cracking on with it.'

'What sort of shop is it going to be?' Hilda wondered. 'Does anyone know?'

'A gents' outfitters, so I've heard,' put in Charlie, walking over to the door and turning the sign to closed. 'That's what they seem to think in the pub anyway.'

'They're certainly having a lot of work done on the place,' remarked Hilda. 'It looks as though it's being gutted. It'll be smart when it's finished, I bet.'

'If it's too smart, it'll make the rest of us look shabby, won't it?' said Jess lightly.

119

'There you are, Charlie,' joshed Hilda, grinning at him. 'That's a hint for you to give the front of this place a lick of paint.'

Going to the till to do the cashing up, he looked at Hilda and indulged in a rare moment of humour. 'Better still, I'll give you a paintbrush and you can do it.'

'You'll be lucky.'

'I thought that would shut you up.'

Looking at Jess, Hilda said, 'If you're ready to go home, I'll wait and we can walk back together.'

'I'm not going home.' She removed her overall to reveal a white broderie anglaise blouse, which she was wearing with a royal-blue dirndl skirt. 'I'm going to the West End to meet Babs.'

The older woman knew Babs vaguely, having met her a few times when she'd visited the Mollitts, and from hearing regular news of her from Jess. 'She's back from her stint in the north then?' she remarked casually.

'Yeah, thank goodness. I can't wait to see her to catch up with all the news.' She paused, looking at her father. 'Lunch is all organised at home. The kids know what's got to be done.'

'Thanks, love.' He was in one of his more amiable moods. 'You go and enjoy yourself.'

'You'll come back with a sore throat after all that talking,' smiled Hilda, walking to the door.

'It'll be worth it,' said Jess.

When Jess met Babs outside the Wimpy snack bar at the corner of Coventry Street, she immediately perceived a difference in her; there seemed to be a glow about her somehow.

'Oh, Babs, it's so good to see you,' she enthused, hugging her. 'I've been positively bereft without you. It seems as though you've been away for ever.'

'It feels like that to me too,' she replied. 'I've missed you, kid.'

Jess moved back and ran a studious eye over her, noticing her shining eyes, her radiant skin. There was definitely a new bloom about her. 'You look terrific,' she complimented. 'The Liverpool air must agree with you.'

Babs gave Jess an odd look. 'It could have something to do with the air, I suppose,' she grinned.

They went into the bright, crowded restaurant and, after quite a long wait, managed to get seated in one of the banquettes. They both ordered their favourite fast food, which had become something of a craze in London since its introduction a few years ago: the Wimpy hamburger and Whippsy strawberry milkshake. Today, however, they were too engrossed in conversation to bother too much about what they were eating as they exchanged news.

'A new man in your life, eh?' said Babs when Jess told her about Don.

120

'You should have written to me about him.'

'I thought it would be more fun to tell you personally,' Jess explained. 'Anyway, it isn't serious.'

'Whatever it is it's good news,' smiled Babs. 'Not least because it'll save me having to nag you about finding a man.'

'So, what's next for you?' Jess enquired, squeezing tomato sauce on to her hamburger from the tomato-shaped plastic container. 'Which show are you going into now?'

Babs gave Jess a mysterious grin. 'None of them,' she announced. 'I haven't said anything to them at Burtons yet. But I'm leaving the company.'

'Ooh, that sounds interesting,' responded Jess. 'Have you got another dancing job?'

'No. I'm leaving the business altogether.'

'You're joking!' Jess was stunned.

'Never been more serious in my life.'

'But why would you do a thing like that?'

'I don't have a choice in the matter.' She had a soppy grin on her face. 'Once my waistline starts to expand I'll be given the push anyway. Pregnant chorus girls aren't in demand.'

Jess's mouth fell open.

'Well, aren't you going to congratulate me?' beamed Babs. 'I'm three months gone.'

'But how . . .?'

'The usual way,' Babs grinned. 'It happens north of Watford, you know.'

'Dickie's . . .?'

'Of course it's Dickie's.' She looked astonished that anyone would suggest otherwise. 'What sort of a girl do you think I am?'

'Sorry.' Jess was still trying to take it in. 'It's just with you having been away . . . I mean, you could have met someone in Liverpool, couldn't you? And you haven't seen Dickie much lately.'

'That's why I'm in this condition,' she laughed. 'When he came up to Liverpool to see me, well, we were so pleased to see each other, we got carried away – threw caution to the wind.'

'No need to ask if you're pleased.'

'Oh, Jess, I'm thrilled. You said I look good and that's why – because I'm so happy. A baby is just what Dickie and I need to cement our relationship.' She was radiant with enthusiasm. 'It'll bring us closer together.'

Jess didn't want to spoil Babs' moment by pointing out that that wasn't the best reason to have a baby and it could have the opposite effect. 'Is Dickie pleased too?'

'He will be.'

Jess's heart sank. 'He doesn't know?'

121

'Not yet,' Babs confirmed cheerfully. 'I've only been back a week and I haven't seen much of him.' She wriggled her shoulders in delight. 'I shall make sure I choose the right moment to tell him but I know he'll be just as excited as I am. This is exactly the incentive he needs to make him pop the question.'

'As you're so pleased about it, then I am too,' Jess told her with a warm smile. 'Congratulations. I know you'll be a terrific mum.'

'I'll certainly do my best.' Babs shot Jess a close look. 'It'll be your turn next, kid, now that you've got a new man. Though I recommend that you do the conventional thing and get married before you fall pregnant. Don't get it the wrong way round like I have.'

'Leave off,' laughed Jess. 'I can't even begin to think of getting married. Not for a few years, anyway. Not until the kids are more off my hands.'

'You're entitled to a life of your own, you know.'

'Yeah, yeah, I know all that,' she sighed. 'But even apart from my family responsibilities, I haven't known Don all that long. It's much too early to be thinking in terms of marriage. Nothing like that has ever been mentioned, not even casually in conversation. It isn't that sort of a relationship.'

Babs' assumption had made Jess feel uneasy, though. She was fond of Don but didn't feel as if he was 'the one', the man she wanted to spend the rest of her life with – not at this stage, anyway. Going out with him was one thing, marrying him quite another. Still, she comforted herself with the thought that it wasn't an issue since Don showed no sign of wanting any sort of commitment from her. So she pushed it to the back of her mind and concentrated on her friend's exciting news.

'I'm putting on weight already,' Babs was saying proudly. 'Especially on my bust.'

'You'll have to disguise it somehow until you're ready for the company to know,' Jess pointed out. 'Not an easy thing in those tight-fitting costumes.'

'There'll be no need for me to hide it because I'll be leaving anyway, as soon as I've told Dickie,' Babs informed her.

'Really?' Jess was surprised.

'Oh, yes,' Babs said in a definite manner. 'The job is far too physically demanding for someone in my condition. I don't want to take any chances with this baby, it's far too precious.'

'Of course not.' Jess studied her friend's face. 'How come you look the picture of health? Aren't you supposed to be sick and pasty-faced in the early stages?'

'I've had very little morning sickness,' she explained. 'I've been lucky in that respect. In fact I feel like the luckiest woman alive in every respect.'

Jess hoped her luck held out after she broke the news to Dickie. She had a sudden flashback of her visit to the flat; of Rose's obvious desire for her to leave and the unexpected meeting with Dickie on the stairs. Babs probably knew from Dickie that Jess had met up with him briefly but she hadn't said anything so it seemed wise not to mention it, somehow. It was probably nothing anyway.

It was Saturday afternoon and Ronnie and his mates were sitting on the grass in Churchfields discussing what to do with the rest of the afternoon.

'Anyone got any ideas?' asked Shifter, a thin, wiry boy with dark hair and sharp features. His nickname came from his agility; he could outrun most boys of his age. Although he was slight of build and was probably the smallest of the three lads, there was no question that he was the leader.

'We could go down the river and do some skimming,' suggested Nifty, who also got his name from his quick way of moving, though he was bigger altogether than his friend. He had ginger hair and masses of freckles.

'Surely you can come up with something a bit more interesting than chucking stones in the water,' scorned Shifter.

'Making 'em bounce across the surface of the river can be quite good fun,' ventured Ronnie.

'Nah,' said Shifter. 'It's too boring.'

'We could go down to the swings then,' was Ronnie's next suggestion.

Nifty gave him a pitying look. 'What are you, Mollitt, two years old or something? We're miles too old for that sort of thing.'

'Climbing up the slide instead of going up the steps and coming down backwards can be quite a laugh, though,' Ronnie pointed out.

Another, even more pitying look. 'You can only do that when there's no one else there,' he reminded him, with seething impatience. 'The place will be teeming with fussy old women and their snotty-nosed little toddlers on a sunny Saturday afternoon like this.'

'Mm. I s'pose so. What about a kick-about then?' said Ronnie, who'd not played much football since he'd been friendly with these two. 'I'll nip home and get my ball, if you like.'

'You know we don't like playing football.' They avoided anything the older generation approved of.

'It was just an idea.'

'A stupid one, an' all,' said Shifter.

'Oh well, I don't know what we can do then.' Ronnie had run out of ideas.

'Let's go to West Ealing and see what we can nick from Woolworths,' was Nifty's bright idea.

'I'm not doing that.' Ronnie didn't mind breaking school rules for a laugh but breaking the law was something else entirely.

'Why not?'

'I just don't want to.'

'You're yella,' accused Shifter.

'He's chicken,' agreed Nifty, flapping his arms as though they were wings and emitting a clucking sound.

'No, I'm not,' denied Ronnie hotly.

'Why don't you wanna do it then?'

'Dunno.' Ronnie daren't set himself up for ridicule by admitting that all his instincts reacted against stealing and he couldn't bear to imagine the row there would be at home if he got caught. 'I just don't happen to think it's much fun, that's all.'

'You're scared.'

'Shut up.'

'Prove you're not scared then.'

Ronnie affected a nonchalant shrug. 'Why should I? We're mates so you should take my word for it.'

'We won't stay mates if you don't prove you've got some bottle,' challenged Shifter.

'By nicking stuff from Woolworths, you mean?'

'It doesn't have to be that exactly, but something along those lines.' Shifter considered the matter for a moment, looking around for inspiration, his eyes lighting up suddenly. 'See that old fogey over there,' he said, looking towards the path where an elderly woman was making her way slowly across the park carrying a shopping bag. 'Go and snatch her bag and scare her to death while you're at it.'

'What's daring about that?' asked Ronnie because he didn't want to do it. 'She's just an old lady who'll frighten easily. And getting her bag will be a doddle so it won't prove anything.'

'But have you got the bottle to do it, though?' challenged Shifter. 'That's the thing.'

'If I thought it would prove anything I'd do it like a shot,' bluffed Ronnie.

'It will. It'll prove that you're not scared to do anything more daring than playing marbles,' Shifter told him.

Ronnie bit his lip. 'But she's old,' he pointed out.

'What does that matter? The meaner the dare, the bigger the thrill,' enthused the heartless Nifty. 'Go on. I dare you to go over there and do it.'

'No.'

'I said you were yella,' accused Shifter. 'I dunno why me and Nifty bother with you. Do you, Nift?'

'Nah. We don't hang out with goody-goodies who are scared to do anything wrong,' said the other. 'If you don't do this, you can forget the idea of hanging around with us.'

Ronnie looked from one to the other, sighing. 'Right, what do you actually want me to do?' he asked.

124

'You've got to go over there and rough her up a bit, then snatch her shopping bag and bring it back here to us, to prove that you've actually done it,' he spelled out for him. 'If there's anything we fancy in the bag, we'll share it.'

The whole idea made Ronnie feel sick but the thought of the derision he would have thrown at him if he didn't take up the challenge was even worse. He was so confused. He hated himself for even considering the idea but felt compelled to go along with them.

'But there's a lot of people about,' he mentioned, casting his eye around the park. There were various children's ball games in progress and people sitting on the benches, some walking dogs, the ping of ball on racket drifting over from the tennis courts.

'All the better,' responded Shifter. 'There wouldn't be much of a risk if the place was deserted and there was no chance of getting caught.'

'Where will you two be?' Ronnie wanted to know.

'We'll be waiting here for you to come back with the bag,' Shifter told him. 'We'll be here, don't worry.'

'What if she screams?'

'All the more fun.'

Still Ronnie made no move.

'Yella . . . yella . . .' Shifter chanted while the other one did another imitation of a chicken.

'I'll soon show you I'm not scared,' declared Ronnie, who felt physically ill at the thought of what he was about to do. 'I'll do it.'

'Bet you won't,' taunted Shifter.

'I bloody well will,' Ronnie told them. 'I'll show you that you've no right to call me yella.'

And with that he swung off across the grass towards the woman, who was walking slowly on account of her age and the weight of her bag. Ronnie had been brought up to respect the elderly, not torment the life out of them. But the fear of his mates was stronger than his abhorrence for what he was about to do. Choking with fear and self-loathing, he approached the woman.

'Your bag looks heavy. Shall I carry it for you?' he offered through dry lips, noticing her thin face, sparse white hair and stooped shoulders.

Her faded eyes rested on him, weighing him up. Apparently deciding that he was to be trusted, she gave him a wrinkled smile and handed him her bag. 'That's a very kind thought, young man,' she said. 'It is a bit of a weight for an old girl like me.'

Make off with the bag, you idiot, he urged himself, feeling his mates' eyes boring into him. Do it, do the dare – *now*. 'Have you been shopping in the Broadway?' he heard himself ask, walking beside her with the bag.

'That's right, son,' she told him in a friendly manner. 'I live on the other side of the park so I usually cut across here. It's quicker. I enjoy it too, if the weather's nice. It's such a lovely place.'

Mortified almost beyond feeling by his failure to do the business, Ronnie told himself it still wasn't too late. He could make off with the bag now. Instead he said, 'We're lucky to have such good parks around here, that's what my mum often said.'

'She must be very proud to have such a polite and thoughtful son as you,' she remarked.

'My mum's dead,' he blurted out.

'Oh, you poor boy,' sympathised the woman. 'Have you got a father to be proud of you?'

'Yeah, I've got a dad.'

'Well, you just tell him from me that he's got a real little gem in you.'

That was the last thing he had in mind but he nodded politely and said, 'Thank you. I'll do that.'

They walked on, out of the park and along the road until she stopped outside a small block of flats. Imbued with an aching sense of failure, Ronnie decided it wasn't too late to do the dare even now; he could still run off with the bag. As long as he delivered it to the others, it would count.

'Thanks ever so much, son,' she said, taking her purse out of her pocket. 'Let me give you something to get some sweets as a little thank you.'

Now he felt really terrible. 'No thank you,' he said in a shaky voice. 'You keep your money.'

'Go on, I want you to have it.'

'It's kind of you but I don't need paying, honestly.'

Determined to show her appreciation, she opened her purse, at which point he put the bag at her feet and fled without another word, leaving her looking puzzled.

Not daring to face Shifter and Nifty, he didn't go back into the park but headed home the road way, his eyes swimming with tears. He'd failed totally and would never live it down with his pals. He'd be an outcast. There would be no end to the abuse he would have to take from them. In fact, they would probably keep their word and cast him out altogether. Even though being friends with them was nerve-racking and made him miserable for most of the time, the thought of being discarded by them bothered him a great deal. Maybe because going around with the daring duo made him feel important; he wasn't really sure.

Still, nothing made sense any more. He felt permanently confused; torn between the principles he'd grown up with and the desire to please his new friends, to be accepted as one of them. Yet the thought of what they'd wanted him to do to the old lady gave him a choking sensation in his throat.

If only Mum was still here. She would have known what to do about this awful confusion that plagued him. Not that he'd have told her what he'd almost done to that old lady; he wasn't that daft. But he knew, somehow, that he wouldn't have even considered going through with the dare if Mum had still been around. He couldn't have borne to let her down in that way. But she wasn't here and not a day went by when he didn't miss her.

He kept his head down all the way home because of the stupid tears that wouldn't stop streaming down his face no matter how hard he tried to make them stop. He'd be finished around here if any of his peers got to know that he'd been blubbering.

'You're very quiet tonight, Jess,' remarked Don that evening on the way home from the cinema in his car. 'Is there anything wrong?'

There was something very wrong – with Ronnie; that was the cause of Jess's preoccupation. The boy was completely impossible. They'd had another scene at tea time, when she'd noticed that he seemed quieter and paler than usual and had dared to ask him if he was all right.

He'd replied with venom, reminding her that she wasn't his mother and she was to keep her nose out of his business. When their father had demanded he apologise, the boy had stormed out of the room. And all because she'd enquired after his health. His behaviour really was beyond the pale.

But fond as she was of Don, she didn't feel able to discuss this with him. Not only because he and Ronnie didn't get along but because everything was black and white to Don. People were either right or wrong – there was no grey area or room for allowances to be made in his mind. And although Ronnie was being an absolute horror lately and causing her no end of grief, she still believed that beneath all that rage, there was plenty of good in him. Anyway, he was her brother and she would defend him against anyone so it wouldn't be wise to give Don cause for criticism and cause an argument between them. She had quite enough of those to contend with at home.

So she replied to Don by saying, 'I'm fine. Just a bit tired. We had a busy day in the shop.'

'That's all right then,' he said, seeming satisfied. 'A good night's sleep will work wonders for you.'

Don came into Mollitts Newsagents one morning a few days later to confirm an arrangement he had with Jess for that evening. The shop was empty of customers so he stayed for a chat with Jess and her father.

'Nice job they've made of the place over the road, don't you think?' remarked Charlie, looking across at the gleaming, modern shop front, as yet empty of stock.

'Yeah. It certainly puts my place in the shade,' replied Don. 'But I'll leave the owners of Dean's Stores to worry about that. I'm paid to manage the store, not worry about modernising it.'

'Quite right,' was Charlie's wholehearted agreement. 'I've no plans to modernise this one either. The traditional look suits us, for the time being anyway.'

'As it's going to be a gents' outfitters, I suppose they want their shop front to be a bit stylish to pull in the punters,' said Jess. 'Personally, I think it looks lovely and it smartens up the Broadway no end. I can't wait to see what it's like when it's finished with the window dressed.'

Both men nodded in agreement and they talked some more until Don had to get back to work. 'See you later, Jess,' he said, heading for the door.

'OK.'

On the way out he almost collided with someone on the way in, a youngish man who was a stranger to Jess, and a rather dazzling one, with an Italian haircut and fashionable casual clothes. Apparently he was no stranger to Don, who seemed to turn to stone at the sight of him, the colour draining from his face.

'You,' he gasped, turning back into the newsagent's and closing the door. His voice was quivering as he added, 'What the bloody hell are you doing here?'

'Looking for you,' the stranger explained breezily. 'I called at your shop and they told me you'd probably be in here.'

'How did you find me?' Don was very pale.

'I learned from your old firm where you were working.'

'I suppose it never occurred to you that if I'd wanted to see you, I'd have given you my address when I moved away,' said Don through gritted teeth.

'Of course it occurred to me, but as I was in the area anyway it didn't seem right not to look you up,' he replied. 'Thought you might be a bit better tempered now.'

'You had no right to come after me, snooping about, making enquiries.'

'Well, I'm here now.'

'More's the pity,' Don growled. 'What are you doing around here anyway? It's miles out of your way.'

'Just checking on my investment,' he explained, looking across the street through the window.

'Investment? What are you talking about?'

'You have to keep these people on their toes.'

'People?' Don seemed bemused.

'The shopfitters,' he explained cheerfully. 'The work's costing me a small fortune so I want to make sure it's done properly. I've left them alone to get on with it for long enough; thought it was time I showed my face and geed them up a bit. I want to get the shop open and trading sharpish so that I can start getting my money back.' He paused. 'Still, with a bit of luck, I should be ready to open by the end of next week.'

128

Jess and Charlie stood quietly behind the counter listening to this conversation, which was taking place by the door. The atmosphere in the shop was so tense, Jess could feel her heart pounding.

'The new shop . . . it's *yours*?' Don muttered, looking angrier than ever.

'That's right,' the other man confirmed proudly. 'What do you think of it so far? Not bad, eh?'

Don ignored the question. 'Men's outfitters, *you*?' His tone was one of disbelief.

'There's no need to sound so shocked.'

'What do you know about men's outfitting?'

'Quite a lot, as it happens,' he informed Don, standing his ground and keeping his temper despite Don's scathing hostility. 'I've been selling clothes on the markets for long enough to have a pretty good idea what a man with an eye for fashion wants and I can offer it to them at a reasonable price.'

'You've only dealt in cheap tat,' Don hit out.

'I'm aiming for the younger "with it" market,' said the other man, ignoring the insult.

'Flashy, you mean,' mocked Don.

'You can call it what you like, mate, there's a market out there for it and I intend to get a share of it,' the other man told him. 'The shop's in an excellent trading position with the bus stop right outside. Once word gets round, I'll draw custom from every town the length of the Uxbridge Road, as far as Shepherd's Bush. They only have to hop on a bus.'

'Gents' outfitters,' scorned Don. 'Rubbish tip more like.'

'One man's rubbish is another man's idea of style,' the stranger returned. 'Though it isn't the sort of gear you'd be seen dead in, of course.'

Suddenly Don seemed to exude such hatred for him, Jess felt her stomach churn with the strength of it. It was frightening to see him like this. The other man seemed much less intense and more easy-going, but that could just be his outward way of coping with Don's barrage of enmity towards him, she thought. She was sure of one thing, though: something very powerful existed between these two men.

'Of all the shopping parades in London, why did you have to choose this one?'

The man grinned uncertainly at Don and even from the other side of the shop, Jess could see what an appealing smile he had. 'I was looking for retail premises and that one just happened to come up,' he explained.

'That's one hell of a coincidence.' Don looked suspicious.

'A happy one too, I thought,' he said, apparently undeterred. 'It's high time I saw a bit more of my brother.'

Jess and her father exchanged glances.

'You bastard,' seethed Don.

'Now then, that's not a very nice way to welcome me to the area, is it?'

Don lunged towards him, grabbed his arms, and began shaking him, growling with rage.

Before things could get any uglier, Charlie made a swift intervention. 'All right, boys, that's enough now,' he said, coming from behind the counter and dragging Don away from his brother. 'You can settle your differences outside. I won't put up with brawling in my shop.'

'Sorry, mate,' apologised Don's brother. 'I didn't intend a fight to break out on your premises.' He looked across at Jess as though to extend the apology.

'Don't listen to him,' Don ground out. 'He doesn't care what trouble he causes – to anyone.'

Charlie opened the shop door. 'Out, the pair of you,' he ordered. 'Don't come back until you've calmed down.'

At this point the telephone started ringing in the office and Jess went to answer it, whereupon she heard news of such a distressing nature it removed all else from her mind. When she came back into the shop the two brothers had left and she was far too preoccupied with the content of the phone call to give either of them any more thought.

Giving her father a brief account of why she urgently needed a few hours off and assuring him that she would be back as soon as possible, she left him to deal with a sudden flurry of customers and hurried from the shop.

'How dare you cause trouble in front of my girlfriend and her father?' Don was talking to his brother in a side street, out of sight of the Broadway. It wouldn't do much for his reputation if he was spotted quarrelling in the street by any member of his staff.

Bruce Day's brows rose. 'Girlfriend, eh?' he said lightly. 'And very nice too. You're a lucky man.'

'Yes, I am extremely lucky,' Don confirmed, looking at his brother coldly, 'though what she'll think of me after that disgraceful scene you've just caused, I've no idea.'

'You caused the scene, mate, not me,' his brother pointed out. 'You were the one who got all stroppy and violent. You really should watch that temper of yours.'

'You're enough to try anyone's temper.'

'I was only trying to be friendly.'

'You're wasting your time.'

'But, Don—'

'I want nothing to do with you,' Don ground out, his voice deep with fury. 'So keep well away from me.'

'That might be difficult as we'll be working in the same parade of shops.'

'Difficult but not impossible,' Don told him. 'Especially as you won't be around outside of working hours. Thankfully for me you'll be in Tottenham.'

'I won't, you know,' Bruce corrected. 'I've moved west. I've got a flat in Ealing Broadway.'

'Oh, no,' groaned Don. 'Tell me I'm not hearing this.'

'It wouldn't be practical for me to travel from North London every day, battling through traffic, would it?' he explained.

'You could have taken the tube.'

'Even then it's a bit of a trek and I need to be close by, to keep on top of the job, with it being a new business venture.'

'Oh, well, I suppose it could be worse,' sighed Don. 'You could live over the shop and be my neighbour.'

'I would have done if there had been suitable accommodation upstairs,' Bruce informed him.

'Thank God for small mercies.'

'Look, mate,' began Bruce, 'don't you think it's about time we stopped all this nonsense and tried to patch things up between us?'

'It isn't nonsense and the answer's no.' Don was adamant.

'But we're the only family we've got now that Mum and Dad have gone,' Bruce reminded him. 'Surely the fact that we're brothers counts for something.'

'Not to me,' Don informed him brusquely.

'That's a terrible thing to say and I don't believe you can really mean it.'

'I do, believe me,' Don told him. 'As far as I'm concerned I don't have a brother.'

Now Bruce was beginning to get rattled. 'That's a silly attitude,' he stated. 'Downright childish, if you ask me.'

'Maybe it is but it's the way I feel and it'll never change.'

'Have you forgotten what good mates we used to be, all the laughs and good times—'

'And who ruined all that?' Don cut in fiercely. 'You did. So don't come crawling to me with any ideas of a reconciliation because there isn't going to be one, *Not now. Not ever.* Frankly, I'm amazed that you think there can be after what happened.'

'Look . . . if we could have a proper talk, you might see things differently.'

'No.' Don was breathless with rage.

'If you'd only listen—'

'Just go away and leave me alone,' Don warned him in a deep trembling voice.

'Don, please, I—'

'I don't want you anywhere near me, do you understand?' Don made clear, his voice gruff with emotion. 'Just the sight of you makes me want to be sick.'

And he turned away and swung off down the street towards the Broadway, leaving his normally irrepressible brother staring sadly at his retreating back.

Chapter Nine

'It's ever so good of you to come, Jess,' said Babs, her voice thick from weeping, eyes red and swollen. 'I didn't intend for you to drop everything and come rushing over here. I was feeling so desperate when Dickie left, I went straight out to the phone box and called you on impulse . . . just needed to hear the voice of a friend, I suppose.'

'I'm glad you called, and I wanted to come,' Jess assured her warmly. 'I wouldn't stay away knowing you were so upset.'

'What about the shop?' Babs fretted.

'Dad'll manage.'

'I don't suppose he was too pleased, though, your just taking off in the middle of a working day.'

'He was very understanding, actually.' Once again Charlie had reminded Jess that her faith in him wasn't misplaced. 'Told me to come straight over.'

'That was nice of him.' Babs blew her nose. 'God, what a mess. There was I, in all my innocence, really believing that Dickie would be pleased about the baby – would want us to be a family. Instead of which he turns up here this morning and tells me it's all over between us, that he's in love with someone else.'

'He didn't come clean about that when you told him about the baby then?'

'No. He was going to, apparently, but I got in first by telling him I was pregnant and he didn't feel he could. I noticed he seemed a bit quiet but I thought that was just shock; that he needed time to get used to it,' she explained. 'He's been trying to pluck up the courage to tell me about him and Rose ever since, and finally managed it this morning,' she said, shaking her head as though she still couldn't quite believe it. 'Oh, Jess, how can I have been so stupid?'

'Not stupid, just besotted,' she corrected. 'It happens to the best of us. Remember what I was like over Jack?'

She nodded absently. 'Rose, though,' she went on dully. 'The girl who was taking my place here at the flat while I was away. I mean, is that below the belt or what? The minute my back's turned he starts sleeping with my replacement here. He even came to Liverpool a couple of times to see me and acted as though everything was the same as always.' She gave Jess a wry look. 'And managed to get me pregnant while he was at it.'

'The two-timing git.' Jess didn't want to turn the knife by mentioning her own suspicions when she'd met him on his way up to the flat while Babs was away; it was irrelevant now anyway.

'He's more than twice her age, too,' Babs muttered, almost to herself.

'Which means it's probably got more to do with his ego than his heart,' opined Jess. 'He's flattered that a young girl will even give him a second glance. Six months, I'll give it.'

The two women were alone in the flat, ensconced in armchairs by the window. Babs' flatmate Pat was out at rehearsal. Babs had called in sick. She'd sobbed until there wasn't a tear left in her when Jess arrived. The fact that she'd let go so visibly indicated the depth of her despair because she hated to show weakness, even to her best friend.

'He seems to be smitten, though,' said Babs miserably.

'I still say it won't last,' stated Jess. 'He won't be able to keep up with her, and she'll soon get fed up with him. I mean, what is he? Just a vain, ageing comedian. She's probably dazzled because he's in showbiz, being new to it. That'll soon wear off when she's been in the business for a while.'

'I expect you're right,' Babs sighed. 'But it doesn't make me feel much better.'

'Give it time.' Jess lapsed into a thoughtful silence. 'In all this talk of him and Rose, what about his responsibility towards you and the baby?'

'He offered me money to get rid of it,' was Babs' bitter reply. 'Even gave me the name of someone who would see to it.'

'Oh, Babs.' This just kept getting worse.

'I told him what to do with his money,' Babs continued. 'I'm not doing that. Not likely! I don't want the baby but as I'm stuck with it I'll see it through.'

'You don't want the baby?' queried Jess. 'But you were so thrilled when you first told me about it.'

'That was when I thought Dickie and I were going to bring it up together. Everything's changed now.'

'It's still your baby, with or without him.'

'It was going to be a joy,' Babs said sadly. 'Now it's just a problem I have to deal with on my own.'

'You're not quite on your own, you know,' Jess reminded her. 'You've got me.'

'Oh, Jess,' responded Babs gratefully. 'It's such a comfort to hear you say that but you've got quite enough problems of your own with your family to look after. The last thing you need is me draining on you as well.'

'I'm not so burdened that I can't help a friend in trouble,' Jess was quick to assure her.

Babs shook her head. 'I know you'll always be there for me, kid, and I'm grateful for it. But when it gets down to the nitty-gritty, I'm on my own with this one.' She paused, casting a wistful eye around the room. 'I'll have to move out of here for a start. Children are strictly banned.'

Jess bit her lip. She wasn't in a position to offer Babs a permanent home with the Mollitts because the house was her father's. But she said, 'You can always stay with us until you get yourself sorted, you know.'

'Oh, yeah.' Babs gave a wry grin. 'I can see your dad putting the welcome mat out for an unmarried mum. What an example that would be to your little sister.'

She did have a point, but Jess was prepared to stick her neck out for her. 'If it's necessary I can probably talk him into it,' she offered. 'But perhaps Dickie will prove he has some decency in him and agree to stump up some cash on a regular basis so that you can afford somewhere decent to live with the baby.'

This produced a harsh laugh from Babs. 'You and I both know that isn't going to happen.' She shrugged helplessly. 'No, Jess, I have to face it. I'm well and truly in the cart.'

'What about your folks?'

'Out of the question,' was her immediate response. 'They'd be too ashamed to have me in the house. Anyway, I'm old enough to sort out my own problems. I can't go running back there like some desperate teenager.'

'Look, I might not be in a position to do everything that Dickie should be doing but I'll do what I can,' Jess offered again. 'You have my word on that.'

'Thanks, kid. You're a good friend.' She attempted a smile. 'But I'll be all right. You know me, I'm a tough old bird. I'll get through it somehow.'

'I meant what I said about staying at our place,' Jess confirmed. 'I'll have a chat with Dad. You only have to say the word.'

'I wouldn't dream of it.' Babs was adamant. 'I'll find myself a little bedsit and get a job in a shop or do waitressing or something to keep me and the kid. I'll be fine, honestly.' Her eyes glistened with tears, which she brushed aside with the back of her hand, and cleared her throat to steady her voice. 'I can't focus my mind on the actual reality of being a mum yet, it's too far into the distance. To be perfectly honest, all I can think about right now is the prospect of life without Dickie.'

'I know how hard it must be for you.' It was true because Jess had been through a similar thing herself when Jack had ditched her. But being pregnant must make it a million times worse.

'I'll get through it, though,' said Babs with a burst of her old spirit. 'Oh, yeah – even if only to show that rotten bugger that I can survive without him.'

'That's the stuff.' Jess looked at the clock on the mantelpiece. 'I'll have

135

to be going soon. I don't want to leave Dad on his own in the shop for too long.'

'No, of course not.'

'But before I go, can I just say again that I'm there for you if you need me?' she emphasised. 'Knowing how fiercely independent you are, I don't want to impose. So promise me that you'll let me know if there's anything I can do.'

'You'll be the first person I'll turn to, I promise.' Babs dismissed the subject and moved on quickly. 'So, now that that's settled let's put the kettle on and have another cup of tea before you go.'

'That'll be nice.'

As Babs disappeared into the kitchen and Jess was left to mull the situation over, she found herself in no doubt that Babs would rise to the challenge ahead, no matter how tough things got for her. Her strength of character would see to that. Jess hoped most fervently that she wasn't going to be too proud to accept help but had the horrible suspicion that she was.

That evening Bruce Day was standing at the bar of The Feathers in Ealing Broadway, idly chatting to the barman, whom he knew from calling in here when he'd been arranging the tenancy of his flat nearby. It never took Bruce long to make friends.

'Well, all settled in then, are we?' enquired the barman sociably.

'I feel as though I've never lived anywhere else,' replied Bruce, taking the head off his pint.

'Nice place you've got, is it?'

'It suits me.'

'You got any people living over this way?'

'Yeah, I have as it happens,' Bruce informed him pleasantly. 'My brother lives just down the road at Hanwell.'

'You won't be lonely then,' commented the man.

Bruce smiled noncommittally in reply, then drifted into his own thoughts as the barman went to serve another customer, recalling the incident with Don earlier. He hadn't expected an easy meeting with his brother by any means but the vehemence of Don's hatred towards him was a shock he was still smarting from, though it wasn't in his nature to put his feelings on show; not when he was upset about something, anyway.

Setting up in business so close to Don's place of work hadn't been entirely coincidental. Bruce had been looking for a shop to rent anyway, and had had an open mind as to its location so long as it was in the London area. When he'd been browsing through some agents' details and happened to spot some retail premises in Hanwell Broadway, he'd immediately recognised the possibility of being able to put things right between himself and Don, and dismissed all the others. He so much wanted them to be on good terms again, and being close at hand must surely offer more opportunity than living on the other side of London.

Bruce was ambitious. His entrepreneurial skills had come to light as a boy when he'd discovered what fertile ground the school playground was for anyone cute enough to invest their pocket money in confectionery they could sell on at a small profit at a time in the day when there was no other means of supply. He'd later progressed to a market stall, trying a variety of lines until finding his niche with men's clothing.

He'd enjoyed market life and was a natural for it. There was nothing quite like being at the grass roots of the retail trade: the buzz, the badinage, the community spirit. But having got that far, he'd aspired to more. Now his hard work had paid off and he was in a position to progress.

But his success had an emptiness about it. Indeed, his whole life was blighted by the continuing feud with his brother. A reconciliation seemed a feeble hope because Don was a very stubborn man and had made his position clear again today. But Bruce could be equally as determined and wouldn't be put off. If he was at it for the rest of his life, he'd keep trying.

Thinking back on that dreadful scene in the newsagent's, and wincing at the memory, he realised that there was something he must attend to first thing in the morning. His thoughts were interrupted by a voice beside him.

'Hello, there,' said one of his neighbours, a pale, quietly spoken man of middle years, who worked as a clerk in the offices at Ealing town hall.

'Wotcha,' smiled the sociable Bruce. 'What are you having?'

The man raised his hands in a gesture of protest. 'No, no. I'll get these,' he insisted. 'I reckon I owe you a drink after what you did for my wife yesterday.'

'You don't owe me anything, mate. I was only too glad to help,' Bruce assured him. 'How is she now?'

'Coming along. The ankle's still painful but she's managing to hobble about indoors on crutches.' The man shook his head, tutting. 'I'm hoping this setback will persuade her to stop using that damned bike of hers. Cycling is too dangerous around here with so much traffic on the road.'

'She only fell off the bike because she swerved to avoid a dog who ran in front of her,' Bruce pointed out. 'There wasn't much traffic about at the time. It isn't a very busy road.'

'Even so, I don't feel happy about her going to work by bike every day,' the clerk said. 'She has to cycle through Ealing Broadway and that's always busy during the working week.'

'Mm, it is,' nodded Bruce. 'She was telling me how much she enjoys the exercise, though.'

'I'd feel a lot happier if she would take the bus but we'll just have to see how she feels when the time comes for her to go back to work,' the man explained. 'Meanwhile, I just want to thank you again.'

137

'It was nothing, really,' he assured him again. 'Anyone would have done the same. It just happened to be me who was passing that way.'

The neighbour's wife – a schoolteacher – had taken a tumble off her bike near the flats where they all lived in a quiet side street near the station. Bruce was driving home and had stopped to assist her. She'd been very shaken and in a lot of pain so he'd taken her to the hospital where she was found to have broken her ankle. On her instructions he'd telephoned her husband at work and waited at the hospital until he'd arrived.

'Well, as far as I'm concerned it was lucky for us it was you. I can see that you're going to be a real asset as a neighbour,' effused the man, smiling. 'Now about that drink . . . what's it to be?'

'If you insist, I'll have a pint of bitter, please,' replied Bruce.

The next morning Jess was holding the fort in the shop while her father went to the bank for change, when she had a visitor.

'I just had to call in,' said a man she recognised as Don's brother; he was looking extremely smart in a pale grey Italian-style suit, his light brown hair fashionably razor cut to an even length all over, 'because I want to apologise properly to you and your father for what happened here yesterday. It wasn't fair to you and I feel really bad about it. I'm so sorry.'

'Dad isn't here but I think I can safely accept your apology for both of us.' Studying him for a likeness to Don, she noted that he was also tall and had a similar shade of hair to Don. But that was where the resemblance ended. This man was broader altogether, his face chunkier and square-jawed; he had a snub nose and a full mouth that seemed permanently ready to smile.

'That's a relief,' he said, and she could see genuine feeling in his shandy-brown eyes. 'I wouldn't want to get off on the wrong foot with my business neighbours. It really wasn't on, turning your shop into a battleground.'

She almost pointed out that Don seemed to have been the instigator of the trouble but it seemed disloyal to him so she just said, 'The shop wasn't busy at the time so it didn't cause too much of a problem for us.' She paused. 'Though you're right, it isn't the place for a fight.'

'Sorry.'

'Forget it,' she said. 'I'm Jess Mollitt, by the way.'

'Bruce Day.'

'Pleased to meet you.'

'I'm glad you're still speaking to me,' he confessed. 'I thought you might have taken Don's side against me, you being his girlfriend.'

'Don's family quarrels are his own business and nothing to do with me.' She paused, looking at him and liking what she saw. 'It does seem an awful pity the two of you can't settle your differences, though. Life's too short to harbour bad feeling.'

'You should tell my brother that.'

'I already have, ages ago.'

He looked surprised. 'He's talked to you about it?'

'No. Not really. He just mentioned the fact that you didn't get on when I first got to know him. It just came up in conversation. But he didn't give me any details,' she explained. 'It's difficult for me to imagine anything being bad enough to cause a permanent rift between siblings. I'd hate to fall out with mine.'

'There wouldn't be a rift if it was up to me,' Bruce confided impulsively. 'But Don can really dig his heels in when he wants to. Still, that's just the way he is. We're all different, I suppose.'

'Indeed.' There was an awkward pause. She glanced towards the window. 'Anyway, how are things going over the road?' she enquired, moving swiftly to a less emotive topic. 'Looks from here as though you're almost ready to open.'

'Next week, unless there's a last-minute hitch.'

She ran her eye over his suit, thinking how good it looked on him. 'Is that the sort of thing you'll be selling?' she asked.

'Among other things, yeah.' Grinning, he gave her a twirl to reveal a boxy jacket, which was slightly shorter than the traditional kind. 'What do you think?'

'I think it's smashing,' she replied. 'I like the continental look. It makes a change from the drab suits most men wear. I'll have to persuade Don to get something like that.'

He burst out laughing. 'You'll be lucky. He'd sooner slit his throat than wear anything like this,' he told her.

She found herself smiling too. 'Yeah, I think you're probably right about that.'

'Mind you, I wouldn't wear some of the things I'm going to be selling,' he went on to say. 'Stuff like the really short bum-freezer jackets and the very tight trousers. They're mostly for teens and early twenties.'

'Sounds as though you really know your market.'

'It pays to, doesn't it?'

'I should say.'

'I enjoy dealing in trendy men's gear.' He grinned and spread his hands. 'To be perfectly honest, though, I'll sell anything if there's a market for it as long as it doesn't put anyone else out of business: clothes, crockery, bedlinen. If it's legal and what people want, I'll set up shop.'

He was like a breath of fresh air, and just what she needed to lift her spirits in the aftermath of the distressing news about Babs, as well as the continuing strain at home over Ronnie's bad behaviour.

'You stick with what you're doing and get some style into the men around here,' she told him. 'God knows, they need it.'

Bruce smiled. 'Have you always worked with your dad?' he enquired conversationally.

'No. I used to be in show business,' she told him.

'Really?'

'Oh, yeah.' She remembered something. 'Talking about men's trendy clothes, the theatrical types I met during that time used to wear really modern stuff. Some of them went over the top – really weird gear, you know. But I prefer it to the boring, traditional clothes most men wear.'

He nodded. 'Showbiz, eh?' he said, encouraging her to expand on the subject.

'That's right. I used to be a dancer,' she told him. 'I was a Burton Girl.'

Up went his brows in unashamed approval. 'Ooh, high-kicking . . . fishnet tights and all of that?'

'That's right.'

'I bet you were sensational,' he complimented in a hearty manner, 'being tall and slim. I'd like to have seen you. Any chance of you going back to it?'

His down-to-earth attitude was very appealing. 'No. Dad needs me here,' she explained.

'I see.' He thought for a moment. 'I suppose an ordinary job must seem a bit dull after doing something like that.'

'I do miss it, I must admit,' Jess said. 'But I had a good run so I mustn't grumble.'

At that moment her father came back into the shop and Bruce repeated his apology, which was accepted. 'Perhaps I can show you how sorry I am by buying you a drink after work one night soon,' Bruce suggested.

'Yeah, I'd like that,' said Charlie. 'I usually pop in for a quick one after work.'

'Excellent.' Bruce looked at his watch. 'Meanwhile, I must be going.'

'Good luck with the shop,' said Jess.

'Thanks. Cheers. See you.'

As the door closed behind him, Charlie said, 'He seems like a decent sort of a bloke.'

'I thought so too,' Jess agreed.

'God knows what's happened between him and his brother for Don to behave like he did yesterday.'

'It obviously goes deep,' observed Jess. 'But we'll probably never know the details. It's one of those things you know instinctively that they'll keep between themselves.'

'That's the impression I got too,' her father agreed thoughtfully.

The leaves began to turn, there was a nip in the air and Jess perceived the surge of energy on the streets that always happened at the onset of autumn. People walked quicker and more purposefully, schools reopened, stew vegetables appeared in the greengrocer's, winter coats adorned shop windows and living rooms became cosier in the evenings with a fire in the hearth.

140

Bruce's shop opened and seemed to be doing well. His friendly personality made him an instant hit with the other traders. No one had a bad word to say about him – apart from Don, of course, who claimed that people trusted him at their peril.

The new season came as something of a relief to Jess because the children were back at school and she hoped that Ronnie might be a little less difficult now that he was occupied all day. She was also pleased to see Todd settled at his new school. He'd been very anxious about it towards the end of the holidays but now that the dreaded first day was over, he went off every morning in his smart uniform with a smile on his face.

Another reason Jess welcomed the new season was the fact that the beginning of the school year meant the resumption of her classes. Life had seemed dull without them to plan and look forward to each week. But now it was September and she was feeling much more positive about everything, including the difficult phase Ronnie was going through. That's all it is, a phase, she told herself, and the worst is probably over.

'This is your last chance to prove yourself, Mollitt,' threatened Shifter, fixing Ronnie with a glare. 'I mean it. If you don't do the business this time you're no mate of ours and we'll make sure you've got no other mates either. You'll have no one to go about with because the whole school will know you've got a yella streak running down your back and everybody will hate the sight of you. We'll make sure you never forget that it doesn't pay to cross us. You'll dread getting up in the morning, I can promise you that.'

'We ought to call you Molly instead of Mollitt,' taunted Nifty. 'As you act like a girl.'

'I don't,' denied poor Ronnie.

'Ooh, not much,' said the other boy. 'You couldn't even take a bag off an old woman. Cor, what a weed.'

'I coulda taken the bag. I just didn't want to, that's all.' Ronnie had taken a terrible beating from them over that. He was no weakling but these two were real ruffians and being up against them both together had meant he hadn't stood much of a chance. And as if giving him a thrashing hadn't been enough satisfaction for them, they'd still continued to taunt him; it just went on and on.

'You've already showed us that you've got no bottle.' Shifter was relentless. 'So if you want us to change our minds you'll have to do this thing today.'

It was Saturday afternoon and the boys were in Hanwell Broadway, sitting on the steps of the clock tower. The pavements were crowded with shoppers, people waiting for buses either side of the street, some mooching along or standing around chatting in groups; there were queues trailing out of bakers' and greengrocers'.

141

'OK, I'll do it,' Ronnie agreed miserably.

'Good, let's get on with it, then, before you have a chance to bottle out,' said Nifty.

'We'll have a look inside first to see what they've got that we fancy, then you go inside and do the business. All right, Mollitt?' ordered Shifter.

'Yeah, all right,' he agreed glumly.

They made their way to Dean's Stores and looked inside through the glass door.

'Wagon Wheels and fruit pies,' observed Shifter. 'There's a box of each on the counter so nicking 'em will be easy.' He looked at Ronnie. 'Go on then, Mollitt. Get it done. We want at least three of each so that there's enough for us all.'

Ronnie felt so sick he wanted to retch. He couldn't do it; didn't want to do it. He hated this trap he was in and longed to be free of his tormentors.

'I reckon he's gonna bottle out again,' Nifty said to Shifter. 'Just like last time. He's got no guts, none at all.'

Looking fearfully into the shop, Ronnie saw his sister's boyfriend behind the counter in his white grocer's coat. His mood changed instantly, fear banished by hatred for Don. Rage flashed through him at the memory of how he'd squealed on him. Anything that caused that slimy creep bother was worth doing. If he got into big trouble himself, he didn't care.

'I won't bottle out,' he announced to the others, contempt for Don giving him an air of confidence. 'You'll have Wagon Wheels and fruit pies and anything else I can lay my hands on. Just wait and see.'

While his friends watched in amazement at his change of attitude, he swaggered into the shop, oozing with self-assurance.

'So, what is it you want to talk to me about?' Jess asked Don that evening when they were settled at a corner table in a pub on the river near Kew. He'd suggested they go for a drink instead of the cinema as originally planned because he wanted to speak to her about something important. 'You seem very tense. What's the matter?'

He looked at her gravely. 'It's that brother of yours again,' he informed her.

'Ronnie. Oh no! What's he done this time?' she asked. 'Don't tell me you've seen him playing truant again.'

'It's a lot more serious than that this time, I'm afraid,' he told her solemnly.

'Oh?'

'It's a criminal matter, actually.'

The colour drained from her face. 'Ronnie a criminal?' she gasped in disbelief. 'What on earth are you talking about?'

'He's been stealing from my shop.'

142

'Oh, Don.' Her hand flew to her brow. 'Surely not. I know he's been a little perisher lately but he wouldn't do that. Not stealing.'

'I'm afraid he has done. He came into the shop this afternoon and – bold as brass – stole some of the stock from under my nose. Wagon Wheels and fruit pies to be exact,' he informed her sternly.

'I can't believe it,' she said, still somewhat bemused. 'You wait till I get my hands on him.'

'He obviously came into the shop with that sole intention,' Don went on. 'He stood there facing me across the counter with an evil look on his face, then just took the things, as though he was taunting me. Then he ran off, laughing at me behind my back with those mates of his no doubt. I saw those young thugs hanging around outside.'

Jess felt bile rise in her throat. 'Oh, Don, I'm so sorry,' she said. 'He obviously did it as a prank to annoy you because he still hasn't forgiven you for that business back in the summer. Did you go after him?'

'There was no point. All that would have achieved was more entertainment for him and his mates at my expense. They'd have thought that was great fun, my chasing after them with not a hope of catching them with the start they had.'

'Why didn't you come over and tell Dad and me about it at the time?'

'Because I wanted to think about what action I should take and I thought it best to speak to you before telling your father.' He paused, his eyes hard and his mouth tight and turned down at the corners. 'This is a very delicate matter. I mean, with you and I being, well . . . close.'

'It's embarrassing for me too, and I feel awful,' Jess said. 'Obviously we'll pay for the stuff he took and he'll be made to pay us back. Dad will give him a thorough wigging and dish out some suitable punishment.'

'I'm afraid it's gone beyond that now, Jess,' he told her with an air of doom.

Meeting his solemn gaze, she asked, 'What do you mean?'

'The boy is out of control and needs harsher punishment than either you or your father can give him.'

'Meaning what exactly?'

'I think I should report the matter to the police.'

She couldn't believe it. 'Surely you wouldn't do that,' she burst out. 'You're a friend of the family.'

'Even more reason to do it,' was his considered opinion. 'Ronnie is bringing disgrace upon your family and he needs correcting before he ends up in real trouble. A brush with the law might be just the thing to bring him to his senses.'

'So you're telling me that you'd be prepared to get my brother a criminal record for some boyish prank.' She was aghast. 'I know it was wrong but there's no need to involve the police.'

'I really do think it would be the best thing for him in the long run,' Don insisted.

'Or the ruin of him,' she argued. 'Something like that could set him on the wrong road for good and all.'

'They won't do anything too terrible to him for a first offence,' he suggested. 'He'll probably get off with a warning.'

'But it'll go on his record.'

'It might scare him into behaving himself.'

With a slow shake of her head, she said. 'Frankly Don, I don't know how you can even suggest such a thing. Not to a member of my family. As if I don't have enough problems already, you feel the necessity to add to them in this horrible way.'

He leaned across the table towards her. 'It's because you're having such problems with Ronnie I feel I must do this,' he explained. 'If we can get him to behave himself it will be one less worry for you to cope with.'

'I've never heard such cock-eyed logic,' she burst out.

'Look, I care about you . . . a lot, and I hate the idea of your having to look after that family when you should be living your own life.'

'I do live my own life.'

'Only after you've seen that they're all right.'

'There's nothing wrong with that.'

'I think there is.'

'Oh, do you now. Well, it's the way it has to be for me, for the moment,' she reminded him fiercely. 'When we first started seeing each other, I told you that I had family commitments. I remember suggesting at the time that you might prefer to go out with someone who is free to do as they please.'

'And I said that it wasn't a problem for me, and it still isn't,' he assured her. 'It's you I'm thinking of.'

'Look, Don, I won't say the weight of family responsibility doesn't ever get me down, because it does at times. It would be lovely to be free to come and go as I please and not have to organise the household beforehand, but no matter how infuriating they are, I love them all, and I won't desert them while they need me.' She paused, looking at him in such a way as to make her message perfectly clear. 'Neither will I stand by and see one of them up in court for a petty crime if I can do anything to stop it.'

'You're too protective of him.'

'Yes, I expect I am,' Jess agreed assertively. 'But if he'd been involved in a real robbery or injured someone, I would report him to the police myself. But not for something like this. Oh, no.'

'There's right and wrong, and Ronnie has overstepped the mark and needs correcting.'

'We can do that within the family.' She stood her ground. 'You don't grass up the brother of your girlfriend – the son of your pal. It isn't the way we do things – not in my world.'

'You're making me sound like some evil bugger when all I want to do

144

is what's right, and what will be best for Ronnie in the long term,' Don claimed.

What made this whole thing even more upsetting for Jess was the fact that she was practically certain that Don wasn't being malicious. He really did believe that his way of dealing with the problem was in Ronnie's best interests. He was a decent man with cast-iron principles and clearly defined guidelines. There was no room for debate with Don.

But she was equally as firm in her beliefs. 'You must do as you see fit, of course, but if you really do care for me, I suggest you think twice about it,' she told him.

'Is that a threat?'

'No, just a fact,' she told him evenly. 'You say you care for me – well, you are going to cause me a whole lot of trouble and heartache if you shop Ronnie to the police. Surely that isn't what you want for someone you care about.'

'But, Jess—'

'I mean it, Don,' she said. 'You go to the police and I'll never forgive you.'

He brooded on this for what seemed ages, drinking his beer slowly. 'All right, you win,' he agreed at last, with obvious reluctance. 'We'll deal with it your way. But don't blame me if he gets into real trouble.'

'I've no intention of blaming you for anything,' she made clear. 'If he breaks the law again in your direction, I won't do anything to stop you handing him over to the police.'

'I shall have to if it happens again,' he warned her.

'OK, I accept that. But I'm grateful to you for letting me do it my way this time.'

He shot her a look. 'You are going to tell your father, though, aren't you? I hope you're not planning on dealing with it yourself.'

'No, I won't do that,' Jess assured him. 'Dad needs to know, needs to read the riot act to him.'

'That's all right then.'

'Ronnie really would be getting off too light if I didn't tell Dad.' She paused, biting her lip. 'But I think it might be best if I break the news to him rather than you did. He's going to hit the roof. No point in subjecting you to that.'

'I'll leave it to you, then.'

'Thanks.'

Don managed a watery smile. 'Right, now that that's settled, I think another drink is in order,' he said. 'We might as well try and enjoy what's left of the evening. Gin and orange?'

'Please,' she said. 'I feel as though I need it.'

Watching him walk over to the bar, Jess wondered what the long-term prospects were for her with Don. They still hadn't talked about a future together, but she guessed he was serious about her now. And she thought

145

a lot of him or she wouldn't continue to see him. But true love? She wasn't sure. Marriage would be difficult for her at the moment, anyway. She wouldn't want to leave home while they still needed her there, and it was asking a lot of any man to expect him to move in with her family. She certainly couldn't imagine Don mucking in with the rough and tumble of family life. Still, that was something for the future. It wasn't an issue that needed addressing for the time being.

More immediate was the problem of Ronnie. What were they going to do about that boy?

Jess told her father about Ronnie's latest transgression first thing the next morning, and everyone kept out of the way while Charlie dealt with his son, his angry voice resounding through the house from the living room.

After the thunder of Ronnie's footsteps on the stairs, Jess left him for a while to calm down, then went upstairs and found him lying on his bed staring at the ceiling.

'I suppose you've come to give me a lecture too,' he said, glaring at her, his eyes hot with resentment. 'As if I haven't already had enough earache from the old man.'

'You're lucky he didn't make your bum ache too,' she told him. 'You deserve a good hiding after what you did yesterday. It's a good job for you Dad isn't a violent man.'

'I'd sooner have had that than what's he's given me.'

'Which is?'

'He's stopped my pocket money for a month, even my paper round money, and I'm not allowed out after school except to help in the shop on a Saturday, filling shelves and tidying up.'

'You got off light.'

He shrugged.

'Helping in the shop won't hurt you.'

'There isn't enough for me to do there so he just invents jobs,' he complained.

'At least we'll know where you are.'

Ronnie sat up and looped his long arms around his knees. 'I wish you'd get it into your head that you're my sister, not my mother,' he told her. 'What I do has nothing to do with you.'

'It does when it's my boyfriend's shop you steal from,' she retorted. 'How do you think that makes me feel?'

'He was asking for it,' he declared. 'Going about so high and mighty. He needs to be brought down a peg or two. I don't know what you see in him.'

'You're not meant to know,' she said.

'He's such a drip, Jess. Surely you can see that.'

'I wouldn't go out with him if I thought he was the idiot you're making him out to be,' she put him straight. 'Anyway, I'm not here to talk about

146

Don. I want to know if that little scam of yours had anything to do with those boys you're hanging out with,' she said.

He looked at her sharply. 'What have they got to do with it?' he demanded.

'I think they were probably egging you on and getting you to do their dirty work,' she told him.

'No,' he denied fiercely, his cheeks flaming. 'No one tells me what to do. I did it because I wanted to.'

'To upset Don?'

He shrugged, giving her a defiant look. 'Anything that ruffles his feathers is worth getting into trouble for.'

Jess emitted a weary sigh, wishing she was able to communicate with him as she had done in the past. 'Why don't you give us all a break, eh Ron, and behave in a normal manner instead of acting like a moron the whole time?' she asked. 'You're making life miserable for the whole family, causing rows and tension in the house.'

'There wouldn't have been a row this morning if you hadn't told Dad,' he accused.

'I had to tell him.'

'Or old ferret face would have done it for you, is that what you mean?'

'No. I told Dad because what you did was wrong and he needed to know about it,' she corrected.

'You're getting as bad as your boyfriend.'

'And you're getting to be a serious liability to this family. If you're not very careful you'll end up in Borstal.'

'Oh, I'm not listening to any more of this,' he hissed, bending his head and clamping his hands over his ears. 'Clear off out of here, go on. Get out!'

As there was no sensible alternative, she did as he asked, feeling sad as well as desperately worried. As she made her way downstairs to prepare the vegetables for Sunday lunch, she was at a loss to know how to steer her brother away from this course of self-destruction he'd got himself on.

147

Chapter Ten

The final class of the morning was almost at an end but Jess still wasn't quite satisfied with a tap routine they were working on, a lively little item performed to the tune of 'Put on a Happy Face'.

'OK, everyone, before we finish I'd like to go through that last bit once more – *and can we have it right this time – please?*' She was smiling, her firm but light-hearted manner drawing an enthusiastic response from the class. She could usually manage to soften her authority without losing control.

'Right. Let's have a few more shuffle-hops-steps, then a couple of time-steps . . . off you go – *now*. Good . . . oh, that's much better . . . Well done! You've all worked really hard this morning.' Patience rewarded by a slight improvement, she beamed at the class. The perfectionist standards drummed into her at Burtons had stayed with her but she tried to make sure that her lessons weren't heavy-going; people would soon stop coming if they didn't have fun. 'I'm sure you'll be relieved to know that I'm letting you go now, girls. I'll see you all again next week. Take care on the way home.'

Chattering and giggling the children went to the chairs at the side of the hall to get changed; a few were being collected but, this being the over-eleven's class, most of them made their own way home. They all lived locally.

'A good lesson, Jess,' praised Hilda, gathering her music from the stand on the piano and putting it into her bag. 'It went really well again today.'

'Thanks. But it's down to a joint effort from all three of us,' Jess returned the compliment. 'We make a good team.'

'Have you thought any more about putting on a Christmas show?' enquired Libby, sitting on the floor to change out of her tap shoes.

'I have actually,' replied Jess, looking from one to the other, 'and I think it might be a good thing. Nothing too elaborate or daunting for the kids, just a short performance for their relatives and friends, involving all three classes. I think that's enough for a first show. What do you think?'

'I think it's a lovely idea,' approved Hilda.

'Me too,' added Libby. 'Doing a show is so exciting: scary but fun too. We all enjoy it, in my regular class, when we're putting something on.'

Grinning, she threw Jess a meaningful look. 'Even though the teacher gets to be unbearable in the run-up.'

'I'll take that as a warning and do my best to stay calm and bearable,' responded Jess lightly. 'As you both approve, I'll start making the arrangements.'

'We'll help to organise it, won't we, Libs?'

Libby nodded, looking at her sister. 'Can I be in it, even though I'm not actually one of your pupils?'

'Of course you can,' Jess told her. 'We'll need an experienced dancer to keep the whole thing together.'

'Where will we have it?' wondered Hilda.

Jess considered the matter. 'I'm not sure. Maybe here, as it's only going to be a small affair,' she suggested. 'It'll be expensive to hire somewhere with a proper stage and curtains and everything.'

'Mm, that's true.' Hilda cast a studied eye around. 'The hall is perfectly adequate for what we've got in mind. Later on we might want to be more adventurous.'

'I'll have a word with the landlord; get it booked for one evening in December,' Jess mentioned thoughtfully. 'In fact, I might as well do it on the way out.'

When all the children had either been collected or left the premises in noisy, exuberant groups, Jess and the others made their way down the stairs. Jess always felt exhilarated after a class, and today she was especially buoyant as thoughts of putting a show together filled her mind. Telling Libby and Hilda she'd see them later, she went into the bar to speak to the landlord.

'So we'd need the hall for a few hours on a weekday evening . . . let's say early or mid-December,' she explained, having outlined her plans. 'It'll have to be early evening because some of the children are quite little.' She pondered on this for a moment. 'Say six thirty until about half-past eight or nine. Is that all right with you?'

The landlord looked at her steadily across the bar. 'Sorry, love. I can't do it.'

'Oh, that's a pity.' She rethought the matter. 'What about the end of November then,' she suggested, 'if the hall is fully booked for December? It's a bit early for a Christmas show, but that isn't really a problem.'

'I can't let you have the hall then either,' he informed her.

'Oh?' Her brow furrowed. 'Why not?'

'Because I'm having billiard tables installed up there.'

'Billiard tables?' She tried to make sense of this rather odd statement. 'Are you saying that I can't book the hall for any evening?'

'That's right.'

She threw him a questioning look. 'But the tables will be put out of the way for daytime bookings, I presume?' she said with growing anxiety.

'My Saturday morning classes, for instance?'

'No. They'll be permanent fixtures. I'm turning it into a billiard hall.' The landlord cleared his throat, looking sheepish. 'I intended to have a word with you about it the next time I saw you.' Pausing, he drew on his cigarette then emitted a chesty cough. 'I'm afraid the hall won't be available for hire any more at all after the first week in November. They're starting the alterations then.'

'Not available to anyone at any time?' She couldn't believe it.

'Exactly.'

This was such a blow. 'But you can't do that,' she burst out. 'I'm just getting my dance school established.'

'Sorry, love. I hate to put you out but business is business,' he told her in an even tone. 'A billiard hall will bring me in a decent, regular income. It was always only ever a casual arrangement between you and me, anyway.'

'Not as far as I was concerned.'

'In that we never had a contract, I mean,' he went on to point out. 'There's nothing in writing.'

Leaden with disappointment, she stared into space, trying to gather her thoughts.

'Look, I really am sorry, Jess. Your dad's a good customer here and I wouldn't do this unless I had to,' he was at pains to make clear. 'But I have to make this business pay and the hall isn't earning its keep as it stands at the moment. I'm sure you understand.'

'But—'

There were several men standing at the bar, impatient to be served. 'You'll soon find somewhere else, I'm sure,' he said with an air of finality. 'Now if you'll excuse me, I have a lunchtime crowd to attend to.'

Realising that his decision was irreversible, she left the pub feeling thoroughly dejected. Problems seemed to come at her from all sides lately.

On her next half-day off Jess whizzed through her chores, slipped a chunky-knit red jacket over her slimline black trousers and headed for Churchfields. A walk in the park always had a soothing effect on her when she was worried or upset about anything.

But not even the autumn trees in their glorious fiery shades, or the crisp fresh air in her face was able to shift the gloom today. Exhaustive enquiries over the past few days had produced the same result as the last time she'd been looking for a hall to hire: there wasn't one available on a Saturday anywhere in the local area. This meant she would have to look further afield and start again somewhere else. To add to her disappointment, she knew she would lose most of her existing pupils because the mothers wouldn't be prepared to let them travel. Anyway, the whole idea had always been for the dancing classes to be a local community event.

It was a lovely day; fresh and sunny with an earthy autumnal tang in the air. Warm and breathless from walking at a brisk pace, Jess sat down on a bench to take a rest. It being midweek and a school day, the park was almost deserted, though she was too preoccupied to notice much about her surroundings.

'Mind if I join you?' asked a voice beside her and, turning, she saw Bruce Day.

'Not at all,' she told him dully, waving her hand absently towards the bench. 'There's plenty of room.'

'Ooh, dear, someone doesn't sound too chirpy,' he remarked amiably. 'Shall I go away and leave you alone?'

She wasn't in the mood for company but there was such a warmth about him, Jess heard herself saying, 'I didn't mean to seem offhand. Of course I don't mind if you join me.' She turned to him. 'It's nice to see that you're finding the time to enjoy one of my favourite local attractions.'

He glanced around. 'It's one of my favourites too.' He gave a wry grin. 'I'm hoping a spot of fresh air will give me the energy to whizz through the pile of paperwork that's waiting for me at the shop when I get back. I can think of things I'd rather do on my half-day than paperwork, but it has to be done.'

'I'm lucky there because Dad does most of ours.'

Bruce was dressed in a thick, cream sweater and casual trousers, his well-cut hair blowing in the breeze, and his rich brown eyes were resting on her approvingly. 'There you are then, it isn't all bad, is it?' he pointed out.

'No, of course it isn't,' she agreed. 'Take no notice of me. I'm just feeling a bit thwarted, that's all.'

'Well, I'm in no hurry to get back to the dreaded office work,' he told her with a half-smile, 'and they say a trouble shared . . .'

Without any prior intention, Jess found herself confiding in him about her threatened dance school. 'I'm not prepared to give up because I adore teaching and I think the kids enjoy it too. But it looks as though I'll have to move the school out of the area and I really didn't want to do that.'

He didn't make any comment, and turning to see that he was lost in thought, she made an assumption. 'I know I must seem to be whining on and my problem is nothing compared to the trouble some people have to endure,' she said. 'But my dance school is really important to me. And you did ask . . .'

'I don't think you're whining on at all,' he said, facing her. 'That's the last thing I would ever think about you. I was quiet because something suddenly occurred to me and I was thinking it through.' He scratched his face absently. 'I think I might be able to help.'

'Really?'

'Yeah. There's a very large room over my shop. I suppose it's big

152

enough to be called a hall but it's full of junk so doesn't look much like one at the moment,' he explained. 'It hasn't been used for anything other than storage for many years by the look of it, and it's a bit of a mess. But from what I can remember the floor seems to be all right and it's a decent size. If it was cleared out and given a good clean, it might be just what you're looking for.'

'Don't you need it as a storeroom?'

'No, I've got plenty of storage space downstairs so I don't use it. The stuff littering the big room upstairs is all rubbish left by the previous tenants – old boxes, bits of broken furniture, that sort of thing. I've been meaning to have a clear-out up there but I've been so busy I haven't got round to it yet.'

'Are you sure you don't need the space?' She didn't want to get her hopes up only to have them dashed. 'If you get extra stock in for any reason?'

'I don't ever carry a huge amount of stock because fashions change so fast at the cheap and trendy end of the menswear market, I try to avoid having too much left on my hands to dispose of at knockdown prices,' he explained. 'I only buy what I know I can sell, and most of what I have is out on display in the shop. Anyway, there's another, smaller room up there that was used as an office at one time, I think. If I'm stuck at any time I can use that. I certainly don't need the main room.'

'Well, if you're positive . . .'

'I am. As a matter of fact, I've been cursing the fact that there's a hall over the shop instead of living accommodation, which would have saved me having to pay rent on a flat. As it is now, it's just wasted space so I'd be glad to see it used. Anyway, you're welcome to have a look at it – see what you think.'

'Is there access to it without going through the shop?' she enquired, her interest rising.

'Yeah, all the shops in that parade have back entrances.'

'That's what I thought.'

'Well, if you think you might be interested, come over and have a butcher's.'

'How much would you charge for three hours on a Saturday morning?'

'I haven't a clue. You'll have to advise me on that one,' Bruce told her. 'If you think it's suitable for you, we'll work something out between us based on what you were paying at the pub.'

'When can I come to look at it?'

'I'll be at the shop until about five o'clock this afternoon, in the office,' he told her. 'I'll be happy to show you the hall at any time until then.'

'Thanks ever so much,' she said, her voice lighter and vibrant with new hope.

He could feel her eagerness, had seen the dull look of worry in her eyes turn to sparkle. 'You want to see it now, don't you?' he speculated with a half-smile.

'That obvious, is it?' she giggled.

'Afraid so.'

'But I don't want to drag you away from here until you're ready to go.'

He stood up with a purposeful air. 'I need to get back to the dreaded paperwork, anyway,' he told her lightly. 'So let's go and let you have a look.'

Jess was about to get up when she had a visitor. 'Hello, there,' she said to an emaciated dog, who limped up to her and sat at her feet. 'You're a sad-looking thing, aren't you? Where did you come from?'

The pitiable creature – who had a tawny-coloured coat with bald, scabby patches and sad dark eyes – looked up at her and whimpered.

'It's in the advanced stages of neglect by the look of it,' observed Bruce, going down on his haunches to the animal, who was so thin its bones protruded and face looked pointed.

'The poor thing,' cried Jess. 'How could anyone let an animal get into such a state?'

'People take them on and then abandon them when the novelty of having a pet wears off,' he said, inspecting the dog. 'They just leave them to roam the streets. It's a him, by the way.'

'He could have just got lost, I suppose,' she suggested without much conviction.

'It's possible. But it's much more likely that he was taken somewhere and dumped by some irresponsible owner.' He stood up, looking grave. 'I think I'd better take him back to the shop with me. I'll ring the RSPCA from there and ask them to come to collect him. They'll look after him and try to find him a home. Pets are strictly forbidden in the flats where I live or I'd take him on myself. And I can't keep him at the shop because he'd be on his own every night, and that wouldn't be fair.'

'Do they put strays down after a certain time if they can't place them?' Jess wondered.

'I don't know but I suppose they might,' he replied. 'They wouldn't have room to keep them all – not in the long term.'

'Oh dear,' muttered Jess.

They were both feeling anxious as they headed home, the dog staying close to Jess's heels. When they got to the end of Park Street, she remembered that she needed to turn the oven on for a casserole, so told Bruce she would meet him at his shop in a few minutes. As they parted company, the dog followed her instead of Bruce and no amount of coaxing would get him to do otherwise.

'Looks as though you've got an admirer,' he grinned.

'Yes, it does seem like it, doesn't it?' she agreed worriedly. 'But I can't take him home with me. We've never had a dog. We don't know anything about them.'

'Don't worry. I'll pick him up and carry him if I can't get him to come of his own accord,' said Bruce. 'Come on, you daft animal. Come with me.'

As he moved towards the dog, so the dog moved closer to Jess, making a low whining sound, his soulful eyes resting persuasively on her. It was too much for Jess's soft-hearted nature. 'It's all right, Bruce, I'll take him home with me,' she decided. 'I'll give him some food and water, then ring the RSPCA.'

'Would you like me to ring them for you from the shop?' he offered. 'I was going to do it anyway. If you give me your house number . . .'

'No, it's all right, I'll do it.' She supposed she was trying to delay the inevitable because she couldn't bear the idea of the dog's possible fate. 'But I'll have to come and look at the hall later on. I need to get this little fella sorted out first.'

'Sure.'

'See you later then.'

'I'll look forward to it,' he said, and meant it. He thought she was lovely.

'Come on then, you scruffy article,' she said to the poor creature who trotted slowly beside her.

'Ugh, what's that?' was Libby's reaction when she came in from school to see the dog sitting in the corner of the kitchen on a blanket, having polished off a large tin of stewing steak – which Jess had had put by for an emergency – some plain biscuits and several bowls of water.

'A jam doughnut,' Jess replied waggishly. 'What do you think it is?'

'I can see that it's a dog,' she tutted. 'I meant, what's it doing here?'

'He's a stray. We're looking after him – just temporarily.'

'It doesn't half whiff.' Libby was holding a handkerchief to her nose.

'He can't help that,' defended Ronnie, who'd also just got in from school. 'He needs a bath, that's all, don't you, boy?' Ronnie was on his knees gently fondling the dog's ears, apparently oblivious to the fact that the fur was matted with filth and a miasma of the foulest kind was emanating from the creature. 'And he isn't an it, he's a he. So show some respect.'

'You'll get germs, touching him like that,' warned Libby. 'Don't come near me with his fleas all over you.'

'As if I'd want to.'

Todd came in the back door, satchel slung over his shoulder. 'Oh, a dog. Is it ours?' he asked, looking hopeful.

'No, we're just giving him shelter for a little while,' explained Jess. 'I've got to ring the RSPCA and tell them to come and collect him. But I'll do it later on. He'll be all right where he is for the moment.'

'He pongs a bit,' observed Todd.

'So would you if you hadn't had a bath in ages,' defended Ronnie.

155

'Anyway, he's an animal so what else do you expect? It's natural for them to smell.'

'Be that as it may,' interrupted Jess, 'I've got to go out for half an hour so you'll have to look after the dog while I'm gone. Dad's out at the wholesaler's and should be back soon. There are some fresh buns in the larder to keep you going until tea-time. Shan't be long. Take care of the dog. If he needs to go out, stay with him in the garden until he wants to come in again. Don't let him wander off.' She grabbed her coat from the chair and headed out of the back door in a rush.'

'It's perfect,' said Jess, running an approving eye over Bruce's hall, which was thick with dust and littered with empty cardboard boxes, newspapers, broken chairs and other nonperishable items that needed to be in the dustbin. 'This is just the sort of thing I'm looking for.' She looked around, frowning as she spotted a snag. 'There isn't a piano, though. Would you have any objection to my installing a piano in here? I can bring ours from home. It never gets used now that Mum isn't around.'

'I've no objections at all.' Bruce cast a studious glance around. 'As I said earlier, the place is in a bit of a mess.'

'Nothing that a bit of elbow grease won't shift.' She gave him a grateful smile. 'You've made a worried woman into a very happy one, do you know that? You've saved my dancing school.'

'As much as I'm enjoying the credit, I think that's a bit of an overstatement,' he suggested with a half-smile. 'You'd have found somewhere else eventually.'

'Not as convenient as this, though,' Jess pointed out. 'I'd have lost a lot of pupils if I'd moved the school away.'

'Well, as long as you're happy, that's the main thing,' he said. 'And it's helped me too, because the place will get used. Now that you've set the ball rolling, I might hire it out for other things, though I'll have to get some chairs and tables that can be stacked around the sides when they're in the way.'

'About the cost . . .' she thought she ought to mention it, 'I was paying ten shillings at the pub.'

'Let's knock a bit off that because you'll be supplying your own piano.' He thought for a moment. 'So, let's say seven and six.'

'You're a gentleman.'

'Deal,' he said, offering his hand.

'Deal,' she said shaking it. 'Right, now that that's settled I'd better get back and see how those kids are coping with the dog.'

'When are the RSPCA coming for him?'

She didn't reply; just stood there grinning.

'You didn't call them, did you?'

'Not yet,' she admitted.

He threw back his head and laughed and she joined in; they both knew

156

that she wasn't ever going to make that call.

When Jess got back the dog was missing from the blanket in the kitchen.

'Where is he?' she shouted into the house. 'I hope you kids haven't let him out to wander off.'

'In here,' called Ronnie.

She went into the living room to see the dog sitting on the mat by the fire with Ronnie beside him. The dog looked like a skinned rabbit; his fur was wet and clinging to his skinny body.

'You should see the bathroom, Jess,' announced Libby. 'There's water everywhere, and Ronnie's used all your Drene shampoo and got all the towels soaking wet.'

'I had to use the shampoo because I though the soap might be too strong for him and make him sore, with his skin being in such a bad state,' explained Ronnie. 'And I'll clean the bathroom up in a minute.'

'You bathed that dog . . . in our bath?' Jess hadn't seen enthusiasm in Ronnie for a very long time, let alone seen him show any initiative.

'Well, yeah, I had to, didn't I? I couldn't leave him as he was with everyone complaining about the smell,' said Ronnie, who seemed to have assumed entire responsibility for the animal. 'And where else would I bath him but in the bath? The sink isn't big enough. He might have hurt himself on the taps.'

Jess wasn't sure how to answer that so she just said, 'Well done, Ronnie.' She couldn't remember the last time she'd had cause to praise him and it felt wonderful.

'I suppose it'll be all right to have him in the house now that he's had a bath,' admitted Libby.

'He'll look nice when his fur dries,' added Todd with enthusiasm. 'It'll be fun having a dog. We can take him out for walks and throw sticks for him and stuff like that.'

Jess bit her lip. 'I haven't actually said we're keeping him,' she reminded them.

'He needs someone to look after him,' came an unexpected contribution from Charlie in his armchair. 'We might not know much about dogs but we can learn, and at least he'll have a good home with this family.'

'But we're out all day, Dad.' She wanted to be realistic about this.

'We can take him to the shop with us,' suggested Charlie. 'Or get Hilda to pop in if we leave him here.'

'He'll be all right with us at the shop, I suppose,' said Jess, thinking it over. 'We can get a basket for him and put him in the back room; there's a yard out the back too. One of us can take him for a walk at lunchtime.'

'So we're keeping him then?' Ronnie thought it was looking hopeful.

'I think we should,' replied his father.

There was a general roar of agreement.

'What shall we call him?' asked Todd.

157

'Doughnut,' said Ronnie without hesitation. 'Jess made a sarky comment about him being a jam doughnut when Libby asked that stupid question, and his fur's a sort of doughnut colour.'

'He's too skinny to be called Doughnut,' Todd pointed out. 'Doughnuts are round and fat.'

'He's only skinny because he's half starved,' Ronnie pointed out. 'He'll be different altogether when he's been looked after properly for a while.'

'He still won't be like a doughnut, though.'

'That isn't the point—'

'Oh, really, will you two stop going on about doughnuts?' Libby objected strongly. 'We are not calling him that because it's a really stupid name for a dog. You can't name a dog after a cake.'

'There's no law against it,' said Ronnie.

'No, but it's a pretty daft thing to do,' she tutted. 'Why can't we give him some normal dog name like Rover or Scamp?'

'Because I like Doughnut.' Ronnie was digging his heels in on this one.

Jess decided it was time to intervene. 'As Ronnie took the trouble to bath him, I think he should be allowed to choose his name.'

'I'll go along with that,' supported her father.

'Doughnut it is then,' smiled Jess.

The news that Jess was hiring the hall over Bruce's shop for her classes created a furious reaction in his brother when she mentioned it to him casually the next day over lunch in Lyons.

'I don't think you should go ahead with it,' he stated forcefully.

'Why on earth not?'

'The man isn't to be trusted.'

'I'm hiring a hall from him for a few hours each week, not giving him my life savings to look after,' she pointed out tartly.

'You're deliberately misunderstanding me,' he said, his voice rising. 'The man is rotten to the core.'

'How will that affect me when all I'm doing is using his hall?' she wondered.

'It will, believe me.'

'He seems a decent enough chap to me,' Jess told him. 'I rather like him actually. He's good fun.'

'Good fun?' He looked about to explode. 'How do you know whether or not he's good fun?'

'I don't,' she replied. 'But he seemed to have a good sense of humour when we were together in the park.'

'You were with him – in the park?' This news appeared really to rattle him.

'That's right,' Jess confirmed and went on to tell him how it had led to her hiring the hall, and gave him a brief account of what happened about the dog.

'If you take my advice, you'll steer well clear of my brother,' he advised her in an authoritative manner.

'Are you saying that I should lose this chance to save my dance school just because you don't get on with him?'

'You'll find somewhere else,' he said dismissively. 'His isn't the only hall for hire.'

'It's the only one available on a Saturday morning in the area that I want it,' she asserted. 'I'll never get anywhere else just across the road from where the classes are held now. This means I won't have to start afresh. All the same people will come.'

Don stirred his coffee so vigorously, it spilled over into the saucer. 'I really would rather you didn't have dealings with him, Jess,' he said, and his voice was shaking.

Now he was going too far and making her feel suffocated. 'This is getting out of hand, Don,' she told him straight. 'You don't own me. I make up my own mind about people. You can't expect me to dislike him just because you do.'

'You don't know what he's capable of.'

'Tell me then.' She was getting really exasperated with him now. 'Tell me what he's done to make you hate him so much so that I can judge for myself.'

His face worked, his little eyes burning with rage. 'There's no need for you to know,' he told her. 'Just trust me when I say that the man is no good.'

She looked at him, perceiving real distress. He obviously had a genuine grudge against his brother and wasn't just doing this to demonstrate his claim on her. She felt a pang of pity for him because there was such inherent melancholy about the man. It couldn't be easy being burdened with such an intensely serious nature. But at the same time she couldn't allow him to dictate to her with whom she could and could not associate.

'Are you afraid he'll make a pass at me or something, is that what's behind all this?' she asked. 'Only there'll be nothing like that at all. He knows that you and I are a couple.'

'That wouldn't stop him.'

'Don't be so insecure, Don,' she admonished. 'Surely you know you can trust me.'

'He's the one I don't trust.'

'In that case you'll have to rely on me to keep things on the straight and narrow, won't you? Because I absolutely insist on being able to have dealings with whoever I chose.' She was determined on this one. 'And I really do need that hall for my dance classes.'

'So my feelings mean nothing to you?'

'Now you really are being ridiculous.' She reached for his hand and gave it a reassuring squeeze because he looked so vulnerable suddenly.

'Of course your feelings matter to me. But I have a mind of my own.'

'I wouldn't dream of saying otherwise but my brother—'

'You're the one I'm going out with,' she interrupted, 'and I'll make sure that he remembers that.'

He managed a smile. 'Promise,' he said, holding her hand in both of his.

'I promise.'

'Good.'

She couldn't leave it at that, though; it was far too serious an issue. 'But you mustn't get angry every time I speak to him,' she told him. 'That wouldn't be fair to me. I intend to be friendly with whoever I choose . . . whether you like them or not.'

'Yeah, yeah,' he sighed. 'I know I'm being unreasonable. I'll watch it in future.'

Despite his apparent good intentions, she didn't think this would be the end of it. It was easy to see how Don might view Bruce as a threat, with his good looks and appealing manner. But there was obviously much more to his hatred of him than sibling rivalry. Don wouldn't be pleased to know that she couldn't help finding Bruce attractive, she admitted with a surge of guilt; her and the rest of the female population probably.

'I'll have to be getting back soon,' she said, looking at her watch. 'I want to take the dog for a walk, or look after the shop while Dad takes him.'

'You took the dog to work with you.' He sounded very disapproving.

'That's right,' she confirmed. 'We couldn't bear the idea of leaving him in the house on his own while he's so new to us, and so weak. He needs plenty of attention at the moment so we've made him comfortable in the back room.'

He shook his head, sucking in his breath loudly. 'Are you sure you've done the right thing in taking in a stray dog?' he asked, as though she'd just admitted to giving a herd of Friesians the run of the house.

'Quite sure,' she assured him, knowing that there was no point in trying to explain why she could speak with such confidence because Don simply wouldn't understand.

'Stay away from her, do you hear?' commanded Don.

'That won't be easy as she's going to be running her dance school from these premises once a week,' his brother pointed out mildly.

'Don't be flippant,' rebuked Don fiercely. 'You know perfectly well what I mean.'

'I've no intention of trying to steal her from you, if that's what you're worried about.'

'Oh, no?'

'No, definitely not.'

The two men were in the office behind Bruce's shop with the door

160

firmly closed against the ears of the staff, Don having stormed in here after leaving Jess. 'Oh, not much,' he said, standing stiffly by the desk at which Bruce was seated. 'She might be taken in by your Good Samaritan act, and grateful to you for letting her hire the hall, but I'm not. I know exactly why you've done it.'

'You've got me all wrong, mate.'

'So you keep telling me but we both know there's been proof to the contrary.'

'Only in your mind.'

'That's it, try and pretend I'm not right in the head.'

'I'm not suggesting any such thing. But I will say that you're a bit too quick to jump to conclusions.' Bruce leaned back, studying his brother's face, noticing the pallor and features drawn tight with tension. 'You really will drive yourself crackers the way you're carrying on, though, making mountains out of molehills the whole time. You've always been a bit too serious for your own good but never as bad as you are now.'

'And we both know why, don't we?'

Bruce met his accusing stare. 'If you say so, mate,' he said with a sigh of resignation.

'You're trying to make out I'm in the wrong just to ease your own miserable conscience,' claimed Don.

The other man stroked his chin, forcing himself to stay calm because it was impossible to reason with his brother in this mood. 'Look, I'm fully aware that Jess is off limits to me and I won't go anywhere near her in that way. Right?'

'You'd better not.'

'I won't.' He was beginning to get impatient now. 'But I'll tell you straight so that you can be prepared. I am going to be civil to her whether you like it or not because it's my way to be sociable. She's a nice woman and I like her very much. So don't go off in a tantrum every time I pass the time of day with her. You can't stop me from talking to her so accept it now, for goodness' sake.'

'If you so much as suggest anything else I'll kill you,' threatened Don.

'Oh, cut the dramatics and calm down, for God's sake, man,' Bruce advised him. 'You must be taking years off your life with all this unnecessary anger.'

'Unnecessary, is it?'

'Yes, it most definitely is,' confirmed Bruce in an adamant tone. 'Your attitude towards me – as well as being hurtful – is nothing short of ridiculous.'

'Don't give me all that innocent stuff.'

'How many more times must I tell you? I am not going to make a move on Jess Mollitt, you have my word on that.'

'Your word,' sneered Don. 'And that's supposed to make me feel better, is it?'

'It's all I have to offer in the way of reassurance,' Bruce pointed out. 'So you can either accept it or spend your life worrying every time I so much as say good morning to her, and working yourself up into a state over nothing.'

Don threw him a look. 'I have no choice but to accept it but if I get the slightest inkling that you've broken your word, you'll regret it. Understand?'

'Don't be tiresome, Don,' said the other man wearily. 'You've made your point and I get the message loud and clear.'

'You'd better.'

'But now I think you should leave before you give yourself a heart attack,' Bruce suggested.

'I'm going,' said Don, and walked out, slamming the door behind him.

Bruce leaned back in his chair, idly tapping a pen on the desk and mulling the situation over. Don really would flip his lid if he knew the truth about Bruce's feelings for Jess – that he thought she was warm and beautiful and he would very much like to know her better. Having those feelings was no betrayal, he reminded himself, as long as he didn't do anything about them. If it was anyone else but Don she was involved with, he might have stood a chance, since Jess wasn't married or even engaged.

But despite the appalling way his brother treated him, he did still actually care about him – a great deal. If Don were ever to lose Jess to anyone but Bruce, he would cope with it, eventually. But if he lost her to his brother, it would destroy Don and any chance of a reconciliation between them along with it. So all he could have with Jess was friendship. He fully accepted that, but it didn't stop him from feeling sad.

Chapter Eleven

'You're looking well, Babs,' commented Jess one evening when she was visiting her friend in the bedsit where she now lived. 'Pregnancy seems to suit you.'

'Give over, Jess,' came Babs' baleful response. 'I feel like a constipated hippo, and I know I look like one.'

'No you don't,' Jess assured her staunchly. 'You look nice – a bit plumper, that's all.'

'*A bit plumper?*' She made a face. 'Come off it. I'll have to hire a crane to get me up the stairs soon.'

'Honestly,' laughed Jess, 'you don't half exaggerate. You're not that big.'

'Considering the fact that I've still got three months to go, I'm enormous,' Babs pointed out, grinning wryly. 'I dread to think what size I'll be by the end.'

'Perhaps it'll slow down at a certain point in the pregnancy,' suggested Jess.

'It damned well needs to,' was Babs' spirited response. 'The rate I'm expanding at the moment, before long I won't be able to get through the door.'

Jess grinned at her friend's tendency to overstate. 'You've a long way to go before there's any danger of your getting stuck in the doorway.'

'I hope you're right,' Babs said. 'I could be stuck there for days before anyone found me, being up here in the attic.'

'You'd soon make yourself heard,' smiled Jess, going along with the joke. 'They'd hear your shouts at Paddington Station.'

'True,' grinned Babs.

'Anyway, changing the subject,' began Jess, 'how's the job going?' Babs had left the Burton troupe and now worked in a greasy spoon café just around the corner from here in a Paddington backstreet.

She shrugged. 'It seems a bit dull after being on the stage, naturally,' she replied, her tone determinedly cheerful, 'but it pays the rent. Beggars can't be choosers and they don't mind that I'm pregnant. As long as I can fry bacon and make tea I can stay for as long as I like.' A mischievous gleam came into her eyes. 'To be perfectly honest, Jess, I don't think they'd care if I dropped the sprog in the staff room and went straight back on duty. That's the sort of place it is – a bit rough and ready – but it'll do for me.'

Sipping her coffee from a cracked mug, Jess cast a worried eye around the cheerless little attic room with its dingy, yellowing walls and dreadful furnishings. There was a small sink and gas ring in the corner, a double bed, two scruffy brown armchairs, which they were sitting in, and a scratched old table suffused with stains. Even a smattering of Babs' personal photographs and knick-knacks failed to make it seem like a home. To add to Jess's concern was the fact that Babs had to climb three flights of stairs to get to it.

'Look, I know how much you value your independence, and the last thing I want to do is encroach upon that,' Jess ventured with caution. 'But I hate the idea of you living here on your own. I know you won't even consider the idea of coming to stay with us but if you were to get a place somewhere nearer, at least I could call to see you more often to make sure you're all right. The streets around Ealing Broadway are riddled with houses converted into bedsits.'

'At a much higher rent than I pay for this, too, I should think,' was Babs' answer to that. 'I'll be fine here, honestly. You've no need to worry about me. It's cheap and they're not fussy. They don't mind about the baby. That's the important thing. At least I don't have to worry about getting chucked out when it arrives.'

'There isn't much in the way of facilities for a baby, though, is there?' Jess felt compelled to point out.

'No. But people have managed with less,' Babs rather wearily replied. 'It's a roof over my head and it's better than a hostel. The child won't be born into luxury, that's for sure, but it'll just have to take its chances.'

Sensing that her friend would be irritated if she were to pursue the subject, Jess decided to concentrate on a more positive aspect of her pregnancy. 'So, what are you hoping for, a boy or a girl?'

'I couldn't care less,' Babs replied dully. 'It's going to be a bloody nuisance, whatever it is.'

It hurt Jess to hear her friend speak like this, especially as she'd been so thrilled initially. 'I'm sure you'll feel differently when it arrives,' she suggested hopefully.

'I very much doubt it,' Babs said with a shrug. 'But can we talk about something else? I try not to think too much about the future because it's too damned depressing.' She sipped her coffee, cradling her mug in her hands. 'How's the dance school coming along now? Are you getting on all right in your new hall?'

'Yeah, it scrubbed up very well. Hilda and I really went to town on it.'

'Good. I'm glad it's worked out for you, kid. I know how much you enjoy your classes.'

'We're putting on a little show one evening soon,' Jess went on. 'Just to give the kids a chance to show off what they've learned to relatives and so on. It'll give them some experience of performing, and should be fun. They're all very excited, and the mums are busy making their costumes.'

'It takes you back, doesn't it?' Babs said wistfully. 'I was in a good few dancing school shows myself when I was little.'

A sudden thought came into Jess's mind. 'Do you fancy coming along?' she asked eagerly. 'I'd love you to be there to see my little band of hopefuls do their stuff.'

Babs shook her head and said quickly, 'Thanks for asking, kid, but I don't go out these days, only to work.'

'This would be a nice change for you then,' Jess pointed out with gentle persistence.

'Sorry, but no.' Babs was beginning to sound edgy.

'You might enjoy it and it'll do you good to get out.'

'Look,' Babs began, seething with irritation now, 'I know you mean well and I appreciate your concern but I'm absolutely fine and I don't need to be patronised. If I wanted to go out I'd go but I don't so I'll stay at home, thank you very much.'

Smarting from her acid tone, Jess was quick to apologise. 'Sorry. I didn't mean to sound patronising.'

Babs clutched her head with both hands. 'No, it's me who should apologise,' she said, looking at Jess with remorse. 'I'm a selfish cow and I shouldn't have blasted off at you like that. It's nice of you to invite me to your show and I didn't mean to seem ungrateful. It's just that . . . well, I don't feel like going out much at the moment. I'm shattered in the evenings after dragging this extra weight around all day.'

'I understand.' Jess paused thoughtfully. 'Look, I know I shouldn't interfere but I hate to think of you being here on your own, coping with your problems. I wish you'd let me do something to help.'

There was a brief hiatus before Babs responded with an explanation. 'When I realised that I was going to be on my own with this pregnancy, I decided right away that it was my problem and I would deal with it without draining on other people.' Her expression became grave. 'And that's exactly what I'm doing. I got myself into this mess and I'll get myself through it.'

'Everyone needs a little help at some time in their life,' Jess pointed out.

'And if I need help I'll ask for it.'

'Oh, yeah,' said Jess with friendly cynicism. 'Knowing you, you'd have to be desperate before you'd do that.'

Babs shrugged. 'Maybe. But it's just the way I am.'

'Yes, it is your way to be independent, I won't argue with that,' agreed Jess. 'But it isn't your way to shut yourself off from your friends; never going out or seeing anyone from one week to another. You used to be the life and soul of the party. I realise that the pregnancy is making you tired but that's no reason to become a recluse.'

'Now you're exaggerating,' Babs denied. 'I'm with people all day at work.'

'Friends, I mean.'

'I see you.'

'Only because I turn up on your doorstep uninvited.' Jess made an absolute point of visiting Babs as often as she could, no matter how busy she was. 'If I didn't do that I'd never see you. I bet I'd have to wait a long time for you to get in touch with me.'

Babs emitted a heavy sigh. 'I wouldn't ever lose touch with you, kid. I promise you that. But something happened to me when Dickie dumped me,' she tried to explain. 'It dragged the heart out of me, somehow, and left me feeling so screwed up inside, I just don't feel as though I want to see anyone.'

'I could kill that bugger.' Jess's voice rose as she was reminded of Dickie. 'I don't suppose he's done the decent thing and offered you any financial support for his child?'

'He doesn't even know where I am,' Babs informed her. 'And that's how I want it to stay. I'll never get through this unless he's out of my life altogether.'

'He should face up to his responsibilities.'

'Of course he should,' agreed Babs. 'And if I made enough of a fuss he probably would – to keep me quiet if nothing else.' She paused, looking into space for a moment before focusing her gaze on her friend. 'But that isn't what I want.'

'But it will be so hard for you, with no financial help from him,' Jess reminded her gently.

'Yeah, I'm fully aware of that. But there's more to this than just the practicalities,' she tried to explain. 'It's an emotional thing.' She pointed to her heart, looking sad. 'A horrible ache deep inside there. I know this'll sound crazy, and I don't understand it myself, but his doing the dirty on me didn't stop me loving him, even though I hate him too. I can only stay strong if I never see him and act as though he doesn't exist. If I so much as hear his voice I'll go to pieces.'

'I understand.' Jess was very subdued.

'You say you want to help me,' Babs went on. 'Well, the best way you can do that is to talk about something other than the abysmal state of my life. Tell me all your news.'

'OK,' agreed Jess, and went on to tell her about the recent addition to the family.

But although she appeared to cheer her friend up with light-hearted tales of a canine nature, Jess wasn't fooled by her false laughter. Babs was in the depths of hell and there didn't seem to be a damned thing Jess could do about it.

'He's like a different boy, Hilda,' Jess told her friend as they walked to the

166

Broadway together one cold and misty November evening; they were going to the hall to work out how many people they could seat for the show. 'He seems happier altogether; not nearly so stroppy. It's amazing.'

'And you reckon it's all down to the dog?'

'I know it sounds a bit fanciful but I think it must be,' Jess replied. 'He absolutely adores Doughnut, and seemed to change the minute he clapped eyes on him.'

'I've heard of this sort of thing before – people having their life transformed by an animal,' Hilda remarked. 'It could be it was just what he needed at this stage in his life. A difficult time, adolescence – full of uncertainty and humiliation. They're betwixt and between – unsure of themselves and easily influenced by other kids. Losing his mum couldn't have helped, either.'

'Well, all I can say is, that from the day Doughnut arrived at the house, Ronnie became less difficult. He seems to have appointed himself as the dog's official keeper; does everything for him when he's at home and tears home from school to see him. None of that hanging about on the way home with those awful boys he was so friendly with. He feeds the dog, takes him for walks, brushes him, talks to him. Nothing's too much trouble as far as Doughnut is concerned. He's so gentle with him too. It's a treat to see.'

'I know. I've seen how he is with him. He's putting on weight.' Hilda chuckled. 'The dog, that is.'

'His coat's improved too now that he's having regular meals and proper care,' Jess told her. 'Ronnie's always buying him special dog biscuits from his pocket money. He rarely goes out without him; would take him to school if he could.' She shook her head. 'Honestly, Hilda, I didn't think it was possible for anyone to change so much and so suddenly. I hope it lasts. That boy had been a headache to us all for long enough.'

'Perhaps having something to love and care for has given him confidence in himself and that's reflected in his general behaviour,' suggested Hilda.

'I'm no expert on psychology but I suppose it must be something like that,' agreed Jess as they turned into the Broadway, bathed in a fluorescent glow from the main road streetlighting, and hazy on this misty night. Some of the shop windows were already dressed with Christmas decorations. 'Just to give you an idea of how much he's changed, he even managed to be civil to Don the other day. He still doesn't like him but at least he isn't rude to him now.'

'That must make life a lot easier for you.'

'Not half. It was agonising before.' Jess paused thoughtfully. 'Don't get me wrong, Ronnie hasn't turned into a plaster saint or anything. He still teases the life out of his sister, leaves his part of the bedroom like a tip and is full of youthful arrogance like any other kid of his age. But at least

167

he isn't like a time bomb waiting to explode around the house any more. I'm keeping my fingers crossed that it'll last.'

Hilda said she hoped so too, and the two women turned their mind to the job in hand as they made their way through the yard at the back of Bruce's shop.

'Nice of Bruce to let us come along to the hall when he isn't here, isn't it?' Hilda mentioned as Jess put the spare key he had lent them into the lock.

'Yes, it is. He seems to be taking a real interest in our little dance school,' said Jess. 'He can't do enough to help.'

'I think he's a smashing bloke.'

'Me too,' said Jess, and they made their way inside and up the stairs.

It was Sunday afternoon and Ronnie was walking the dog in Churchfields when he was faced with an unwelcome meeting.

'Well, well,' said Shifter in a mocking tone. 'If it ain't old Molly Mollitt.'

'Wotcha, Molly,' added Nifty.

'Hi,' said Ronnie.

Shifter cast a disapproving eye in Doughnut's direction. 'If you wanted to get a dog, you should have got a decent-looking mutt,' he sneered. 'Not one that looks as if it's just crawled out of somebody's dustbin.'

'He doesn't look like that at all,' objected Ronnie. 'He looks really good now.' He was immensely proud of Doughnut's improved condition but this confrontation had sent him into such a panic he wasn't brave enough to make too much of a stand.

'If you think that, you wanna get your eyes tested, mate,' said Shifter.

'Yeah,' agreed his pal.

'Anyway, we don't wanna waste time talking about some pathetic mongrel,' Shifter told him. 'We wanna know why you've been avoiding us.'

'Yeah,' added the other one. 'We take a dim view of being ignored.'

'We don't like it at all,' persisted Shifter. 'In fact, we don't tolerate it.'

'I was grounded for ages after the scam at Dean's Stores,' explained Ronnie, his old fear of them making him tremble inside, 'and since then I've been busy.'

'You've been keeping well away from us at school,' Shifty mentioned disapprovingly.

'Well, we're not in the same class, are we?' The other two were in the lowest grade at the secondary modern; Ronnie was in the highest. He'd been studiously avoiding them ever since the scam at Dean's Stores, partly because he didn't want to get into any more trouble, and also because their appeal for him had faded to the extent that he couldn't think what he had ever seen in them. He longed to tell them to go away and leave him alone but couldn't quite muster the courage.

'That never stopped you looking for us before during break,' Shifter pointed out. 'We always used to see you in the playground but you seem to prefer your old mates these days.'

'As they're in the same class as me, it's only natural we'd hang out together.'

'Oh, yeah?' came Shifter's mocking tones. 'You used to say they were all creeps.'

'Maybe I did think that at one time—'

'But you don't think that now?' Shifter cut in.

Ronnie hesitated, striving for the mettle to be honest with them. 'No, I don't think that now,' he managed to utter finally, without sounding too terrified.

Shifter took a loud breath, shaking his head slowly. 'Ooh, I don't like the sound of that one little bit,' he told him. 'We don't like being dropped, do we, Nift?'

'Not only do we not like it, we don't put up with it,' his mate agreed.

'I think you're going to have to do something to keep us sweet, Molly,' threatened Shifter. 'We can be really awesome when we're angry.'

'That's right,' put in his shadow.

'And we're angry with you.'

'Very angry,' added the other one.

'We think you're avoiding us because you haven't got the bottle to hang out with people like us – people who aren't scared of a bit of danger,' accused Shifter.

'Is that right?' said Ronnie, clinging for dear life to his courage. 'So what was I doing at Dean's Stores then? I proved I had bottle then. I'm not doing anything else.'

'You are, you know,' corrected Shifter.

'That's what you think, mate.'

Shifter moved towards Ronnie but had cause to shrink back quickly when Doughnut barked, then growled; he was straining at the leash to protect his master.

'Bloody dog,' cursed Shifter, glaring at the animal. 'Get that mangy mutt away from me.'

'You're not scared of a pathetic mongrel who looks as though he's just crawled out of someone's dustbin, surely,' challenged Ronnie, courage rising.

'Course, I'm not, but that thing's wild . . .'

'It needs putting down,' declared Nifty as Doughnut's growls grew fiercer. 'I'd shoot the bugger if I had a gun.'

Shifter turned away and looked around until he found a large stone, which he aimed hard at the dog, hitting him on the back and making him yelp. Instantly Ronnie became fearless. Commanding the dog to stay, he let go of the lead and lunged towards Shifter.

'Don't you dare hurt my dog,' he hissed, grabbing hold of Shifter and wrestling him to the ground while Nifty stood aside, watching in astonishment and Doughnut barked like mad. Strengthened by his love for the dog, Ronnie held Shifter down firmly by his arms. 'I've finished with you and your mate and want nothing more to do with either of you – *ever.*'

'Here, get off of me.' He was wriggling and twisting to get free but all to no avail. In defence of his beloved pet, Ronnie was invincible. 'Do something, Nift.'

But Nifty didn't fancy the idea of a dog bite, and was standing well back.

'You're just a couple of wasters,' Ronnie went on, pinning the struggling Shifter to the ground. 'So leave me alone in future. Or you'll get more of this. And if you ever come near my dog again, you'll have a long spell in hospital. Understand?'

No reply.

'Understand?' repeated Ronnie in a harder tone.

'Yeah, yeah, just get off of me,' Shifter conceded at last.

Ronnie got up feeling ten feet tall as his tormentors scurried away. He was somewhat dismayed, however, to discover that the rumpus had attracted a crowd; people were out enjoying the winter sunshine and the clear blue skies, albeit that there was a frosty nip in the air. But even the unwelcome sight of Mr and Mrs Pickles didn't lessen his immense satisfaction in standing up to Shifter and Nifty at last. He knew instinctively that he wouldn't have any more trouble from them and it felt *so good.*

'What a disgusting display of loutish behaviour, Ronnie Mollitt,' rebuked Ada Pickles as Ronnie went down on his haunches to calm his troubled dog, who was still barking. 'Fighting like a ruffian in a public park. I shall see to it that your father gets to hear about this.'

Before Ronnie had a chance to respond there was an intervention from a man he knew by sight to be the owner of the new men's shop in the Broadway. 'I saw the whole thing,' he told Ada. 'The boy was protecting his dog and no one can blame him for that. One of those yobs threw a ruddy great stone at it.'

'Be that as it may, this is a public park where decent people should be able to walk in peace on a Sunday afternoon,' declared the outraged Ada. 'We don't come out walking to see boys rolling about on the ground brawling. It's nothing short of a disgrace.'

'Calm down, dear,' put in her peace-loving husband. 'The boy was provoked. He was looking out for his dog, that's all. There's no need to bother Charlie with it. Boys will be boys.'

'Delinquents, the lot of 'em,' she pronounced. 'You haven't heard the last of this, young Ronnie Mollitt.'

And with that she marched off, muttering to her husband about the degenerate behaviour of young people these days.

'Are you all right, son?' enquired Bruce as Ronnie dusted himself off, having quietened Doughnut.

'Yeah, I'm OK. Thanks for sticking up for me.'

'That's all right.'

Ronnie made a face. 'I won't half cop it at home when Mrs Pickles has had her say,' he told him gloomily. 'My pocket money'll be confiscated for at least a month. And I probably won't be allowed out after school until after Christmas.'

'I'll put in a good word for you, if you like,' offered Bruce. 'I know your dad and your sister. I'll make sure they know the truth about what happened.'

'Ooh, would you?' said Ronnie gratefully.

'Course I will.'

'It was lucky for me that you came along when you did,' Ronnie went on to say. 'At least I'll have someone on my side.'

'I wouldn't normally be over this way on a Sunday. I was at the shop because I'm behind with the office work, and I got so fed up with it, I thought: to hell with it, let's go for a walk.' Bruce kneeled down and fondled the dog's head. 'My word, you've come on, haven't you, boy?'

'You know Doughnut?'

'Yeah, I know him. I was with your sister when he limped into her life,' Bruce explained. 'He was in a sorry state then. You've done wonders with him.'

'Thanks.'

'If you're going home we may as well walk back together,' Bruce suggested casually. 'The sooner we tell your folks your side of the story the better, I reckon. That woman looked as though she couldn't wait to drop you in it.'

'She's a neighbour of ours – a bit of a dragon.'

'I gathered that.' With Doughnut trotting beside them, they made their way across the park, conversation flowing easily.

'I suppose you'll be leaving school soon,' assumed Bruce.

'Next summer.'

'Are you going into the family business.'

'Not likely.'

'You don't fancy following in your father's footsteps then?'

'No. I'd rather do something different.'

'Want to establish your own identity, eh?'

'I suppose so,' replied Ronnie, who hadn't thought about it in any depth.

'Have you anything particular in mind?'

'Not really,' he confessed. 'But I've still got plenty of time to think about it.'

'True.'

'I really hope Dad doesn't stop my pocket money because I've been in

171

a fight,' mentioned Ronnie as they approached Park Street. 'I'm going to need every penny I can get with Christmas coming up and all the presents to buy. I want to get Doughnut a really good collar with his name engraved on it.'

'Perhaps when your dad knows that you were provoked by those boys, he'll let you off lightly.'

'He might do but I'm not banking on it,' Ronnie said. 'He doesn't approve of me fighting under any circumstances. So he's bound to hit the roof.'

'You'll just have to hope for the best then.' Bruce didn't consider it his place to comment further on the subject. The mention of Ronnie's finances had set him thinking, though. 'Do you fancy making a bit of extra dough in your Christmas holidays?' he asked.

'Phew, not half,' the boy enthused. 'How?'

'I'm looking for someone to help in my shop during the Christmas rush,' Bruce explained. 'It'll be pretty boring stuff – just running errands, making the tea, tidying up, packing the customers' goods and so on. But it would be some extra cash for you.'

'Cor, that would be smashing,' enthused Ronnie without a moment's hesitation.

Bruce had a sudden thought. 'As long as your dad doesn't need you in his shop.'

'No, he won't need me because he and Jess can manage.' Ronnie frowned. 'Though if I'm grounded because I've been fighting, I won't be able to do anything.'

'Let me know what happens, and if you are able to work for me, I'll have a word with your dad about it because I don't want to do anything unless he's happy about it. But, all being well, you've got yourself a holiday job.'

'Thanks ever so much,' the boy enthused.

What a day this was turning out to be, he thought. Not only had he got Shifter and Nifty off his back, he'd got access to some extra dosh too, as long as he wasn't confined to the house for weeks. Still, even if that did happen, the fight with Shifter had been worth it.

Hilda met Ada Pickles by chance in the haberdashery department of Rowse's department store in West Ealing.

'I'm getting some ribbons for young Libby Mollitt's costume in the show Jess is putting on,' explained Hilda, who was waiting for her change to come down the chute from the cashier's office. 'They always have a good selection in here.'

'I've just popped in for some buttons for a cardigan I've knitted for our Maureen's eldest,' Ada informed her.

'Are all the family well?' enquired Hilda politely.

'Yeah, they're all right.' She shot Hilda a look. 'Jess is putting on a show then?'

172

'That's right,' nodded Hilda. 'Just a little one for the parents and friends of the pupils. It gives the kids something special to work for. They're all very excited.'

'Talking of the Mollitts,' Ada pursed her lips and sniffed, 'they've really gone down hill now, haven't they?'

'Not that I know of.' Hilda's defences were up. 'What makes you say that?'

'We all know that their standards have been steadily slipping ever since Joy died but I think they've gone altogether.'

'In what way exactly?'

'With Charlie spending all his spare time down the pub and letting the kids do just as they like, of course,' Ada went on heatedly. 'It's getting on for a year and a half since he lost his wife. It's high time he pulled himself together.'

'He has . . . up to a point.' In all honesty she had to add that qualification. Although Charlie had improved to a certain extent and spent less time at the pub, he still wasn't the same man he'd been when his wife was around.

'I haven't noticed it,' Ada declared forcefully. 'He always seems to be in a world of his own whenever I see him. Usually stinks of booze an' all.'

'Charlie does his best,' said Hilda, who would never admit her own disapproval to Ada on principle and couldn't understand why Ada persisted in bitching about the Mollitts to her. Surely she must know by now, that Hilda would never speak ill of them. 'Personally, I think he and Jess are doing a good job between them.'

'Those kids are at an age when they need their father to keep them in order but he lets them do exactly what they like,' Ada snorted. 'No discipline whatever. That Ronnie's a right little heathen.'

'That isn't fair,' Hilda disagreed heatedly. 'He went through a difficult patch but he's a lot better now.'

'Better, my Aunt Fanny,' ranted Ada, really into her stride now. 'I saw him fighting in Churchfields only the other day. Rolling about on the ground like a ruddy hooligan. And how does his father react when I take the trouble to tell him about it? He turns round to me and says the boy was just protecting his dog from yobs and he had every right to give the other boy a hiding. I mean, honestly . . . instead of punishing him, he was praising him! What sort of a way is that for a responsible father to carry on, eh? That boy will be in Borstal before very much longer, you mark my words, Hilda.'

'I don't agree with you.'

'I might have known you'd side with them.'

'Why say these horrid things about the Mollitts to me when you know they're friends of mine and I always take their side?' Hilda asked.

'I've a right to voice my opinion,' Ada asserted.

173

'And I've a right to mine,' returned Hilda. 'I happen to think the Mollitts are a smashing family.' Mercifully, her change arrived and the sales assistant handed it to her with the receipt. 'But I must go now. I hope you find some nice buttons. Ta-ta.'

'Ta-ta.'

Hilda left the store and joined the bus queue. Charlie Mollitt didn't always find favour with her but she did think he'd made the right decision in taking Ronnie's side about the fight in Churchfields, which she'd already heard about from Jess. That dog had done wonders for Ronnie, and vice versa. The dog must be in seventh heaven with Ronnie as its champion. It was a family pet but everyone knew that it was Ronnie's dog. Well done, Charlie, she thought as she got on the bus.

'You're spoiling me rotten tonight, Don,' said Jess as the two of them lingered over coffee after a meal in a restaurant in Leicester Square. 'You've really pushed the boat out.'

'I thought you deserved a treat.'

'Oh, and why is that?'

'Just because you're a beautiful woman and I felt like spoiling you,' he told her.

'Spoil away, boy,' she chuckled, winking at him, her hair falling loosely around her face, the red jersey dress she was wearing looking good with her dark colouring. 'You certainly won't get any objections from me.'

'I didn't think I would.'

The restaurant – which was new and furnished in contemporary style – overlooked the square where the Saturday night crowds were out in force: walking along in groups, studying menus in restaurant windows, laughing and pushing, the atmosphere of gaiety increased by the dazzling Christmas decorations. Everyone was swathed in coats and scarves but didn't seem bothered by the cold weather.

Jess had thought that she and Don were going to the cinema locally this evening but Don had sprung a surprise on her by driving them into the West End.

He was looking smart but more than a touch middle-aged in a blazer and grey flannels, his hair slicked down with Brylcreem. He was being especially charming this evening. The conversation had flowed naturally over the meal and the atmosphere between them now was warm and tender.

'Seriously though, Don,' Jess said, reaching over and touching his hand in a gesture of affection, 'you don't need to take me to the West End to wine and dine me. I enjoy myself wherever we go when we're out together.'

He gave her an odd look. 'Actually there is a particular reason why I organised something special for tonight,' he informed her, looking solemn.

'Oh, really? Have you had a promotion at work or something?' she asked him lightly.

'No, nothing like that.'

'Come on then, spill the beans,' she urged. 'Don't keep me in suspense.'

He reached into his pocket and took out a small box, which he opened and held out to her. 'This is the reason, Jess,' he said, looking at her lovingly. 'I hope you don't mind my choosing it for you.'

'Well, no . . .'

'I wanted it to be a surprise but the jeweller has agreed that we can change it if you don't like it.'

Staring at the solitaire diamond in a bed of red satin, she said, 'It's beautiful, Don.'

'I'm hoping you'll do me the honour of wearing it on your engagement finger,' he told her ardently. 'Will you marry me, Jess?'

Surprise was her immediate reaction. She'd known Don was serious about her but hadn't expected him to propose this soon; didn't think he was ready yet to replace his much-loved wife. There was a feeling of joy too, albeit not ecstasy, but it was clouded by personal uncertainty and family problems lurking at the back of her mind. 'Oh, Don,' she said, looking into his questioning eyes, 'I wasn't expecting anything like this, not yet anyway. I mean, it isn't as though we've known each other all that long.'

'I didn't expect it either,' he confessed. 'After Sheila died, I didn't think I'd ever want to share my life with anyone again. But you've changed everything. You've given me a reason to get up in the morning.'

'Don, I'm very flattered but—'

'Before you start worrying about that family of yours, I know you're not free to leave home just now – at least you think you're not because of your devotion to them all,' he said, pre-empting the objections he'd guessed she would make. 'And I'm not suggesting that we get married right away. But in a year or two you might feel able to fly the nest. The kids are almost grown now and the time has surely got to come when you will feel you can have a life of your own. But there'll be no pressure from me, I promise. If we're engaged, I'll be happy with that – for a while, anyway.'

It was a huge relief that he wasn't going to try to push her into an early marriage. The reason his proposal made her feel trapped must be because she wasn't ready actually to marry him; she needed more time to get used to his serious ways. 'I really am quite overwhelmed, Don,' she told him.

'You'll make me a very happy man if you'll agree to wear the ring,' he proclaimed. 'You mean everything to me.'

'And you mean a lot to me.' Something she couldn't quite put her finger on was causing her to hesitate in giving him the answer he was waiting for.

'Perhaps you need a little time to think about it,' he suggested helpfully.

Why didn't she grab the opportunity with both hands? She asked herself. Here was a good man offering her marriage with no immediate pressure, just the security of knowing that he was there for her, and a wedding could happen whenever she was ready. How many women received that sort of an offer? She trusted him never to betray her as Jack had. He was a decent man and she'd be a fool to refuse him. Pushing lingering feelings of suffocation to the back of her mind because it seemed so cruel, she said softly, 'No, Don, I don't need time to think about it. I'd be honoured to wear your ring.'

'I'm the luckiest man in London,' he said, eyes shining with triumph. 'You've made me so happy.'

As he slipped the ring on to her finger, the hovering doubt she hadn't been able to identify suddenly became clear. Was he putting his ring on her finger just to make sure of her against Bruce? Was the ring simply a 'Keep off' sign for his brother? She remembered him once saying that Bruce wouldn't be deterred by a couple's commitment to each other, so surely an engagement ring wouldn't make him feel any safer. No, it was unkind of her even to think such a thing.

'I'm the lucky one,' she said. 'And I'm happy too.'

'I think this calls for champagne, don't you?' he said, looking around for the waiter.

'That would be lovely,' she smiled.

The hall was beginning to fill up with people and the anteroom room that Jess was using as a communal dressing room for the performers was buzzing with nervous excitement as the children got changed into their costumes; the smaller ones were assisted by their mothers, with Libby on hand to help out too. Every child in the school was taking part in the show, albeit that the little ones had nothing too complicated to do.

Jess was standing by the piano with Hilda, and Bruce, who had come upstairs to the hall after closing his shop to make sure all was well and to wish them luck. He had been completely unprepared for what Jess asked of him on a sudden impulse.

'Compere the show – me?' he said in astonishment. 'Oh, no, Jess. You can count me out on that one.'

'Oh, go on Bruce,' she persisted in a light-hearted manner.

'No.' He was adamant. 'I was only too happy to do the other things that needed doing – organise the hire of extra chairs and find a portable stage for you and so on – but I'm not being master of ceremonies as well. Absolutely no way!'

'I reckon you'd make a smashing compere,' muttered Hilda, sorting through her music.

'Of course he would,' added Jess, giving him an encouraging smile.

'With your personality, you're absolutely made for the job.' The idea had popped unexpectedly into her mind a few minutes ago and she'd come right out with it, such was her desire for the show to be a success. 'That's the only reason I'm asking, because I know that your gift of the gab will help things to go with a swing. Of course, I realise it's short notice.'

'It doesn't come much shorter than the last minute,' he pointed out, giving her a wry grin.

'I planned to do it myself but when you turned up, it suddenly came to me that you'd do the job a whole lot better,' she explained.

He shot her a look. 'Flattery won't work, Jess.' He was smiling but firm.

'I'm amazed that you're not jumping at the chance,' put in Hilda craftily. 'The way you've been taking such an interest this past few weeks, helping us with the practical side of things, I should have thought you'd want to be involved on the night.'

'Taking an interest is one thing, actually taking part is quite another.' He was determined not to give in.

Libby – stunningly attired in the red sequined costume with tight bodice and floaty skirt that she was wearing in the opening number, her face liberally spread with stage make-up – came over in search of some assistance backstage, and joined in the light-hearted discussion. 'Please say you'll do it,' she pleaded. 'Then Jess can concentrate on helping me with the kids. There's an awful lot to do and I've still got my own headdress to fix.'

'All we're asking you to do is introduce the various items,' said Jess. 'It isn't as though we're asking you to do a tap dance or anything.'

'I wouldn't put that past you either, if you thought it would help the show,' he said, grinning. 'You're a very determined woman.'

'I do have certain standards, though,' she giggled. 'And I'm not sure that the spectacle of you on stage tap dancing is something I'd wish to see.'

'Thank God for that.'

'You two keep on at him until he does agree to do it, then one of you come and give me a hand,' said Libby, before dashing off to attend to something in the dressing room.

'Honestly I only popped in before leaving to see if everything was all right for the tenants of my hall,' he said with a slow smile. 'I'd have steered well clear if I'd known I was going to get nagged and bullied by you lot.'

'Why don't you want to do it anyway?' Jess wondered.

He gave an eloquent sigh. 'Isn't it obvious?'

'No.'

'I'd feel like an idiot,' he explained.

'Why?'

'Because this is no place for a man.'

177

'Rubbish,' disagreed Jess.

'It's a woman's thing,' he stated categorically. 'The place is crawling with women and little girls, hardly a man in sight. As I told you just now, I only popped in to see how you were getting on. I didn't intend to stay. And I'm not going to be made to look like a prune by you lot.'

'There are some men here,' mentioned Hilda, glancing towards the chairs where a few of the dads had dutifully come along with their wives.

'Well, I'm not joining them. I'm getting out of here sharpish,' he declared.

'Coward,' laughed Jess.

'I'd sooner be a coward than a laughing stock,' he riposted.

'You wouldn't be.'

Over the past few weeks Jess had got quite pally with Bruce. She and her helpers had spent more time at the hall than usual, for special rehearsals and preparations for the big night, and he'd taken an interest in the show over and above what would normally be expected of a landlord. They'd usually arrived in the early evening before he'd left the shop and he'd stayed on and made himself available for practical tasks like furniture shifting, seeming to want to be involved. She'd enjoyed his company; had found the repartee between them very uplifting and just what she needed to lower the tension that inevitably arose in the production of any show; professional or amateur, the nerves got just as frayed.

She'd grown fonder of him than she dared to admit. It was difficult not to warm to his jokey charm and generosity of spirit. Hilda and Libby thought he was a great bloke too. Jess didn't try to hide from Don the fact that she got on well with his much-loathed brother, but neither did she emphasise it, or mention the extent of Bruce's helpfulness these past few weeks. Ignorance definitely was bliss in this particular instance.

'I'll be off then,' said Bruce, turning to leave.

She touched his arm in a restraining gesture. 'Being serious for a minute,' she said, wanting to put the record straight. 'Thanks for everything you've done for us. You've been great. We had no right to try and twist your arm into doing the compering when you've done more than enough already.'

He shrugged. 'Don't worry about it,' he smiled.

She wrinkled her nose. 'You're a star,' she grinned. 'But I must stop yapping now and get on. There are a million and one things I have to do. See you, Bruce.'

'Good luck. Hope all goes well.'

'Me too, and thanks.'

He strode towards the door and Jess turned to Hilda for a quick last-minute run through the music for the show. She was just about to go to the dressing room when Bruce reappeared.

'OK, I'll do it,' he said with a sigh of resignation. 'Give me the damned script.'

The two women beamed at him.

'It's very good of you,' praised Jess.

'You're a real gentleman,' added Hilda.

'Enough of all that old toffee.' He spread his hands in a helpless gesture. 'Why am I doing this?'

'Because you're a lovely fella?' suggested Jess.

'I'll second that,' added Hilda.

'You're a couple of con women,' he grinned. 'No man stands a chance against you.'

Over the next couple of hours the children danced their hearts out and did Jess proud on the portable stage Bruce had obtained and erected for them. They didn't have stage curtains, special lighting or much in the way of scenery. But the costumes were lovely, the dancing a joy to watch, and, having a raised platform meant that the performance could be seen by the whole of the audience.

There was the usual cluster of disasters: children getting the jitters and forgetting their steps. One little girl was sick, another was made helpless by a fit of nervous giggles in the middle of a routine and one of the tinies got so overexcited she wet herself.

But the show was an unqualified success, the warmth from the audience proved that. Afterwards Jess was inundated with compliments about the production.

'Thanks for being the compere, Bruce.' She had a quiet word with him when everyone except she and her helpers had gone and the latter were busy putting the chairs away. 'I know you only did it under protest but you were brilliant, and it left me free to do other things. I'm very grateful.'

'I rather enjoyed it, actually.' He gave her a grin. 'Even though you bullied me into it.'

Laughing, she thanked him again and hurried away to help the others with the last of the clearing up. Seeing her lovely face flushed with success and her eyes shining, he knew there was nothing he wouldn't do for her. Being with her so much this past few weeks had stirred something very special in him. But he couldn't tell her that, not ever; it was especially important now that she was officially engaged to Don. Trust me to fall for someone I can never have, he thought miserably.

179

Chapter Twelve

Christmas was a time of poignancy for the Mollitts again but emotions weren't quite so raw as last year – the first without Joy – so it was slightly less of an ordeal. As always, Hilda joined them for Christmas Day and Don came along too. Being the season of goodwill, Jess considered the idea of inviting Bruce as he didn't have family to go to. But care for the general good finally prevailed since bad feeling between the brothers would sour the atmosphere and make things awkward for everyone.

Babs declined Jess's invitation; said she was spending Christmas with someone from work. Jess guessed it was just an excuse and could hardly bear to think of her friend alone in that terrible bedsit. But as any hint of concern was seen by Babs' as charity and offended her independent nature, there was nothing Jess could do except continue to make it clear that she was there if Babs needed her. Once so gregarious, she seemed to become more of a loner every time Jess saw her. Deeply worried, she lived in hope that her pal might revert to her old self after the baby was born, when her hormones had settled down and she didn't have the pregnancy to contend with.

Despite Jess's very best endeavours, she didn't feel comfortable when Don was in the house. He got on well enough with her father but she sensed that he wasn't easy with the children's youthful exuberance; and his sombre personality definitely made them edgy. But even Ronnie – who was pleased with life in general at the moment, having been offered a Saturday job by Bruce as a result of his diligent approach to his work during the holidays – made a special effort.

It just didn't come off somehow, though. It wasn't a question of her siblings being rude or hostile; more that they just didn't know what to say to him, or him to them. Jess spared no effort to put him at ease, constantly striving to include him in the conversation and explain family jokes. But he didn't fit in and it must have been as obvious to him as it was to her. She hoped the awkwardness would recede with time. Family occasions would be awfully difficult otherwise, as he was going to be her husband.

Quite often over the holiday she found herself with happy thoughts of Bruce and the light-hearted atmosphere he'd created in the run-up to the show. Everything seemed to shine when he was around. For most people, a good rapport with a future relative would be cause for joy, she imagined. But not for her; not with the way Don felt about Bruce. There was also the added complication of her getting on rather too well with Bruce; in moments of honest introspection, she could admit that her feelings weren't entirely those of a sister-in-law. She tried not to feel bad about this, though, since natural impulses couldn't be helped. As long as she didn't act on them there was no harm done. She would never hurt Don in that way.

Despite her doubts about Don's place in the family, the holiday passed without any major upsets or serious rows. Even the twins seemed to bicker less over Christmas. A household without problems was a rare and wonderful thing for the Mollitts, and Jess revelled in it, hoping it would last.

It didn't. A week or so into the new school term she noticed a dramatic change in Todd. He was pale and anxious; seemed nervous about going to school and was unusually subdued when he got home.

'What's the matter, love?' she asked when he came in from school on the verge of tears and struggling not to show it.

'Nothin'.'

'There obviously is . . .'

'There isn't.'

'Is the work bothering you?' she asked kindly. 'Some difficult lesson perhaps?'

'No.'

'Just wondered if there's anything I can do to help?'

'No.' He was snappy, which was most unusual for him. 'Everything's fine.'

'We're not blind, Todd,' she persisted gently. 'Anyone can see that you've not been as happy with school since you went back after the Christmas holidays.'

He shrugged. 'Nobody jumps for joy about going to school,' he said dully.

'He's right there,' came Libby's wholehearted agreement.

'I'll say he is,' added Ronnie, who was busy foraging in the biscuit tin; he always headed straight for the larder when he got in from school.

'But Todd's always enjoyed it until now, haven't you, love?' Jess reminded them.

'It's probably all those grammar school drips getting up his nose,' suggested Ronnie, munching a ginger nut and looking at his brother thoughtfully. 'Am I right, mate?'

'I've told you there's nothing wrong,' he said through gritted teeth, angry colour rising in his cheeks.

'I should hate to see you when there is then,' joshed Ronnie. 'You've got a face like Libby's school drawers – long and dark and horrible.'

'You're disgusting,' objected his twin sister, flashing her eyes at him furiously. 'Tell him, Jess. Tell him to wash his mouth out.'

'Give over, you two, for goodness' sake,' admonished Jess. 'I'm trying to find out what's the matter with Todd—'

'Why can't you all mind your own business?' came a vociferous interruption from Todd before he slammed out of the room in an almost unprecedented show of temper.

He still seemed troubled the following week and refused to tell Jess what the problem was, or even to admit that there was a problem. It upset her to see this naturally sweet-natured child so miserable and she did everything she knew to coax it out of him.

'Honestly, what a family,' she confided to Hilda. 'We just get Ronnie sorted and another one of them starts acting up.'

'It's the age they're at,' suggested the other woman. 'It'll be just growing pains.'

'I'm not so sure it is just that with Todd,' Jess told her. 'I think he's been fighting and that isn't like him at all.'

'No, it isn't,' Hilda agreed worriedly. 'He's usually such an amiable little soul.'

'He broke his glasses the other day,' Jess went on to say. 'He says he dropped them but I don't believe that for a minute. They looked to me as though someone had stamped on them.'

'One of the other boys?' surmised Hilda. 'Do you think he's being bullied?'

'It has crossed my mind.' Jess chewed her lip. 'At first I thought perhaps he was having trouble with the work but now I suspect it's got more to do with the other kids.'

'The poor lad,' said Hilda.

'Do you think I should go to the school and find out if the teachers have noticed a change in him? Bullying does seem the most likely explanation for his unhappy state and I'm not having that, Hilda. I'll murder any little perisher who's giving my kid brother a hard time.'

Hilda's brow furrowed. 'If you do go the school, you'll have to be very discreet about it, love,' she advised. 'You could make things worse for him if that is what the problem is. If the bullies get to know you've been to the school they might think he's told tales on them and give him an even worse time.'

'Mm, there is that,' agreed Jess. 'But I can't just stand by and do nothing, can I?'

'No, you can't do that.' She considered the matter. 'Give it a bit longer, just to see if it blows over. If he's no better in a few days, have another chat with him and if he still refuses to tell you what's wrong, you'll have to go to the school to find out what's behind it. As you say, you can't just leave it.'

'I hate to see him so miserable,' Jess told her. 'He's always been such a chirpy kid, much easier than the twins, and he was so thrilled when he got into the gram.'

'I remember.'

'He was happy as a sand boy last term; seemed to settle in really well,' Jess continued thoughtfully. 'It's odd that it's now in his second term that there are problems. If there were going to be any, you'd expect them at the beginning, wouldn't you?'

'You would, yeah,' agreed Hilda. 'Still, it might just be something and nothing. You know what kids are like.'

Jess emitted a sigh. 'Do I ever? Honestly, if it isn't one thing it's another in our house.'

'The joys of family life, eh.'

'You can say that again,' replied Jess with a wry grin. 'Anyway, I'll take your advice and leave it for a few more days. I don't want to make things worse for him so I'll see how it goes.'

One evening that same week, Charlie was getting quietly sozzled at the bar of the Red Bear. He was thoroughly glad to see the back of Christmas. It reminded him too much of Joy and how different life had once been. The kids missed their mother, of course, but they had the resilience of youth on their side, and life was an adventure still to come for them. For him it was loneliness for as far ahead as he could see.

His children meant everything to him; if it wasn't for them he'd probably fall apart completely. Jess was a little diamond, the way she'd stepped into her mother's shoes. Maybe he didn't show her his appreciation as often as he should but his immense gratitude was all there, in his heart.

'Wotcha, Charlie boy,' said a voice beside him and, turning, he saw Vernon Peck, the owner of a sweetshop in Hanwell Broadway, and two other retail outlets in nearby suburbs.

'Hello, Vern. How's it going?'

'Not so bad, mate,' he replied. 'What are you having?'

'I was just leaving actually . . .'

'You've got time for a quick one,' Vernon egged him on, 'just to save me drinking alone.'

Charlie was by no means sober but he wasn't too far gone to remember that Jess would be out this evening; she was doing an extra dance class for the older children, and had said she would leave his meal ready for him to heat up when he got in. So his staying on here for a while longer wasn't going to upset her.

'OK. You've twisted my arm,' he conceded. 'I'll have a whisky, please.'

The two men got talking and Charlie lost count of the drinks he consumed.

'Fancy a game of darts, Charlie,' suggested Vernon. 'The board's free.'

'Yeah, if you like,' replied Charlie, who was mellow enough to agree to anything. 'I might be too squiffy to hit the board but I'll have a go, just for a laugh.'

'Loser pays for the drinks,' suggested Vernon as they made their way to the dartboard.

'Fair enough,' agreed Charlie.

Had Charlie been sober he might have been surprised to notice that he was beating Vernon hands down, since he'd never been much of a darts player. As it was, he was delighted at his excellent performance.

'I didn't realise you were so good at the game,' complimented Vernon.

'Me neither,' confessed Charlie.

Vernon suggested that they make it a bit more exciting by playing for money. 'A fiver,' he proposed.

'You're on,' Charlie approved.

After he'd won the game and pocketed the other man's money, Charlie said, 'I think it's time I was making a move.'

'Oh no you don't. You can't leave while you're on a winning streak. That just wouldn't be sportsmanlike,' chided Vernon. 'You must give me a chance to win my money back. It's the only decent thing to do.'

'I really ought to go . . .'

'We'll make the game shorter, if you like. We'll start at one hundred and one instead of three hundred and one.'

'Oh, go on then.'

'How about making this one even more interesting,' suggested Vernon. 'Let's raise the stakes – say two hundred quid.'

'Don't talk daft, man,' responded Charlie. 'I haven't got that sort of money going spare.'

'I'll make it easy for you then,' offered the other man. 'If I lose I'll pay you two hundred pounds in cash. If you lose you give me your newspaper licence. That way you don't have to find the dough.'

'You know I can't let that licence go,' protested Charlie in a slow drunken tone. 'We've been through it all before.'

'The way you've been playing tonight there's not a chance of your losing it, is there?' urged Vernon. 'You'll keep the licence and be two hundred quid better off.'

'No. My luck might change and I can't afford to lose my licence to sell newspapers,' said Charlie, though he was too inebriated really to care.

'Luck doesn't come into it,' pointed out the determined sweetshop owner. 'You've been beating me because you're better than me at the game. All I want is a chance to win back my pride. I'm feeling in the mood for a challenge.'

Charlie squinted at him through a drunken haze, still capable of remembering that Vernon had three shops in West London and wasn't short of a few quid. He had the look of affluence about him, with his big cigars and camel coat. Losing a couple of hundred pounds wouldn't make much difference to him. But winning that money would make a huge difference to Charlie. He would share it among his children. Even divided by four it would still be a nice little wad for each one as a gift. They were all at an age where they needed spare cash and his income didn't run to anything much beyond basic pocket money.

Jess could put her share towards her wedding trousseau, Libby could get some of the modern teenage clothes she was always yapping about lately, and he was sure that the other two wouldn't have any trouble finding a use for their portion. 'All right, you're on,' he agreed. 'Two hundred pounds against my licence to sell papers.'

'Right,' said Vernon, poising his dart ready to aim. 'The nearest to the bull's-eye starts. OK?'

Swaying slightly, Charlie nodded.

Vernon Peck had been after Charlie's licence to sell newspapers for years because it would enhance his turnover at the Hanwell shop. The legal right to sell papers was given only to traders within a certain distance of each other and the only way Vernon could ever obtain one was to buy Charlie's. But he'd never been willing to sell because it was the main part of his livelihood.

Being an astute and not particularly honest businessman, when Vernon had come into the pub this evening and seen Charlie standing at the bar on his own and already three sheets to the wind, he'd seen the perfect opportunity, not only to get his hands on Charlie's licence but to do so without handing over so much as a penny. As luck would have it, Vernon had never played darts in this particular pub so Charlie had no idea how good he was or how easy it was for him to seem hopeless when he needed to.

'Looks like I get first go then,' he said as Charlie's dart missed the board and fell to the floor.

Struck with horror, Jess stared at her father. 'Tell me it isn't true, Dad, please,' she implored him. 'For pity's sake tell me that you're just kidding and you haven't really gambled away our licence to sell newspapers.'

'I wish I could say that, love,' he said, a monumental hangover still burning in his head, 'but it wouldn't be true. I've lost the licence. God knows how I could have let it happen. But I got drunk and Vernon Peck conned it off me.'

'You fool, Dad, you bloody fool,' burst out Jess, her voice rising to a shout of despair. 'You know that Vernon Peck's been after that licence for years. How could you have been so stupid as to let him win it off you in a darts game?'

'It's all a bit hazy but I do remember bits of what happened and I reckon that he must have deliberately led me to believe he was no good at the game by losing at first,' he told her.

'The oldest trick in the book and you fell for it,' she admonished. 'Honestly, Dad, how could you?'

'We seemed like mates having a few drinks together so I wasn't on my guard,' he told her, thinking back, 'I thought I could win some money for

186

us. I'd had a bit to drink and I suppose I wasn't thinking straight.'

She was fierce in her rebuke. 'I really don't know how you could have made yourself that vulnerable when you've still got three kids of school age to support,' she told him.

'Because, as you say, I'm a bloody fool,' he sighed, hardly able to look her in the eyes. 'I'm so ashamed.'

'And so you damned well should be.'

It was the afternoon of the next day and Charlie had finally plucked up courage to make his confession, having struggled through the morning, guilt-ridden and hungover. They were in the staff room at the shop. Charlie was sitting at the table, whey-faced and shaky with the shock of what he'd done and the lingering effects of the excessive amount of alcohol. 'I only popped into the pub for a quick one after work. I didn't intend to stay.'

Jess was standing up, her face pinched with worry. 'How many times have I heard that?'

'All right, I know I've done wrong,' he said meekly. 'You've every right to be angry.'

'Angry?' she exploded. 'I'm absolutely furious.'

He sat there, hanging his head. The dog, who was asleep in his basket, stirred and emitted a low growl at the sound of raised voices. Jess fondled him for a moment to calm him and lowered her voice when she spoke. 'No one minds you having a drink, Dad,' she went on, feeling a stab of pity for him, despite everything. 'God knows, I know how bad you must have been feeling since Mum died. But having a companionable pint is one thing and drinking the pub dry is quite another. You've really dropped us in it this time.'

'I know.'

'So, tell me, what exactly are we supposed to live on,' she demanded, 'now that you've given away a large chunk of our livelihood?'

He clutched his sore head. 'I'll just have to work something out. It's my responsibility,' he muttered.

'It certainly is.' She wasn't going to be too easy on him; not this time.

'I'll think of something,' he said but he didn't have a clue at the moment.

She shot him a look. 'Perhaps Vernon will release you from the deal as you didn't know what you were doing when you entered into it,' she suggested hopefully. 'He might do it as a gesture of goodwill from one local trader to another.'

'Not a chance. Vernon's far too canny for that,' Charlie informed her. 'I've already tried it. I went round to see him this morning. He won't budge.'

'We'll soon see about that,' declared Jess, taking her coat off a hook on the back of the door and slipping into it. 'I won't be long. Listen for the shop bell while I'm out, please.' She paused and added a parting shot because she was so angry with him. 'If you're not too damned hungover to serve the customers, that is.'

'I won that newspaper licence fair and square and your father must honour the deal by signing it over to me,' insisted Vernon Peck, who'd ushered Jess into the office behind this shop rather than risk having customers get to know his private business. The mood she was in she might have blurted it out and made him seem like the villain of the piece. There was an assistant on duty behind the counter so he could leave things to her. 'I made that clear to him this morning when he came round here begging and pleading to have the arrangement cancelled.'

'But I'm asking you not to hold him to it, as a fellow trader,' Jess entreated, trying to keep it friendly at this stage. 'He just can't afford to lose his legal right to sell newspapers and periodicals. It's the mainstay of our business, as you very well know.'

A short fat man of about fifty with several chins, greying hair and puffy lips, Vernon had the look of good living about him and was dressed in an expensive-looking suit. 'If your father couldn't afford to lose, he shouldn't have entered into the wager,' he pointed out coolly.

'He wasn't in any condition to take on a challenge like that,' she said, 'and I think you knew that.'

'I can't be held responsible for another man's drinking habits,' objected Vernon. 'If people can't hold their liquor, they should stay off the stuff.'

Jess's attitude hardened as she realised what a slippery customer Vernon Peck was. 'You've been after that licence for years, that's common knowledge around here,' she told him, 'and I reckon you deliberately set out to get it off my dad last night. You got him drunk with that intention.'

'With respect, my dear, your father is quite capable of getting himself drunk without any help from anyone,' Vernon pointed out, his cold grey eyes resting on her superciliously. 'He was already well tanked up when I went into the pub. He's only got himself to blame if people take advantage of him.'

'So you admit that's what you did?' she accused.

'He's a grown man and he knows the score as far as bets and business are concerned.'

Deciding it was time to grovel, Jess said, 'Look, Mr Peck, my father has already taken a big enough knock with the death of my mother, so please don't make him lose his business too. Without the newspapers I doubt if we'll survive. Whereas you have several shops and you don't need our newspaper licence to stay in business.'

'A good businessman strives for more than just survival,' he announced smoothly. 'He aims to improve his profits and that's what being able to sell newspapers will do for me.'

'I'm asking you, not as a businessman but as a human being,' she went on, 'to release my father from the wager.'

'Nothing doing. Sorry.'

'But he has three children to support.'

'His responsibility, not mine,' he made clear. 'He should have thought about that before he agreed to do it.'

'You're a hard man.'

'You don't get a chain of shops by being soft,' he informed her coldly. 'I've done nothing illegal, nothing I'm ashamed of.'

'That doesn't say much for your values.'

'My values! That's rich.' He gave her a close look, eyes glinting icily, mouth set in a grim line. 'What about your father's values?' he queried. 'What's he doing spending his money at the pub if he's so worried about supporting his children?'

'He's been through a bad time,' she defended but knew it was a lame excuse. 'He needs some relaxation.'

'We all have bad times at some time or another, my dear,' he pointed out evenly. 'But we just have to pick ourselves up and get on with life.'

'Some people are better at it than others.'

'I agree. Anyway, your dad is going to have to show us all what he's really made of now that he's lost his newspaper licence because I am not going back on the deal we made last night.' He met her eyes. 'Now, if you'll excuse me, I have a business to attend to.' He paused momentarily. 'Please tell your father that I want the licence signed over to me within the next few days.'

He held the door open for Jess and she had no option but to leave the premises.

She didn't go straight back to the shop because she needed time to cool down before facing her father. If she went straight back in the mood she was in she was likely to give him another tongue-lashing. He'd been stupid and irresponsible – she'd already told him that, and he was painfully aware of it anyway, so there was no point in ranting on at him even more.

Remembering that she'd left some notes she'd jotted down about a dance routine she was working on at the hall last night after class, she decided to retrieve them so that she could work on them further before the next lesson. Being a time when she didn't officially have access to the hall, she went into Bruce's shop and asked permission to go upstairs, as a mark of courtesy. Friendly as ever, he didn't mind at all.

She found the notes in the piano stool where she'd put them for safekeeping. Stuffing them into her pocket, she was about to leave when she was suddenly infused with the calming atmosphere of this place. Here – especially when she was in front of a class – she felt set free. Nothing could touch her then; not the latest family crisis or problem at the shop because when she was taking her class she was totally absorbed.

For a few hours every week, she was able to shed her troubles.

Sitting down on the piano stool now, she lingered, searching her mind for a solution to this mess her father had got them into, and knowing that there wasn't one because Vernon Peck was determined to press his claim.

'What's all this then?' grinned Bruce, appearing in the doorway. 'Skiving off work in the middle of the afternoon. Tut-tut. I'll have to have a word with your dad about that.'

'I was just enjoying a few minutes of peace and quiet,' she told him, standing up guiltily. 'But I'll be off now and out of your way.'

'How can you be in anyone's way when the place is empty?' he asked, coming over to her. 'I just came up to see if you were all right. You were looking worried when you came in the shop.'

She gave a humourless laugh. 'That's an understatement,' she said with a bitter edge to her voice.

'Sounds serious.'

'It is.'

'Well, you talked to me before when you were worried, remember, when you lost the hall. I came up with a solution then,' he reminded her. 'It could work again.'

'I don't think there is a solution to this one. Anyway, I don't want to burden you,' she told him. 'I'm sure you've got work to do.'

'I pay staff so that I'm not chained to the counter.' He went to the side of the hall to get a chair and sat down near the piano stool. 'So why not sit down and tell me all about it?'

Jess sighed, shaking her head. 'I know you mean well but this really is a tough one.'

'You might feel better for talking about it, though, even if we can't come up with an answer,' he suggested. 'So take a pew and tell your Uncle Bruce all about it.'

So she told him the whole story. 'I'm dreading going back to the shop,' she said in conclusion. 'Because I'm going to have to tell Dad that I failed to get Vernon to change his mind. I know it's all Dad's fault but I can't help feeling sorry for him.'

Bruce stood up purposefully. 'Don't go away,' he said with an air of command. 'Stay here and enjoy the ambience for a bit longer. I'll be back in about ten minutes. Don't leave until I get back.'

'OK. But where are you going?'

'Tell you later.'

And before she could say another word, he was striding across the hall to the door.

'How dare you come round here interfering in a business arrangement I have with Charlie Mollitt?' fumed Vernon Peck.

'Business arrangement, my arse,' responded Bruce, who had been

190

shown into the same office as Jess a few minutes ago. 'From what I've heard it was a right old con job.'

'He would say that, wouldn't he?'

'He's said nothing to me,' Bruce informed him. 'I've just put two and two together from what his daughter's just told me.'

'Yeah, well, his daughter's bound to try to find a get-out for her old man, isn't she?' he said. 'She won't want to admit that he lost that licence through his own stupidity. Anyway, as you've been talking to her about it, you'll know that I am not backing down on the arrangement. I hope I made that clear to her.'

'You made it crystal clear,' Bruce confirmed.

Vernon shot him a look. 'So if you know that, why are you wasting my time?'

'Because I have a very different perspective from that of Jess Mollitt.'

'Well, you would do, wouldn't you?' Vernon said, misunderstanding Bruce and thinking that he was on his side after all. 'You're in business, a man of the world. She's just a chorus girl turned shop assistant.'

'I think she's a lot more than just a shop assistant,' Bruce disagreed, 'but that isn't what I meant.'

'Get to the point then, man, and don't take up any more of my time,' commanded Vernon impatiently. 'Time is money to me. What's all this about a different perspective? There's only one way to look at it: I won that newspaper licence off Charlie Mollitt fair and square and he's duty-bound to honour the agreement.'

'It isn't quite as cut and dried as that from my point of view, Vernon,' Bruce told him meaningfully.

'What are you on about?'

'I saw you in The Feathers the other night,' Bruce informed him, brows raised slightly, 'and I'm pretty certain that Mrs Peck would be interested to know how cosy you were with your assistant from the Ealing shop.'

Vernon's eyes popped; his mouth dropped open. But he quickly recovered his composure. 'Doris has worked for me for many years and has become a family friend. My wife knows that I sometimes have a drink with her after work,' he said, not very convincingly. 'I was just buying her a gin and orange to show my appreciation for the extra hours she's been putting in at the shop lately; we've been stocktaking.'

'Oh, she's been putting in extra hours all right,' returned Bruce, 'but what she's been doing has nothing to do with humbugs or liquorice allsorts.'

Vernon narrowed his eyes. 'You want to be careful what you're saying,' he advised him coldly.

'Oh, stop messing about, Vernon,' said Bruce impatiently. 'I saw you leave the pub together and get into your car. You were wrapped around each other like a couple of lovesick teenagers. A family friend? Do me a favour.'

191

'I've told you, I've known her a long time,' Vernon blustered. 'Anyway, don't you have anything better to do with your time than to spy on people?'

'I wasn't spying on you. I just happened to be in the same pub as you and left at the same time. Pure coincidence,' he explained. 'I wouldn't have given it another thought if you hadn't conned the Mollitts out of their livelihood. Anyway, if you hadn't been so busy entertaining your lady friend you might have noticed me. You're lucky it was only me who saw you. Throwing caution to the wind like that, you're asking for trouble. You really ought to be more careful.'

'I've no need to be because it was all perfectly innocent,' the sweetshop owner continued to insist.

'In that case you won't mind if I tell Mrs Peck about it, will you?' Bruce threatened.

'You don't know my wife.' Now he did look worried.

'I'm not on Christian-name terms with her. But I know who she is and where I can find her. She's the grey-haired woman with fancy glasses who comes to your shops in a fur coat. I've seen her at your Ealing branch. I'm partial to something sweet and I quite often call in there for a bar of Cadbury's. I'll tell her what you've been getting up to the next time I see her.'

'You wouldn't dare.'

'Try me.'

Vernon scratched his head, sighing heavily. 'All right, so what's the deal?'

'You go over and tell Charlie Mollitt that you've decided to forget the arrangement you made with him last night and he can keep his newspaper licence, and I'll forget what I saw you getting up to with Doris the other night.'

'That's blackmail.'

'That's right, and what you did last night to Charlie Mollitt was extortion,' Bruce spelled out. 'Add adultery to that and you beat me hands down in the sin department.'

'All right, all right, don't keep on about it,' Vernon said with seething irritation.

'So, do we have a deal?'

He pondered on the question. 'I could agree to what you want and still be at risk because the story could get about,' he suggested. 'If you tell the Mollitts what you know, they could pass it on and it'll be all around the Broadway.'

Given the man's total lack of discretion, it was only a matter of time before that happened anyway, in Bruce's opinion. But it wasn't in his interests to point that out to him. 'If you agree to let Charlie keep his newspaper licence, not a word will pass my lips on the subject of your private life,' he told him. 'You have my word on that. Even Charlie won't

192

know why you changed your mind. Not from me, anyway.'

'He'll think my sudden change of heart a bit fishy, though, won't he?'

'Not if you tell him you've been thinking about it, and you want to do the decent thing as you're both local traders,' he suggested. 'What could be more believable than that? Anyway, he'll be too relieved to care why you changed your mind.'

There was a silence while Vernon thought about it. 'Oh, all right, then,' he agreed, tutting loudly. 'Charlie keeps his lousy licence. I'll go over and tell him in a minute.'

'Good. Now that that's settled, we can both get back to work,' said Bruce.

'I'll second that,' said Vernon, with a mixture of relief and disappointment.

Bruce came bounding into the hall to find Jess standing looking out of the window.

'I hope I haven't been too long,' he said.

'Of course not.' She looked at him expectantly.

'It's all sorted,' he smiled. 'Vernon is going to see your dad to tell him he won't be holding him to the agreement. So Charlie keeps his licence.'

'Really?' She looked at him puzzled. 'But how? I mean Vernon was so adamant.'

'Maybe he isn't such a bad bloke after all,' he grinned.

Jess gave him a suspicious look. 'You know I'm not daft enough to believe that,' she said. 'So how did you persuade him to change his mind?'

He tapped the side of his nose mysteriously. 'It isn't important.'

'It is to me.'

'Then it shouldn't be,' was his answer to that. 'The important thing is that your dad keeps his licence. So just forget all about it – pretend last night didn't happen. And make sure your dad does the same. Vernon will explain why.'

In a sudden impulse she threw her arms around him, looking into his rich, warm eyes. 'I don't know how you did it but thank you so very much.'

'A pleasure.'

In a great outpouring of gratitude she kissed him, full on the lips. Only it turned out to be rather more thorough than she intended and neither of them did anything to end it.

'That shouldn't have happened,' she murmured eventually.

'No.'

'I don't know what came over me.'

'No harm done.' He moved back quickly, his face unusually serious. Being Bruce she expected him to laugh it off but he didn't seem to be in that sort of a mood.

'I was so grateful to you,' she went on as though further explanation was necessary. 'I suppose I got a bit carried away.'

'And now you'd better carry yourself away back to your dad's shop and take over at the counter so that he can pay attention to Vernon,' he said, reverting to his usual self and making a joke of it; except that it sounded false.

'Yeah, OK.' The atmosphere between them had become tense and awkward. He was avoiding her eyes.

'I need to go back to work anyway,' he said meaningfully.

'Of course,' Jess said, smarting with a feeling of rejection. 'It was good of you to spend so much time helping us. I don't know what you did but I do appreciate it.'

'Forget it.'

'Thanks again.'

They made their way down the stairs together, shrouded by an uncomfortable silence, and she left him in his shop. Seeing the door close behind her, Bruce's expression became grim. That hadn't been just a kiss of gratitude. She felt the same as he did, and his feelings for her were growing stronger all the time. This was one complication he hadn't expected when he'd decided to move to the same area as his brother.

Jess was the loyal type. She probably wouldn't admit her feelings, even to herself, because she wouldn't want to be disloyal to Don. What she didn't know was that Bruce couldn't, *under any circumstances*, let things go any further. Jess was engaged to Don and it was absolutely imperative that Bruce didn't do anything to destroy their relationship. He wasn't going to stop being friendly with her because that would make things difficult for them both – with her running her dance school in his hall – but he must make sure it didn't ever go beyond that.

Jess was feeling tense as she walked back to Mollitts. She'd obviously embarrassed Bruce with her impulsive action. He'd seemed cool and distant after that. But she was certain there was something special there between them; it was tangible every time they were together, an underlying passion beneath the light-hearted banter. He inspired feelings in her that she hadn't ever felt for Don and knew she never would.

Despite what Don thought about Bruce, she had an instinctive belief that Bruce wouldn't knowingly do anything to hurt his brother. And the last thing she wanted to do was cause Don any pain. So, she told herself, no more throwing your arms around him, girl. Strictly platonic from now on. She also decided that she wouldn't embarrass Bruce by mentioning the subject again. The next time she saw him she'd behave as though nothing had happened.

Chapter Thirteen

The pupils of the boys' secondary modern were sent home early one afternoon a few days later because the central heating had broken down and the sub-zero temperature in the school wasn't considered healthy. Offering silent thanks to the faulty boiler for saving him from the volatile temper of the history teacher, Ronnie headed homewards with his mates, calling at his father's shop on the way to collect Doughnut.

Having raided the larder – with meagre results since it was midweek – and had a leisurely look through this week's *Beano*, he decided to take a stroll down to the Broadway to get a bar of chocolate. Although it made a nice change to have the place to himself, he had to admit that it was, actually, a bit dismal without the others for any length of time. Thanks to his Saturday job, he could afford to splash out on sweets more often now.

Grabbing his coat and scarf and putting the dog on the lead, he left the house. School was out for everybody now and he met Libby walking home from the girls' school with a crowd of friends. Unable to avoid them – much to his annoyance – he greeted them as briefly as possible and hurried on his way. His twin sister's mates were a bit too loud for his liking; always giggling and teasing and prone to shriek out such crippling embarrassments as, 'Fancy coming to the pictures, Ron?', or 'How about a snog?'

The weather was raw, and dusk already falling, the damp of evening settling over everything. As the cold bit into his bones, he quickened his step, taking a short cut to the Broadway down a narrow side street. The dog growled suddenly. 'What's the matter, boy? Too cold for you?' he asked in a manner to suggest that his beloved pet might reply. 'I won't hang about so you'll soon be home by the fire.'

The weather was obviously not the problem because Doughnut continued to emit hostile rumblings from the back of his throat, pulling at the lead too. The reason became clear when Ronnie heard the sounds of a scuffle: a groan, a shout, raised boyish voices. There was a rumble somewhere, he thought, but there was no sign of it in the street. Realising that the noises were coming from an alleyway between the houses, he decided to take a look.

What he saw turned his blood cold as the reason for his brother's uncharacteristic behaviour recently became horribly obvious. It wasn't

195

kids from Todd's school who were giving him bother but secondary modern boys. Three of them of about Todd's age had him pinned against a high brick wall. Two were punching him while the other was emptying the contents of his satchel on to the muddy path.

'That's what we think of stuck-up grammar school kids like you,' declared the satchel emptier, stamping on Todd's precious exercise books with a dirty shoe and tossing the satchel to the ground.

'Dunno who you think you are with your sissy school uniform,' jeered another. 'You think you're better than us just 'cause you go to the gram. But you're nothing. We're the business around here and you're the lowest of the low – just an 'orrible little four-eyed worm. And I'll tell you what we do to worms, shall I? We tread on 'em – crush 'em to death.'

'Yeah,' chipped in the third boy.

Ronnie had heard more than enough. 'Oi, you lot, leave him alone. Three against one isn't fair,' he declared, dragging one of the boys away and setting about him. 'If you wanna fight, at least have the bottle to fight fair. Come on, Todd, let's give 'em a pasting. Give 'em a taste of their own medicine. They chose the wrong one when they picked on a Mollitt.'

While Doughnut yapped supportively on the sidelines, Ronnie gave the satchel saboteur one almighty shove, which sent him flying to the ground. He then laid into his mate with his fists while Todd took on the other one, able to fight back now that the numbers were more evenly balanced, though he wasn't quite as bold as his brother. Being a streetwise sort of a lad, Ronnie knew that Todd must take part in the brawl himself if he was to gain freedom from his tormentors. If he stood back and let Ronnie sort this by himself, they would taunt Todd for evermore about having his big brother fight his battles for him.

'That's quietened you down a bit, hasn't it?' said Ronnie when he and Todd had the two up against the wall. The third boy had vanished; frightened off by the appearance of Ronnie, who was in the fourth year and known in their school as a bit of a hard man. 'Now you can wipe the dirt off my brother's books and put them back in his satchel.'

They did as he said without argument.

'You can wipe the muck off the satchel too,' added Todd bravely.

'What with?' one of them asked.

'Your hanky'll do,' replied Todd, gaining in courage by the second. 'And if you haven't got one, do it with your coat or your jumper. I'm not having my satchel back in that filthy state.'

'But—'

'Just do it,' ordered Todd and, much to his amazement, the boy did as he said.

'Now clear off,' commanded Ronnie when the condition of the satchel was improved and returned to its owner. 'And if you ever go near my brother again, your mum and dad will be visiting you in hospital.'

196

'They wouldn't dare, bruv,' put in Todd, keen to assert himself now that he'd tasted bravery.

The boys scuttled away.

'Thanks, Ronnie,' said Todd.

'That's all right, kid,' his brother assured him. 'I know that I sometimes take the mick 'cause you go to a poncy school, but I'm not having the likes of them beat you up 'cause you're brainier than they are.'

'Thanks for . . . well, not making me look like an idiot,' added Todd.

'They needed to see what you were made of and you did well,' praised Ronnie. 'You really showed 'em. They'll think twice before picking on you again. I doubt if you'll have any more trouble with them.'

'I'm not scared now, anyway.'

'That's the main thing. They can smell fear, that sort.' He thought for a moment. 'They've been duffing you up every day on the way home, have they?'

'Yeah.'

'You should have told me about it sooner,' Ronnie admonished. 'You shouldn't have kept it to yourself, letting them make your life a misery.'

'I daren't say anything at home,' Todd confessed, 'because if Jess had found out about it she'd have gone after them and made me look a right ninny.'

'Mm. I can understand why you kept quiet,' said Ronnie sympathetically. 'But if anything like that ever happens again, you tell me about it and we'll sort it together; just you and me. No need to involve the others. OK?'

'Thanks.'

Seeing his brother in a new light, Ronnie turned to him and grinned. 'You're all right, as kid brothers go,' he told him. 'Fancy coming down the Broadway to get some sweets?'

'I do but I'm skint,' he admitted. 'I've spent all this week's pocket money.'

'I've got some spare dosh,' his brother told him. 'I'm a working man now, remember.'

'OK then,' Todd agreed happily.

The two brothers and their dog walked towards the lights of the Broadway in the gathering dusk.

During the following week, Jess made an observation to the twins when the three of them were finishing their breakfast. Charlie was at the shop and Todd had already gone to school; he left earlier than his siblings because he had further to go.

'Todd seems to have been a lot happier this past few days, don't you think?' she mentioned.

'Mm,' muttered Libby, rather absently because she was thinking about the day ahead.

197

Ronnie didn't say anything.

'He seems just like his old self, in fact,' Jess continued. 'Doesn't seem worried about going to school and he's lost that awful sickly look that's been hanging over him lately. I think he seems on really good form. Have you noticed?'

'Now you come to mention it, I suppose I have,' replied Libby, finishing her porridge.

'It's a big relief to me, I can tell you,' Jess went on in chatty mood. 'I was going to the school to see the headmaster if he'd carried on as he was.'

'Just as well he seems better then, because he wouldn't have liked that one little bit,' proclaimed Libby. 'It would have been *so embarrassing*.'

'That's what I thought,' said Jess, who wasn't so far removed from her own schooldays to forget the sort of things that had mattered then. 'Still, all seems to be well with him now, thank goodness.' She sipped her tea. 'I wonder what it was that was worrying him.'

'Dunno,' said Libby truthfully.

'Whatever it was, he seems to have sorted it,' added Ronnie.

Something about the way he avoided her eyes caused Jess to ask, 'Do you know anything about it, Ron?'

'No. Not a thing,' he fibbed, deciding that there were some things that were best kept between brothers because sisters just wouldn't understand.

When Jess next saw Bruce, he was his usual charming self, full of warmth and goodwill.

He came into the shop for a morning paper and to tell her that he had become the owner of the portable stage she'd used for the Christmas show and it would be at the hall permanently from now on. This had come about as a result of her request to hire it on a permanent basis. Her classes were well attended, so she could afford to pay a bit extra for the hall. Having a platform had proved to be invaluable, in that it allowed her to see and be seen by those pupils at the back of the class when she was demonstrating the steps.

Glancing at the front page of the newspaper as Charlie took his money, Bruce commented on the plane crash in Munich yesterday that had killed several members of the Manchester United football team as well as some journalists covering the match and three members of the club's staff. He shook his head sadly. 'A tragedy, all right,' he said. 'I couldn't believe it when I saw it on the television news last night.'

'Shocking,' agreed Charlie.

'The plane crashed on the runway in the snow, apparently,' Jess put in gravely.

Bruce nodded. 'It's a sad business; the pride of English football, gone just like that.'

They chatted some more about the awful news, then Bruce made as if

198

to leave. 'I'd better go and earn a crust.' He grinned, immediately lifting the atmosphere. 'See you, folks. Keep smiling.'

The door had closed behind him when Jess realised that she hadn't thanked him properly for making it possible for her to have the use of the stage, or discussed the extra cost. She rushed out of the shop after him.

'Thanks for organising the stage for me,' she said, catching him up just before he crossed the road; she was shivering because the weather was bitter.

'No trouble at all,' he assured her. 'It only took one phone call to fix it.'

'I didn't realise you were going to buy it,' she told him. 'I thought you would just keep it on hire and I'd pay you the hire charge.'

'I thought I might as well buy it because it'll be useful to have it there when I hire the hall out for other things,' he informed her. 'Most functions need a platform, don't they? People expect it when they book a hall.'

'Yeah, there is that,' she agreed. 'Anyway, just put the extra cost on my bill.'

'I won't be charging you for it,' he informed her, looking surprised at the suggestion. 'There should be a platform there. You shouldn't have to pay extra for it.'

'Thanks, but I'd rather pay,' she asserted. 'I'm not looking for favours.'

'And I'm not giving any.' He was equally as firm. 'If you're paying to hire a hall, you're entitled to the basic necessities. It was only because you took the hall on unexpectedly that there hasn't been one there before. When you mentioned keeping it after the show, it nudged me into putting it right.'

She gave him a hard look. 'Are you sure?'

'Positive.' He gave her a half-smile. 'You're quite awesome when you're being forceful, aren't you?'

Infected by his mood, she laughed. 'You should see me when I really get going.'

Before he could reply, Don appeared, his expression thunderous. 'You'll freeze to death out here without a coat, Jess,' he told her with seething disapproval.

'I'll leave you to it, then. See you around,' said Bruce, glancing at Don before making a hasty retreat, marching across the road, an impressive figure in a stylish light grey overcoat.

Jess turned on Don. 'I'm not a child, for heaven's sake,' she admonished. 'I don't need to be ticked off for being outside without a coat.'

'I was concerned about you, that's all,' he told her in a querulous manner.

She was imbued with a mixture of irritation and remorse. She didn't doubt his concern but was it about her exposure to the weather or to his brother? Either way she felt stifled by him when he was in one of his overbearing moods. Deciding to give him the benefit of the doubt, she said, 'I appreciate your concern and I shouldn't have snapped. But I really am old enough to go out without a coat if I want to, you know.'

'All right, all right; point taken.'

She moved on swiftly to avoid a full-blown argument. 'Were you on your way to see me?' she asked.

He nodded. 'Just to say that I'll pick you up about seven tonight for the cinema.'

'That'll be fine.' She was shivering violently now, thus giving an air of plausibility to his claimed concern for her wellbeing. She turned to go. 'See you later then.'

There was an odd atmosphere between Jess and Don that evening. They went to see a war film with rather too many battle scenes for Jess's taste. Not in the mood to persevere with it, she found herself staring blankly at the screen, thinking about Bruce. His warmth, his wonderful sense of humour and good looks were a potent combination, and she was shocked by the growing intensity of her feelings for him; she wanted to be with him now instead of here with Don. That's enough, she admonished sternly. You're engaged to Don so grow up and stop harbouring ridiculous notions.

Noticing that Don seemed preoccupied on the way home in the car, she asked him if anything was the matter.

'Not especially, no.' His manner indicated otherwise; he'd obviously taken umbrage about something.

'As you're making it obvious that I've upset you in some way, you'd better tell me what it is I've done so that I can try to put it right,' she suggested.

'All right, I'll tell you,' he said brusquely. 'I don't like the way you're getting so friendly with my brother.'

'Oh, not that again.' He must have been simmering ever since the incident this morning. 'We've been through all this before and I've told you that I am not going to be horrid to him just because you don't like him.'

'You were so keen to talk to him you were even standing out in the cold,' he said accusingly.

'I was thanking him for organising something for me at the hall, that's all,' she explained through gritted teeth. 'I didn't even realise it was cold until I got out there. Anyway, if I want to stand out in the cold talking to him or anyone else I'll do so. Being engaged to you doesn't mean I have to ask your permission.'

'He's trying to get you to fall for him,' he stated, ignoring her comments. 'He's an expert at that.'

'Oh, don't be so ridiculous,' she retorted. 'You're paranoid about the man.'

'You know nothing about him.'

'I know all I need to know for the amount of contact I have with him,' she returned. 'As far as I'm concerned, he's a nice bloke who lets me have the use of his hall, and I am not going to stop having a laugh and a joke with him just because you've got some vendetta against him.'

They pulled up outside her house. He switched the engine off and turned to her. 'Bruce is not a nice bloke, Jess. I can promise you that,' he stated categorically. 'He's not nice at all. In fact I'd go as far as to say that he's thoroughly evil. He takes what he wants and doesn't care who he hurts in the process.'

'What did he do, for goodness' sake?' she asked with an impatient sigh. 'Steal your sweets when you were kids or something?'

'No. He stole my wife and then killed her,' he burst out.

The silence was piercing. Jess felt his words reverberate right through her; it was as though the breath was being squeezed out of her.

'Are you saying that Bruce murdered your wife?' she managed to utter at last.

'He killed her, yes.'

'I just can't believe it,' she gasped. 'Actually murdered her, you mean?'

'He didn't stab or strangle her,' he explained. 'But he was responsible for her death.'

Jess was trembling all over. 'What . . . what actually happened?' she forced herself to ask.

Don stared straight ahead of him, his sharp-featured profile gleaming in the pale glow from the streetlights. 'He was having an affair with her,' he began, his jaw rigid. 'They were running away together when his car crashed. It went out of control and hit a tree on one of the main roads out of Essex. She was thrown through the windscreen and killed instantly. He got off more or less scot-free – just a few superficial injuries.'

'Oh Don,' she said, putting a sympathetic hand on his arm. 'How terrible for you.'

'Yes, it was awful,' he said bitterly. 'Horrendous, in fact. The worst time of my life.'

'Were they running away because you'd found out about them?' she enquired tentatively.

'No. I knew nothing about it until after the car crash,' he told her. 'They say the spouse is always the last to know, don't they? Well, I certainly was. Though it all fell into place once I did know what had been going on.'

'I'm so sorry.'

He turned to her. 'So, now you know why I don't have any time for my brother.'

'Yeah, I certainly do.' She bit her lip, thoughts spinning around in her head. 'What caused the car crash?'

'Careless driving.'

'Was that the official verdict?'

'No. They reckon the car skidded on black ice; that's why it went out of control.'

'So he wasn't prosecuted for dangerous driving then?' She so wanted Bruce not to be guilty.

'Oh, no, this is Bruce we're talking about, remember,' Don snorted. 'He talked his way out of it as usual. That man can make anyone believe anything.'

Jess was more affected by this than, perhaps, she should be. As well as being overcome with compassion for Don, her faith in her own judgement was shaken to the core. Charming, warm-hearted Bruce, whom she'd trusted instinctively, was actually a man who would sink low enough to steal his brother's wife.

She found it hard to believe that Bruce would do such a thing, though it was easy to understand how Don's wife had fallen for him. Reading between the lines, she thought the car crash probably had been an accident, despite Don's natural tendency to blame his brother for every single thing that was wrong with his life. But Bruce *had* been going away with another man's wife; that was bad enough in itself. At least now she knew why Don got into such a feverish state every time she had anything to do with Bruce. And she'd spent all evening wishing she was with him instead of Don. How awful! How lucky she was to have Don. A little too strait-laced perhaps but at least he saved her from any more heartache.

'The whole thing must have been very traumatic for you,' she said.

'Very,' he confirmed with emphasis. 'I thought I'd never get over it.' He looked at her, his expression becoming tender. 'I probably wouldn't have if you hadn't come into my life.'

'You would have . . . eventually,' she said, holding his hand in both of hers, feeling deeply sorry for him. 'Everything gets better in time.'

'You've given me a reason to live again,' he told her. 'I feel as though I can cope with anything with you beside me.'

'I'm glad to have helped.'

He lapsed into thought for a moment, then said, 'Look, I know I said I wouldn't put pressure on you about setting a date for our wedding, but I'd like to get it settled.'

'But we agreed to wait . . .'

'Yes, I know. But there's no harm in making a provisional arrangement, is there? Just so that we know what we are aiming for,' he said. 'No need to start actually on the preparations or anything.'

Jess felt cornered but didn't want to hurt him by putting him off altogether now that she knew what he'd been through in the past. He was obviously feeling insecure and wanted to make sure of her. 'OK. Let's say that we'll make it no later than next year, possibly in the spring,' she suggested. 'The twins will have left school by then and Todd will be older. Dad should be able to manage, and as long as we live locally I can call in and help out if necessary.'

'Next spring it is then.'

His obvious delight felt like a burden to Jess in her current mood. Being

202

the controller of someone else's happiness was a huge responsibility.

When half-day closing came round the next day, Jess was very glad of it. Having been awake for several nights in turmoil over her feelings for the Day brothers, she felt in need of an afternoon off. Her father usually stayed at the shop to catch up on paperwork, the others were all out at school, so she planned to do a few chores then put her feet up by the fire.

But she was feeling too restless to sit down for long. So she put a coat on over her sweater and trousers, wrapped a red woolly scarf around her neck, put the dog on the lead and headed for Churchfields. It was one of those cold February days with bright, heatless sunshine and the feel of frost waiting to descend when the sun went down. It was wonderfully invigorating, though, and she was glad to be out in the fresh air.

She was so engrossed in her own thoughts, she was startled when someone tapped her on the shoulder.

'You,' she blurted out when she found herself face to face with Bruce.

He started back in mock fear. 'Well, don't sound so pleased to see me.'

'You took me by surprise,' she said coolly.

'It's my afternoon for office work and you know how much I love that,' he said with irony. 'Any excuse for a break.' He hesitated for a moment. 'Mind if I walk with you?'

She didn't reply. She was so disappointed in him it was almost a physical pain and she was finding it hard to be civil to him. 'I'm going right down to the bottom of Brent Lodge Park,' she informed him briskly. 'I need the exercise and I want to give Doughnut a really good walk.'

'Suits me.'

They walked on in silence. She made no effort at conversation whatever.

'Have I upset you, Jess?'

'No.'

'Why are you being so cold towards me then?'

'I'm not.'

'Yes, you are,' he said, halting in his step and taking her arm so that she couldn't avoid turning to face him. 'And you know you are. So tell me what's the matter.'

There was a brief hiatus while she tried to gather her scrambled emotions. 'Don told me what happened to his wife,' she blurted out. 'He told me you were having an affair with her.'

'Oh . . .'

'At least I now know why he nearly has a fit every time I talk to you,' she said.

'I was *not* having an affair with her.'

'I don't believe you,' she said. 'Don wouldn't lie to me.'

'Neither would I.'

'I know who I'd rather trust.'

203

'That's up to you. But because of what Don believes happened between Sheila and me this thing between you and me can never come to anything.'

'What thing?'

'You know perfectly well.'

'No . . .'

'Don't insult my intelligence by denying it,' he cut in, his tone ragged with emotion. 'You want me as much as I want you.'

'You flatter yourself.'

'Not at all,' he denied. 'I'm just being honest. Now that you know why Don hates me so much, we might as well have this other thing out in the open.'

'What makes you think you're so irresistible that every woman you meet is going to fall at your feet.'

'That's the last thing I would ever think but I do know that you and I are drawn to each other,' he stated categorically. 'I felt it the first time I saw you and it's been getting stronger ever since.'

'What is it with you that you want to make any woman of Don's fall in love with you? You did it to his wife, now you're doing it to me,' she accused bitterly, her cheeks flushed from the cold, the wind lifting her hair. 'I suppose it flatters your ego to do that to him?'

'No . . .'

'Isn't it enough that you're the brother with the looks and the charm?' she ranted on. 'Do you have to keep proving it by spoiling things for him?'

'I have no intention of spoiling anything for Don and I never have,' he informed her firmly. 'But you and I are intelligent adults and we both know that something has happened to us.'

'Rubbish.'

Taking her off guard, Bruce pulled her out of sight behind a tree and kissed her hard. 'That is what I'm talking about,' he said breathlessly, drawing back and staring into her face. 'That is what you and I both want and can never have because – regardless of what you might think of me – I wouldn't do that to Don. Not ever!'

She was very shaken; too emotional to speak.

'Are you still denying it?' he asked.

'No . . . no, of course not.' She was very subdued and there was something she felt compelled to ask. 'Were you very much in love with Don's wife?'

His face worked and he didn't reply; just stared into space. 'I wasn't in love with her but she did mean a lot to me,' he said at last.

'At least you could have the decency to admit the truth,' she said.

He threw her a hard look. 'I'm not prepared to discuss my feelings for Sheila any further.' His tone prohibited argument. 'And I am only telling you about my feelings for you because I think we both need to know where we stand.'

'Which is nowhere.'

'Exactly.'

She gave him a thoughtful look. 'The tragedy of the past doesn't seem to have affected you,' she mentioned. 'Life is just a bit of fun to you from what I can make out.'

'We all have our own way of coping.' There was nothing light-hearted about his manner now. 'If everyone went about like Don the whole world would sink into a sea of despair.'

Jess couldn't truthfully deny that but said defensively, 'It's just his way.'

'And being cheerful is mine,' he told her. 'Whether I feel like it or not.'

She emitted a heavy sigh. 'So, where do we go from here?' she wondered.

'There are two ways we can handle it,' he proposed. 'We can either avoid each other altogether, which means your finding another hall for your dancing school. Or we can carry on as we have been but make sure that nothing ever happens. Now it's out in the open, we'll be on our guard.'

Standing there in the freezing weather with the wind whistling through the skeletal trees and flattening the grass in patches, the familiar sound of a train thundering over the viaduct, she knew she couldn't bear not to have his cheery presence around her now and again, no matter how painful.

'It would be stupid for me to give up the hall now that I've got the classes established there,' she pointed out.

'And I don't want to feel that I can't get my morning paper at your shop or come walking here in case we meet,' he added.

'So we carry on as before then?'

'Suits me.' He forced a grin. 'And right now let's finish our walk. We might as well as we've come this far.'

They headed towards Brent Lodge Park with Doughnut trotting beside them. Despite their intentions to carry on as though nothing had happened, and their brave attempt at ordinary conversation, they both knew that it would never be the same between them again.

It was Saturday night and Charlie had the house to himself. Jess was out with Don, Ronnie had gone to some sort of a social evening at the youth club, Libby had gone to her friend's house to play records and Todd was at the pictures with a friend from school and his family. The place was usually a circus of noise and activity to the point where Charlie often longed for peace and quiet. But now that he had it, he wasn't too keen. He found himself depressed at the thought that this was how it would always be in a few years' time when they'd all left home.

There was a play on the TV – some sort of a mystery – but he couldn't follow it properly because that awful business of his almost gambling away the newspaper licence kept coming into his mind. He'd been that close to losing his livelihood, it scared him. If it hadn't been for Vernon being so decent about it in the end, God knows where they'd be. He was deeply ashamed.

He'd not been to the pub since for fear he might overindulge and do something stupid again. It was so easy to get chatting and have more to drink than he intended. He missed it, though; the company as much as the booze. There was always someone in there he knew to talk to. But if he couldn't trust himself, the only answer was to steer clear altogether.

It was lonely sitting here with only Doughnut for company, though, and his sense of isolation was hardly bearable. Surely it could do no harm to go down there if he made absolutely certain that he didn't have more than one drink. At least being out among people would ease the constant self-castigation. Just an hour out of the house, that was all. One pint. No more!

He got up, settled the dog in his basket in the kitchen, put his coat on and left the house. Immediately he entered the pub he was cheered by the warmth of the welcome.

'Wotcha, Charlie, me old mate,' said one of a group of men who were standing at the bar. 'Haven't seen you lately. You been going somewhere else?'

'No, I've been staying in, as it happens.'

'Ooh, that's a bad sign,' said one of the men. 'Too much of that can make a man maudlin.'

'Good to have you back, anyway,' said another. 'What are you having?'

'I'll have a pint of bitter, please.' He was very glad he'd come.

Hilda got off the bus and headed home. It was a cold night but dry and clear, a full moon spreading a pearly glow over the serried ranks of houses. She'd been to the cinema in Ealing Broadway on her own. She would much rather have had company but had learned over the years of widowhood that if you waited for someone to go out with you'd spend your whole life at home and lose confidence in yourself altogether.

Having the Mollitts next door had been a lifeline to her over the years; more recently, her involvement in Jess's classes had given her a new interest. It was so good to feel part of something. But the young ones had plans of their own on a Saturday night and didn't want an old girl like her tagging along.

Turning into Park Street she became aware of a noise; a sort of droning sound. Or was it someone crying in pain, she couldn't be sure. Standing still to listen more carefully, she realised that it was someone singing out of tune and the noise seemed to be coming from the other side of the street. Simultaneous with her identifying the awful racket, the purveyor of the discordant rendering walked under the lamppost.

'Charlie Mollitt,' she gasped, hurrying over to him. 'You'll have all the neighbours out on the street with that bloody din. Keep it down, man, will you?'

'Well, if it isn't Hilda, a pillar of the com— com— a pillar of the commoonity.' He could hardly get the words out, he was so drunk. 'How are you, love?'

'In better shape than you, by the look of it,' was her stern reply. 'I've never heard such a terrible noise.'

'Don't you like my singing?'

'You're no Perry Como.'

'I wouldn't be living around here if I was,' he said, lids drooping, body swaying.

'I'm really surprised at you, Charlie.' Jess had told Hilda in confidence, as a friend, about the near-loss of the newspaper licence. 'I didn't think you'd get yourself into this state again, not after what happened the other week.'

'I've only had one.'

'One dozen, more like.'

'Well, maybe I have overdone it a bit . . . but what's a man to do when he needs some company?'

'There are other places besides the pub to go,' she pointed out curtly. 'But you'd better come to my place and get sobered up before you go home.'

'Whyzat?'

'Because it would be better if Jess and the others didn't see you like this,' she stated firmly. 'They've had more than enough of it.'

'Don't nag,' Charlie said in a slurred voice. 'Why is it that you women always want to nag?'

'Probably because we have men like you to put up with,' she replied, taking his arm and guiding him in the right direction.

'Where are we going?'

'I've just told you. You're coming home with me and no argument about it. I'm not having those kids upset by your nonsense again.'

'My head feels like a carpenter's workbench,' he complained, a couple of hours and several large black coffees later, ensconced on Hilda's sofa, tie loose, hair dishevelled. 'It's as though there's someone inside there hammering bloody great nails into my brain. My stomach's none too happy either.'

'I hope you're not expecting sympathy because you'll get none from me.' The booze was still in his system but at least he wasn't in such a bad state now, Hilda observed, and wouldn't be staggering when he went home to his family.

'That's the last thing I'd expect from you,' he said, 'you being so self-righteous and all that.'

'Me? Self-righteous?' She was amazed that she should be seen in such a light.

'That's right,' he confirmed. 'Always so good and clean-living. Never put a foot wrong. Always ready to point the finger at me when I don't come up to scratch.'

'That isn't fair, Charlie,' she objected.

'You can't wait to have a go at me.'

She threw him a withering stare. 'Someone has to stand up to you. Your kids can't tell you what they really think because you're their dad and they're supposed to look up to you – though God knows how they manage it the way you've been carrying on since Joy died. Even Jess can only go so far when she makes a stand. But I'm not family so I can tell you the truth and I damned well will. It's time you pulled yourself together and started giving your children the consideration they deserve.'

'All this because I went down the pub for a bit of company,' he complained.

'No. All of this because I found you drunk and disorderly in the street,' she corrected briskly. 'Your children would have been mortified if they'd happened to come along and seen you like that. You're letting your family down, Charlie.'

'You've never liked me.'

'Ooh, I think the boot is on the other foot there, don't you?' she argued. 'You've never had a civil word for me in all the years I've known you. I think Joy even used to be embarrassed by it at times.'

'That was all a joke,' he was keen to point out because he had never intended to hurt her. 'Surely you knew it was all in good fun.'

She gave him a questioning look. 'Was it, though, Charlie?' she asked him. 'I was never really sure. I went along with it but I never quite knew how to take it.'

'Oh,' he said in surprise. 'You never seemed short of an answer.'

'I had to give back as good as I got because I didn't want to fall out with you. I didn't want to stop popping next door because Joy was my dearest friend,' she explained. 'And the children meant a lot to me – still do. But I always sensed that you thought I spent too much time in your house when Joy was alive.'

His head was beginning to clear now. 'It was just that . . . well, you always seemed to be there.'

'I was lonely,' she confessed.

He nodded in a knowing sort of way.

'You didn't know the meaning of the word then but you do now, don't you?'

'Not half.'

'Drowning your sorrows in drink won't help.'

Looking at her, Charlie felt his mouth trembling suddenly, and he lowered his head, his whole body beginning to shake. 'I know that.' He covered his face with his hands as tears began to fall. 'And for what it's worth I know I've been useless since I lost Joy and I'm fully aware of the fact that I'm letting my kids down.' The words were choked out between sobs. He dragged a handkerchief from his pocket and held it to his face.

'You don't let them down all the time,' Hilda pointed out, softened by his admission.

'Yes I do, all the time,' he corrected.

'It isn't as if you don't go to work or anything.' Sorry for him now, she was trying to make him feel better. 'You don't sit at home all day wallowing in self-pity. It's just this tendency you have to hit the bottle that lets you down.'

'There isn't a day goes by when I don't feel ashamed,' he confessed. 'I try to do better but I just don't seem to have the strength. Jess has got more guts than I'll ever have. I'm a complete dead loss.'

'Come on, Charlie, you're not all that bad a person,' she assured him with compassion. 'You're just not very good at coping with grief, that's all.'

'You've just finished having a go at me for being a useless father,' he said thickly.

'I was angry with you for getting drunk again,' she explained. 'I said that in the heat of the moment.'

'You meant what you said and you were right,' he told her. 'I am letting the kids down.'

'Stop doing it then,' was her advice. 'Joy's gone. You have to make the best of things.'

'Easier said than done.'

'It can be done, though,' she said. 'I know because I've been there.'

He looked at her enquiringly. 'How did you manage when you were first widowed?'

'With a great deal of difficulty,' Hilda admitted. 'You can either get on with it or go under. I suppose I went for the second option, though I didn't realise that's what I was doing at the time. I just tried to get through it one day at a time. You don't get a rehearsal for these things. We can all only do our best.'

'You didn't have any kids to help you through it, did you?' it suddenly occurred to him.

'That's right. I couldn't toddle off to the pub for company either because it isn't done for a woman to do that – not a woman like me anyway.' She paused thoughtfully. 'I suppose that's why I turned to Joy and the children.'

Charlie was feeling much less muddled now; clearer in fact than he'd been in a long time. 'Yeah, I can understand that now,' he told her. 'I was so used to your being around, you were just a part of the furniture. I don't suppose I ever really thought about how you might be feeling.'

'I was just that nosy woman from next door.'

He made a face. 'Yeah, I suppose it was something like that, if I'm really honest,' he admitted.

'I'm glad you feel you can be honest with me.'

'But I do know and appreciate how much you've done for my family since Joy's been gone,' he quickly pointed out. 'Being around for the kids while Jess is out at work, doing any number of favours, and, of course, more recently you've been a godsend to Jess with her dance classes.'

'Being involved in Jess's classes is an absolute joy for me, not a favour.' She grinned. 'A crusty old widow like me needs something to do.'

'I suppose you're too used to being without your husband to miss him,' he surmised.

'I'll always miss him but obviously the pain of it does lessen with time.' She paused then added, 'I still get lonely, though.'

'Not desperately so, though, like I do. Not after all this time.'

'Sometimes.'

'Oh.' He seemed surprised. 'But you seem so sorted—' he pointed out – 'involved in things. I mean you've been out somewhere tonight, haven't you?'

'On my own, though, Charlie. I'd been to the cinema when I met you. It isn't much fun going by yourself but if I waited for company I'd never go anywhere.'

'I didn't think of that.'

'Being out among people who are all with someone is the loneliest feeling of all,' she went on to say.

'That's why the pub is such an attraction for me,' he told her. 'There are always men in there on their own so I don't feel out of place, even though most of them have their wives to go home to.'

'It's easier for men in that way.'

'Mm.' He looked at her. 'Look . . . I'm sorry I was so rude to you earlier on. It was the drink talking.'

'I know that,' she assured him with a half-smile. 'Anyway, you've said a lot worse to me in your time.'

'Yeah, I know.' He made a face. 'It really was done in fun when Joy was alive, you know. I'm sorry if I hurt you.'

'Don't be soft.' She was embarrassed suddenly. 'I'm a tough old bird. It'll take more than a bit of kidding around from you to upset me.'

'That's all right then.'

She looked at the clock on the mantelpiece. 'Anyway, I think it's safe to send you home now. You seem sober enough not to make a fool of yourself in front of the kids.'

He stood up. 'Thanks for everything,' he said.

'That's all right,' she replied, leading the way into the hall and handing him his coat off the hallstand. 'Now do us all a favour and stay out of trouble, for God's sake, Charlie. Make those lovely kids proud of you again.'

'I'll try.'

She opened the door to a rush of cold air. 'If you need a friend at any time, you know where I am,' she said on an impulse. 'I might be a nosy old bag but I'm a good listener and I'll always be here for you as well as the rest of your family.'

His emotions were so acutely sensitised, her kindness sent hot tears rushing into his eyes. He would never have believed that Hilda could touch him so deeply. 'Thanks. I'll bear that in mind,' he said thickly.

'G'night, Charlie.'

''Night, Hilda.'

Chapter Fourteen

'Oh, Babs, she's beautiful,' said Jess of Babs' baby daughter, wrapped in a white honeycomb blanket and sleeping in a wooden drawer on the table.

'She is rather gorgeous, if I say so myself,' agreed Babs.

'You must be *so* proud,' Jess further enthused, admiring the little pink face, topped with wisps of fair hair, hands splayed out in repose with tiny fingers curling.

'Course I am,' she confirmed but her voice lacked enthusiasm, somehow.

'Have you decided on a name for her yet?'

'I thought I'd call her Cindy,' she replied. 'It's a name I've always been fond of.'

'That's really pretty,' smiled Jess. 'I like that.'

'Well, the poor mite has to be called something and that's as good as anything, I suppose,' she sighed.

Perceiving an underlying depression but deeming it wise not to probe, Jess moved on swiftly. 'So, you did it then, kid; you gave birth, you clever thing,' she said lightly.

'I only did what nature forced on me,' her friend pointed out with a wry look.

'It's still a major achievement,' Jess opined. 'It's more than I've ever done, anyway.'

'It's only a matter of time for you, though, isn't it?' suggested Babs. 'As you're engaged to be married.'

The casual remark startled Jess. She and Don hadn't discussed the future in terms of children, and she realised with a shock that she found it almost impossible to imagine him as a dad; she certainly couldn't visualise him with a small baby. That would be far too messy and unpredictable for his highly developed sense of order. But to put her thoughts into words seemed disloyal so she just said, 'Maybe.'

'I'll be an old hand at motherhood by the time you do your stuff,' Babs mentioned, her light-hearted tone obviously forced. 'So you'll be able to benefit from my experience.'

'It'll be handy, having someone to turn to for advice,' Jess said, keeping the conversation casual. 'Meanwhile I'll practise on this little one. Can I pick her up?'

'Better not, as she's sleeping.' She visibly tensed. 'If we wake her up she'll only start yelling and that really sets my nerves on edge.' She made a face. 'She only does four things at the moment: sleeping, feeding and crying are three of them.'

'I think they start to do interesting things quite soon; after just a few weeks, so I've heard,' said Jess. 'Proper smiling is one of the first.'

'So they tell me.'

'Anyway, what's childbirth like?' Jess asked, turning away from the makeshift cot. 'Is it as painful as everyone says?'

'Unimaginable,' Babs told her. 'I'm told I had an easy birth. God knows what a difficult one must be like.'

'I wish you'd let me know when you were going into labour.'

'You couldn't have done anything.'

'I could have got Don to drive me over here and we could have taken you into hospital.'

'You were too far away and it all seems so urgent when the pains start coming,' she explained. 'All I wanted to do was get into hospital and get it over with. One of the other tenants here called an ambulance for me.'

'But you didn't even let me know you'd had the baby until you'd been out of hospital for over a week,' said Jess with just a shadow of reproach. 'You could have at least given me the opportunity to visit you while you were in there.'

'Sorry.' Babs looked extremely pale and drawn; her cheeks were slightly sunken and her normally luxuriant blonde hair was scraped back off her face into an elastic band. 'I just didn't want you to have to come and see me in that awful place. I hated it so much. All the other mums were married and as smug as hell about it. Downright nasty, some of them. Treated me like scum just because I didn't have a husband.'

'I'd have soon told them where to get off, if I'd come to visit,' responded Jess. 'It might have made it easier for you, having someone on your side.'

'Yeah, well, it's all over now, thank God.'

'It's just that I'd like to have helped – been more involved.'

'I wanted as little fuss as possible,' Babs went on to say, as though finally realising she might have hurt Jess's feelings. 'I don't see why anyone else should be put out by my problems.'

'I'm your friend. I want to help.'

'I know, and you've been brilliant,' Babs told her. 'Thanks for the presents you bought for the baby. The pram set and the nighties will be really useful.'

'I'm glad you're pleased.' Having received a phone call from Babs this morning at the shop, Jess had got here as soon as she could after work. 'I dashed out to get something at lunchtime but there wasn't all that much choice locally. I shall be getting something else but I didn't want to come empty-handed.'

'You shouldn't have, but thanks anyway.'

Babs made some coffee and they settled in the armchairs while little Cindy slept on.

'So, now that she's actually here, what are your plans for later on?' Jess enquired chattily. 'As regards work, I mean?'

'I shall take her to the café with me. The staff room is warm and cosy so she'll be all right,' Babs replied. 'They don't mind. I arranged it with them ages ago.'

'You won't be going back for a while though, will you?' queried Jess, thinking how ill her friend looked and knowing that she wouldn't thank Jess for mentioning it so she needed to be tactful. 'You'll need a bit of time to get back on your feet. Most people do after having a baby.'

'I shan't leave it too long,' Babs stated. 'I don't want them finding a permanent replacement for me. Employers who'll let you take your baby to work are few and far between.'

'You must look after yourself, though,' Jess couldn't help reminding her. 'Don't let yourself get run down.'

Babs gave a dry laugh. 'It's just me and Cindy, Jess,' she pointed out, her tone noticeably harsh. 'There's no devoted husband to look after us. I'm the only breadwinner around here and babies are expensive.'

Jess stared into her coffee mug. 'I was wondering if you'd let me help in some small way,' she offered cautiously.

'Definitely not. You've got enough to do with your money without giving me handouts. I know you work in a family business but I don't suppose your dad pays you a fortune, and you'll be getting married soon. You need what you get if you're going to be setting up home.'

'Have you got a pram for her?' Jess wasn't easily put off.

'Not yet,' Babs replied. 'I didn't want to get anything major like that until she was actually here, safe and sound. I'll have to get one now, though, somehow. I don't really fancy second-hand but I can't afford a new one.' She threw Jess a warning look. 'And don't you dare offer to buy her a pram because they cost a fortune and I know you can't afford it.'

'I certainly can't afford a coach-built one,' she was forced to admit. 'But there's a folding pram available that's much cheaper. I saw one in a baby shop in Ealing. It isn't nearly as classy or nice-looking as the other kind but at least you'd have something to take Cindy out in, and she could sleep in it when you take her to work.'

'Yeah, I've seen one or two of those around.'

'They're not nearly as popular as the traditional prams but they're a lot more useful because you can fold them up and take them on the bus or train,' she continued effusively. 'It wouldn't break the bank and at least it would be new. I've got a little bit put by and I'd really enjoy getting you one of those. Please say you won't be offended.'

Babs pondered the matter. 'Well, as long as it isn't too much,' she said. 'Promise you won't leave yourself short.'

215

'I promise,' smiled Jess.

They chatted for a while until Jess said she had to go. 'I hope you're going to come and visit us with Cindy,' she suggested. 'I'd love the family to see her. And once you get your folding pram, the journey shouldn't be too difficult.'

'Will a scarlet woman be welcome in your house, though?' Babs wondered.

'Don't be daft. My dad's not that narrow-minded,' Jess assured her. 'You could come for lunch one Sunday.'

'When I get properly organised.' Babs was evasive as usual.

'In the meantime, you know where I am if you need me.' Jess was determined to offer assistance whether it was wanted or not. 'You can always reach me at the shop if I'm not at home. Anything . . . anything at all, just give me a bell.'

'Thanks, Jess.'

'I'll see about the folding pram tomorrow.'

'Don't spend too much, though.'

'I won't.' Jess gave her friend a hug and left.

On the way down the stairs she heard the loud and persistent wail of a baby crying. Cindy's got an excellent pair of lungs on her, she thought.

Babs stood at the attic window nursing her crying baby and watching Jess in the lamplight glow, striding off down the street. Turning back into the room, she sank wearily into the armchair and put her baby to the breast. Cindy wouldn't feed and became hot and agitated, screaming even louder and making Babs' already ragged nerves feel as though every one had been individually severed. She made several more attempts until, eventually, the baby began to suckle. Breastfeeding hadn't been a success; it didn't seem to satisfy Cindy. Babs was going to have to talk to the health visitor about putting Cindy on the bottle soon anyway. Her employer had agreed to let her take the baby to work with her but would draw the line at breastfeeding.

Tears began to meander down Babs' cheeks. She couldn't remember ever feeling so alone and miserable before. She'd never been a particularly nervous person; now she felt sick with nerves the whole time. Everything frightened her; looking after the baby, earning a living, going out. Her stomach felt tight and she couldn't keep food down. Despite the brave front she had put up for Jess, she felt feeble and inadequate to the responsibilities that now burdened her. Her life as it had become seemed too much to bear.

The baby stopped feeding and began to whimper. She put her on to her shoulder and rubbed her back gently. 'What are we going to do, eh, baby?' she sobbed. 'Did a child ever have such a useless mother as you've got? You're completely reliant on me and I don't feel able to look after myself, let alone you.'

216

As the baby's cries rose in a nerve-shredding crescendo, Babs sobbed even more.

Libby was still awake when Jess went to bed that night and was in a chatty mood so they lay there in the dark talking in low voices.

'So what's Babs' baby like then?' Libby asked.

'She's a lovely little thing.'

'Aah,' murmured Libby. 'I hope we get to see her.'

'So do I,' said Jess. 'I shall try to persuade her to come over when she's more used to being a mum. It's all a bit new to her at the moment and she probably doesn't want to go far. Having a baby to look after takes some getting used to, I should imagine, especially when you're on your own.'

'It must be awful for her, not being married,' observed Libby.

'It isn't easy for any woman in her position,' agreed Jess.

'And being so old.'

'Old!' exclaimed Jess. 'She's only twenty-seven.'

'Exactly. You'd think she'd have had more sense than to get herself knocked up at that age,' was Libby's considered opinion.

'These things happen to the best of us,' Jess pointed out. 'It doesn't do to judge people.'

'I wasn't judging her,' Libby was eager to point out. 'I wouldn't do that to her. I'm sorry for her, that's all. She seemed so nice when she's been here. Glamorous, sure of herself, funny. Now her life's ruined. She's had to give up her career, and do some awful job. Seems a shame.'

'She'll come through it,' said Jess, her stomach churning at the thought of Babs in that terrible bedsit with the baby, and seeming so sick and sort of isolated within herself. 'I'm sorry for her too. Though she's very proud, so I daren't mention it.'

'Poor thing.'

'She'd have a fit if she thought anyone was thinking of her in that way,' mentioned Jess. 'She likes people to think she's invulnerable.'

'I'd never let that happen to me,' declared Libby. 'I wouldn't let some bloke ruin my life.'

'I'm very glad to hear it,' was her sister's predictable response.

They lapsed into silence for a while, then: 'Changing the subject,' said Libby, 'I've been thinking about my audition for the Burton troupe, and wondered if you could give me any tips.'

'I didn't know you had an audition arranged,' was Jess's astonished reaction.

'I haven't yet. But I will have in the not-too-distant future, I hope. I'm going to contact them fairly soon. I want to start there when I leave school in the summer.'

'You know I don't approve of your going into it straight from school,' Jess reminded her.

'I haven't forgotten. But a career as a dancer is a short one,' Libby

217

pointed out, 'especially in that line of dancing, so the sooner I get started the better.'

'I can't disagree with you about that, but I still say that straight from school isn't a good idea.'

'The younger I start the better, surely.'

'That is one way of looking at it. But my objection has more to do with experience than age,' Jess amended. 'If you've never done a day's work in your life and you go into Burtons straight from the classroom you'll find it dreadfully hard-going. If it was a ballet school or something it would be different, even though that's tough enough.'

'I'm stronger than you think.'

'Even so, being a Burton Girl is very demanding, both physically and emotionally, as I've told you before,' Jess went on. 'It's a job, not a college, and you earn every single penny they pay you. That's why I think you should have a year doing an ordinary job just so that you have some experience of the world other than as a schoolgirl. You'll still only be sixteen and you can keep up with your dance class during that time. Sixteen is quite young enough.'

'I want this more than anything else in the world, Jess.' Libby was adamant. 'You won't put me off, no matter what you say.'

'I'm not trying to put you off joining the Burton troupe, as such,' insisted Jess. 'I'll do everything I can to help you when the time is right. But that time isn't now.'

'I'm going all out for it, Jess.' Her voice rose determinedly. 'And nothing you say or do will stop me so you might as well get used to the idea.'

'We'll just have to agree to differ on this one then,' stated Jess. 'Do it if you must and I'll do what I can to help but don't expect me to approve.'

'I won't.'

A heavy silence descended over the darkened room, a beam of moonlight shining on the ceiling through a crack in the curtains.

''Night, love,' said Jess, to ease the tension.

''Night, Jess.'

Much to her astonishment, the following evening Jess found herself in conflict with Don over the pram she'd bought that day for Babs and arranged to have delivered directly to her friend.

'Using your savings for some mate or other,' he disapproved. 'It really isn't on, Jess.'

'Babs isn't just some mate or other,' she corrected firmly. 'She's a very dear friend and she needs help.'

'She can't expect you to shell out your hard-earned money on her,' he objected.

'She doesn't expect anything from anyone,' Jess informed him coolly.

'I *want* to do this for her. God knows, I can't do much for her but I can do this.'

'She isn't your responsibility.'

'For heaven's sake, Don, I know that,' she chided. 'But the woman is in trouble and the father of the child doesn't want to know.'

'It's her own fault she's in trouble. It's up to her to get through it.'

They'd gone out for a drink at a pub in Ealing Broadway and were ensconced at a corner table. But now Jess was on the verge of walking out. His harsh attitude had shocked her. 'I don't know how you can be so callous,' she told him. 'I really don't.'

'And I don't know how you could have spent all that money without talking to me about it first,' he retaliated. 'I thought we were supposed to be a team.'

'Oh, so I have to consult you every time I want to spend any money, is that it?'

'Don't be ridiculous.'

'I don't ask you what you do with your money, do I?' she challenged.

'This isn't about money,' he told her. 'It's about your making decisions without discussing them with me first.'

'Look, Babs means a lot to me and I want to do what I can for her, little though that may be,' she announced, anger rising with every word. 'You've never even met her so I didn't think it should be a joint decision. It never occurred to me that you'd be all that interested, to be perfectly honest.'

'Of course I would have been interested.'

'All right, if you say so. But it's important to me that I do this or I wouldn't have gone ahead.' She refused to be bullied. 'The last thing I expected was trouble from you. I thought you had some humanity in you. I thought we shared the same values.'

'We do, but I still think you should have consulted me before going ahead.'

'Being engaged doesn't mean owning each other,' she pointed out.

'It does mean being seriously involved in each other's lives, though. Well, that's what I've always believed, anyway,' he persisted in a querulous manner that Jess found immensely irritating. 'And I think I have the right to give my opinion when I think someone is taking advantage of your good nature.'

'Babs taking advantage?' she returned cynically. 'She wouldn't know how. She's the one who's been taken advantage of, in the worst way possible.'

'She could have always said no, Jess,' he pointed out brutally, words pouring out of him as though of their own volition because his inability to control Jess was filling him with fury. 'I've heard no mention of rape here. She sounds like a right old scrubber to me.'

The glass containing the remains of Jess's gin and orange was on the table. In a moment of blinding rage, she picked it up, threw the contents in his face and marched towards the door, leaving an electric silence behind her.

Too upset about the argument with Jess to be unduly embarrassed by the fact that everyone was staring at him, Don mopped his face with his handkerchief, then went after her.

'Come and get in the car, Jess, please,' he urged her as she marched along the Uxbridge Road with her head in the air. 'We can talk about it there.'

'There's nothing to talk about,' she stated categorically. 'I want nothing to do with a man who's so entirely without compassion as you apparently are.' Turning to him, she twisted her ring off her finger and pushed it into his hand. 'Here, you can have this back too.'

'Now you're just being silly.'

'Don't you dare to patronise me,' she blasted, walking on. 'I'm just glad I found out what you were like in time to do something about it. I wouldn't want to be married to anyone so mean-spirited he disapproves of my helping a friend.'

'Look . . . I was out of order, I admit it, and I'm sorry,' he told her, his mood made conciliatory by the fear of losing her. 'Please come to the car with me so we can put this right.'

'Go away.'

'I don't want to lose you,' he said, frantic to appease her. 'Please let me explain.'

'What is there to explain?' she asked in a rhetorical manner. 'I heard what you said. You've shown your true colours and you are not the sort of person I want to share my life with.'

Going after her, he took her arm in a firm grip. 'As you've just humiliated me in front of a pub full of people by throwing a drink over me, I think you owe it to me to at least let me try to put things right,' he pointed out assertively. 'I'm not asking for an apology but I am asking for that.'

'Me apologise?' she burst out. 'Don't make me laugh.'

'All right, so I'm the one who needs to apologise, and I have already done so,' he reminded her. 'So now, please listen to what I have to say.'

There was a pause while Jess considered the matter. Maybe it was a bit drastic to throw a drink at him. 'OK. I'll come back to the car but I'm promising no more than that,' she made clear. 'You've shown a side to your nature tonight that I don't like at all.'

As they walked back to the car in stony silence, Don found himself wondering why he'd had such an angry and heartless reaction to Jess's good-natured gesture towards her friend. He wasn't normally so lacking in compassion. Could it be that he was jealous of Jess caring for anyone other than him – albeit just a woman friend – because he wasn't secure in her love for him? He'd never been sure of her feelings for him, or indeed of his for her, if he was really honest. But he did know that he couldn't bear to be alone again, to go back to the grinding loneliness of his life before she'd come into it. So he would fight tooth and nail to get her back.

'I'm a brute and I don't deserve you,' he said when they were in the car.

'I won't argue with that,' she told him. 'Not based on your behaviour tonight, anyway.'

'I don't know what came over me,' he confessed truthfully. 'I think I must have been jealous.'

'Of a woman who's been left in the lurch and has very little going for her?' Jess challenged. 'Surely even you wouldn't be that small-minded.'

Priding himself on being a man of integrity, Don really did want to be honest about his feelings; he also wanted to understand them himself. 'No, not exactly. I think it was more a jealous reaction to your affection for Babs and the fact that I was excluded from your decision.'

'Oh . . . oh, I see.'

'It wasn't that I needed to approve of what you were doing but that I wanted you to share it with me,' he struggled to explain, working it out as he spoke. 'You see, I want to be a part of your life, fully involved, not just hovering around in the background. It's the only thing I can put my reaction down to. I was lashing out without really knowing why. I've been thinking about it on the way back to the car.'

'At least you're being honest about it,' she said, softening towards him slightly. 'That's something, I suppose.'

'I always try to be honest, you know that.'

'Yes, and I respect that, but I must be allowed to have some independence,' she asserted. 'I don't want to have to refer to you about every little thing.'

'And you won't have to, I promise,' he assured her. 'I accept that I was wrong and I'll try not to do it again. Give me another chance so I can show you that I mean it.'

He was so genuinely contrite, Jess relented. 'Well, maybe I could have mentioned the pram to you,' she felt compelled to admit. 'And I would have if I hadn't been in such a hurry to get it to her because she needs it so urgently.' She made a face. 'And I really am sorry about the drink in your face. I shouldn't have done that.'

'Let's call it quits then, shall we?' he suggested. 'A new start as from now.'

'OK, Don.'

'Thank you,' he said, slipping his arm around her.

Although she responded and behaved normally towards him for the rest of the evening, the feelings the incident had evoked in her continued to play on her mind. Not for the first time she'd felt suffocated by his possessiveness and had experienced a moment of longing for escape from both him and the engagement. The feeling had passed eventually but the fact that she'd had it at all made her wonder if they were right for each other. Still, she supposed everyone had similar doubts from time to time when they were committed to someone for life. It was only natural.

'Well, what do you think?' asked Libby, bounding into the living room where the rest of the family was gathered on this midweek evening. Dressed in a loose-fitting sweater and black pedal pushers, her dark hair tied back in a ponytail, she studied herself in the mirror above the fireplace for a moment then turned towards them for the verdict.

'About what?' enquired Jess.

'My hair, of course,' she informed them. 'I've just cut myself a really trendy fringe.'

Jess studied her sister's dubious handiwork. 'It's a bit uneven, love,' she remarked.

'That's the whole idea,' she tutted. 'It's supposed to look like Audrey Hepburn's.'

'Oh . . . oh, I see.' The resemblance wasn't striking. 'Well, I suppose it could look like hers, with a bit of imagination.'

Clearly disappointed at Jess's half-hearted reaction, Libby burst out, 'Well, I think it looks all right. At least I look a bit more modern than I did before.'

'It looks nice,' Jess assured her. 'But you didn't need to mess about with the scissors. Your hair was lovely before. You're a very pretty girl.'

'Don't tell her that, for goodness' sake,' put in Ronnie, grinning. 'She's big-headed enough as it is.'

'Ooh, listen to him,' riposted Libby. 'Mr Style himself, or so he thinks. Just because he's got a Saturday job in a trendy men's shop he thinks he's an expert on what's in and what's not.'

'I know more than you do.'

This produced an eruption of cynical laughter from his twin sister. 'You're a Saturday boy, for goodness' sake. All you do is make the tea, do the errands and sweep the floor.'

'That's where you're wrong, Clever Cloggs. I do other things as well,' he corrected. 'Bruce says I've got a way with the customers. He says I've got potential.'

'For what – packing the customers' bags?'

'I served a customer the other day because the sales staff were all busy,' he informed her. 'I didn't actually finalise the sale or take the money because I'm not trained to do that but I set it up and Bruce said I did very well and used my initiative.'

'Got a problem up there, has he?' she asked, grinning and pointing to her head.

He looked at her thoughtfully and she could almost hear his mind working in search of a put-down. 'You do look like someone in films, you know,' he remarked.

'Oh, yeah?' She was expecting an insult but couldn't resist saying, 'Come on then, let's have it.'

'The Beast from *Twenty Thousand Fathoms*.'

'Oh, ha, ha,' she mocked. 'That's just the sort of childish remark I'd expect from you. You're such a bird-brain.' She turned to her sister. 'Isn't he, Jess?'

'Leave me out of it,' was the way Jess dealt with it. 'You're both as bad as each other.'

'I think you look a bit like Audrey Hepburn, anyway, Libs,' said Todd, who rather admired Libby; he thought she was very good-looking, and knew some of his friends fancied her.

'Crawler,' teased Ronnie.

'Both of you should take a leaf out of Todd's book and be nicer to each other, isn't that right, Dad?'

Charlie lowered his newspaper. 'Yeah, that's right, Jess,' he supported. 'Whatever you say.'

He'd only been half listening. The constant banter between his children was as familiar a sound in the house as the clock ticking or the kettle whistling, and he left them to get on with it. He took in enough to be able to comment if required but it was essentially between them and he was only included as a referee.

On this particular occasion he hadn't actually been concentrating properly on the newspaper either because he'd been preoccupied with something that had been on his mind for the last few weeks; something he couldn't quite make up his mind about and was rather afraid of. It wasn't anything monumental but it did require a certain amount of courage.

Finally making a decision, he put the newspaper down and got up. 'I'm just popping out for a few minutes,' he told his children. 'I won't be very long.'

And because he was their father, no one asked him where he was going.

The following Saturday evening, while her father was upstairs, Jess had a few private words with her siblings in the kitchen. 'I've got something to tell you,' she said in hushed tones, 'and I don't want any wisecracks or sniggering. OK?'

Intrigued, they looked at her, waiting.

'Dad's going out tonight—'

'To the pub, I suppose,' assumed Ronnie. 'So what's new about that?'

'No, not to the pub. He's going to the cinema with Hilda,' she announced in a low voice.

Nobody said anything at first, then: 'Dad never goes to the cinema,' said Libby in a surprised whisper. 'He knows nothing about films.'

'Well, he'll know a bit more after tonight, won't he?' Jess pointed out. 'I think it'll be nice for him.'

'With Hilda, though,' pondered Todd. 'Why on earth would he be going with her?'

'He knows that she enjoys the cinema and often goes on her own so he invited her to go with him for company, apparently,' she explained. 'He told me about it at the shop today and asked me to tell you lot. He probably feels a bit embarrassed about it, you know . . . being that he's going out with a woman.'

'She isn't a woman, as such, though, is she?' observed Todd. 'It's only Hilda.'

'I don't suppose Hilda would be very flattered to hear you say that,' laughed Jess. 'But I know what you mean. She's just like one of the family. It isn't as though he's gone out and found himself a girlfriend or anything.'

Ronnie had been silent so far and was looking extremely doubtful. 'He isn't going out with her, though, is he?' he said. 'I mean, not as in "going out"?'

'Of course he isn't, dumbo,' Libby put him straight. 'They're both far too old for anything like that.'

Knowing what a difficult time Ronnie had had over their mother's death, Jess said, 'He isn't looking for a replacement for Mum, if that's what's worrying you, Ron. No one will ever replace her. But he does need some company of his own age and if he and Hilda get on well together tonight, it would be nice for him to have her as a friend, just to go out with now and again, wouldn't it? I mean, I have Don and you lot all have your friends, Dad doesn't have anyone.'

'He's got us,' was Ronnie's immature reaction.

'Yes, that's true,' agreed Jess, 'and we all care about him. But would you want him to go with you when you go out with your mates? I don't think so.'

'Of course I wouldn't.'

'Exactly,' she said. 'We each have our own lives outside of this house and it's time Dad had some life outside too. He and Hilda are both lonely and they've known each other for years. They both miss Mum like mad so it would help them if they could keep each other company now and again.'

'I've always had the impression that he didn't like Hilda much,' mentioned Ronnie.

'He used to tease her a lot when Mum was alive,' Jess remembered. 'And I don't think he likes the fact that she speaks her mind to him. But they must have sorted out their differences or he wouldn't have asked her out, would he? At least we all like her, don't we? She's been very good to us since Mum died.'

'She always sticks up for us,' Todd pointed out.

Ronnie nodded thoughtfully. 'She's helped us when he was drunk, and in lots of other ways, I suppose,' he agreed.

'I look at it this way,' Jess went on to say. 'If going out with Hilda gives him somewhere to go other than the pub then it can't be a bad thing.'

'There is that,' said Ronnie.

'And we all know that Mum wouldn't mind because she thought the world of Hilda,' Jess added. 'Hilda would never try to take her place or hurt Dad in any way.'

There was a murmur of agreement.

'Seems really weird, though, doesn't it?' remarked Libby. 'I mean, Dad going to the pictures is strange enough in itself, but going with Hilda—'

'I quite agree with you, it is very odd and most unexpected,' interrupted Charlie, appearing at the door, having overheard the last part of the conversation. 'I can hardly believe it myself. But it'll do me good to do something different and I'm looking forward to it. It'll make a change, anyway.'

There was an embarrassed silence as Charlie's children realised that they'd been overheard.

But the tension soon melted away when Libby burst out laughing. 'I'd better warn you, though, Dad, in case the shock gives you a heart attack or something,' she said with a mischievous grin. 'We've got talking pictures now.'

'You cheeky little madam,' he said, but he was smiling with his children as their laughter filled the room.

'I'm glad you enjoyed the film, Charlie,' said Hilda as they got out of his car in Park Street and stood talking at her gate. 'I wasn't sure if you would, you not being a film-going type.'

'Neither was I,' he confessed. 'But much to my surprise, it had me gripped from start to finish.'

'That's the art of Alfred Hitchcock, isn't it?' They'd been to see *Vertigo* with Kim Novak and James Stewart, an exciting suspense story about a detective with a fear of heights. 'No one sleeps in one of his thrillers.'

'They'd have a job.'

'I must say, though, that when you first mentioned the idea of going to the cinema with me, I thought you'd be dragging me off to the pub halfway through the film,' she mentioned in her usual outspoken way.

'I wouldn't have dared.'

'I'm not that much of a dragon, surely.'

'Just kidding,' he grinned. 'Anyway, we did go for a quick one afterwards, didn't we?'

'Yeah, and I enjoyed it too,' she admitted readily. 'So we've both broken new ground tonight; you went to the pictures and I went to the pub.'

'Perhaps we can go out again sometime,' he suggested. 'If you fancy a night out.'

225

'I'd really like that, Charlie. Going out is much more fun when you've got company.' She paused, wondering about something. 'In the meantime do you fancy coming in for coffee just to finish the evening off?'

'That would be lovely,' he enthused. 'It'll be quieter in your place than mine.'

'I'll say.'

As she opened her gate, a nearby front door opened and Ada Pickles put a milk bottle on the step. Looking around as she stood up, her eyes bulged as she spotted Charlie Mollitt and Hilda going into Hilda's together; at a time of night when decent people were thinking about going to bed, too. Well, really . . .

Anyone else would have closed the door quietly but diplomacy never had been Ada's strong point.

''Evening,' she called over.

'Hello, Ada,' said Hilda.

'How are you?' added Charlie. 'Ted all right?'

'We're both fine, thanks.' A short pause, then with all the subtlety of a brick through a window she asked, 'Been anywhere nice?'

'We've been to see the new Hitchcock thriller,' informed Hilda, walking to her front door with Charlie behind her.

'Was it good?'

'Smashing,' replied Charlie.

Hilda turned the key in the lock and opened the door. 'Good night, Ada,' she shouted.

''Night, Ada,' Charlie added.

Inside Hilda's hallway with the front door closed behind them, they both went into fits of laughter. 'That's given her something to think about,' chuckled Hilda.

'Knowing her, she'll put two and two together and make five,' he said.

'You can bet your sweet life on it,' she agreed. 'But let's forget about her. Take your coat off and make yourself comfortable in the other room while I put the kettle on.'

Chapter Fifteen

As the class came to the end of a routine they were learning with a collective lack of co-ordination and style, Jess glanced at her watch and frowned. She always seemed to run out of time; just a few minutes left and the standard fell far short of what she was aiming for. Not a single pupil was doing the steps with the proficiency and verve she knew they were capable of.

'OK, everyone,' she began in a friendly but authoritative manner from her vantage point on the platform, 'we're almost out of time; there's just a few minutes left. Hands up all those who want to leave it there and go home.'

Not a single hand went up.

'Hands up those who would like to spend the final few minutes improving that last routine.'

A forest of arms shot up.

'Good. So let's go through it again with more enthusiasm and poise. Do it as though you're really enjoying it. Be confident; I know you can do it.' She leaped off the stage and stood in the centre of the hall, a willowy figure in a loose white blouse and black tapered trousers with short slits at the sides. 'I'll just run through it to remind you . . . we're going to do tap, step ball change with the right foot, then tap, step ball change with the left foot; six each of those then we'll finish off with twelve high kicks holding on to each other. OK . . . with the music on the beat – follow me.'

And off she went, tapping and stepping around the room, moving with the ease of a juvenile, her eager band of hopefuls following. 'On your own now,' she said, running across the room and jumping back on to the stage so that she could see what they were doing. 'Better, girls, much better . . . keep those legs up . . . Oh, that's much more like it. That's really good.' When she finally ended the lesson, there was a ripple of laughter from the class, born both of enjoyment in what they were doing and relief that they'd got it right. 'Well, you took your time but you finally managed to please me so we'll end it there. See you all next week. Take care now.'

Watching from the back of the hall – having come upstairs to see Jess about something – Bruce thought she was magnificent; her gracefulness, her skill, her energy and joy in the job. The way she communicated with those children must surely be a special gift. They loved her, you could feel it. Every one of them wanted to dance like her, and she had the ability to bring out the best in them all, even those with two left feet. He was imbued with love and admiration for her. Brother's fiancée or not, he couldn't help it.

Noticing him suddenly, she slipped into a sweater and came over. 'Hi,' she greeted him coolly.

'Sorry to intrude,' he apologised. 'I thought you'd be finished by now. Wanted to catch you before you left.'

'You're not intruding,' she said in an even tone. 'It's your hall.'

'And you're hiring it so it's yours while you're paying,' he pointed out.

She shrugged. 'There is that, I suppose,' she agreed. 'But it doesn't matter.'

'I'm glad I was early, actually,' he confessed. 'It gave me a chance to see you in action. You're very good.'

'Thank you,' she said politely. 'I do my best.'

'It's almost inspiring enough to make me want to take lessons myself,' he joshed.

'Somehow, I don't see you as the new Fred Astaire.' She couldn't help grinning.

'Me neither.' He looked at her. 'Seriously, though, I need to talk to you.'

Her brow drew tight. 'That sounds ominous. I hope you haven't decided to expand your shop to this upper floor so that I can't have the use of the hall any more,' she said worriedly.

'No, nothing like that,' he put her mind at rest. 'I just wanted to tell you that I'm going to get it done up – I'm having a painter in.'

'That's a relief. But what's brought this on?'

He cast a critical eye around the room. 'I noticed the other day that it needs a lick of paint. I don't think it's been done for yonks,' he explained. 'I know a bloke who'll do it for me at a cheap price but he can only do it in his spare time when he's not at his regular job. I'm thinking of getting it done over Easter.'

'I see.' She looked at him, wondering what he was leading up to.

'So I just wanted to check that it'll be all right with you, that you won't be having classes over the holiday period,' he explained. 'I wouldn't want to interfere with your arrangements.'

'We'll be taking a break over Easter so you can go ahead and arrange it,' she told him. 'It's very good of you to consider me and I appreciate it.'

'Just keeping my part of the hire agreement.' He paused, grinning. 'I reckon there'd be a parental uprising if your pupils were to go home with wet paint all over their clothes.'

'It doesn't bear thinking about.'

A silence. The atmosphere had been strained anyway; now that the reason for his visit had been dealt with, it was fraught with tension.

228

'So, how have you been?' he asked at last.

Their eyes met. She'd seen him in passing since the incident in the park, and briefly when she paid for the hall. But this was the first time they'd been alone together for any length of time and the emotion was intense. 'I've been fine. Yourself?'

'OK. How's Don?'

'He's all right.'

'Still taking life too seriously?'

She found herself with a vivid memory of the argument she'd had with Don over Babs' pram and how trapped she'd felt then. Overwhelmed by that same feeling again now, she finally faced the awful truth; that she was engaged to one brother and in love with the other. She wanted to be with Bruce; to talk and laugh and make love; to share life's experiences with him. It wasn't just a fusion of sexual chemistry but something far more profound.

What a mess! She didn't want to be in love with a man who'd lied to her. She couldn't have him anyway – he'd made that very clear; neither could she break off her engagement because it would destroy Don. So she was just going to have to make a go of it with Don and hope her unwanted feelings for Bruce faded in time. There was no point in hankering after what might have been if the circumstances were different because nothing was going to change. All right, so Don wasn't the love of her life but she trusted him never to betray her and that was worth a lot. She wouldn't let him down either.

But now she said in reply, 'He wouldn't be Don if he wasn't. I don't suppose he'll ever change.'

'No.' He looked sad.

'Nor would we want him to.'

'Oh, I'm not so sure about that.'

She shrugged noncommittally and, afraid she might be disloyal to Don by agreeing, affected a swift change of subject. 'By the way, I've been meaning to thank you for giving Ronnie so much encouragement when he works for you on Saturdays. He's thrilled to bits with the job.'

'Thanks aren't necessary,' Bruce made plain. 'He's a good little worker and very useful to me. He really earns his money, that boy.'

Such a different attitude to his brother, she found herself thinking as she remembered having to beg Don not to involve the police after the incident at Dean's Stores. If Don had had his way Ronnie would be branded a juvenile delinquent by now, his chances of a decent future limited.

She admonished herself for making comparisons. The Day brothers were two separate individuals, each having the usual human mix of strengths and weaknesses. Bruce was more fun to be with, it was true, and less judgemental. He was also a wife stealer and a liar. Don was a decent bloke with a lot of good points and he deserved her loyalty. In her present mood she needed to get away from Bruce because she couldn't trust herself.

'I'm very pleased to hear it.' Glancing towards the piano where Hilda and Libby were standing chatting with their coats on, she added quickly, 'I must go. Hilda and Libby are waiting for me.'

'Off you go then,' he said, and walked briskly out of the hall and down the stairs.

'You're in a good mood tonight, Jess,' observed Don that same evening when she was ensconced on the sofa with him at his place, having dined on a meal that she had prepared for them. On impulse she'd gone to see him at work this afternoon and suggested that – instead of going out to the cinema or for a drink as they usually did on a Saturday night – she cook for them at his flat and they have an evening in. They were luckier than most courting couples, in that they had somewhere to go to be on their own. She'd then shopped for steak and all the trimmings and got some wine, organising fish and chips for the others at home as she wouldn't be there to cook for them. 'Why am I getting all this loving care and attention?'

'Because you deserve it,' she replied lightly.

'I'm not complaining but what have I actually done to deserve it?' he asked.

'You don't have to do anything in particular to receive a bit of pampering from your fiancée, surely,' she pointed out. 'Just being yourself is enough for me.'

'If I was a cynical man, I'd say you've got a guilty conscience about something,' he mentioned.

'But you're not a cynical man, are you?' she smiled. 'Well, not all the time, anyway. So stop wondering why; just sit back and relax and enjoy it.'

He was, in fact, absolutely right. Her conscience had been giving her hell ever since her meeting with Bruce this morning when she'd faced up to the actual seriousness of her feelings for him. This whole charade was all part of her plan to salve her conscience, and try to get some discipline into her emotions. The theory was, if she made an extra effort with her relationship with Don, it would stand a good chance of working. Many a marriage had been successful on less than they had.

'I will then,' he said happily.

God help you, Jess Mollitt, she thought.

'Well, you certainly know how to give a girl a good time, Bruce,' said Brenda, who worked in the baker's near Bruce's shop where he was a regular customer for currant buns and doughnuts. Being a sociable sort of a fellow he always stayed long enough for a bit of a chat when he called there.

Brenda had been sending out signals for weeks and this afternoon, after being in such turmoil over Jess this morning, he'd finally invited her out on a date. Why not? It was what Brenda obviously wanted and he had to do something to get his brother's future wife off his mind. A twenty-five-year-old redhead with inviting blue eyes might help to that end.

'I do my best,' he said, looking around the West End nightclub, which was classy and intimate, with soft lighting, plush furnishings, a four-piece band and a small dance floor where couples were smooching. 'There'll be a cabaret later on. They put on a good show here. Always use quality performers.'

'I can't wait,' enthused Brenda, who could hardly believe her luck in getting such an exciting date for a Saturday night.

Jess had stayed in contact with the Burton Company ever since she left the troupe. It had been such an important part of her life, she didn't want to lose touch. Her usual method of communication was to visit the Burton premises on her half-day off to catch up on all the gossip and see old friends, especially now that Babs had left and she didn't get news through her.

There were practical advantages too. Because she was an old girl, she was allowed to sit in on rehearsals, which she found particularly useful now that she was teaching. Watching professionals at work inspired her and reminded her of the high standards she wanted her own pupils to aspire to.

Calling in there one afternoon a few days after she'd got her Saturday class to work so hard and watching Elsie Tucker ordering the girls to 'liven up for God's sake and put some oomph into it', Jess realised just how much of her Burton training went into her own teaching.

After the rehearsal, she stayed to socialise with the dancers. There were several new faces but those from her own era were eager for news of Babs, who hadn't stayed in touch with anyone except Jess.

'If we'd known she'd had a little girl we'd have had a collection for her,' said someone when Jess told them about Cindy. 'We could have got her something nice between us. But we don't even know where she lives.'

Someone suggested that it wasn't too late to have a collection to buy a gift and wondered if Jess could deliver it to Babs when she next saw her. The idea quickly gathered momentum; Babs had been a very popular member of the troupe in her day. Elsie chipped in. Even Miss Molly stumped up a few shillings.

Jess suggested that the cash might be more useful to Babs than a present because it would enable her to get something she really needed for the baby. She agreed to make a diversion on her way home today to deliver the money, guessing that Babs would be home from work by the time she got there because it would be evening by then.

Delighted to have something to give Babs as well as her friends' good wishes, she got a greetings card at a shop in Oxford Street, signed it from everyone at Burtons, then hurried to the station, stopping only to telephone home to tell them that she'd be late.

Babs took her sleeping baby out of the pram in the hall, carried her up the stairs to her room and lay her on the bed while she went back downstairs to get the folded pram. Wearily opening it up again and settling Cindy into it, she then turned on the gas fire and put the kettle on for tea. She'd had a terrible day and her nervous system was in shreds. Cindy had cried with hardly a break throughout the whole of her shift.

Fortunately the boss gave Babs a free hand to run the café and wasn't there for a lot of the time because he had other business interests. If he'd been there today she would almost certainly have lost her job. When people went into a café for a cup of tea and a bacon sandwich they wanted to have it in peace; they didn't want their nerves shattered by a squalling baby, especially as most of the customers were men: labourers, building workers, van and lorry drivers, garage mechanics.

For much of the session, Babs had been frying bacon and eggs while holding the baby. It was the only way she could get her to quieten down, though she didn't stop even then. But the danger of all that hot fat splattering about worried Babs terribly. The fact was, the kitchen of a greasy spoon café just wasn't a suitable environment for a small baby.

To add to her problems, Babs had lost her concentration; she felt woolly-headed and couldn't gather her thoughts sufficiently to work out a solution. So she carried on, struggling through the days as best as she could. A recent attack of flu – which had left her with a sore chest and a stubborn cough – didn't help because she felt physically ill as well as nauseous with nerves. In a permanent state of illogical panic, the first thing she did most mornings was vomit. Her mouth was permanently parched and she couldn't eat. And the worst part was the all-consuming blackness that dogged her every waking moment; a feeling that dragged her down, making her weaker with every day that passed.

The kettle had just started to whistle on the gas ring when someone knocked at her door. She immediately tensed, fearing it might be her landlord giving her notice because the baby's crying at night was disturbing the other residents.

When she saw Jess standing there, the relief was so great she burst into tears.

'It's sweet of the girls to have a collection for me,' said Babs later when she was more composed. 'I really am very touched.'

Jess heaved a sigh of relief. Babs was so sensitive lately, there had been the possibility that she might take offence and see the money as an act of charity instead of friendship. But thankfully she'd accepted it in the spirit with which it had been given.

'They were really keen to do it,' Jess told her. 'And they were eager for news of you. They didn't even know that you'd had the baby or where you were living, or they'd have sent you something before. Why haven't you kept in touch with any of them?'

'I didn't see the point.'

'Oh, Babs,' said Jess in a tone of friendly admonition, 'you'll lose so much if you turn your back on your friends. You're very highly thought of among the dancers at Burtons.'

'Everything's different now. I don't have anything in common with them any more,' she pointed out dully. 'I'm not the same person as I was when I was in the troupe.'

You can say that again, thought Jess, observing how thin and ill her friend looked. She'd noticed, too, that her hands were trembling when she'd poured the tea, and she'd sobbed inconsolably when Jess had first arrived, claiming afterwards it was just because she was so pleased to see her. Jess didn't believe her but Babs was so touchy these days she daren't ask too many questions or show concern because she got spiky.

'Your circumstances and priorities have changed, obviously,' said Jess, 'but you're still the same person.'

Babs shook her head. 'No, I'm not, not at all. I feel quite different now.' She stared into the distance for a few moments then said, 'But I'm grateful to the girls for their collection and I'll write and thank them for it. The money will come in very useful for Cindy.'

'More useful than a present because you know what you need,' Jess suggested.

'Exactly.' Babs sat up straight as though trying to shake off her depression. 'Anyway, that's enough about me,' she said. 'Let's hear your news.'

Jess toyed with the idea of telling her about her trauma as regards the Day brothers but finally decided against it. Talking about her feelings for Bruce only brought them back to the forefront of her mind and got her all steamed up. So instead she said, 'My dad's found himself a friend to go out with . . . a woman.'

'No!'

'Yeah, and you'll never guess who.'

'Go on, tell me.'

'Our next-door neighbour Hilda.'

'Ooh, that was a crafty move on his part,' commented Babs, showing a hint of her old capacity for humour. 'He doesn't have far to walk her home.'

'I didn't think of that,' grinned Jess.

'I take it you don't mind then.'

'I'm delighted,' Jess confirmed. 'Hilda's a dear.'

'So what sort of thing is it? Romantic?'

'Oh, no, nothing like that,' Jess was quick to make clear. 'They're just keeping each other company because they're both lonely. They've known each other for years so it's the sensible thing to do.'

'Sounds like a good idea to me.'

'They only go out together on a Saturday night,' Jess went on to say. 'But Dad sometimes pops next door of an evening during the week if it's too rowdy in our place, what with the twins arguing about who's turn it is to use the record player they had between them for their last birthday, and Libby playing Elvis records nonstop. I think Dad finds it all a bit too much and it's a relief to have somewhere to go for a break.'

'It's nice for him.'

'I think so too,' nodded Jess. 'He's a lot more cheerful lately anyway, thank goodness. He'd been a real misery guts since Mum died until now.'

'Good.' Babs sipped her tea, looking at Jess. 'So, what about this bloke of yours? Is he still in the picture?'

Jess nodded.

'You've never said much about him,' Babs remarked. 'What's he like?'

'Don's all right.'

'Only all right. Not heart-stoppingly gorgeous?'

'Oh, no. Not at all. He's just ordinary-looking but a thoroughly decent bloke.'

'There's something to be said for that too,' was Babs' earnest opinion. 'The good-looking ones need watching. Dickie was gorgeous and look what happened to me.'

The conversation came to an end when a soft grunting sound from the pram rose to a piercing howl. Jess watched Babs' face tighten and turn even paler. 'She wants her bottle, I expect,' she said shakily.

'You get it ready and I'll give it to her if you like, to give you a break,' suggested Jess.

'Thanks.' Babs was already getting a bottle out of the sterilising unit.

'Can I pick her up while you do that?' asked Jess.

'Please do,' invited Babs. 'Perhaps that will shut her up. She's been an absolute horror today.'

Jess picked the tiny thing up and held her against her shoulder, walking up and down with her, talking to her gently and breathing in the soft baby scent. 'I think I must have the magic touch,' she said as Cindy stopped crying and began to emit little contented noises.

Getting a tin of milk powder out of the cupboard, Babs looked over and the sight of Jess holding the baby with such obvious affection touched her heart and brought a glimmer of light into her dark world. 'It does seem like it,' she agreed. 'I could do with you being around more often.'

'If you lived nearer, I could be.'

'You know I can't do that so don't start nagging me again,' said Babs, testing the milk on the soft part of her arm.

'Come and visit us then,' invited Jess. 'The family would love to see you, and my sister is dying to see this little thing.' She paused. 'Anyway, it's about time you met my intended.'

'Yeah, yeah, I know all that. But going anywhere is such a performance when you've got a baby, I tend to avoid it,' she said, prevaricating as usual. 'But I will come over sometime.'

'I shall keep on at you until you do,' Jess told her. 'You'll get so fed up with it you'll come just to keep me quiet.'

'I know what to expect then.' She handed Jess the bottle. 'Here, you feed her and I'll make some more tea.'

'Sure,' said Jess settling down in the armchair with the baby.

By the time Jess got home the family had eaten and all the washing-up was done. Jess had had beans on toast with Babs, in an effort to encourage her to eat, but the poor thing had managed little more than a mouthful. Jess was very worried about her indeed.

She was still thinking about her when she got into bed that night. But she wasn't left alone with her thoughts for long because Libby was still awake and in one of her talkative moods. Having been given details of the baby, she began to quizz Jess about her trip to see the Burton Girls, which Jess had just happened to mention in conversation. Libby could never get enough of that subject.

'I didn't realise you were going there today,' she remarked.

'I didn't know myself until around mid-morning,' Jess informed her. 'I suddenly decided it was time I paid them a visit as I've not been for a while. And I didn't have anything else on.'

'No particular reason then?'

'No. Just wanted to see them all, and watch them rehearse,' she explained. 'It helps with my own classes.'

'Are any of the dancers who were there with you still in the troupe?'

'Yeah, quite a few. Some have left though.'

The questions kept coming until Jess could take no more. 'Flipping heck, Libs, what is this? The third degree? I'm tired and I'd like to go to sleep.'

'Just interested, that's all.' Libby sounded sulky.

'I know you are, and we'd talk about Burtons all night if you had your way but we both need to get some sleep,' Jess told her. 'So don't go into a strop about it, please, love. Just turn over and go to sleep. G'night.'

''Night.'

Jess turned on to her side but it was a very long time before she actually dozed off. She couldn't stop thinking about Babs and how desperate she obviously was, despite all her attempts to hide it.

Babs was awake until the small hours too. She couldn't remember the last time she had a decent night's sleep. She always ached with exhaustion when she got into bed but could never sleep properly. Her nerves were so raw, the slightest sound from Cindy's pram shot right through her.

She had a sudden vivid memory of Jess, earlier on, holding her daughter. She'd seemed so completely at ease with her. The two of them looked so right together. It had warmed her heart then and it did again now.

Through the depths of despair she glimpsed the beginnings of an answer to her problems. Lying there in the dark it all became clear suddenly; she knew what she must do.

Jess had been at school with Brenda Baxter. They'd never been friends as such but knew each other vaguely and usually stopped for a chat if they happened to meet around the town so were quite up to date with each other's news. Brenda was in very high spirits when Jess met her in the post office one morning a few days later. Jess was in the queue waiting to get served; Brenda was on her way out, having finished at the counter.

'I'm glad I've seen you, Jess,' said Brenda, 'because I've got something really exciting to tell you.'

'Oh?'

'Yeah.' Her eyes were gleaming. 'Don't be surprised if you find yourself out in a foursome with me and your boyfriend's brother,' she informed her gleefully.

Jess's heart lurched. 'Really?' she said. 'Are you and Bruce seeing each other then?'

'Not half,' she confirmed, bubbling with enthusiasm and having no idea of the crushing effect this was having on Jess. 'I've been out with him on the last two Saturday nights. Cor, does he know how to treat a girl?'

'He obviously does, by the look on your face.' Jess tried to look pleased.

'I'll say he does. None of this taking you to the pictures or down the local pub and buying you a bag of chips afterwards if you're lucky, like most of the blokes around here.'

'No?'

'No. That isn't the way he does things at all.' She was full of it. 'He took me to some classy West End nightclub and we had the works. A posh meal and as much as I wanted to drink. Talk about doing things in style.'

'Lucky you.' Jess forced the words out. 'Sounds as though he's a man who knows his way around.'

'I've never been out with anyone like him before.' Brenda paused, her face flushed and animated. 'It could be a bit of a laugh, eh, Jess, us going out with two brothers?' she went on to enthuse. 'I mean with us being old school mates.'

It seemed churlish to point out that they'd only ever known each other

236

at a distance, so Jess said, 'Yeah, it might be fun.' She knew it would never happen anyway.

Brenda leaned towards her in a confidential manner. 'I don't know if you've realised it but you and me are about the only two left out of our class at school who aren't married and settled down with kids,' she informed her knowingly.

'Are we?' responded Jess, struggling to show an interest in this dismal news.

'Oh, yeah,' she confirmed with an air of the well informed. 'Mind you, I would have been married long ago if I hadn't got mixed up with some lowlife and wasted my best years on him.' She put her head at a saucy angle and clicked her tongue twice. 'Still, things are on the up for us both now. You're almost at the altar with Don Day and with a bit of luck I won't be far behind with his brother.'

'Isn't it a bit early to be thinking of marriage?' Jess suggested warily. 'If you've only been out with him a few times.'

'Yeah, I suppose it is really, but you can't help hoping when you meet someone new, can you?' Her optimism didn't seem the slightest bit dampened by Jess's mention of reality. 'We all do that, don't we? Us single girls.'

Jess nodded, longing for the queue to move on so that she could do what she had to and escape. Bruce's love life shouldn't matter to her, but it did – agonisingly so.

'As you say, it's still early days for me and Bruce.' Brenda was unstoppable. 'But if we do carry on seeing each other, shall I suggest a foursome with you and his brother?'

Jess decided it was time to be frank about this aspect. 'Bruce might be all for it but Don definitely won't,' she stated categorically. 'The two of them don't get on.' In this particular instance, Jess was very glad that they didn't. She could hardly bear to imagine the misery of an evening spent in some pub or restaurant watching Bruce and Brenda drooling over each other.

'Oh, that's a shame,' Brenda said, shrugging. 'Still, never mind. It was only a thought.'

Much to Jess's relief, the queue inched forward.

'Anyway, I'd better be getting back to work,' said Brenda at last. 'See you around.'

'Yeah, see you, Brenda.'

The post office was crowded with people, a low drone of conversation filling the room. Standing there wishing the counter assistant would shift herself, Jess became aware of a familiar voice rising above the general hubbub.

'I wouldn't have believed it if I hadn't seen it with my own eyes,' the voice was saying. 'But there they were, as large as life, going into her place together.'

'No.'

'Yeah, I know it's hard to believe but it's true as I'm standing here talking to you. It must have been turned eleven o'clock at the very least. I mean, you don't go visiting at that time of night, do you? Not ordinary decent visiting.'

'You don't,' agreed a voice Jess didn't recognise.

'Some people have no shame.'

'That's very true.'

'Of course, that was a good few weeks ago,' said the first woman. 'He's in and out of there all the time now. You don't need much imagination to work out what's going on there.'

'Well, well, Charlie Mollitt and Hilda Hawkins, who would have thought it?'

'It's downright disgusting, if you ask me,' the first woman went on. 'I mean, what way is that to carry on?'

'No way at all.'

'First he's down the pub every night staggering home paralytic, now he's started womanising. Not much of an example to set to those kids of his, is it?'

If Jess hadn't been so angry she might have seen the funny side of any man being accused of 'womanising' with a pillar of respectability like Hilda. But this was no time for humour. Deciding to come back for her stamps another time, Jess left the queue and walked to the end where Ada Pickles was holding forth.

'Jess,' said Ada looking extremely uncomfortable, 'I didn't see you there.'

'Obviously.'

The other woman, whom Jess recognised as a local resident but knew only by sight, lowered her eyes to the floor, cheeks flaming.

'I was only saying—' began Ada.

'I heard what you were saying, every single word,' Jess interrupted. 'And now I'm going to say my piece and you are going to listen, whether you like it or not.' Jess had raised her voice and people were looking this way, enjoying the entertainment.

Ada was visibly squirming. 'I didn't mean any harm,' she began feebly.

'Oh, yes you did,' the young woman disagreed hotly. 'You always do with that evil tongue of yours.'

'Here, you wanna watch what you're saying—'

'Like you do, you mean?' Jess cut in. 'You are one of the nastiest, most mean-minded people I have ever had the misfortune to come across. My father and Hilda Hawkins are good friends, and his children are delighted that he has found someone to help him through the loneliness he's had to endure since my mother died.'

'Yes, I—'

'As for that rubbish about him setting a bad example,' Jess went on, 'he's doing exactly the opposite. He's illustrating to us the joy of friendship and how it changes lives for the better. But I shouldn't think your life is touched by friendship because no one would want to make a friend of a nasty piece of work like you.'

'Oh really—'

'You're a vicious woman, Ada Pickles, and if I ever catch you spreading malicious rumours about any member of my family again, I won't be responsible for my actions.'

With that she marched from the premises, leaving Ada shame-faced and not knowing where to look, with every eye in the room upon her.

Having had the unwelcome update on Bruce's love life from Brenda, followed immediately by the altercation with Ada Pickles, Jess was none too happy when she got back to the shop. But she said nothing to her father about the set-to with Ada because she didn't want to spoil things for him.

What a day this is turning out to be, she thought miserably. Roll on bedtime.

Things took a turn for the better, however, around lunchtime when Babs turned up at the shop with the baby asleep in the pram.

'What a lovely surprise,' welcomed Jess.

'I fancied an outing and thought perhaps we could have lunch somewhere,' she explained.

'That would be smashing.' Jess thought Babs seemed slightly more cheerful than she'd been lately. She was still pale and drawn but at least she seemed to have made an effort with her appearance, in that her hair was freshly washed and worn loose and she was wearing lipstick. 'It's really cheered me up, seeing you and the little one. It's quite made my day.' She paused, looking at her. 'But how come you're not at work?'

'I've got a day off. So I thought I'd make the effort and come over. You've asked me enough times.'

'I told you I'd wear you down with my nagging, didn't I?' said Jess in a jovial manner.

'The folding pram you gave me really came into its own today,' Babs mentioned, sounding pleased. 'I managed all right with it on the tube and the bus.'

'Good.'

Charlie appeared from the door behind the counter.

'Hello, Mr Mollitt,' Babs greeted him politely. 'How are you keeping these days?'

'Not so dusty, dear, thanks. Yourself?'

'Mustn't grumble.'

He came out from behind the counter. 'Let's have a look at this nipper of yours then,' he said, peering into the pram. 'Aah, she's fast asleep, bless her.'

'Good job too,' said Babs with a wry look. 'She's a noisy little so-and-so when she's awake.'

'They usually are at that age,' he mentioned, smiling. 'They've got to exercise their lungs somehow. She's a lovely little thing. A real credit to you.'

He was right about that, thought Jess. Although Babs was obviously not well and she had very little in the way of facilities, she kept the baby spotless: a pink bonnet and mittens showing above the pram cover, the pillowcase as white as snow.

'Thanks, Mr Mollitt.'

'If we're going out to lunch you'd better come through to the back while I comb my hair and put some lipstick on,' Jess told her. 'I can't go to the café looking like this.'

'Well, look . . . I need to pop to the chemist for some baby cream because Cindy's a bit sore in her nether regions,' explained Babs. 'So I'll do that while you get ready. Can I leave her here with you while I dash over there? It'll be quicker if I go on my own. I'll only be a minute.'

'Of course you can leave her here,' said a delighted Jess, lifting the counter flap and wheeling the pram through towards the staff room.

'I won't be long,' said Babs.

'Take your time. There's no hurry,' Jess told her. 'She'll be fine with us.'

Babs got off the bus and walked around the corner to Ealing Broadway station in such a hurry she broke into a run. She could hardly ask for her ticket because she was sobbing so much and trying to stifle it. The man in the ticket office paid little attention. He was more concerned with getting the queue down than some neurotic woman who couldn't keep her feelings under control.

Sitting on the train she stared unseeingly ahead of her, her face soaked with tears. The lie about the urgent visit to the chemist had worked exactly as she'd planned. She'd done the right thing, she was sure of it. It was the best thing for Cindy and that was all that mattered. Her own pain wasn't important, even though it was hardly bearable. The tube rumbled out of the station with that familiar whining noise. Babs looked out of the window through a blur of tears. Soon the nightmare would be over and she'd be safe; more importantly, so would her daughter.

Jess didn't think anything of it at first. She'd told Babs not to hurry and she'd taken her literally, that was all; she'd obviously got chatting to someone in the shopping parade, though Jess couldn't imagine who, since Babs was a stranger round here.

Half an hour passed; forty-five minutes. Where the devil had she got to? Panic beginning to well up inside her, Jess left the sleeping baby with her father and went out looking for her friend in the Broadway. The chemist's shop was just closing for lunch but Jess managed to speak to the counter assistant, who didn't recall serving anyone of Babs' description.

So where was she? If she'd been taken ill before she'd reached the chemist, someone would have notified them, so it couldn't be that. With a shiver of fear, Jess began to wonder if perhaps her friend hadn't intended to go to the chemist's at all. Maybe it had just been an excuse to leave the baby for some reason.

Dark thoughts began to form at an alarming rate. Perhaps Babs wasn't coming back at all. Maybe she'd abandoned her baby. You read about that sort of thing in the paper: new mothers, feeling unable to cope acting out of desperation. Jess had noticed that she'd seemed brighter today, had had a new sense of purpose about her, somehow. Could that have been because she knew she was about to set herself free from her awesome new responsibilities?

No. Babs wouldn't do such a terrible thing, Jess told herself firmly. At least, the person Babs had once been certainly wouldn't. But there had been little sign of that woman just lately. Telling herself that she was letting her imagination run out of control, she made her way back to the shop.

'She'll turn up,' her father said a bit later as Jess beat a path from the backroom to the shop door to peer out into the street. 'She wouldn't just walk off and leave her baby.'

'But where is she?' Jess was frantic with worry now. 'She's been gone for over an hour.'

Her father pondered on this. 'I don't know where she is, love. But women get funny moods when they've had a baby, don't they?' he reminded her. 'Nippers can be very wearing in the early days. Maybe she just wanted some time to herself.'

'She'd have asked me to look after Cindy for longer if she just wanted a break,' Jess pointed out.

'There is that. But she could have acted on impulse,' he suggested, though he was worried too. 'She's been under a strain. Perhaps it all seemed too much for her suddenly and she decided to take an hour or so away from it all.'

'Or perhaps she suddenly lost her mind and went wandering off,' added Jess.

'Now don't start dreaming things up,' he advised her.

'She's not been herself for ages, Dad – even before the baby was born,' Jess told him, thinking back on Babs' behaviour. 'In fact, she's not been right since her boyfriend ditched her.' She bit her lip anxiously. 'Oh, Dad, what are we going to do?'

'There's no call for alarm at this stage. I'll go out and have another look for her,' he suggested. 'If there's no sign of her in a little while, I suppose we'll have to think about notifying the police.'

'Meanwhile I'd better see if she's left any baby food and nappies and so on,' said Jess, taking a bag that was hooked on to the pram and opening it. 'The poor little mite will be waking up soon and need feeding.'

Charlie put his coat on. 'I'll put the closed sign up while I'm out just in case you're busy with the nipper,' he said. 'I'll be back as quick as I can.'

'Thanks, Dad.'

The bag was neatly packed with clean nappies, bottles and milk powder and other essentials such as clean bibs, some muslins and a nightdress. A nightdress? So she had planned to leave Cindy here overnight.

Then Jess saw the note pinned to it with a nappy pin that set alarm bells ringing in her head as soon as she'd read the first few words. Jess tore after her father and caught him at the shop door.

'You won't find her around here, Dad.' Her voice was distorted as she handed him the note with a trembling hand.

Dear Jess,

I can't look after Cindy so I'm asking you to do it for me. I know it's a terrible thing that I'm doing, and more than I have a right to ask of anyone, but please take care of her for me. She'll have a chance with you, a chance of a decent life that I can't give her. I'm too broken inside to be a mother to her. I know you'll be kind to her. Try not to hate me too much. There really is no other way.

  Your friend,
  Babs

'She must have been in a hell of a state to leave her kid like that,' Charlie said, handing the note back to her; his hand was shaking a little too.

'Well, yes,' Jess agreed. 'No one in their right mind would do a thing like that.'

'It could just be a cry for help,' he suggested, but he couldn't hide his concern. 'I mean, she must know that you'll just take the baby straight back to her.'

'Unless she's gone away somewhere, somewhere we won't find her,' Jess speculated.

He stroked his chin, mulling the situation over, his expression becoming graver by the second.

'What is it, Dad? Tell me.'

'Nothing, love.'

But she knew something had occurred to him, the same awful thought that had just come into her mind, she suspected. She read the letter again, the notepaper shaking so much in her hand she could barely read the writing. There was something so dreadfully ominous about the final sentence – 'There really is no other way.' She looked at her father and saw her own fears reflected in his eyes.

242

Chapter Sixteen

'No, Jess, I can't just drop everything and go to Paddington now, this minute.' Don was horrified at the thought of such a disruption to his well-oiled routine. 'It just isn't possible in the middle of a working day. Surely you can see that.'

'I realise it's difficult but I wouldn't ask if it wasn't an emergency,' she persisted.

'Oh, come on now, this isn't an emergency,' he disagreed, frowning at her. 'As I've said, willingly I will do it for you but not until tonight after work.'

'That might be too late.' She was sick with worry. 'Someone needs to go to Babs' place right away. I've got a really bad feeling about this.'

'You're overdramatising the whole thing,' he responded impatiently. 'Of course your friend won't try to kill herself.'

'We can't be sure of that.'

'I can,' was his categorical reply. 'She just wants to offload her responsibilities so that she can have an easy life, that's what all this is about.'

'She isn't like that,' Jess asserted. 'Please do this for me, Don. I need you to go there; I need to know if she's all right.'

'Sorry, Jess, it can't be done.'

'I wouldn't ask you if I wasn't desperate.' Her first impulse had been to enlist Bruce's help because he had a car and she knew instinctively he wouldn't have hesitated. But that would have infuriated Don. 'Someone needs to get there sharpish and Dad's car is off the road being repaired. I'd go myself but it'll take too long on public transport. Anyway, I have to stay here and look after the baby.'

'Even if she did have something like that in mind – which is most unlikely – she wouldn't necessarily do it at home.'

'No, but it's the only lead we've got.'

This conversation was taking place in the manager's office at the back of Dean's Stores. Don was standing by his desk looking through the glass partition into the shop, which was crowded with customers. 'How can I just walk out of here when the store is busy?' he wanted to know.

'You've got staff,' she pointed out. 'They can manage without you for a couple of hours.'

'But I'm being paid to be here,' he reminded her. 'We're short-staffed too.'

'Give your head office a ring and clear it with them if you're that worried.'

'It won't do much for my reputation for reliability, will it?'

'Come off it, Don. An hour or so off isn't going to put a black mark against your name.' His reluctance to help was really beginning to annoy her and she wished she had asked Bruce to do it. 'I know it's asking a lot but it could be a matter of life and death.'

'Oh, Jess, really,' he said with an edge to his voice. 'Your friend is just making excuses for herself, that's why she put that in the note about there being no other way. Can't you see that?'

'If I could I wouldn't be here asking you to go to Paddington to check on her, would I? I'm not the sort of person to ask for help unless I really have to, you know that.' Her mouth was parched with anxiety, her voice quivering slightly. 'Still, I might have known you wouldn't be willing to help. Once again you're showing just how lacking in compassion you are, like you did when I bought Babs the pram and you were so mean about it.'

He tutted. 'Look, it might seem as though I'm being hard but I'm just being realistic, which you're unable to be at the moment because you've worked yourself up into an emotional state,' he lectured. 'This Babs woman has walked out on her baby because she doesn't want the bother of it. It's as simple as that. I can see that she needs to be confronted and made to face up to her responsibilities because you can't possibly be expected to look after her child for her. And I am quite willing to go to Paddington to see her but it will have to wait until I've finished work for the day.'

'Perhaps you're right and I am making a fuss about nothing but if there's one chance in a thousand that her life is in danger, it's worth making the effort to save her.'

'I won't argue with you about that. If I really thought anyone's life was at risk, I'd move heaven and earth to save them.' He waved his hand towards the glass partition. 'But you can see how I'm fixed at the moment. I'm being paid to do a job and I can't just go swanning off because you've got a bad feeling about something. If it was a genuine emergency it would be different but it isn't. I'll go as soon as I finish here tonight.'

Jess's fears for Babs were all consuming, and making her nerves jangle. 'Don't bother,' she snapped. 'I'll go myself – I'll get a taxi and take the baby with me. I can't leave her with Dad because he's got the shop to look after.'

'Don't be so damned ridiculous,' he retorted. 'From here to Paddington a cab will cost an arm and a leg.'

'This is no time to think about money. If there's no other way, it's what

'I'll do.' Being practical, the baby would be a hindrance, especially if her suspicions were confirmed but she'd take her if she had to. 'I'll either go myself or get Dad to go.'

'All that money for a taxi because you've got an overactive imagination, he disapproved.

'If it means saving Babs' life, it'll be worth it.' She walked to the door, turning as an idea occurred to her. 'Maybe I should ring the police and get them to send someone round there.'

'You'll be in trouble for wasting police time.'

'Better that than take a chance.'

He stared at her, cold-eyed and tight-lipped. 'Oh all right,' he said at last, with an exaggerated sigh of resignation. 'I'll go. It's a bloody nuisance and completely unnecessary but I'll do it if it means that much to you.'

'Thanks, Don, I owe you one.' She walked back into the room and handed him a slip of paper with Babs' address on it, far too tense to make much of his change of heart. 'She lives upstairs in the attic bedsit, the door at the top of the stairs. The street door's always open. Please hurry.'

'I'll just ring the office to clear it with them and I'll be on my way,' he told her.

'Can you call me from a phone box to let me know the situation as soon as you've checked it out?' Jess asked.

'Yeah, yeah,' he agreed with seething impatience. 'Whatever you say.'

Don got angrier and more frustrated with every second that passed as he fought his way through the traffic in central London, at a complete standstill for a while in Shepherd's Bush. He wouldn't mind if the journey was necessary but the whole thing was a ridiculous waste of time. He'd been forced to lie about it too. He'd told head office he had to go out on an urgent family matter. Well, he could hardly tell them the truth: that his fiancée's irresponsible friend had walked out on her baby and thrown everyone into a panic. About the only good thing to come out of this trip was the opportunity for him to give the wretched Babs woman a piece of his mind. If she was there, that was. She was probably miles away by now, laughing her head off in the thought that she'd left her friend literally holding the baby.

Turning off the main road at Notting Hill Gate, he pulled into the side of the road and consulted his A to Z. It occurred to him that a less honest man might be tempted to stop wasting time and go back without finishing the job; just tell Jess that he'd been to the address and there was no one at home. But he was a person burdened with integrity and some old tart of a friend of Jess's wasn't going to make him lie twice in one day.

Having done everything she could think of to stop Cindy's relentless shrieking – she'd fed, changed, winded and cuddled her – Jess took her for a walk in the pram because having a screaming baby in the shop wasn't conducive to a smooth-running business. The racket she was making was enough to shatter even the hardiest nervous system. However, the motion of the pram seemed to settle her so Jess stopped off at Hilda's to give her an account of what had happened.

'Oh my Lord, how dreadful,' was her concerned reaction. 'That poor little child.'

They discussed the situation some more until Jess said she had to get back to the shop.

'Why not leave the baby here with me until you finish work?' offered Hilda.

Jess hadn't planned to ask that favour of her, but since she was offering . . . 'That would be a great help, if you're sure you don't mind,' she said.

'Course I don't mind. A busy shop's no place for the poor little mite,' she said, peering into the pram. 'She'll be better off staying here with me.'

'Thanks ever so much, Hilda.'

The older woman tutted. 'Let's hope your fears prove to be unfounded,' she muttered worriedly.

'I'm praying that they are.'

'It's a terrible thing for a mother to do, though, to go off like that and leave her baby,' Hilda went on. 'The poor girl must be at her wits' end to have done such a thing.'

Jess nodded. 'It's her state of mind that's worrying me,' she told her. 'If she feels bad enough to leave her baby, God knows what else she might do.'

'Well, try not to let your imagination work overtime, dear,' Hilda suggested wisely. 'You'll hear from Don soon enough.'

What a dump, thought Don, when he finally found the bedsit house, the front garden of which was strewn with litter. There were broken bricks, old bicycle wheels, bits of rusty metal along with sweet wrappers and broken bottles. What a terrible place to bring up a child. When he entered the building through the unlocked door, he was even more disgusted. Squalid was an understatement. There was peeling wallpaper and broken floorboards, and the revolting stench was suggestive of rotting cabbages and an unclean lavatory.

There didn't seem to be anyone about so he made his way up to the attic and rapped his knuckles on the door at the top of the stairs. As predicted, there was no reply. It was as he'd thought, she was long gone from here. He knocked again just to make sure. Not a sound. He tried the door and it was locked. No surprise there. You didn't leave your door unlocked when you went out. Good, he'd done what Jess asked, now he could go home with a clear conscience.

246

He'd just started down the attic stairs when he heard something from inside the room; some sort of a human sound. He stopped in his tracks and listened hard. All was silent. He must have been imagining things. Continuing on his way, he stopped suddenly when he heard it again. It was the sound of someone coughing. All at once the locked door and lack of a response to his knock had alarming significance and he was at the top of the stairs before he'd had time to think about it. With uncharacteristic spontaneity, he threw himself against the door, shoulder on. It took several attempts and he ended up on the floor, but he was inside. And what he found there shook him to the very core and made him deeply ashamed for doubting Jess's instinct.

'Christ Almighty,' he gasped at the sight of a woman he presumed to be Babs, lying on her back on the bed fully dressed. She seemed to be either unconscious or dead, her face a greyish white, blonde hair strewn about the pillow. Even as he stood there horror-stricken, she coughed and eliminated the latter theory. An empty pill bottle was on the floor by the bed. His first instinct was to find a phone box and ring for an ambulance. But by the time it got here it could be too late. It made more sense to take her to the hospital in the car.

So he heaved her into a sitting position then lifted her into a standing position. She was grunting and objecting in a barely intelligible manner. 'Leeme alone, shurrup, geroff,' he managed to discern.

'As much as I'd like to I can't do that,' he muttered. 'You've got to stay awake, do you hear me. Stay awake.'

Her legs buckled and she began to slither to the floor. With physical strength born of necessity, he lifted her up and carried her over his shoulders in a fireman's lift, down the stairs. Somehow he managed to get her into the passenger seat of his car where she immediately went to sleep.

He knew vaguely from a film he'd once seen that you were supposed to keep an overdosed person awake. The only thing he could think of to this end was to talk to her, even though he knew she wouldn't respond and probably couldn't even hear him. He didn't know if it would work but it was worth a try.

'You're not going to die, you know, Babs, as much as you might want to,' he said, using her name in the hope that it might register and help somehow. 'I'm not going to let you slip away so you can get that idea right out of your head. Do you understand me? You've got too much to live for, a young woman like you. You've got a beautiful little daughter, so I'm told. What's going to happen to her if you're not here, eh? Who's going to bring her up? She needs you so you've got to stay around.'

She grunted something incomprehensible. He felt compelled to keep talking, even though she was too far gone to comprehend what he was saying. He found himself telling her that he'd felt like doing the same thing in the early days after he'd lost his wife. 'I didn't have the bottle when it came down to it, though. And I'm very glad I didn't because I met Jess and things turned out all right for me in the end. They will for you too, you'll see. Life can be a bugger, I can vouch for that. But you can't just give in and let it beat you, and I'm not going to let you do that. Apart from anything else, my name will be mud with Jess if I let that happen. She's relying on me to save you. Mind you, I thought she was talking rubbish when she said she thought you had something like this in mind. How wrong can you be, eh?' He paused, sighing with relief. 'Thank God for that, we've arrived at the hospital. Now we can get help.'

Half dragging, half carrying her to the entrance, he handed her over to a nurse and explained the situation. As they took her away on a trolley, having told him to go into the waiting room, he was surprised to realise that tears were streaming down his cheeks. It was the relief of getting her here alive, he supposed.

'It was a good job you did twist my arm into going to Paddington right away, as your instinct proved to be correct,' Don told Jess later, when he called her from the hospital pay phone and brought her up to date. 'I should have known better than to doubt you in the first place. I'm really sorry.'

'It doesn't matter about that,' she was quick to assure him. 'You did actually go, that's the important thing. So, she's going to be all right, you say?'

'Yeah, apparently. They've pumped her stomach and she's sleeping now.'

'Thank God for that.' There was a brief pause. 'You saved her life, Don.'

'The credit for that must go to you,' he corrected. 'You nagged me into going to Paddington. I wouldn't have done it if you hadn't kept on at me; and anyone would have done the same, finding her like that.'

'Even so—'

'She's all right, that's all that matters now,' he cut in.

'That's true,' Jess agreed. 'So are you coming back now?'

'No. I thought I'd stay until she wakes up, which should be soon,' he said, surprising her. 'They said I can see her for a few minutes when she comes round even if it isn't the official visiting time. I think she might be a bit panicky, finding herself in hospital with no one around apart from the hospital staff. Don't you?'

'Yeah. But I'll get there as soon as I can, so you can make your way home if you like. Hilda will look after the baby.'

'I'd rather stay.'

'That's kind of you.'

'Well, the poor thing needs all the support she can get at the moment.'

'You've changed your tune,' Jess couldn't help mentioning. 'You've never had a good word to say for Babs before. So what's happened?'

He didn't reply right away because he was as amazed as Jess was that he didn't want to hightail it out of here with all possible speed. 'I suppose I just want to finish the job,' was the only way he could describe it.

'As long as you don't mind.'

'This is me you're talking to,' he reminded her with an unusual stab at humour. 'You'd soon know about it if I minded.'

'Yes, there is that,' she agreed with a smile in her voice.

'See you in a bit then.'

'Just as soon as I get the baby settled with Hilda,' she told him. 'And thanks for being so good about everything, Don. I do appreciate your help.'

'It's the least I can do for the woman I love,' was his tender response.

'Hello,' said Don.

Babs squinted at him through half-closed eyes, which were sore and swollen. 'Who the hell are you?' she asked in a drowsy voice.

'Don Day. Jess's fiancé.'

'Oh, right,' she mumbled. 'What are you doing here?'

'I brought you in.'

'Oh, it was you, was it?' she said dully. 'Why didn't you just leave me alone?'

'And leave Jess with your child to look after?' was his unsentimental reply. 'Not likely. When I marry Jess, I want first call on her attention. It's bad enough having to compete with that family of hers. If she's landed with a baby as well, I'll stand no chance at all. It's time she had a life of her own and I intend to see that she's able to start married life unburdened by someone else's child.'

'I suppose I deserved that.'

'You certainly did.'

'Do you know if my baby is all right?' she enquired, blinking as though to clear her head.

'She's fine,' he assured her. 'I spoke to Jess on the phone just now. She'll be here as soon as she can. Her neighbour will look after the baby while she's out.'

'I knew she'd be all right with Jess.' She brushed a weary hand over her brow.

'Jess never lets anyone down,' was his response.

'No she doesn't.' Her sad eyes rested on him. 'But me, I'm just a mess and here I still am with all the same problems,' she muttered sleepily. 'I can't get anything right. I can't even make a decent job of doing myself in.'

A fierce stab of pity for her shocked him because excessive compassion wasn't in his nature. 'Self-pity won't get you far,' he said in a determinedly firm manner to hide his feelings.

'Do you think I don't know that?'

'Yeah, I suppose you do. Sorry.'

'That's all right.' She looked at him more closely, noticing the short-back-and-sides haircut and the dark grey suit. 'You're not Jess's usual type,' she observed. 'You're a bit ordinary for her.'

'Thanks,' he said with a wry look. 'You really know how to make a chap feel good.'

'I didn't mean that as it sounded,' she tried to explain, but her head was still muzzy from the effect of the pills. 'I meant traditional rather than ordinary. When you're in show business you meet a lot of flashy blokes. Good-looking ones who throw their money about to impress you, then break your heart.' She managed a weak smile. 'I suppose I'm trying to say that I'm glad Jess has found someone decent.'

'That's better.'

Suddenly overcome with the bleakness of her own situation, her eyes filled with tears. 'So what do I do now, Mr Good Samaritan?' She emitted a deep chesty cough and began coughing and crying simultaneously. 'You've brought me back from the dead,' she sobbed. 'Now perhaps you can tell me what a useless human being like me is supposed to do next.'

He handed her a handkerchief. 'You could try facing up to things,' he suggested.

'If I knew how to do that I wouldn't be here, would I?'

'No, I suppose not. But I didn't mean now, this minute,' he amended, his tone softening more by the second. 'I meant when you're well again. Right now you need to sleep. Things might seem different in the morning.'

'If only . . .'

'Look, I'm no expert on this sort of thing but I think you'll have to give it time,' he advised.

'Hobson's choice, mate, as I'm too weak to get out of this bed,' was her weary answer to that.

Seeing her lids droop, he said, 'I must go now and let you get some rest.'

'OK.'

Her face was bloodless and her eyes were so shadowed they looked bruised as her puffy lids began to close. She'd done a terrible thing today; an unforgivable thing. But she looked so wretched lying there, so isolated within her own inner hell, he ached with compassion for her. On impulse he brushed her brow with his lips and walked quietly from the ward.

Babs could barely look at Jess when she visited her on the ward the following evening. Babs had been asleep when Jess came yesterday. 'What can I say?' she said, keeping her eyes fixed on her hands clasped together on the bed sheet. 'It was such a dreadful thing that I did, there are no words to justify it.' She paused, then raised her eyes warily to meet her friend's. 'Now I can see how bad it was but at the time it seemed like the only decent thing to do. I must have been crazy, leaving my own child and expecting you to look after her.' She shook her head. 'I don't know myself any more, Jess, and it scares the hell out of me.'

'You're very depressed and not thinking straight, that's all,' suggested Jess kindly.

'I couldn't have been thinking straight to walk out on my baby, could I?' she agreed. 'It's terrifying to think that I could do such a thing. She could have been taken into care as you're not a relative. God knows what could have happened to her.' She held her head in despair. 'None of the practicalities occurred to me at the time; things like you might not want a baby suddenly foisted on you, or that anyone might be upset by my demise. I felt so ill and incapable. Everything was black; everything a problem. All I could see was that I was a hopeless mother with nothing to offer, and you were a good, responsible person and part of a loving family who would be kind to my baby. I just felt too awful to go on. Oh, Jess, I'm so ashamed.'

Jess took her hand. 'Look, it happened and it's over,' she soothed. 'And you'll make things worse if you keep beating yourself up over it. You weren't meant to die yet so put the whole thing behind you and look to the future.'

'The doctors here tell me that I'm clinically depressed,' she went on to say. 'In other words they think I'm a loony.'

'Oh, Babs . . .'

'It's true. After what I did how can it be otherwise?' She looked sad. 'They don't think I'm in a fit state to be discharged from hospital so they're sending me to a funny farm: some place in Tooting for an assessment and possibly some sort of treatment. They seem to think it all dates back to my being dumped by Dickie; that and postnatal depression, and the worry of having to bring Cindy up on my own. I'm obviously not as strong as I thought I was.'

'We're all only human, and at least you're going to get help now,' Jess pointed out. 'Some sort of specialist treatment can only be a good thing.'

'I don't get a say in it, apparently. I have to do what they say whether I like it or not,' she explained. 'It's standard procedure for attempted suicides. I can't leave hospital until they decide that I'm in a stable condition.'

'It's the best thing, even though it might not seem like it to you at the moment.'

'As I don't have a choice I've just got to accept what they say.' Babs looked worried. 'I know it's a lot to ask but do you think you could hang on to Cindy for a bit longer? I'm scared they'll take her into care if I don't have someone reliable to look after her.'

'Of course I'll look after her until you're fit enough to do it yourself,' Jess assured her. 'Do you honestly think I would stand by and let your daughter be taken away?'

Babs squeezed Jess's hand. 'It's just that you've enough to do already, and you have to work.'

'I'll manage somehow, with Hilda's help,' Jess assured her. 'You concentrate on getting better and let me worry about little Cindy. I'll make sure she's well cared for, you have my word on that.'

'You're such a good friend,' said Babs, her eyes filling with tears. 'I don't know how I'll ever thank you.'

'You get better,' Jess urged her. 'That'll be thanks enough for me.'

They fell silent, both feeling emotional.

'Talking of thanking people,' Babs said at last, 'did you say that that boyfriend of yours brought you here in the car?'

'Yeah, bless him. He insisted on it, even though it'll make him late for his Rotary Club meeting,' she told her. 'He's waiting outside. He thought we'd want to be on our own.'

'I wonder . . . could I see him just for a few minutes?' Babs requested. 'I think I might have been a bit rude to him yesterday when I woke up. I was still feeling groggy and wasn't really in control of what I was saying. I don't think I thanked him properly for saving my life either. I'd like to do it now, if I may.'

'Sure,' agreed Jess readily. 'I'll go and get him.' She paused wondering if they might want to talk alone after what had happened yesterday. 'I'll wait in the car while you have a chat. See you in a little while.'

'Thanks, Jess.'

'A pleasure.'

Don strode down the ward and up to Babs' bed, smiling. 'Well, you're looking better,' he said.

She was still very pale, and wearing no make-up, but her hair was freshly combed and her eyes looked a little brighter. He supposed it wasn't possible to go through something as deeply personal as what had happened yesterday with someone without being affected in some way. This must be the reason she touched something deep inside him. She was a stranger to him but he found himself wanting to help her through this bad time in her life.

'I'm feeling better than I deserve,' she told him. 'I should be burning in hell for what I did.'

'I won't argue with that,' said the plain-speaking Don. 'But the gates were closed to you yesterday so you've got to put it behind you and look forward.'

'That's what Jess has just been telling me.'

'You've been given a second chance,' he reminded her. 'So make the most of it.'

She told him that she wouldn't be leaving hospital yet and he said that could only be a good thing.

'That's all very well,' she said. 'But there are practicalities to be

252

considered. As well as needing to take my daughter off Jess's hands, I also need to get back to work. They'll find a replacement for me at the café if I'm away for too long and I can't let that happen because I need the money.'

'You can't go until they discharge you so you'll just have to stop worrying about it,' he suggested in a kindly tone. 'If the worst comes to the worst and they do replace you, there are other jobs, and the state won't let you starve until you find one.'

'I bet I'll have the devil's own job getting anything out of the welfare for Cindy, though, as I'm not married.'

'The only thing you can do is take it one day at a time,' he said with gentleness he hadn't known he was capable of. 'There's nothing you can do about anything until you're better so there's no point your lying there worrying about it.'

'Yeah, yeah, you're right.' She looked at him and managed a half-smile. 'Anyway, I didn't ask to see you so that I could give you earache about all my troubles. I just wanted to thank you for saving my life.'

'Ooh, there's a change,' he grinned. 'I was in the doghouse for doing it yesterday.'

'Sorry about that.' She bit her lip. 'I was still feeling a bit woozy. I didn't really know what I was saying.'

'Don't worry about it,' Don told her. 'My back is broad. Anyway, I think I said a few things myself.'

'That probably needed saying.'

He acknowledged it with a wry grin. 'Look, let's forget all about that conversation and make a new start.' He thrust his hand forward. 'I'm Don Day, Jess's intended.'

She shook his hand, managing a watery smile. 'And I'm Babs Tripp, close friend of Jess.'

They both laughed, a little nervously.

Don didn't come in with Jess when they got to her place. He went straight on to his meeting.

Hilda was there looking after Cindy and the family were all at home so Jess gathered everybody together in the living room and turned the television off.

'I want to tell you while we're all together that Babs will be in hospital for a while yet, which means we are going to be looking after the baby for as long as we're needed.' She turned to her father. 'I knew I'd have your blessing in promising her that.'

'Too right,' he said. 'She's your friend and she's in trouble. We must do what we can.'

'It won't always be easy,' Jess continued. 'Babies are hard work and noisy and we're not used to having one around. But if we all muck in there shouldn't be a problem.'

253

'Muck in?' Ronnie looked worried. 'Do you mean changing nappies and feeding and that?'

'Yeah, you've gotta do your share of that,' declared Libby.

Neither Ronnie or Todd liked the sound of that. 'We're boys,' Ronnie pointed out.

'Go on, I'd never have noticed,' chortled Libby.

'Boys don't do those things.'

'They do in this house, mate,' said his irrepressible twin sister. 'If we're all helping, then that means you.'

'Don't listen to her, boys,' laughed Hilda. 'She's only pulling your leg.'

'I'm not, you know,' Libby made plain. 'I don't see why they should get away with it.'

'Stop quibbling over trivia,' Jess intervened. 'The important thing is that I've got you all behind me in this. It won't be for too long but it will make a difference, having a baby in the house.'

'What will happen to her while we're all out during the day?' wondered Libby.

Jess threw Hilda a questioning look.

'You don't even need to ask the question,' the older woman assured her. 'Of course I'll look after her.'

'You're a good sort, Hilda,' praised Charlie. 'Always there when we need you.'

'She's one of the family, aren't you?' said Jess.

'I like to think so,' she beamed.

The sound of Cindy reminding them of her presence came from upstairs, where she'd been put to bed in the girls' room in a cot Charlie had managed to find second-hand. 'I'll go and get her,' offered Libby, and hurried upstairs before anyone else had a chance.

'She's potty about that baby,' mentioned Todd. 'She's always fussing over her. She says all that stuff about us doing our share but no one else can get a look in.'

'Girls are like that over babies,' said his worldly-wise brother with a knowing nod. 'They can't help it.'

'I'm really proud of you, Don, for being so kind to Babs and running me to the hospital in the car to save me going on the bus and train,' said Jess a couple of weeks later on their way home from visiting Babs. 'It's quite a way to Tooting and it's been a real help, with me being more tied because of the baby.'

'It's a question of, if you can't beat 'em, join 'em, I suppose,' he said lightly. 'If you're engaged to someone who doesn't think twice before taking on other people's problems, it's the only thing you can do if you want to stay sane.'

'I'm very grateful, anyway.'

'We're a team, you and me.'

Given Don's initial reaction to Babs' suspected suicide attempt, and his general attitude towards her, Jess had been astonished by his behaviour since saving her life. Jess had expected him to criticise her for offering to look after the baby, and to go on *ad infinitum* about her taking on other people's problems when she should be having a life of her own. She thought he'd be unforgiving about Babs' attempt to end her life, and say she didn't deserve help or sympathy because she'd committed a sin. Given his strong views on morality, she'd been ready for him to paint Babs in the blackest tones. Instead he'd been sweet to her, taken an interest in her baby, and made himself available as a chauffeur to Jess when she went to the hospital to visit.

Seeing the kinder side of his nature warmed her heart. It also made her feel even more guilty about her feelings for Bruce, which hadn't faded despite her new respect for Don.

But now she cast her mind back to their visit to Babs. 'I think she seems a lot better, don't you?'

'Yes, she does seem to be responding well to the medication,' he replied.

'Tablets are all very well in the short term but she can't stay on them indefinitely.'

'No, of course not.'

'To tell you the truth I'm a bit worried about when she's discharged from hospital,' confessed Jess. 'She's being well looked after now. But I'm afraid she'll sink back into that low state in no time at all in that awful bedsit and having to drag the baby to work with her, terrified the whole time that Cindy will cry and she'll lose the job, or that she'll scald her with hot fat.'

'She can't go back there.' He was adamant.

'Try stopping her,' Jess reminded him. 'She's always been so damned independent.'

'Leaving your baby with a friend to look after while you try to kill yourself wasn't the act of an independent woman, though, was it?' he pointed out.

'She only did that because she wasn't well.'

'Exactly, and she won't be completely restored to her old self the day she's discharged from hospital, I should think,' he said. 'That sort of thing takes time. She's bound to feel a bit vulnerable for a while, which means she might be more persuadable.'

'Mm, that is a point,' Jess agreed. 'She needs to be nearer to us, her friends. She needs somewhere decent to live and a job in our neighbourhood so that she feels she's got some back-up support close to hand.' Jess frowned. 'But with the best will in the world, she and Cindy can't live with us permanently because we've got a full house.' She paused. 'But I'll think of something.'

★ ★ ★

255

When Jess got in – Don having gone straight home to do some paperwork – there was great excitement.

'She smiled,' announced Libby who was holding baby Cindy. 'It wasn't just wind either. She really smiled, a proper great whopper of a grin.'

'She did an' all,' said Ronnie in a rare moment of agreement with his sister. 'She was looking directly at me too.'

'Don't kid yourself.' Libby was nothing if not predictable. 'It was me she was smiling at. I was the one who'd given her her bottle and I was holding her so of course it was me. Anyway, she wouldn't want to smile at your ugly mug. It was me, wasn't it, Hilda?'

'Leave me out of it,' said the older woman. 'There'll be plenty of smiles to go round now that she's started doing it. You don't have to fight about it.'

'Oh, but they do, Hilda,' Charlie put in. 'Those two aren't happy unless they're arguing.'

'Aah, look, she's doing it again, bless her,' said Libby, peering at the baby. 'Look, look. Quick.'

Everyone gathered around. There was a collective cry of delight when this scrap of humanity showed off her new ability. As they all stood around her grinning sentimentally, Jess thought what joy this baby had given to her family. It was an ill wind because Babs' near tragedy had brought such happiness into this house and they were all going to miss Cindy like mad when she left.

'We ought to put her to bed now,' suggested Jess.

No one took any notice.

'Babies need routine,' she added.

'Yeah, yeah,' said Hilda, making clicking noises with her tongue at the baby. 'In a minute.'

The enveloping warmth so palpable here at this moment made Jess even more determined that Babs and her daughter wouldn't return to their former bleak life when Babs was discharged from hospital. A couple of ideas she'd been mulling over began to come together into a possible solution.

'I've got a suggestion to make,' Jess told Babs when she next visited her, 'and I want you to promise me that you'll hear me out before you dismiss it out of hand.'

Babs looked wary. 'Sounds as though I'm likely to object. But go on then.'

'It's about when you come out of here.'

'I thought it might be. We've been through all that and I'm going back to my bedsit and my job at the café,' she stated firmly. 'The job is there for me whenever I'm ready to go back. I rang them from here to confirm that. And my rent was paid in advance so they can't throw me out, not just yet anyway.'

256

'You and Cindy need to be near your friends, near to us,' Jess pointed out.

'There's a lot of things we need but we are dealing with reality here,' Babs said.

'What about if something better for you both is now possible?' Jess went on.

'Whatever it is I won't be able to afford it.'

'Oh, but you will.'

'I'm not going to sponge on you, Jess,' Babs made clear. 'You've done more than enough for me already.'

'There'll be no sponging,' Jess was eager to point out. 'You'll be paying your way.'

Babs gave her a wary look. 'You'd better tell me what you've got in mind then, hadn't you?'

'You and Cindy stay with Hilda and you work in Don's shop,' Jess burst out excitedly. 'Hilda looks after the baby while you're at work. How does that sound?'

Her eyes lit up momentarily but she soon came down to earth. 'It sounds wonderful and it would be if Hilda happened to want a lodger and a job as a babysitter, and Don was looking for staff,' she said dully.

'Surely you know me well enough to realise that I wouldn't mention it to you if I hadn't checked everything out first,' Jess told her. 'Don has been short-staffed for ages and Hilda rattles around in her house on her own and would welcome a lodger. She adores Cindy and has offered to look after her while you're out at work without any prompting from me. She already does it while I'm at work anyway, as you know, so both she and Cindy are used to each other. I know how independent you are and that you'll want a place of your own eventually, but staying at Hilda's would give you a base while you get back on your feet and look around to see what's about in the way of accommodation to rent.'

A suspicious look came Jess's way. 'It's one hell of a coincidence, isn't it, Don being short-staffed just at the time you happen to be trying to fix me up with a job?' she queried.

'It's quite genuine, though,' Jess assured her. 'He really does need staff, honestly. He's always going on about it. I don't know why I didn't think of it before. But, of course, you might not want to work in a grocery shop.'

'All jobs seem a bit dull after being on the stage, as we both know,' Babs pointed out. 'But it can't be worse than the café.' She made a face. 'Ugh. The steam, the constant smell of frying has put me off of bacon for life.'

'You wouldn't earn a fortune at Don's place but you should make enough to pay your way at Hilda's, and be able to give her a little something for looking after the baby,' Jess told her. 'Knowing Hilda, she'd willingly do it for nothing but I know you wouldn't want that.'

'I certainly wouldn't.'

'All the details you'll have to discuss with Don and Hilda,' Jess went on. 'I just wanted to put the idea to you.'

Babs nodded.

'If you don't fancy it, no one will be offended. But there'll be a lot of smiling faces around Park Street if you do decide to go ahead. The Mollitt family are all besotted with Cindy and would hate it if you dragged her off to Paddington.'

Babs thought back to the dark days at the bedsit, and Jess's suggestion sent a gleam of hope into the bleakest corner of her mind. Babs had always prided herself on being a strong, independent woman. The daughter of strict, unloving parents, she'd left home as a teenager and had never gone back to ask for help no matter how desperate and hard up she'd been.

When she'd found herself in trouble after Dickie left her, she'd been determined to get through it herself without asking favours or accepting help from anyone. So much for that tough old bird now. She wanted to stay true to herself and her ideals but all she seemed to be doing lately was grabbing help with both hands. And it was being offered in spades because of someone who had turned out to be such a true friend. She lowered her head as she could hold back the tears no longer.

'Oh, Babs,' said Jess, putting her arms around her, 'don't upset yourself.'

'Sorry.'

'It was only an idea,' Jess soothed. 'But you must do what you think is best for you and your daughter.'

'It isn't that, kid,' Babs mumbled into her handkerchief. 'I'm crying because you're all so good to me and I don't deserve it.'

'You daft bat,' said Jess in a tone of friendly admonition. 'You'll have me in tears in a minute.'

'I'd love to come and live near you all.'

'Smashing.'

'I don't know how I'll ever repay you.'

'Repayment won't be necessary,' her friend assured her. 'So that's another thing you can stop worrying about.'

Chapter Seventeen

Most stage performers found ordinary employment a little dull in comparison, and Babs was never more aware of this than on her first day in her new job. The actual work as a counter assistant wasn't a problem – indeed, it was much less gruelling than the café – but the working environment was more suggestive of a convent than a grocery shop.

The customers at the café had been mostly men who enjoyed a spot of light conversation with the person who served them. Even at the depths of her depression, she'd usually managed some sort of cheerful dialogue because it was all part of the job. Here at Dean's Stores, friendliness towards customers was positively discouraged in favour of formality and staff deference. Don was an absolute dear, and she was deeply indebted to him for his kindness to her, but he was agonisingly serious and had some very odd ideas.

In his brief initiation speech, he was at pains to point out to her that the company had a long-term reputation for good manners, and familiarity towards the customers was strictly forbidden; he seemed to be under the strange impression that a friendly manner meant a lack of respect. It was a dark and dismal, old-fashioned shop with an atmosphere to match, and didn't suit Babs' personality at all. She seriously doubted her ability to conform to this dreary regime, and hoped she didn't lose the job over it because it was so convenient and had been offered to her in good faith.

To help boost her confidence – left frail by her illness – she had decided to make an effort with her appearance and turned up for work with a liberal spread of make-up, a blouse showing more than a hint of cleavage and high-heeled shoes. When she put on the shapeless, mud-coloured overall that Don supplied her with, she couldn't help blurting out, 'Good God, I feel like an inmate of Holloway Prison in this. It's the ugliest thing I've ever had on in my life. Surely you don't really expect me to wear it.'

Her workmates – three middle-aged women of matronly appearance – stifled their nervous giggles behind their hands because their employer took a dim view of laughter among the staff when they were on duty.

'Well, yes, I do, I'm afraid,' said Don uncertainly. 'I haven't had any complaints before.'

'That's a mystery in itself because the things are hideous, aren't they, girls?' Babs said, grinning at the others, who were all looking bilious in the ghastly brown garments, which had a draining effect on the freshest of complexions. 'No self-respecting woman should be made to wear these. They're enough to make the customers think there's still a war on.'

'The job doesn't require glamour,' Don pointed out rather feebly.

'No, but this is taking drabness too far.'

'The staff uniform has nothing to do with me,' he informed her, looking worried; he wasn't used to members of staff speaking up, and was fazed by someone as assertive as Babs. 'They're standard Dean's Stores' issue, worn by staff in all branches. They've been that style for years. The higher management at Head Office seem quite happy with them.'

'They don't have to wear them, do they?' she piped up. 'If I were you I'd have a few words with your superiors about the changing times.' She couldn't hold back her opinion, though was gloomily aware that it wasn't conducive to long-term employment here. 'I mean, as well as depressing the staff, these dreadful outfits can't do much for customer morale either, especially on a wet Monday morning. People want to see something bright and cheerful when they go into a shop, not a bunch of women looking like detainees. This is the late nineteen fifties, for goodness' sake.'

The rest of the staff listened with bated breath, waiting for the explosion, certain that it would come because the boss was known as a tartar. To their amazement, he said reasonably, 'I'll pass your comments on to Head Office but I can't promise anything. They're a bit set in their ways.'

'Set in their ways? I reckon they must have got stuck in a time warp,' she burst out. 'Still, as you can't do anything about it I'll have to put up with it.'

'For the moment, yes,' Don said with patience that astonished Babs' colleagues.

Despite her frivolous manner, Babs was a diligent worker and quick to learn. One of the perks of the job was being able to go home in her lunch break to see Cindy. Her confidence in herself as a mother was still somewhat shaky, but having Hilda around was a great help. Living in a pleasanter and more secure environment was assisting her recovery in general. Even thoughts of Dickie were beginning to lose some of their sting.

She had a sandwich with Hilda and a cuddle with Cindy, and went back to work feeling refreshed. During the afternoon her outgoing personality caused her to bend the rules in her attitude towards the customers, as she had suspected it would. But as they seemed to enjoy a more personal approach, she didn't get a dressing-down from Don. Having made a stand against the management about the overalls, she was already in favour with her workmates, despite the fact that she was clearly the odd one out among these very traditional married women. At the end of the day she was cautiously optimistic about her chances of being kept on.

'So, how do you feel after your first day with us?' Don asked as Babs was about to follow her new friends out of the shop.

'Not so dusty,' she replied. 'Once I get all the prices off pat, I'll be fine.'

'Good.'

'There's one thing I will do to improve things tomorrow, though,' she told him thoughtfully.

He looked at her, hopeful of some promise of moderation to her outgoing demeanour.

'I'll wear flat shoes,' she informed him. 'My plates of meat are killing me in these damned stilettos.'

Much to his own astonishment he burst out laughing.

She picked up on this. 'You look nice when you smile, Don, a lot younger and more handsome,' she observed. 'You should do more of it.'

Unexpectedly embarrassed, he turned pink. 'I'll try to remember that,' he said.

'Good.' She turned towards the door. 'Well, I must be off. I can't wait to get home to see my daughter.'

'I can imagine.' He cleared his throat. 'It's nice to see you looking so much better.'

'Yeah, well, I've had a lot of help, haven't I?' She smiled at him, her eyes a vivid cornflower blue, her face plumper and healthier now. 'Not least from you. Thanks for giving me this job, as well as everything else.'

'I needed someone in the shop so we've done each other a favour,' he said.

'See you tomorrow, then. G' night, Don.'

'Good night.'

Watching her walk away, hips swinging, high heels clicking against the pavement, he found himself wishing she could have stayed to talk for longer. Everything was usually clear cut to Don and he wasn't accustomed to having the fabric of his life thrown into disarray. He had certain principles and knew exactly what he liked and disliked. He couldn't stand women like Babs, with her cheap looks and extrovert behaviour. She was an unmarried mother, and so mentally unstable she'd even tried to kill herself.

Not the sort of person they normally employed at Dean's Stores or that he would have any truck with as a rule. He was happily engaged and devoted to Jess and didn't lust after other women; that wasn't his style. But there was something about Babs that touched his heart and imbued him with a feeling of longing and excitement. He just couldn't wait to see her tomorrow.

★ ★ ★

Babs was thinking about Don at that time too, as she walked home in the spring evening. He was too serious for his own good, and far too pompous for anyone's comfort. But he was a good man; his kindness to her had proved that. There was something else too; something about him that made her want to be with him, to know him better and teach him how to smile more often.

What was she thinking of? Not only was he not her type, he was engaged to her best friend, the woman to whom she owed so much. She shouldn't be harbouring any notions of him other than as her employer and Jess's man. Maybe it was natural to feel something over and above the norm for someone who'd brought you back from the dead; perhaps that was why she was having these strange thoughts and feelings. Whatever the reason, she couldn't deny that she felt something special for him and had from the first moment she'd set eyes on him, as ill as she'd felt at that time. It'll pass, she told herself, and no one except me will ever know about it, so there'll be no harm done.

Jess went walking in Churchfields with Doughnut on her half-day off one Wednesday a week or two later. It was a fine spring day with a fresh breeze and gentle sunshine beaming from a sky suffused with white wispy clouds, floating and racing across the pale blue dome.

As her thoughts turned to Babs, she found herself with a feeling of relief that her friend was so much improved. Her illness and recovery had seemed like Jess's sole responsibility in that she had no one else. So, as well as being pleased for Babs, she also felt personally unburdened. Babs still had to take medication and attend an outpatients' clinic every so often, but she was better than Jess had seen her in ages. She still had periods of unnatural bleakness – you could see some inner torment in her eyes sometimes – but she was able to cope now. She seemed to enjoy the job too. Having her get on so well with Don pleased Jess no end, especially as her siblings still couldn't take to him.

Someone tapped her on the shoulder. 'I thought I might find you here,' said Bruce.

'Oh, hi.' She couldn't help being pleased to see him. Despite everything she was warmed and uplifted by his smile. 'I usually try to escape on my own on a Wednesday afternoon.'

'I know.'

'You came looking for me then?'

He made a face. 'I'm afraid I did.'

'I thought we agreed not to seek each other out . . .'

'I was weak today, sorry.'

'You shouldn't have been!'

'I've no intention of starting anything,' he assured her. 'I just wanted to see you, that's all.'

262

'You see me every Saturday morning when I do my class,' she reminded him sharply.

'That's different.'

She ignored this and walked on. He fell into step beside her.

'How are things at home now?' he asked. 'Are you enjoying the peace and quiet now that your friend and her baby have moved out?'

'Peace and quiet in our house?' she laughed, trying to behave normally. 'It's never been known.'

'It must be a bit less chaotic, though.'

'I suppose so. We still see a lot of Babs and the baby, though, as they're living next door – just temporarily until she finds a place of her own,' she explained. 'The whole family is completely besotted with baby Cindy.'

'So I've heard from Ronnie,' he told her. 'He keeps me up to date with odd bits of Mollitt news.'

'Both the boys are completely enslaved to her, which surprised me,' she told him. 'Boys of that age are sometimes a bit awkward with babies.'

He nodded. 'Your friend is better now then?' he went on to say. 'Ronnie said she'd been in hospital. Some sort of a breakdown, I gather.'

'Something like that. She wouldn't be here now if it wasn't for Don,' she informed him. 'He's been wonderful.'

'Really? I know he gave her a job but Ronnie didn't say much else about it.'

'Probably thought he didn't ought to go into all the personal details, for Babs' sake. But Don did a lot more than just give her a job,' Jess said, and went on to tell Bruce of his brother's kindness.

'Well, well, so he's a bit of a hero?'

'After being forced into taking action initially, yes he did come up trumps,' she confirmed. 'I didn't realise he had it in him to be so softhearted. Neither, I suspect, did he. We all know he's a decent and clean-living man but he's usually so disapproving of anything he doesn't understand and completely intransigent on situations he doesn't approve of.'

'That's always been his trouble.'

'But he's proved just how kind-hearted a person he can be over this.'

'Quite the golden boy in your eyes then?'

'Very much so.' She moved on quickly. 'How are things with you and Brenda?'

'All right. She's a nice girl and I enjoy her company.'

'Good.'

They walked on, stopping every so often to throw a stick for the dog and making a fuss of him when he retrieved it.

'So, now that the crisis with your friend is over and Ronnie is settled in his Saturday job, I suppose things are pretty calm on the Mollitt front.'

'For a change, yes,' she replied. 'It would be nice if it stayed that way too.'

263

She could have no idea then the magnitude of the family crisis that was already in the making . . .

'What do you want?' Don asked of his brother in an aggressive manner that same evening.

'That's a nice way to greet your brother, I must say.'

'You're no brother of mine, so clear off.'

'Five minutes, surely you can spare me that.'

'I've just finished a load of paperwork and I'm about to make myself something to eat.'

'You won't die of starvation for waiting another five minutes,' persisted Bruce. 'I've just finished doing the same thing myself and need food so I won't stay long.'

Don emitted an eloquent sigh and ushered him inside to the living room, scrupulously tidy but predictably plain, with dark furnishings, grey carpet and not an ornament or vase in sight. 'So, what's all this about?' he demanded.

'I've been hearing some really nice things about you,' replied Bruce.

'Oh?' Don looked wary. 'Who from?'

Bruce told him.

'I'm engaged to Jess. The least I can do is help her when she needs it,' Don explained.

'You were very kind to her friend, I understand.'

'Yeah, well, Jess's friends are my friends too. Jess is the type of person to get involved in other people's troubles so it makes sense for me to get used to it and take an interest, as I'm going to be her husband.'

'It's nice to hear that you're prepared to co-operate.'

Don threw him a look, narrowing his eyes suspiciously. 'Have you come round here just to tell me that you approve of my behaviour?' he asked.

'No.'

'I thought there would be more to it than that,' Don groaned. 'So say what you have to say and get out.'

'OK. I'll come straight to the point,' Bruce told him. 'I want us to put the past behind us and be mates again.'

'Oh, not that old chestnut again,' tutted Don. 'You know the answer, so why waste my time by bringing it up again?'

'Stubborn optimism, I suppose,' replied Bruce. 'Hearing good things about you made me think you might have softened a little, become more tolerant.'

'Where you're concerned, not a chance.'

Why do I bother? Bruce asked himself. Why do I want to be friends with someone so cold and uncompromising?

It wasn't as though Don was any fun to be around these days. Bruce supposed the reason must be because what stood between them was a thing unfinished. Or was it that Bruce couldn't forget how good it had once felt to have a brother in the true sense of the word, someone of his own kind, always there in the background?

'That's a pity, Don, a real pity,' he said with feeling. 'It isn't right, the way things are at the moment.'

'Maybe not, but you ruined it, not me,' Don pointed out coldly. 'If you think I'll ever forgive you for what you did, you're living in a dream world.'

'Don't you think you've punished me enough?' Bruce persisted. 'Punished yourself, too, in the process.'

Don looked at him for a moment, his lean face set in a grim expression, thin lips pressed together and turned down at the corners. Then he marched across to the living-room door and swung it open forcefully. 'I don't want to hear any more of this drivel from you. So on your way,' he commanded through gritted teeth.

Bruce stayed where he was. 'Look, we're still brothers, whether you want to admit it or not,' he pointed out. 'It isn't going to go away, that bond between us, no matter how much you deny it.'

'You didn't let that bond stop you—'

'If you'd only listen.'

'I did all my listening years ago,' Don snapped. 'The subject is closed as far as I'm concerned.'

'Things aren't always what they seem.'

That simple statement touched something inside Don and brought his current confused feelings into focus. Despite all his efforts to fight it, he felt increasingly drawn to Babs. He didn't want to feel this way and didn't understand why he couldn't control it because he'd always been such a disciplined man. Jess was the only woman for him and he was in love with her; there was no question in his mind about that. So why did Babs creep into his thoughts all the time? He could feel himself become more fascinated with her with every day that passed and there wasn't a thing he could do about it. She was feisty and outspoken and set great store by her independence but she was achingly vulnerable somehow too. He couldn't possibly be in love with her so it must be just lust, plain and simple.

This must be what Bruce had experienced for Sheila. For the first time, Don could understand something of the agony of his brother's temptation. But unlike Don, Bruce had just gone ahead and followed his instincts, regardless of other people's feelings. Don wasn't going to do that so his conscience could remain clear. He was committed to Jess and that was how it was going to stay. He had no intention of hurting anyone just because of an infatuation that would pass in time if not given too much attention.

'You're just making excuses for yourself and I don't want to hear about it,' Don responded now. 'So, just get out of here and leave me alone.'

265

'All right, I'll go,' agreed Bruce sadly. 'But I think you're hurting yourself as much as you're hurting me over this, but you're too damned stubborn to let go and make things better.'

'You can think what you like,' blustered Don. 'Just keep away from me.'

'OK, Don, you win,' he sighed with an air of finality. 'I won't bother you again.'

Bruce followed his brother through the small hall to the front door and left without uttering another word.

Shutting the door behind him, Don leaned against it, trembling and fighting against tears, memories of happy times with Bruce flooding into his mind with aching poignancy. What was happening to him lately that his errant brother could make him want to weep, and his fiancée's best friend could set his pulse racing with just a smile or a certain tilt of her head? He simply had to pull himself together and not let such fanciful influences destroy his long-held principles.

Jess and Don had gone to a pub on the river near Kew Bridge, as it was a fine spring Friday evening. Ensconced at a table by the window outside of which a glorious willow embraced the river bank and people strolled along the towpath, Jess was feeling relaxed and comfortable in Don's company. Casually chatting about the twins and the fact that they would be leaving school soon, she just happened to mention that Libby was still keen to go into the Burton Girls straight from school.

'I don't think it would be the best thing for her, though,' she said conversationally. 'But it's her life. If she's determined to try for it, what can I do? I can't stop her.'

His reply was a noncommittal grunt.

'I'm trying to persuade her to go into an office for a year or so before she auditions for the troupe,' she continued, 'but if she's determined to go for it sooner then I'll be behind her all the way, even though I don't approve.'

Silence.

'Talk to yourself, Jess, why don't you?'

'Sorry, what was that?'

She repeated what she'd just been telling him and was amazed when he flew into a rage.

'It's time you stepped back and let that family of yours get on with their lives without your damned interference,' he stated cruelly. 'You can't protect them for ever.'

'Interference?' She was shocked and hurt that anyone could think that of her. 'I've never thought I was interfering,' she uttered in a bemused tone. 'I thought what I was doing was giving them support, as mum isn't here to do it.'

'You can dress it up any way you like,' he snapped. 'It's still interference in my book.'

266

'But she's only fifteen, Don,' Jess pointed out. 'She still needs some sort of guidance.'

'Oh, do what you like,' he growled. 'You will anyway, whatever I have to say on the subject.'

Smarting from this unexpected display of animosity, she asked, 'Whatever's the matter with you?'

'I'm sick to death of hearing you drone on about your bloody family, that's what's the matter with me,' he declared irritably. 'If it isn't one of them with a problem it's another. You're always going on about them.'

'Am I?'

'*Ad nauseam*. They are not your responsibility so stop behaving as if they are.'

Her face burned, then became bloodless; she felt sick with humiliation. 'I didn't realise I was being boring,' she uttered through dry lips. 'I'm so sorry. I'll watch that in future.'

He stared at her, her worried brown eyes like huge dark pools in her pale face. Had he really just said all that? How awful that he should hurt her in that way. He was turning into some sort of a monster. 'No, it's me who should be sorry, not you,' he said, reaching for her hand and squeezing it hard. 'Take no notice of me. I'm just a crusty old sod and I don't deserve you.'

But she couldn't ignore what he'd said. 'There must be some truth in it or you wouldn't have come out with it,' she speculated. 'Do I really get on your nerves talking about my family so much?'

'Of course you don't,' he was keen to assure her. 'I don't know what possessed me to say such things.'

'They all mean so much to me, you see,' she explained. 'I suppose I'm just not aware of how often I mention them. As you're going to be part of the family I thought—'

'Look, I'm at fault, not you,' he cut in, keen to put things right. 'I didn't mean what I said. You go ahead and talk about your family as much as you like.'

She eyed him suspiciously, realising that this wasn't the first time he'd been offhand with her recently. He'd been snappy on several occasions. 'Is there something worrying you, Don?' she enquired. 'You've been in a funny mood with me lately.'

'Have I? Sorry.'

'There's no need to apologise but I'd rather know if you've got something on your mind,' she told him. 'If there's anything wrong I need to know about it.'

The thought of how hurt she'd be if he were to tell her what was making him so touchy gave him an ache in the pit of his stomach. What sort of a man spent all his time thinking about the best friend of the woman he was engaged to, and wondering if that friend was thinking about him? A scoundrel, that's who. And it had to stop. His future lay

267

with Jess and he had to put this other nonsense out of his mind. But it didn't feel like nonsense when he was with Babs. Their contrasting personalities just seemed to merge somehow. He felt softer, less serious.

'There's nothing wrong, honestly,' he assured her. 'I just seem to be feeling bad-tempered lately. The stress of the job probably.'

'As long as it is only that.'

'It is,' he confirmed. 'I'll try not to take it out on you in future.'

'Good.'

'So, am I forgiven?'

'Of course you are.' She was puzzled, though, because she didn't think he was being honest with her.

The next day all thoughts of Don's strange behaviour were pushed to one side by a family matter.

Ronnie came home from working at Bruce's shop, looking worried and miserable. This was most unusual these days because he loved his job and was always full of chat about it when he got in. At first he wouldn't tell Jess what the trouble was. But when she finally got him on his own and prised it out of him, she was as angry and puzzled as her brother to hear that Bruce wouldn't consider him for a full-time job when he left school.

'He's always given me the impression that there would be a proper job for me when I left school,' he told his sister. 'But today when I mentioned it to him, because I wanted to know if it's definite, he said that he didn't have anything to offer me.'

'Perhaps there isn't a vacancy at the moment,' suggested Jess.

'But there is,' Ronnie informed her. 'The shop is getting busier all the time. He needs more staff.'

'Curious . . .' said Jess.

'That's what I thought. Anyway, he can stuff his rotten job,' stated Ronnie with typical youthful umbrage. 'I'll soon find something else.' He paused. 'It's just that . . . well, I'd rather he'd been straight with me in the first place, instead of stringing me along. He knows how much I want to work for him full time when I leave school. I really trusted him to be honest.'

'You're better off not working for someone who doesn't keep their word,' muttered Jess, furious at this further proof of Bruce's untrustworthiness.

'Yeah,' agreed Ronnie gloomily.

On Monday morning Jess told her father she had to pop out for a few minutes, and headed for Bruce's shop.

'Ronnie doesn't know I'm here so don't go thinking I'm fighting his battles for him because I'm not,' she informed Bruce in his office at the back of the shop. 'But I'd like to know what's going on. He's really upset that there's not a full-time job for him here and I'm wondering why you've changed your mind. I mean, up until now you've indicated that you're pleased with his work and more or less told him the job was his. Has he done something to upset you?'

Bruce went over to the door to make sure it was properly closed, then sat down at the desk opposite her. Speaking in low tones, he said, 'No, Jess, Ronnie hasn't done anything to upset me at all. Quite the opposite, in fact. I would love to have him working for me on a full-time basis.'

'So why tell him there's no job for him?'

He lowered his eyes and doodled with a pen on the blotter. 'The reason I can't promise him a job is because I'm selling up and moving away.'

It was like hitting a wall at high speed. 'What!' she gasped.

'It wouldn't be fair to have him start work here, only to lose the job if the people I sell to don't want to keep the existing staff on,' he continued. 'I know I was being devious on Saturday but I couldn't tell Ronnie the truth because I'm not ready for the full-time staff to know yet. I shall be straight with them when the time is right but there's no point in unsettling them at this very early stage because these things take time. It might take me quite a while to find a buyer willing to pay the asking price.'

'I just don't know what to say, Bruce, except that I'm shocked and very sorry.' Suddenly she could admit it. She loved him whatever he had done in the past and she didn't want him to go away.

He looked at her. 'I will make it a condition of sale that you are able to hire the hall with no increase in the fee, though, so your classes are safe.'

'Oh, good, thanks.' The dancing school was the least of her worries. 'But why, Bruce?' she asked, her voice ragged with emotion. 'Why would you want to move away?' She waved a hand towards the shop. 'I thought the business was doing really well.'

'It is.'

She threw him a knowing look. 'Aah, is that the reason you're selling up, because you'll make a good profit if you sell while it's a thriving concern?'

'No. It isn't a business decision,' he informed her. 'It's purely personal.'

Narrowing her eyes on him, she said, 'It's something to do with Don, isn't it?'

He nodded. 'Partly. I came here to be near to him in the hope of patching things up between us,' he informed her. 'But I now realise that I must accept the fact that that isn't going to happen.'

'It might, in time.'

'No, it won't, and I have to stop kidding myself,' he said, shaking his head. 'He's absolutely determined not to let me back into his life and that isn't going to change. He's adamant about it. There's no shifting Don when he wants to be stubborn.'

'But that's no reason to leave,' she pointed out, desperate at the thought of never seeing him again. 'You've managed well enough so far without

269

his friendship. You like it here, don't you? You seem to fit in with all the other shopkeepers.'

'Yeah, I like it.'

'Stay then, Bruce,' she begged him. 'I can't bear the idea of not seeing you around.'

His eyes seemed to draw her into their immeasurable depth. 'And I can't bear to see you around and not be able to have you in my life,' he explained. 'That's the main reason I'm leaving. I said Don was only part of it.'

'Oh, Bruce, surely you don't need to do anything so drastic.'

'I do. If it was just the situation with Don, I might be able to consider staying but this thing with you as well is just too much to bear,' he explained. 'I know we agreed that we could go on just seeing each other in passing, so to speak, but it isn't working – not for me, anyway. It must be difficult for you too. You'll never settle properly with Don while I'm close at hand.'

'Just seeing you around the town now and again is better than not seeing you at all.'

'For how long can we keep it up?' he asked her. 'How long can we carry on pretending?'

'We've managed so far.'

'It's been tearing the heart out of me, though,' he confessed.

'Me too,' she admitted. 'But not to see you at all, Bruce . . . that would be worse.'

'Anything will be easier for me than it is at the moment,' he confessed. 'I'll be honest with you, Jess. I can't trust myself not to come between you and Don and that mustn't happen. Absolutely not – *not ever*!'

'I know, Bruce,' she sighed. 'I know.'

'Anyway, I haven't even found a buyer for the shop yet and when I eventually do, it'll take a while for everything to go through,' he pointed out. 'So I'll be around for a while longer.'

'Small consolation.'

'Look, I don't want to go but we both know it's the only way,' he said, spreading his hands helplessly. 'Other than telling Don the truth and destroying him.'

'Which neither of us could ever do.'

'Exactly.'

She studied her fingernails. 'How are things with you and Brenda?' she asked, looking up.

'All right,' he replied. 'We get on well but she isn't you. While I'm still around here every day hoping for a glimpse of you, I'll never make a go of it with her, or anyone.'

'No. I suppose not,' Jess said miserably. 'So your moving away seems the only sensible thing to do.'

He nodded.

She stood up as if to go. 'What shall I tell Ronnie?' she asked.

'In fairness to him you'd better tell him the truth but ask him to keep it to himself for the moment. I'm not having a "For Sale" board put up because it isn't good for business or the mood of my staff. I've told the agent he can put "Sold" up only when we have a firm deal.'

'I'll dread seeing that.'

'Yes, me too.'

Tension drew tight. Jess hardly dare look at him for fear that her emotions would get the better of her and make it even harder for them both. 'Still, we'll be seeing each other before then so we must be adult about it,' she said bravely. 'It isn't as though we're a couple of kids.'

'No.'

'I'd better get back to work. Dad will be wondering where I am,' she said, turning towards the door.

'Sorry to hurt you, Jess,' he said tenderly. 'If there was any other way . . .'

'I know there isn't and it's all right,' she burst out and rushed from the room, leaving the premises through the back entrance rather than the shop because she was in a highly emotional state and didn't want to arouse the curiosity of his staff.

The Youth Employment Officer studied some papers on the table in front of her then looked across at Libby, who was sitting opposite; they were in a room at the school that had been allocated to her for the purpose of interviewing pupils who were leaving at the end of the summer term. 'So, my dear, do you have any idea what sort of a job you'd like?'

'Oh, yes, Miss,' said Libby without hesitation.

'Well, that's a good start anyway.' This was a refreshing change for the older woman, who spent a lot of time seeing school leavers from the secondary moderns who didn't have a clue what they wanted to do when they walked out of the school gates for the last time; except – the girls, anyway – to get married at the earliest possible opportunity. Not that there was much choice for this unqualified, nonacademic sector of young people. Shop, factory work or an office job with the chance to learn shorthand and typing was about it, apart from the handful of those with some special skill or artistic talent, and there weren't many of those around. 'Would you like to tell me what it is then.'

'Sure. I want to be a dancer.'

'Oh. Oh, I see.' She should have known it was too good to be true; the child obviously had a vivid imagination. 'I'm sure that would be a very nice thing to do, as a hobby.'

'I already do it as a hobby,' she explained. 'When I leave school I want to be a professional.'

The woman gave her a studied look. She was a bright-eyed little thing with a pretty face and bags of enthusiasm. But she had to be brought

271

down to earth. 'We all have dreams, my dear, and what would life be without them?' she said, seemingly unaware of her patronising attitude. 'I think I wanted to be a ballet dancer for a while when I was about your age too. But we have to keep our feet on the ground and find you some steady employment.'

'I'm not talking about being a ballet dancer,' Libby swiftly pointed out.

'But you said—'

'I want to be a Burton Girl,' Libby explained. 'My sister was one for years. She earned her living dancing.'

'A chorus girl?'

'That's right,' Libby confirmed with a steely look in her eye. 'That's the only thing I want to do and I won't consider anything else.'

The woman looked at her watch; she had a queue of youngsters still to see after this one. 'I'm afraid I don't have anything at all in that line to offer you,' she stated.

'I guessed you wouldn't have because . . . well, show business is a specialised sort of thing, isn't it?' Libby said with youthful candour. 'I only came for this interview because my teacher said I had to.'

The woman tutted and moved on swiftly. 'There are several firms needing office juniors at the moment,' she informed her, leafing through some cards. 'They're all fairly local so you won't have to do much travelling. Some of them even offer a day-release scheme for you to go to college to learn shorthand and typing, when you've been there for a while.'

'I'm not interested in anything like that.'

'You could do well,' the woman pointed out. 'You could get to be a secretary.'

'I don't want to do that, thank you, miss.'

'We all have to do things we don't want to do,' declared the woman with growing impatience. 'It's all part of being an adult, and you're going to have to earn your own living when you leave here.' She paused and forced a smile. 'You can't expect your parents to keep you for ever, can you?'

'Of course not. But I can earn my living as a dancer,' insisted Libby. 'My sister did, I told you.'

Glancing at her watch again, the employment officer was mindful of all the others she was due to see today. 'Well, take the details anyway,' she suggested. 'Have a look through them at home and talk to your parents about them. When you've chosen the one you might like to try for, let us know and we'll arrange an interview for you. The telephone number is on the card.'

'I really don't—'

'Take them anyway,' insisted the woman, eager to bring the interview to an end so that she could move on to the next child waiting outside in the corridor. 'I'm sure you'll feel differently when you've thought about it.'

272

'Thank you,' said Libby politely, taking the cards with apparent submission, and rising to leave.

'Will you tell the next one waiting to come in on your way out, please?' the woman requested.

'Certainly, miss.'

Libby did as she was asked, then made her way back to her class, across the playground. On the way, she tore the cards into little pieces and disposed of them in one of the school dustbins.

Chapter Eighteen

Although Babs was extremely comfortable at Hilda's, her independent spirit wouldn't let her rest until she had a place of her own. Hilda's warm heart and wonderful cooking made staying on a tempting option but Babs was the sort of person who needed her own home, no matter how humble.

'I need to stand on my own two feet again before I get so used to being spoiled, I'll be too damned lazy and pampered to fend for myself,' was the way she explained it to Hilda. 'I've loved being here, though, and I'll miss it like mad – all the delicious meals and the million and one other things you do for Cindy and me.'

Hilda had enjoyed every moment of their stay but had always known it was only a short-term arrangement. So when the tiny flat above the shoe mender's in the Broadway became available to rent and Babs and Cindy moved into it, Hilda took it in her stride. Or pretended to . . .

'It feels like a morgue without them,' she admitted to Charlie one evening over a quiet cup of tea together in her place. Their friendship was close enough now to inspire confidences they might not feel inclined to share with anyone else. 'I loved having them around the place; didn't mind their noise and clutter because they breathed new life into the house. It seems so gloomy rattling about here on my own again, though it shouldn't do as I'd been here on my own for so long before they came.'

'You're still looking after the baby during the day while Babs is at work, though, aren't you?' Charlie reminded her. 'So you still get to see plenty of them.'

'Oh, yeah, and Babs still comes for a bite to eat with me in her lunch hour and usually stays for a chat when she comes to collect the baby after work,' she explained. 'It's just that the house seems so silent and empty at night now.'

'You'll soon get used to it.'

'Course I will. I don't have much choice, do I?'

'Not really.'

'Trouble is, Charlie, I'm one of these people who enjoys company. I like to feel people around me.' She gave him a wry grin. 'Which is probably why I've spent so much time in your place over the years.'

Returning her grin, he said meaningfully, 'You're not as lonely as you used to be, though, are you?'

'No, not now that you and I have become pals,' she said with emphasis. 'It's made a huge difference.'

'It has for me too.'

'It's surprising what a difference it makes, having someone to go to the flicks with, or just a chat of an evening now and again.' She gave him a slow smile, her eyes twinkling. 'And at least it stops you spending so much time in the pub.'

Not so long ago Charlie would have taken offence at that. But now he just laughed and said, 'Yeah, that's another good thing to come out of it.'

Drifting into thought, the embryo of an idea began to form. Deciding it was too outlandish even to consider, he pushed it to the back of his mind.

When Jess got home from work one day a few weeks later, she found herself under attack from Libby as soon as she set foot through the kitchen door. So ferocious was the onslaught, it sent their brothers scurrying from the room.

'It was you, wasn't it?' Libby accused, standing by the table, hands on hips, eyes hot with tears. 'You messed it up for me. You told them to turn me down, you rotten cow.'

Baffled, Jess stared at her. 'Told who to turn you down for what?' she asked. 'I haven't a clue what you're talking about.'

'Don't come the innocent,' her sister spat at her. 'I know you fixed it so there's no point in your denying it.'

'Honestly, Libby, I really don't know what you're on about,' Jess told her again.

'You've never wanted me to join the Burton Girls so you made sure you got your own way by telling them to turn me down when I auditioned.' Her voice was quivering on the verge of tears.

'*You've auditioned for Burtons?*'

'I wouldn't have said it if I hadn't, would I?'

'When?'

'Today.'

'But you've been at school.'

Libby shook her head. 'Not today, I haven't.' Her eyes gleamed with rebellion. 'I took the day off.'

'You bunked off school to go for an audition?' Jess was horrified.

'That's right,' she confirmed with fierce aggression. 'I knew that Burtons sometimes see girls without an appointment so I took a chance and went along. And before you start lecturing me, I kept quiet about it because I knew you would try to stop me. I thought if I got the job you and Dad would be so pleased for me, Dad would sign the contract that would need his signature because I'm under eighteen and you'd be proud that I'd got it and forget your disapproval. Little did I know that my so-called loving sister had already put the boot in, told her cronies at Burtons that if I applied for a job to turn me down.'

'How can you possibly think I would do such a thing?' Jess was very hurt.

'You'd do anything to stop me getting a place at Burtons,' she pronounced. 'Making out it's to protect me when all the time it's probably because you're afraid I'll do better than you did when you were there.'

'None of this is true,' denied Jess, smarting from the accusation. 'I have never said that you shouldn't try to get into the troupe.'

'Ooh, not much! You're always going on about it. Trying to get me to go and work in some stuffy, boring office, doing a job that isn't right for me.'

'Only temporarily,' Jess amended. 'And only because I think you shouldn't go into the Burton Girls straight from school. I've never said you shouldn't go into it at all.'

'You fixed it so I wouldn't get in.'

'Honestly, Libby, I don't know how you can say such a terrible thing,' said Jess miserably.

'And I don't know how you could have done what you did to me – *your own sister*.'

Jess thought for a moment, then threw her a questioning look. 'How exactly am I supposed to have done this dreadful deed?' she wanted to know. 'I have no influence at the Burton Company whatsoever. I'm just one of their ex-dancers. Even if I had wanted to scupper your changes because I think you're too young, I would have had no way of doing it.'

'I don't believe you. You still have contacts there,' Libby stated, her eyes simmering with resentment. 'You sometimes go there on your half-day off.'

'Only to see old friends and watch rehearsals—'

'And while you were there recently, you had a word in somebody's shell-like,' Libby burst out. 'Telling them that if I were to apply to make sure I didn't get a job.'

'Who am I supposed to have said all this to?' Jess demanded.

'Someone on the management, of course.'

'I'm not on close terms with anyone in that sort of position, I've told you.'

'Don't lie to me . . .'

'Look, I hate to disappoint you, and I realise it must be hard not to have anyone to blame but yourself,' began Jess, her manner more assertive, 'but if you failed the audition, it has nothing to do with me. The management at Burtons wouldn't take any notice of anything I had to say.'

'It has to be that,' ranted Libby, savage in her disappointment and desperate for a scapegoat. 'What else could it be? I've worked hard on my dancing and I'm good, you can't deny that.'

'I wouldn't dream of denying it,' Jess was keen to assure her. 'You're a very good dancer.'

'So why did they turn me down?'

'Didn't they give you a reason?'

Libby thought about this for a moment. 'After I'd done a tap routine, they asked me to smile and show them my legs,' she said. 'Then they told me I'm not quite what they're looking for at the moment.'

'There you are then; they said "at the moment", which probably means they're looking for dancers a little older than you are at this particular time,' Jess suggested. 'They only have so many of the very young dancers in the troupe at any one time. There's nothing to stop you trying again in a year or so.'

'And have to do some rotten office job in the meantime.'

'What about shop work then?'

'That's even worse,' Libby complained bitterly. 'And I wouldn't even have to think about doing either if you hadn't ruined everything for me. It isn't fair.'

'Look, love, I know rejection is hard to take but we all experience it at some time in our life and we just have to face up to it and get on with things,' Jess pointed out, struggling to stay patient. 'There's no point in blaming other people when it happens. That audition was down to you, no one else. If you'd had what they were looking for they'd have given you the job. It had nothing to do with me.'

'You don't understand what getting into the Burton Girls meant to me,' Libby told her. 'I wanted it so badly.'

'If anyone knows what that feels like, it's me,' Jess reminded her. 'But anything worth having is worth waiting for.'

'Dancing is a short career.'

'Not that short,' her sister was quick to point out. 'Every branch of show business is riddled with rejection. You won't get far if you give up after your first taste of it.'

'You still don't get it, do you?' the girl went on, her face white with temper, red blotches suffusing her neck and cheeks, her eyes bright with angry tears. 'I can cope with rejection, as such. It's the reason I was turned down that's upset me. I'd have got that job if Mum was still alive, no doubt about it.' She was weeping now. 'She would have encouraged me, not deliberately set out to ruin it for me.'

'I didn't do it, Libby.'

'Yes, you did,' she wept. 'You're always sticking your nose into everyone's business; telling us all what to do, trying to rule the roost in the family.'

The words pierced to the depth of Jess's being, even though she knew they were symptomatic of her sister's own wretchedness. 'How many more times must I tell you? I had nothing to do with it, I swear,' she tried to convince her.

278

'Oh, do me a favour, I'm not that dumb . . .'

'You're not behaving as though you're very bright, though, are you? You're acting like a spoiled little brat,' rebuked Jess. 'OK, so you've had a disappointment and it hurts like hell. But that's no excuse to take it out on me. Pick yourself up, girl, and get on with your life.'

'I hate you,' sobbed Libby. 'And I want nothing more to do with you.'

'That'll be difficult as we share a bedroom, won't it?' Jess pointed out.

'I'll manage.' Libby stared at her sister across the kitchen, undiluted hatred exuding from every pore. 'And just to keep you up to date, I'm not going to get a job in an office or a shop.'

'Oh? What will you do then?'

'I shall go into a factory. Some of the girls from school are going to do that,' she announced.

'And you reckon an office job will be boring,' was Jess's scathing response. 'A factory will be a million times worse.'

'The money is miles better than in an office,' she informed her coldly. 'If I'm forced to do some awful job that I'm not suited to, I might as well do one that pays a decent wage.' She shot Jess a venomous look. 'And because I'll be working and paying my way here, you won't be able to interfere in my life. I shall come and go as I please once I get rid of my bloody gymslip for good.'

'There's no need to swear.'

'Oh, shut up, you old has-been,' snapped Libby, her tone shrill. 'You're nothing; a complete dead loss. You can't even get a decent bloke so you're going to marry drippy old Don Day, who's so desperate he'll marry anyone.'

It was as much as Jess could do to keep her hands off her, but she managed to hold back because she knew she was just taking the brunt of Libby's disappointment. 'That's enough, now,' she said.

'Who are you to say what's enough?' Libby shouted, her voice loud and ragged with emotion. 'You've no right to lord it over us. You're not our mother. You're nobody. You're not even my sister after what you've done.'

Ronnie appeared from the other room, looking worried. 'Hey, keep it down, Libs,' he urged her in a manner that wasn't unkind. 'They must be able to hear you in the street; in fact, they can probably hear you in Ealing Broadway. Dad will be home soon. He'll go mad if he hears all this shouting from outside.'

'That's right, take her side,' wept the distraught girl. 'I hate the lot of you. Hate you all.'

And with that parting shot, she fled from the room and rushed upstairs to the bedroom.

Ronnie went to go after her.

'I should give her a little while to calm down,' Jess advised him. 'She won't be willing to listen to any of us, the mood she's in at the moment.'

'No, I suppose not. She didn't mean those things, Jess,' he comforted, having heard most of what had been said. 'She's a good kid at heart. She's in a strop, that's all, and taking it out on you. She'll get over it.'

'Yeah, I know.' But even though Jess knew the reason for Libby's outburst, and was trying not to take it personally, she felt raw from the viciousness of her words. 'I just hope she gets over it soon.'

She didn't get over it. From that day on she was a changed person. Her childhood seemed literally to disappear overnight. The lovable, exuberant girl became a silent and sulky young woman. As soon as she left school, she started work in a biscuit factory in Acton, and became increasingly objectionable with every day that passed.

She spent all her spare cash on clothes: the tightest skirts and sweaters she could find and the lowest-cut blouses, which crudely emphasised her willowy young figure. Her lovely face was copiously spread with cheap cosmetics when she went out dancing at a dance hall with a dubious reputation in Acton. When she got home late and was chastised by her father, she answered him back in a way that was unheard of at one time.

The atmosphere in the house was fraught with tension, and rows abounded. Jess was exhausted from trying to defuse the situation between Libby and her father. 'You're fifteen years old and you look like a twenty-five-year-old tramp,' he would lecture her. 'God knows what you get up to, staying out until all hours.'

'I'm always in by midnight,' she would argue. 'I have to be because I have to catch the last bus home to this stupid backwater. I'll be glad to get out of here and into my own place and I shall go as soon as I can afford it.'

Despite Jess's very best endeavours, Libby continued to believe that her sister had been instrumental in her lack of success at the audition. She only spoke to her, or any of the family, when it couldn't be avoided, she stopped attending her own dance class and no longer helped Jess with hers. Babs got one Saturday off in four and stepped into the breach on those days. Other times Jess and Hilda managed between them.

Even though she was desperate with worry and needed someone to talk to about it, Jess couldn't bring herself to discuss the situation with Don. When she'd mentioned it to him initially, he'd been harshly critical of Libby, made no allowances whatsoever and didn't have any helpful suggestions to offer. In his opinion it was simply a matter of discipline; he thought Jess's father should teach the girl a lesson by throwing her out of the house until she'd learned to behave. Another reason Jess didn't feel inclined to say much to him about Libby was because she'd never quite got over him telling her he was sick of hearing about her family. She'd never been convinced when he'd said he hadn't meant it.

She did confide in Babs, though.

'It's upsetting the whole family,' she told her friend, who was up to date with the rest of the details. 'The boys are sick and tired of the rows. And my poor father just doesn't know which way to turn. He can't handle the person she's become any more than I can. She's so rude to him, Babs. Calls him a silly old fool – and worse.'

Babs tutted and shook her head.

'Of course, Dad loses his temper and lies awake all night worrying about her and she just carries on regardless,' Jess went on. 'She doesn't seem to give a damn about any of us. All she cares about is her social life and her mates at the factory. She's a changed person.'

'Can't Ronnie make her see reason,' wondered Babs, 'him being her twin?'

'He's tried but he's the last person she'll listen to,' Jess replied. 'Honestly, if it isn't one of them it's the other in our house. It isn't so long since Ronnie was giving us all a load of grief. But he's a smashing lad now.'

'How's he getting on in his job?' She was referring to Ronnie's full-time job in a gents' outfitters in Ealing Broadway that he'd taken when he left school.

'All right, I think. He doesn't enjoy the working environment as much as Bruce's shop because it caters for a different sector of the market – more expensive traditional menswear – you know, like my dad wears. But as there wasn't a job for him at Bruce's, he seems to have settled in quite well at this other place. I wouldn't say he's mad keen but he goes off every morning with a willing heart. It's all good experience for him in menswear, which will stand him in good stead for the future. He doesn't have to stay at that particular shop for ever.'

'There is that.'

'But getting back to Libby,' sighed Jess, 'I just don't know what we are going to do about that girl.'

'I can't say I do either,' added Babs sadly.

Babs was really enjoying motherhood now. At six months old, Cindy was pink-cheeked and chubby with spiky golden hair that stood up on top in a cute little quiff. She chuckled, could sit up and usually slept through the night.

That bleak period was behind her, but Babs never forgot the blackness that had plagued her then, and still occasionally got tension knots in her stomach even now. Memories of her illness made her appreciate the current quality of her life with vividness that had her wanting to weep with joy and gratitude. And to think that she could have lost it all if Jess hadn't nagged Don into going to Paddington that terrible day.

Her flat was small and basic: just one bedroom, a living room and tiny kitchen and bathroom. But it gave her independence and was a palace compared to the Paddington bedsit. It might be a bit cramped when Cindy got bigger but it would do for now.

She considered her quality of life to be better than ever; better even than during those halcyon days before things had gone haywire. The job at Dean's Stores had proved to be more enjoyable than she'd expected, especially since she'd taken over as cashier and now worked in the cash desk at the back of the shop. The customers came to her to pay, having had their bills added up by the counter assistants. The job lacked the glamour of the stage, of course, but other things were more important to her now.

Over the time she'd been there, she'd managed to introduce a friendlier atmosphere to the shop. The customers didn't seem to object, and if Don disapproved he hadn't said so. According to her workmates, he was a changed man since she'd been there; much more cheerful and sociable.

Don – he was her only problem. What was it with her and men, she asked herself, as she settled her daughter into her cot one late summer evening; why did she always manage to fall for the wrong ones? First there had been Dickie, who didn't have a moral bone in his body, now there was Don, who was riddled with principles and belonged to her best friend.

Nothing had been said by either herself or Don. But they both knew it was there: this growing attraction between them that drew them closer together with each passing day. The odd thing was, he wasn't the sort of bloke she was normally attracted to at all. Far from it. Even though he smiled more than he used to, he was still a very serious man, much too solemn for her. And it wasn't even as though he was good-looking or sexy.

At first she'd put her feelings down to lingering gratitude to him for saving her life, and had thought it would pass in time. But the opposite had happened. She thought about him all the time, inside and outside of working hours, and looked forward to going to work so that she could be with him. Nothing could come of it because she would *never, ever* betray Jess, not after all she'd done for her.

She stood beside the cot, watching until her daughter fell into a sound sleep, then left the room quietly, went to the kitchen and made herself a cup of coffee, which she took into the living room, looking forward to a spot of relaxation.

Something outside caught her eye through the window as she was about to sit down. Libby Mollitt was standing at the bus stop on the other side of the street. Babs' first thought was how gorgeous she was with her tall slim figure and dark hair falling to her shoulders; her second thought was that she looked like a tart.

It was a warm evening and the window was open. On impulse, Babs poked her head out and called across to her to come up to the flat for a minute.

'I can't. I'm going somewhere,' was Libby's predictable response. 'I'll miss my bus.'

'Get your arse up here – *now*,' shouted Babs, causing every head in the bus queue to turn towards Libby. 'Or I'll come down there to you and say what I have to say. Do you want everyone to know your business. Or are you coming up?'

'How dare you scream out at me like that as though I'm some naughty little kid,' objected a furious Libby a few minutes later when Babs answered the door to her and led her upstairs to the living room. 'Who do you think you are that you have the right to order me about?'

'I've been waiting for an opportunity for a private word with you,' she explained. 'And I just spotted the perfect moment.'

'You had no right to show me up like that; anyway, I don't have time to talk to you,' proclaimed Libby, who was wearing a black, clingy skirt with a wide belt, and a white low-cut top that was barely decent. 'I'm meeting some mates of mine in a coffee bar in Ealing.'

'If they're good friends they won't mind waiting a few extra minutes,' Babs pointed out. 'There'll be other buses.'

'That isn't the point.'

'The point is, young lady, that you are causing that lovely family of yours a lot of grief.'

Libby's face worked and her eyes watered momentarily but she soon composed herself. 'What happens between me and my family is none of your damned business.' She tapped her nose with her finger. 'So keep this out.'

'Your sister happens to be a very dear friend of mine so I'm making it my business,' the older woman informed her in a firm tone. 'You're not being at all fair to her, you know.'

Libby gave a dry laugh. 'I think you've got that the wrong way round,' she informed her curtly.

Babs threw her a sharp look. 'You're wrong about her, you know,' she informed her evenly. 'She didn't muck up your audition.'

'You're her friend so you would say that, wouldn't you?'

'No. if she had done it, it would have been with your best interests at heart so I wouldn't have considered it necessary to lie about it.' Babs was very frank. 'But she didn't do it. She wouldn't do something like that, anyway. But she couldn't have because she doesn't have that sort of power in the company. That isn't how it works at Burtons. They know exactly what they're looking for in a girl, and if they see it in someone, they snap her up.'

Libby winced, then shook her head vigorously. 'I can't accept that I don't have what it takes to be a Burton Girl. I'm a good dancer and I look all right so there's no reason why they wouldn't have taken me on if she hadn't stuck her oar in.'

'If show business was that easy, the labour exchange wouldn't be full of thwarted performers,' the older woman pointed out. 'There are a million good dancers out there, Libby, and lots of them knock on Burton's door every day of the week. Some of them audition by arrangement with the stage schools, others just come in off the street like you did. The Burton Company is very democratic. If you have the talent, you're in, no matter what your background.'

'So you're saying that I don't have talent?'

'Of course I'm not saying that,' Babs assured her with emphasis. 'It could be that you weren't right for Burtons at that time, probably because they didn't need any more very young dancers. There's nothing to stop you trying again later on.' She paused, resting her eyes on Libby. 'But you do need to bear in mind that only a tiny proportion of those that audition are actually hired. More people are disappointed than get taken on. Because your sister got in you might have thought it was easy.'

'Of course I know it isn't easy,' Libby said with seething impatience. 'But I also know that it's possible for someone with the necessary dancing ability to get in.' Libby gave an arrogant shrug. 'You can say what you like and you won't make me change my mind. I know that Jess was behind my rejection.'

Patience stretched beyond the limit, Babs grabbed hold of Libby by her arms and pushed the astonished girl down into an armchair, temporarily lost for words.

'As I've just finished telling you, you silly little girl, it's very hard indeed to get into the Burton troupe,' she told her. 'Your sister was one of those who made it and she worked hard, loving every single moment. Much more so than I did. I enjoyed it up to a point but it was more than that for Jess. Dancing on stage thrilled her as though every time was the first.'

'You'd think she'd be more understanding of how much I want to do it then, wouldn't you?'

'Shut up and listen to me for a minute,' ordered Babs in a manner that shocked Libby into silence. 'Jess was at the top of the tree, a brilliant dancer respected by everyone in the company, dancers and management alike. And what did she do? She gave it all up to look after you and the rest of the family when your mother died. How do you think that must have felt?'

Libby lowered her eyes and stayed silent. She didn't even want to think about that because it made her hate herself even more than she did already.

'Jess won't have told you because she doesn't like to worry people with her problems but I know for a fact that it broke her heart to give up that job,' Babs went on heatedly. 'And you repay her by accusing her of something she would never do, not in a million years. And as if that isn't enough you're making life a misery for the whole family by being hateful to everybody and coming in at all hours and being rude to your father when he tries to talk to you about it. You're a selfish little brat and you don't deserve their love.'

'I don't have to listen to this.' Libby tried to get up but was pushed back down by Babs.

'Just look at the state of you.' Babs' voice rose. 'You look as common as muck in the cheap low-cut tops and tight skirts you go about it in. You're worth better than that.'

She shrugged. 'Thanks for the compliment,' she said through dry lips.

'You're a beautiful young girl, Libby. Anyone can see that. You don't have to wear skin-tight clothes to advertise it like you're going to lose it all tomorrow,' Babs continued. 'You're fifteen years old going on twenty-five. If you're not careful you'll end up in the same boat as me with a kid to bring up on your own.'

'You're a fine one to lecture me,' Libby retaliated.

'I'm going to have my say whether you like it or not,' Babs continued. 'I was at an age to know better when I fell pregnant and was promptly dumped and left to cope with it on my own. It's very hard, I can tell you. I got so low I tried to end it all, as you know.'

'That's got nothing to do with me.'

'Even now, every day I have to put up with insults and it still hurts,' Babs went on as though the girl hadn't spoken. 'Don't let it happen to you, Libby.'

'You've got a cheek to suggest such a thing about me,' the girl objected. 'I don't do that. I never have. I dress this way because my friends do and it's what smart girls wear at dance halls. And yeah, I know that boys admire me and I like the feeling. But I don't do anything.'

'They'd admire your looks if you went about in old newspapers fastened up to the neck and down to the ankles because you're a good-looking girl,' Babs told her. 'They'd admire you even more if you were a bit more subtle about the way you dress – the decent ones would, anyway.'

'The square, drippy boys, you mean,' Libby protested. 'I'm not interested in that sort. I like the boys who dig the scene, the ones who know their way around.'

'I'm sure you can look up to date without looking so cheap,' Babs persisted.

'It's the fashion for smart girls of my age.'

'For a certain type of girl, yes.'

Libby stared up at her, full of umbrage. 'I always used to admire you when you were a dancer, you know,' she informed her coolly. 'I thought you were really glamorous. Now look at you: you're just a fat old frump.'

'I have more important things to think about now than fashion and staying thin,' came Babs' unoffended response.

'Which shows how much you've changed.'

'Yes, I have changed but we're not talking about me,' she reminded her.

285

'I realise that you want to hurt Jess and your dad and the whole world because you failed your audition, but in the end you're the one whose going to suffer if you carry on as you are.'

Libby's mouth twisted. 'Have you quite finished?' she demanded through parched lips. 'Can I go now?'

Babs moved back. 'Not quite,' she said, her tone softening.

'Well, hurry up then,' snapped Libby. 'I've a bus to catch. I can't stay here all night.'

'You've made it clear that you think I'm just some old boot who has no right to poke my nose into your business—'

'That's right,' interrupted Libby.

'But, although you might find this hard to believe,' continued the indomitable Babs, 'I do actually care about you for your own sake as well as for what you're doing to Jess and the others.' She paused, looking at her, considering. 'No matter how much front you put up I don't think you're happy with the way you're behaving. I don't think you're enjoying it one little bit.'

The young girl sat very still for a moment, then she got up with a purposeful air. 'You can think what you like,' she said breezily.

'I'm right, aren't I?'

'Oh, I'm not listening to any more of this rubbish,' she replied impatiently. 'Now that you've got it out of your system, perhaps you'll leave me alone because you'll *never ever* get me to change my mind about Jess's part in my failed audition.'

Realising that she'd gone as far as she could and there was no point in continuing, Babs emitted a weary sigh and led Libby downstairs to the front door. She left without another word.

Libby sat on the bus staring out of the window through a blur of tears, though why she'd let Babs upset her she couldn't imagine. I mean, it wasn't as though the woman was even family, just some meddling old cow who was a friend of her sister's.

There was a horrible dragging ache inside her. It had been constant since she'd fallen out with Jess but had been there intermittently since Mum died. Libby's stage ambitions had been a comfort during those first black days of grief. The idea of being in the Burton troupe had been a distraction; it had lifted her spirits, been something to aim for to take her mind off the misery of missing Mum.

When her dream had crumbled at that awful audition, the disappointment had festered into uncontrollable rage that wouldn't go away. Her feelings were so confusing she didn't even understand them herself. She hated everyone at home, especially Jess, but loved them all too – desperately. She wanted to separate herself from the family and be independent but longed to be one of them again like before. She wanted to hurt Jess for ruining her life but wished they were back on their old footing.

Being horrid to the family was both painful and compelling. She loathed herself for doing it but the more ashamed she became the more impossible it was to stop. And as for believing that Jess hadn't wrecked her chances at the audition, that hurt too much even to contemplate because if Jess hadn't been responsible then Libby had failed because she was lacking in some way herself. And that she really couldn't take.

When she was with her friends her anger faded. Then she could forget the loathsome job at the factory that she would never admit to hating because she wouldn't give Jess and Dad the satisfaction of knowing that they were right. In the glittering ambience of the Silver Cellar Dance Hall, with the soft lights and the band playing all the latest hits that she and her mates jived to, she could forget her unfulfilled stage ambitions. When she was with her friends she felt worth something because she was one of their gang and they didn't go about with girls who weren't 'with it'. They were streetwise and witty. They wore four-inch stilettos and bleached their hair. They told breathtaking tales of sexual adventures with boys that both shocked and excited her.

Libby was too scared to do anything like that herself, but knowing she was fancied by boys gave her back some of the confidence she'd lost when she'd failed the audition. Her friends weren't scared of anything and Libby wanted to be like them.

Tonight they were all meeting in a coffee bar because it was a weekday and there were no dances on anywhere for people in their age group; only old fogeys doing foxtrots and waltzes. She and her mates would talk and giggle over numerous cups of espresso coffee; they'd discuss the latest teenage clothes and pop music. Boys would probably be mentioned too.

Suddenly she didn't want to go. Instead, she wanted to go home to bed and put the covers over her head and weep until there wasn't a tear left in her. She wanted Jess to hug her like their mother always had when things went wrong. She wanted to be joshing with Ronnie like they used to, and talking to Todd and Dad and Hilda. She wanted everything to be as it was before.

Admonishing herself for her appalling feebleness, she dabbed her eyes – cursing the fact that she'd ruined her mascara – and stood up and made her way down the aisle of the bus, ready to get off at the next stop to meet her friends.

Chapter Nineteen

As the mornings became misty and the nights drew in, Don's feelings for Babs continued to trouble him. Far from being a passing phase, the whole thing was becoming an obsession. Try as he might, he couldn't get her out of his mind, and this was particularly traumatic for a man who'd always been so scathing about this sort of thing. He didn't want any of it; Jess was the woman in his life and that was how he wanted it to stay.

But his heart said otherwise to the point where work had become his *raison d'être* because it was there that he saw her. Every morning he went downstairs to the shop brimful with almost childlike anticipation of Babs' arrival. Personal contact was easier now that she was cashier because the cash desk was next to his office so he could go in there on some pretext without setting tongues wagging among the rest of the staff.

It wasn't that she was especially beautiful; she certainly wasn't as lovely as Jess. But Babs was the most alluring woman he'd ever met; she possessed a raw sexuality that he found irresistible. He liked her as a person too; enjoyed the cheery warmth she exuded to everyone around her. She was quite different now from the sad and broken victim he'd encountered at that first terrible meeting.

Although he'd said nothing to her about his feelings and had tried hard to conceal them, he had a very strong suspicion that she knew. There was an intimacy about their relationship, even though he'd never so much as touched her hand.

Now that she was living just across the street, he was in a state of constant temptation because he knew he could call on her out of the glare of the staff's prying eyes and without Jess being any the wiser – underhand thoughts, he knew, but this was the level he had come down to. Again he found himself understanding something of what had driven Bruce and Sheila to betray him. Thank God he had the strength of character not to succumb.

One autumn evening, however, all his good intentions deserted him. Throwing caution and integrity to the winds, he went to call on her. She looked surprised to see him.

'A visit at home from the boss, eh?' she said in a questioning manner, having invited him in and made coffee and light conversation. 'It must be something serious. I hope I'm not about to get the sack.'

'Nothing like that,' he assured her. 'This is purely a social visit.'

Sitting opposite him by the fire, she paused with her cup in mid-air, looking at him enquiringly. 'Oh, really?'

Down went his cup on the coffee table with such a shaky hand that the liquid spilled into the saucer. 'Oh, I can't stand this,' he burst out. 'I'm going to come right out and say it.'

Her heart leaped as she realised why he was here.

'The thing is, Babs . . . my feelings for you have—'

'Stop right there and don't say any more,' she cut in swiftly, her cheeks flaming. 'It's better left unsaid.'

'You know?'

'Of course I know.'

'You feel it too?'

She gave him a look of tender reproach. 'You already know the answer to that, don't you?' she said gently.

'Let's just say I was hopeful.' He gave her a nervous smile.

'At first I thought it was just gratitude to you for saving my life but realised later that it was more.' She shook her head gravely. 'It was the last thing I wanted, I can tell you.'

His face lit into a beaming smile. 'Oh, Babs,' he said, standing up and going towards her. 'You can't know how much I've longed to tell you how I feel.'

She shot up and faced him, her expression grim. 'It's going nowhere, though, Don,' she made clear, her voice quivering slightly. 'I would never do that to Jess.'

'Me neither.'

'Why are you here then?' Her manner was determinedly cold now. This thing mustn't be allowed to develop.

'I was sitting at home thinking about you and my willpower just sort of went,' he explained ruefully. 'I just had to know if you felt the same.'

'You shouldn't have . . .'

'I know.'

'All you've done is made things worse.'

'Sorry.'

'You don't look it.'

'I'm doing my best.'

They stared at each other in silence, a fusion of shared emotions drawing them together. It was suddenly too much and they fell into each other's arms – but only briefly.

'Don't do this to me,' Babs begged, pulling away. 'Don't make me betray my dearest friend.'

'I'm not going to make you do anything,' he said thickly. 'I don't want to hurt Jess either.'

'Then you should have left well alone,' she admonished sternly, forcing herself to be strong. 'It isn't fair to me or Jess. Or to you, for that matter.'

'I just couldn't help myself.'

'You should have tried harder, then, shouldn't you?' she rebuked. 'This really isn't on.'

'Oh, Babs.' He looked distraught.

'Look. I don't want to leave my job and move away but I will if I have to,' she made perfectly clear. 'I'll do whatever it takes to do right by Jess.'

'Oh no, please don't move away,' he urged her. 'I can't bear the thought of not seeing you at all.'

Her face was paper white with two patches of high colour staining her cheeks. 'And I can't bear the idea of cheating on someone who has done so much for me.' She was very firm.

'I don't want to do the dirty on Jess any more than you do,' he said, spreading his hands in a helpless gesture. 'I think a lot of her, despite my feelings for you. I didn't want this to happen. I didn't plan to fall in love with you.'

'But it has happened and we have to live with it as best as we can because there's a line over which we are not going to go,' she spelled out for him in a tone that prohibited argument. 'We can be work colleagues and nothing more. If there's so much as a hint of anything else, I shall immediately leave the job and move out of the area.'

He looked crestfallen but knew what she said was the only option open to them. 'I understand,' he sighed.

'I think you'd better go now.'

'Yes, all right,' he sighed.

She showed him down the stairs in silence. At the door, she spoke to him in a tone that left no room for discussion. 'Tonight didn't happen, Don. OK? Tomorrow at work we carry on as before. I want no mention of it – ever.'

Nodding in agreement, he left hurriedly.

He should be grateful that she'd taken the decision out of his hands, he thought, as he walked home. This way no one got hurt. But it was too late to save himself and Babs from pain. And plenty more to come, he suspected.

It was Saturday night and the dance at the Silver Cellar was nearing the end. The lights were low and Libby was smooching around the floor with a boy called Pete who was extremely 'with it' in a boxy bum-freezer jacket, tapered trousers and winkle-picker shoes. He was tall, blond and handsome, and had the most fantastic Italian-style haircut. He'd come to the dance tonight with three mates, who were all dancing with her friends. Libby thought it was great fun.

She was feeling particularly relaxed and jolly on account of the fact that the boys looked old enough to get served with alcohol in a pub and had taken the girls to the one across the road in the interval and bought them some drinks. They'd all had to stand well away from the bar in case the landlord noticed what they were drinking. It had been tremendously exciting, and so grown up. Libby had had a couple of gin and oranges. She'd hated the taste but loved the way it made her feel; sort of warm inside and very happy. A bit like Christmas morning used to be before Mum died.

As the dance came to an end, Pete said, 'Will you be here next Saturday?'

'Oh, yeah,' she said, looking up into his eyes. 'We come here every week. I wouldn't miss it for anything.'

'See you next week then.'

'That'll be smashing.'

She took a lot of teasing from her friends on the way home because Pete hadn't asked to see her home. They were also extremely vocal on the subject of his arranging to see her *inside* the dance next week, which meant she'd have to pay for her own ticket. But she reminded them that none of them had got anywhere at all with his mates, and that soon shut them up. Libby was on too much of a high to be unduly upset, anyway – what with meeting Pete and going in the pub and everything. She couldn't wait for next Saturday to see him again. It seemed so far away, though, with a week in that abysmal factory to be endured first.

She could hardly bear to imagine what Dad or Jess would say if they knew she'd been drinking alcohol. Still, she wasn't going to spoil it by thinking about that; she certainly wasn't going to tell them. It was none of their business. That's funny, she thought, noticing a sudden change of mood; that sweet, heady feeling just seemed to evaporate and she couldn't get it back. By the time she and her friends got off the bus and went their separate ways, she was feeling quite miserable and couldn't understand why.

'We're really doing things in style tonight, Don,' remarked Jess the following Saturday evening as she struggled with her main course of Dover sole and a variety of vegetables in the restaurant of a posh hotel near Marble Arch.

'I thought it was about time we did something special,' he told her.

'It's lovely.'

He frowned towards her plate on which the meal was barely touched. 'Not hungry?'

'Just taking it slowly,' she told him, forcing a smile. 'I'm not used to such extravagant meals.'

'We should do it more often so that you do get used to it,' he suggested. 'We don't have enough special nights out.'

'Only because we're saving up to get married,' she said absently; she was very preoccupied.

Panic and compunction consumed him in equal measures; panic because the thought of getting married to Jess terrified him now that his

292

emotions had been turned upside down by his feelings for Babs; compunction because this whole charade tonight had been organised because he felt so bad about it.

In a moment of peculiar inspiration, he decided to try to make the wedding plans definite. He had to go through with it now, whether he wanted to or not, so if he set things in motion perhaps he might feel more positive. 'And while we're on that subject, I suppose it's time we set a date for the wedding as it's getting towards the end of the year,' he suggested.

Jess felt the blood drain from her face and struggled to compose herself. 'Yeah, I suppose we ought to do something about it some time soon.' She put her knife and fork down. She hadn't had much of an appetite before. Don's talk of wedding plans had destroyed it completely.

'What's the matter?' he asked. 'You've turned deathly white all of a sudden.'

'Just a bit of a headache,' she fibbed. 'I've had a stinker all day.'

'You should have said,' he admonished in a gentle tone. 'I wouldn't have dragged you to the West End if I'd known you weren't feeling well.'

'I didn't want to spoil it for you.' Oh, what a tangled web, she thought. 'Anyway, it's nothing much.'

He felt worse than ever now. She was so good, so thoughtful. She'd been feeling off colour and not said a word because she didn't want to spoil the evening for him when all he was doing was trying to assuage his guilt for having fallen in love with her best friend. 'Would you like to go home?' he asked in a caring tone.

'No, I don't feel that bad,' she assured him. 'I don't think I can eat any more of this, though. Sorry. It must be costing you the earth.'

'It doesn't matter about that.' He was full of concern. 'Would you like a drink of water?'

'No, I'm all right with this,' she said, picking up her wine glass and sipping from it.

'Shall I see if they have anything for a headache at the reception desk?' he suggested.

She reached her hand across the table and gave his a reassuring squeeze. 'Stop worrying,' she soothed. 'You get on and enjoy your meal and I'll join you in dessert if there's something light on the menu. It's just a headache, really.'

'If you're sure . . .'

'I am.'

She felt really terrible now. He'd gone to all this trouble and expense for her and she didn't want to be here; she didn't want to be anywhere with him. She didn't have a headache, not so much as a twinge. Heartache was what she had in abundance, the same malady that had been tormenting her ever since she'd fallen in love with Don's brother. Today it had been exacerbated by a 'Sold' sign, which had appeared on

Bruce's shop. He was leaving and she didn't know how to bear it.

It was the interval at the Silver Cellar and Libby was in the pub with Pete. The others had gone back to the dance but Pete had wanted to stay a bit longer. He wanted her to himself, he said, and she was *so flattered*. The week had seemed endless as she'd longed to see him again. But it had been well worth the wait. She was having the most fantastic time.

'Another drink?' he offered.

'I'm not sure if I should.' She couldn't remember exactly how many she'd had but it was definitely more than a couple. She felt *so good*. Even better than last Saturday. She was floating on air.

'Go on, be a devil,' he said with a persuasive smile.

'All right then,' she giggled. Everything was such a laugh, and Pete wasn't some silly kid of her own age. He was self-assured and grown up; must be nearly eighteen. He knew how to do things and did them in style.

The liquid went down like water; she didn't even mind the taste now that she was used to it. She couldn't wait to tell her friends how well she and Pete were getting on and how smitten he was with her.

'Shall we go back to the dance?' she tried to suggest, but her mouth didn't seem to be working properly and the words came out slow and slurred.

'Yeah, if you like.'

She stood up but felt giddy.

'Here, lean on me,' he suggested.

'Thanks.'

They walked out into the street arms entwined. She'd not known it was possible to feel this happy. When they got back to the dance and the girls saw them together like this they would have to believe that he was interested in her.

'You're going the wrong way,' she pointed out as he led her off the main road into a side street. 'The dance is that way.'

'Yeah, I know. But we don't want to go straight back to the dance, do we, sweetheart?' he said, turning into a dark alley between some houses.

'Don't we?'

'Of course we don't. Not just yet,' he said.

It was late when Jess and Don got back from the West End and everyone in the Mollitt house was in bed. Jess was relieved when Don said he wouldn't come in for a coffee. She was afraid that if she was with him any longer without a break she would blurt out the truth. She was suffering a reaction to Bruce leaving and needed time to get used to it. She'd promised herself she wouldn't destroy Don by giving him up and she was determined to stand by that.

As she slipped into bed, careful not to wake Libby, she realised that her sister wasn't asleep. The sound of stifled sobbing was coming from her bed.

'Libby,' she hissed, 'what's the matter?'

Silence.

Jess got up and padded over to the other bed. 'What's the matter, love?' she asked again.

'Nothing,' came the muffled reply.

'There obviously is.'

'No there isn't.'

'I might be able to help.'

'You can't so go back to bed and mind your own business,' she choked out.

'Libby . . .'

'Leave me alone, please.'

Jess went back to her own bed. But she didn't sleep because the sound of her sister weeping went on until the small hours. And when it eventually stopped, Jess was far too distressed about Libby's unhappiness to doze off, her own problems pushed to the back of her mind.

A month or so later, on an afternoon off, Jess strode out across Churchfields with the dog. It was a misty November day, cold and cheerless, with a pewter sky and dampness in the air that permeated everything; the sort of weather that inspired most people to stay indoors. Jess had come out to give Doughnut some exercise but she also thought a walk might help to clear her head of tormented thoughts.

She took the dog off the lead and let him run free to sniff and poke about in the grass and fallen leaves, the old trees along the river bank shadowy in the mist, the church spire barely visible. It still gave her pleasure to see their much-loved family pet enjoying a healthy life. She'd never forgotten the neglected state he was in when she'd found him, on this very spot as it happened; the day Bruce had offered her the hall for her classes.

She'd had a terrible few weeks since that night out with Don in the West End, as she'd become increasingly desperate about Bruce's imminent departure. She'd only seen him in passing and had studiously avoided the subject of his leaving. He was determined to go and she didn't want to make it more difficult for him by trying to persuade him to change his mind.

Another reason she'd been feeling so tense this past few weeks was Libby's latest personality change. In the same way that she'd changed almost overnight from a warm-hearted, family-loving girl into a teenage monster who was rarely at home, now she was indoors every evening. She still didn't join in family life, though; unlike the girl she had once been, she was quiet and withdrawn and spent most of her time upstairs in the bedroom on her own. The tarty gear she'd been so keen on wearing was replaced by ordinary things: sweaters and skirts or trousers.

She was obviously very troubled about something, but as she refused to admit that there was anything wrong Jess was unable to help. She assumed her sister must have fallen out with her friends from the factory in that she never went out of an evening, but the girl admitted nothing; just told Jess to mind her own business when she asked. It pierced Jess's heart to see her so unhappy and she wished there was something she could do.

Her thoughts turned back to her own personal problems as she walked on towards Brent Lodge Park, keeping a close eye on the dog. Engaged to one brother and in love with the other, that was some complication. She stopped dead in her tracks. Maybe the calming influence of the park had cleared her mind or perhaps she would have come to her senses anyway, eventually. But suddenly she knew what she must do. Maybe she didn't have it in her power to help her troubled sister but she could help herself. It wouldn't be easy but she mustn't be deterred now that she'd made up her mind. And there was no time like the present.

She called the dog, put him back on the lead and headed for home.

Don stared at her in bewilderment. 'You're saying that you want to break off our engagement?' he gasped.

They were in his flat, having moved up here from the office of Dean's Stores, where she'd found him doing paperwork as he always did on half-day closing. Now she bit her lip; she felt terrible but this had to be done. There had been too much pretence; too much self delusion. 'Yes. I'm so sorry, Don. I really am.'

He was very pale; even his lips seemed bloodless. 'Why?' he asked in a subdued tone.

Her face creased with the pain of knowing how much she was going to hurt him but there was no other way. 'Because, er . . . because I'm not in love with you,' she said in a rush.

'Oh . . . Oh, I see.'

'I'm very fond of you and none of this is your fault,' she was quick to add. 'I'm to blame for the whole thing. You see, I never was in love with you, not really. I wanted to be so much, and tried hard to pretend to myself that I was. I thought it was enough to be fond of you. But I now know that it isn't.' She lowered her gaze for a moment. 'I shouldn't have let things get this far. I'm sorry.'

'It's Bruce, isn't it?' he blurted out. 'You're in love with him?'

That was the last thing she'd expected; she hadn't realised she'd been so transparent. But she'd promised herself that there would be no more lies, no more deceit. 'Yes, I am.' She looked at him, puzzled. 'But how did you know?'

'My suspicious nature, I suppose. I could feel a change in you whenever he was around, or when his name was mentioned,' he told her.

'There was just something about you then. That's why I used to get so jealous.'

'He isn't the reason I'm breaking off our engagement,' she went on, too concerned for his feelings to notice that he was speaking in the past tense. 'I'm ending it because, although I do think an awful lot of you, my feelings aren't what good marriages are based on.'

'And Bruce feels the same about you?'

She nodded sheepishly. 'But nothing has happened between us, I swear. Bruce wouldn't do that. He thinks too much of you. And so do I.' She paused, fiddling with her fingernails. 'I know what a stickler you are for morality, Don. But Bruce and I didn't plan to fall in love, honestly. It just happened. Looking back I can see that we were smitten the minute we clapped eyes on each other.' She gave him a wry look. 'I know it sounds far-fetched and I don't expect you to understand.'

'Oh, but I do, Jess. I do.'

Her brows shot up. 'What?'

'I understand because the same thing has happened to me,' he confessed. 'I've fallen for someone else too.'

'You're joking.'

'I've never been more serious.'

'I can't believe it.'

'I'm still having difficulty believing it myself.'

Realising now that what he said was true and not some sick joke, her relief was so great, she felt positively light-headed. 'So that's why you've been so touchy.'

'Sorry, I've tried to act normally.'

'And you did, up to a point. But I knew there was something bothering you.' She shook her head in disbelief. 'I never dreamed it would be anything like this, though.'

'I'm still in shock myself,' he confessed. 'This sort of thing isn't my style at all.' He paused. 'Nothing's happened, though. Neither of us wanted to hurt you.'

She threw him a quizzical look. 'Sounds as though I know this mystery woman.'

He made a face. 'Er, you do . . . rather well, as it happens,' he said sheepishly.

Jess looked at him curiously, waiting for him to continue.

A little later on she found Bruce in his office in the empty shop, and came straight to the point and told him the astonishing story that had just enfolded.

'Don and your best friend – well, stone me,' was his amazed response.

'You couldn't be more surprised than I was when he told me,' she said. 'They're about the last two people on earth I would have expected to get together.'

'It must have been quite a shock to Don to realise that he's only human like the rest of us.'

'It's shaken him, he admitted it.' She was sitting on a chair near his desk. 'God knows how long the four of us would have gone on suffering unnecessarily if I hadn't decided to come clean with Don. I'd decided to end it, anyway, never dreaming he was going to drop that bombshell on me.'

Bruce beamed at her across the desk. 'Thank the Lord you spoke up when you did.'

'My thoughts exactly.' She looked at him. 'Fancy Don letting himself fall for someone else when he's engaged, though. I mean, Don, who never steps outside of his own guidelines.'

'Perhaps he won't be quite so high and mighty in future,' suggested Bruce.

'Mm,' she agreed thoughtfully. 'I reckon it will give him more understanding of how these things work, and how it was with you and Sheila.'

He gave her a dark look. 'Since we're having everything out in the open, I shall tell you the truth about Sheila and me . . .' Bruce began.

'Go on. I'm listening,' she said, half dreading what she was about to hear.

'There was never anything apart from friendship between us,' he informed her. 'I wasn't lying when I told you I wasn't having an affair with her.'

She narrowed her eyes. 'But you were running away together.'

'No. That was all in Don's mind.'

'But I thought you were actually in the car together when it crashed.'

'We were, and she was leaving him,' he explained. 'But she wasn't going away with me. She wasn't going away with anyone. She was going to stay with her mother in Essex until she found somewhere more permanent. I was just driving her there.'

'I don't understand.'

'To cut a long story short, their marriage hadn't been working for a while. They were never really suited. Don was far too serious for Sheila. He made such heavy weather of everything, it got her down. In the end she just couldn't take any more.'

'Why did they get married in the first place?'

'They must have thought it was right at the time, I suppose,' he suggested. 'You don't know someone until you live with them, do you? By the time she realised that they were incompatible, it was too late. Sheila wasn't the most relaxed of people. She needed someone a bit more light-hearted.'

'Babs is very down to earth,' Jess mentioned. 'She just won't put up with too much doom and gloom. Maybe that's just what Don needs.'

He nodded. 'Sheila relied on me to make her laugh; we were good friends, that's all.'

298

'Didn't she tell Don how she felt about the marriage?'

'Many times,' he replied sadly. 'But he wouldn't admit that there was anything wrong; just wouldn't face up to it.'

'Why have you not told him that you and Sheila weren't having an affair?'

'I have, more times than I care to remember,' he explained. 'But he refused to accept the truth.'

'I'm sorry I didn't believe you. I should have trusted my instincts about you.'

'Don can be a persuasive influence.'

'I think you ought to try to make him accept the truth now,' was her opinion. 'This is a time of new beginnings for all four of us, not a time to hang on to old grudges. He should be feeling a whole lot happier and more secure in himself now that he can be with the woman he really loves. He might be ready to listen.'

'Don't bank on it. You know how stubborn he can be,' Bruce sighed. 'Families, eh. Who'd have 'em? If it wasn't for the bad feeling between Don and me everything would be perfect.'

'Don't remind me about families,' she said ruefully. 'I'm worried to death about my little sister, and if it wasn't for that, everything would be perfect for me too.'

'Tell me about it in a minute,' he said, holding out his arms to her. 'But before that, come here . . .'

Bruce intended to go to see his brother the following evening but – much to his astonishment – Don pre-empted the situation by calling at Bruce's shop the next morning and inviting to join him in the pub for a drink after work that evening.

'I know I've always said there's no chance of you and I patching things up,' began Don, as they stood at the bar together. 'But I've had a change of heart. I think it's time we put the past behind us.'

'Blimey,' responded Bruce. 'What's brought this on?'

'Experience,' he replied. 'Until I met Babs, I thought feelings could be controlled. Now – having broken all the rules and fallen in love with my fiancée's best friend – I know different.' He sipped his beer. 'I understand something of how it was for you and Sheila.'

Bruce stared at him over the rim of his glass. 'I'm glad to hear that you've come to your senses, mate,' he said. 'But you've still got it all wrong. Sheila and I were only ever good friends. There was never an affair.'

'Come on, Bruce, there's no need to lie about it now,' Don urged him. 'It's water under the bridge.'

'I'm not lying, Don, I never was,' Bruce informed him evenly. 'And, as you say, there's no need for me to lie about it now.'

Don took a large swallow from his glass, the truth finally beginning to dawn. 'So . . . what you said about giving her a lift to her mother's really was true?'

'Every single word,' Bruce confirmed. 'Everything I've been trying to get you to believe all these years. Not so much as a fib anywhere.'

His brother put his glass down on the bar and clasped his head, his thoughts spinning. 'God, how awful. I just couldn't accept it . . . I wouldn't accept that the marriage wasn't working.' He looked up. 'I can see now that it was easier for me to think that you'd stolen her and she was leaving because of you. Her wanting to leave simply because of me was just too painful to bear.' He shook his head. 'I've given you a really bad time.'

'It hasn't been easy.'

'I really don't know what to say.' Don was full of contrition. 'Sorry seems so inadequate.'

'Sorry will be fine.'

'I came here tonight to tell you that I'd forgiven you. It turns out I'm the one needing to ask you to forgive me.' Don gave a wry grin. 'Can you?'

'Course I can,' replied Bruce without hesitation. 'You know me. It isn't in my nature to bear a grudge.'

'Mates again then,' Don said, offering his hand.

Bruce grinned and shook his brother's hand.

Charlie and Hilda had been to the cinema and were having a cup of coffee and a chat in her place to round the evening off.

'So, there's been a bit of a shake-up among the young 'uns then,' he said.

Hilda nodded. 'You could have knocked me down with a feather when I heard about it,' she told him. 'Jess and Bruce are so right together, I've often thought so when I've seen them together at the hall. But Babs is the last person I thought would be suited to Don. They're such different types.'

'Must be the attraction of opposites,' Charlie suggested.

'Must be, I suppose.'

He looked awkward suddenly. 'As a matter of fact, Hilda, I've been doing some serious thinking myself lately,' he began.

'Ooh, you be careful,' she chuckled. 'You'll do yourself a mischief with too much of that.'

He didn't appreciate the joke. 'I'm being serious,' he informed her gravely.

'Come on then,' she said, with a straight face. 'What's on your mind?'

'Well, it's just that . . . you and I . . . I mean, we spend a lot of our spare time together and you're just like one of the family but you still live in here all on your own.'

'Yeah, so what of it?' She squinted at him. 'What are you trying to say?'

'There's always something that needs sorting in my family,' he went on nervously. 'If it isn't one of the kids causing a problem it's another. Jess is sorted and the boys seem settled at the moment but we've still got Libby going about like death warmed up. Jess is worried to death about her.'

Hilda frowned. 'She is being difficult at the moment. I suppose it must be something to do with her growing up.'

'That doesn't mean she has to go about the house like a sick cat, does it?'

'Have you never heard of hormones, Charlie?' She didn't wait for a reply. 'Anyway, what's all that got to do with whatever it is you're leading up to?'

He stood up and paced the floor. 'The thing is . . .'

'Spit it out, man, before you wear my carpet out.'

'I'm trying to say that you might not want to take me on, with the family and all their noise and rows and everything.'

Hilda looked at him with a half-smile. 'Get on with it, for goodness' sake,' she urged him.

He stared at the floor. 'I was thinking that we got on well and we think a lot of each other . . . we're not young but neither are we too old to make a new start . . .?'

'Is this a marriage proposal, Charlie Mollitt?'

He nodded, looking wary. 'I realise that you'll need to think about it,' he mumbled. 'I know the kids can be a bit overpowering.'

'If you think I'd be put off by those lovely children of yours, you don't know me at all,' she admonished.

He raised his eyes rather fearfully to meet hers. He wasn't an eloquent man in this sort of situation and it was difficult for him. 'Sorry, Hilda, I didn't mean to offend you.'

'Stop apologising, you daft devil.' She was fully aware of what had been left unsaid in all this but knew Charlie well enough to understand why. 'It'll take more than that to offend me.'

'You mean . . .?'

'I don't think much of the way you proposed – all that muttering and mumbling – but I liked what you said even if you did have a funny way of saying it. So, if you think your kids will be willing to put up with me as your wife, I'd love to marry you.'

'Oh, Hilda, you've made me a very happy man,' he beamed, going towards her.

301

Chapter Twenty

Preoccupied with her own distress, Libby was only vaguely aware of what was going on around her. The family had been summoned to the living room where Dad and Hilda had just announced their plans to marry to a great whoop of delight, but Libby felt so distanced from the whole thing she might as well not have been there.

She didn't mind having Hilda as a stepmother. As far as she could feel anything outside of her own personal hell, she thought it was a good thing. Dad needed someone and Hilda was already just like one of the family. Thoughts of the older woman's endless capacity for kindness combined with the general sense of excitement and goodwill currently present in this room, made Libby want to weep. Nothing new there; she seemed to spend all her time shut away somewhere in tears: her bedroom; the bathroom with the door locked; the toilets at work. She felt so utterly alone, so isolated from everything, especially her family. They were all good people and she longed to feel part of things again. But she was a degenerate outsider because of the mess she'd made of her life.

Realising with a start that her father had said something to her and she hadn't heard a word, she said, 'Sorry, Dad. What was that?'

'Have you got cloth ears or something, girl?' he asked good-humouredly. 'I've asked you twice if Hilda and I have your blessing. The others are all thrilled to bits but the cat seems to have got your tongue.'

'Sorry. Yeah, I'm all for it,' she said absently.

'Is that all you have to say?' was his disappointed response. 'Aren't you going to congratulate us?'

Suddenly her surroundings became so vivid they seemed to close in on her. Dad, Hilda, Jess, Bruce, Ronnie and Todd were all looking at her expectantly. And all she could do was stand there like some gormless twit. She felt so dull-witted and close to tears, she couldn't speak.

'How about giving them a hug, eh, Libs?' came Jess's helpful suggestion.

'Yeah, yeah, of course.' She went over to the couple and gave them each a dutiful peck on the cheek and said she was really pleased for them and hoped they would be very happy. Then – when the clamour of conversation rose again and everyone was occupied – she slipped out of the room and left the house, grabbing her duffel coat off the hall-stand on the way.

She headed off down the street in the direction of the Broadway with no idea of why she'd come out or where she was going. It was a cold and windy night with needles of rain stabbing her face as she walked passed the closed shops, head down, hands in her pockets. This being midweek, there weren't many people about. Those who were around were hurrying, eager to get inside out of the weather, the chilly mortals in the queue at the bus stop shifting from foot to foot impatiently.

Undeterred by the weather, a crowd of loutish boys were congregated by the clock tower, the rough tones of their youthful voices rising above the howling wind. Knowing that to walk past them would create an eruption of whistling and catcalling, she crossed the road, panic rising in the fear that they might come after her. She wasn't usually daunted by a few wolf whistles but her nerves were so raw she was oversensitive and frightened of everything. What was she doing, walking the streets like this? Why had she left the house when she had nowhere to go?

A light in an upstairs window caught her eye. She halted in her step, looking up at it, thinking, a gleam of hope rising within her. In that flat lived the only person she felt able to talk to about her dreadful plight; the one human being who might possibly understand. Taking her courage in her hands, she walked up to the front door and knocked on it.

'Are you sure this boy didn't force you to have sex with him, Libby?' asked Babs, having had the whole miserable story sobbed out to her. 'From what you've said, it sounds as though he did.'

'He was very persistent but I can't honestly say that he forced me,' she admitted, looking very shamefaced. 'I just sort of went along with it even though I didn't really want to do it. I'd been feeling terrible about myself because I'd got into this awful mood at home and couldn't get out of it. I thought sex would be different to what it was; thought it would be romantic and loving, not rough and scary. I suppose I thought it would make me feel better about myself somehow. I mean, everyone's always going on about how wonderful it is and everything. But I didn't think much of it and I was even more depressed afterwards.'

'That's because you're not ready,' suggested Babs.

'I can't believe I would let myself down by doing something I didn't want to do,' Libby went on, needing to talk about it. 'I always wanted my first time to be special. Instead of that I go and do it with someone I hardly know in some horrible back alley.'

'We all make mistakes,' said Babs kindly.

'I couldn't stop crying afterwards,' said Libby, fresh tears forming as she thought back.

'Did he try to comfort you?'

'Oh, no. He didn't want to know about me afterwards,' she explained. 'Told me to grow up and stop snivelling. Then he said he was going back to the dance and walked off as though nothing had happened.'

'The pig,' tutted Babs, shaking her head. 'He wants locking up.'

'I didn't want to go back to the dance,' the young girl continued. 'I haven't been near the place since and don't want to *ever* because he'll be there. I never want to see him again.'

'You don't still fancy him then.'

She shook her head vigorously, her eyes brimming with tears. 'The thought of him sickens me now. I was disgusted with myself that night. When I got home, I couldn't face anyone so I went to bed and hid under the covers. I couldn't stop crying.'

'That's understandable,' soothed Babs. 'You're too young to cope with something like that. One day, when you meet someone nice, it will be different.'

'Jess asked me what was wrong when she came to bed. I couldn't tell her.'

'You should have,' was Babs' opinion. 'Talking to her might have helped.'

'I was too ashamed to say anything.'

'Jess would have understood.'

'She'd have gone mad.'

'Initially, yeah. That's only natural because she's your big sister and wants the best for you. But when she'd calmed down she'd have helped you.'

'I keep thinking that it might not have happened if I hadn't had those drinks.'

'The boy should have known better than to buy drinks for a fifteen-year-old girl.'

'I shouldn't have had them.'

'No, you shouldn't,' the older woman stated firmly. 'But I still think the boy has a lot to answer for.'

They were sitting on Babs' sofa. The baby was asleep in the bedroom and Don wasn't here so they were alone. Libby had collapsed into tears as soon as Babs had opened the door to her, and blurted out the whole sickening story. Babs hadn't scolded her. She'd just put a comforting arm around her and let her tell her tale.

'I feel so cheap, Babs; the feeling just won't go away.' She dabbed at her eyes with her hanky.

'It will do in time, love. I think you'll feel better when you've spoken to Jess about it,' suggested Babs. 'You've been through a trauma. You need your sister.'

'I can't face telling her because I feel as though I've let the family down,' she said. 'It was different telling you.'

'It's often easier to talk to a stranger,' remarked Babs. 'Not that I'm a stranger but I'm not family either. Is that why you came to me?'

'Partly that and partly because you've raised a few eyebrows yourself,' she explained. 'I thought you might be less shocked than Jess.'

'I see.'

'Thanks for being so nice to me, especially as I've been so horrible to you,' she said ruefully. 'I'm sorry about that.'

'Forget it, kid. It's all in the past.' Babs thought the girl was barely recognisable without the heavy make-up and those awful clothes she used to go about in. She looked about nine years old in a sweater and trousers, her huge eyes swollen from crying, dark hair dishevelled. 'Once you've talked to Jess and calmed down a bit, you must concentrate on the future and put this wretched business behind you.'

Libby lowered her eyes. 'That won't be possible,' she said, biting her lip.

'Why not?'

'My period hasn't come,' she burst out, eyes wide with fear. 'I'm more than a month overdue and I feel sick in the mornings.'

'Bloody hell, Libby,' gasped Babs. 'That really has torn it.'

'Libby doesn't seem to be anywhere in the house,' observed Jess worriedly.

'That's typical of the way she's been behaving lately,' opined Charlie. 'It's very rude of her to go swanning off in the middle of a family celebration. I shall have a few sharp words with that young lady when she comes back.'

'She's probably gone to meet her terrible friends,' suggested Ronnie.

'I don't think she sees them now,' mentioned Jess. 'She hasn't been out of an evening for ages.'

'There is that,' agreed Ronnie.

'She won't have gone far,' put in Hilda, ever the peacemaker. 'Probably just fancied some fresh air.'

'Maybe you're right,' said Jess, but she was deeply worried about her sister. As well as being moody and withdrawn, she'd not been looking well lately.

'Shall I go out looking for her?' offered Bruce.

The sound of the telephone interrupted the conversation and sent Jess hurrying to the hall to answer it.

'Jess, it's Babs. I'm calling from the phone box near my flat,' she explained in an anxious, rapid tone. 'I think you'd better come over to my place right away. I've got Libby with me and there's something you should know.'

Stopping only long enough to tell the others that Libby was safe and that she had to go out, Jess grabbed a coat and left the house.

Such was Jess's concern for her sister on hearing the news, her immediate reaction was one of fury.

'Oh Libby,' she burst out. 'How could you have been so stupid?'

'Steady on, Jess,' warned Babs. 'She didn't get pregnant on her own.'

'She shouldn't have put herself in such a vulnerable position,' returned Jess, worry about her sister's future manifesting itself in anger. 'Mixing with yobs and drinking in pubs when she's under age. That's just asking for trouble.'

'Sorry, Jess,' the girl muttered, looking very downcast. 'I know I've been stupid.'

'I hope you do,' returned her sister, softening slightly. 'Who is the lowlife who did this to you? Let's go and get him. I'll murder the bugger.'

'Please don't, Jess,' Libby protested, her voice muffled from crying. 'He didn't force me.'

'He got you pregnant, though, and he can't be allowed to get away with it,' Jess declared. 'He must be made to face up to his responsibilities and give you some support.'

'He'll say the baby isn't his; he'll tell everyone that I'm a tramp who's done it with other boys and I haven't,' said Libby, her voice small and shaky. 'I don't want him to know.' Despite being enfeebled by trauma, her spirit hadn't completely deserted her. 'I'll *never ever* tell anyone who he is, no matter how many times you ask me.'

As much as Jess wanted support for her sister, she knew they wouldn't get it. The boy would doubtless cause even more humiliation for Libby if they tried to pursue it. Anyway, whether or not to name the father must be her decision; as young as she was it was her right. 'All right, love. Calm down. I won't press you.'

'You're not going to try to get it out of me?'

'No, I won't do that.'

'Thanks.'

Jess still wasn't quite ready to forgive her for taking those first steps that had got her into bad company, which had led to the pregnancy and ruined a potentially golden future. 'So much for your dancing career now,' she said.

'I'd lost the chance of that anyway.'

'No you hadn't,' Jess disagreed. 'You could have auditioned for Burtons again.'

'I'd stopped going to classes and got rusty,' she reminded her. 'I wouldn't be good enough to audition for an amateur troupe, let alone a top professional outfit.'

'You'd have soon got it back if you'd started going to classes again. After all those years of training you wouldn't have lost it because of one short lapse,' Jess pointed out. 'But you chose to turn your back on everything because of one lousy rejection.'

Libby was whey-faced and full of remorse. 'I was wrong, I know,' she said.

This was the first time Jess had heard her admit it. 'Oh really?' she said in an enquiring tone.

Libby nodded. 'I'm sorry I blamed you when I failed the audition,

Jess,' she said tearfully. 'It was terrible of me. I just couldn't face up to the fact that I wasn't good enough to be chosen by Burtons. I was so disappointed, I kept telling myself it wasn't my fault. I sort of went off the rails.'

'I'll say you did,' confirmed Jess, 'and got yourself pregnant as a result.'

'I'm really sorry,' she wept. 'I don't know what I'm going to do. Will I have to go to one of those women you hear about . . . who see to these things?'

'Is that what you want?'

'No, I don't think I could go through with that.'

Jess looked at her and saw a frightened little girl who had lost her mother at a tender age. She wasn't emotionally mature enough to look after herself, let alone a child. But mollycoddlying wouldn't give her the strength she was going to need to cope with the problems ahead. 'In that case you'll have to face up to the pregnancy,' Jess told her gravely. 'You'll need to be very strong.'

'Will I have to give the baby up for adoption?'

'I don't know what will happen yet,' Jess told her. 'We'll need to give it a lot more thought; see what Dad says.'

'Couldn't I . . . couldn't I keep it?'

Jess combed her hair off her brow with her fingers distractedly. 'I don't know if that'll be possible, love. We have to do what's best for you and the baby. You're only fifteen, still a child. You'll find it very hard if you do keep it.' Jess wanted her to be prepared. 'It's a huge responsibility for someone of your age and you'll have to grow a good few extra skins because you'll get abuse from all sides. And the gossip will be the least of your worries. There'll be no going out just when you feel like it to have fun. It'll be your baby, your responsibility. You'll have to look after it and bring it up.'

Libby looked desolate.

'But I'll be there for you,' added Jess. 'I'm marrying Bruce but I'll still be around.'

'Even after the way I've treated you?'

'Yes, even after all of that. You're my sister and I love you. I'll never desert you, I promise you that.'

'Oh, Jess, that means so much to me,' the girl cried, throwing her arms around her sister and hugging her. 'I can cope with anything if I've got you on my side. And I know I don't deserve it.'

Jess was crying too as she held her sister's thin body in her arms. The relief of being on good terms with Libby again was so intense it made her feel physically weak. But there were enormous problems ahead.

'We'll have to see what Dad thinks is the best to do,' she mentioned when they were both more composed.

'Dad,' said Libby, making a face. 'Oh God, Jess. He's gonna kill me.'

'It'll be the boy who did it he'll want to kill,' corrected her sister. 'He'll be after him with murder in his heart.'

Seeing Libby's worried reaction, Babs made a swift intervention. 'Your dad can't go after him if you're not going to tell him who the boy is, can he?' she pointed out.

'Whatever happens about that, you'd better brace yourself for a trouncing,' Jess told Libby. 'To say he'll be upset is an understatement. But he has to be told and there's no time like the present.'

'Good luck,' said Babs as the sisters got up to leave.

'She's going to need plenty of that,' replied Jess, putting a comforting arm around Libby. 'But I'll be with her, every step of the way.'

'I'll ask you again,' ranted the devastated Charlie at his younger daughter. 'What's this boy's name? I'll break every bone in his body. There won't be a doctor alive who can put him right when I've finished with him.'

'I can't tell you, Dad.'

'You can and you bloody well will.'

'And have you go chasing after him and get yourself hurt?' she said, her eyes raw and swollen from fresh tears. 'He's young and strong and probably wouldn't think twice about having a pop at you. He could seriously injure you if you try to make trouble for him.'

'I'm not exactly in my dotage, you know,' he pointed out. 'I can still give some whippersnapper whose done wrong by my daughter a run for his money.'

'I'm not telling you his name and you can't make me,' she insisted.

'Oh, I see,' he ground out. 'So I'm told that my daughter is pregnant by some dirty little yob and I'm supposed to just sit back and do nothing.' He puffed out his lips, shaking his head. 'I don't know what you take me for but you've got me all wrong.'

'Be realistic, Dad,' put in Jess. 'Even if Libby were to tell us who he is, he'll only make things worse for her if he turns nasty. He'll defend himself by telling lies about her to other people as well as to us, and she's going to have enough to cope with, without having everyone thinking she's been sleeping around.'

'Jess is right, Charlie,' supported Hilda.

There were only the four of them in the room. The boys had been sent upstairs and Bruce had made a diplomatic exit at Jess's request. She'd thought it best for everyone at this emotional stage. They would all be told the full story later. Charlie's reaction to the news had been predictably explosive. But his rage was directed almost entirely towards the boy. His temper was frayed with Libby now because of her refusal to give him a name.

'So you've brought disgrace on the family and you won't even tell me who did it.' His voice was breaking. 'It isn't good enough, Libby. I'm your father; I do have certain rights.'

309

Hilda looked at the sisters. 'Look, why don't you girls go up to your bedroom for a little while?' she suggested. 'Leave your dad and me alone for a few minutes.'

Catching the message in her eyes, Jess said, 'Yeah. OK. Come on, Libs,' and they left the room.

'If it isn't one damned problem it's another in this family since Joy died,' complained Charlie, pacing up and down. 'But this one really takes the biscuit. God knows how we're going to get through it.' He stopped and looked at Hilda. 'What a family to marry into, eh? I'll understand if you want to change your mind.'

'You know me better than that, Charlie,' she admonished. 'I agree we have a major crisis on our hands, but it isn't the end of the world. Your daughter is in trouble and it's up to us to stand by her and give her our support.'

'Which is what I'm trying to do,' he snapped. 'But how can I if she won't tell me who did it?'

'Chasing after the boy won't help anybody,' Hilda wisely pointed out. 'The sort of lad who would do that to a girl in a back alley isn't the sort to want to take responsibility for the consequences. It'll just make things worse for Libby.'

Charlie put his hand to his heart. 'It hurts here, Hilda,' he said, tears running down his face. 'Not for me but for her. To think of my little girl having some lout take advantage of her . . . I'll kill him if I ever get hold of him. I'll kill him . . . I swear I will.'

'It's just as well she isn't going to tell you who he is then, isn't it?' she told him in her down-to-earth way. 'About the last thing we need is you up on a murder charge.'

'But what are we going to do, Hilda?' he asked, clutching his head in despair. 'She's fifteen years old and in the family way. God Almighty!'

Hilda put her comforting arms around him. 'We're going to help her through it, that's what we're going to do,' she told him softly. 'All of us. We're going to talk it through and see what best can be done. It'll take more than an unexpected pregnancy to get the Mollitts down.'

He mopped his face with a hanky, managing a smile. 'You're a good sort,' he praised her. 'Always so strong.'

'I've got to be,' she grinned. 'I'm going to be one of the Mollitts soon and they've no time for quitters.'

'I'm so lucky to have you by my side at a time like this,' he said. 'And I know Joy will be glad too – wherever she is.'

Hilda bit back the rising tide of emotion because she needed to stay in control for him as well as Libby. 'I think so too.' She cleared her throat. 'But now I think you should have a few minutes on your own with Libby,' she suggested. 'I'll go and make some tea and leave you alone. I'll give her a call on my way to the kitchen.'

When Libby came into the room, looking pale and uncertain, Charlie opened his arms to her and she rushed into them. Words weren't necessary. They both knew that whatever horrors lay ahead, it was going to be all right between father and daughter.

A few days later, Hilda called on a neighbour.

'Oh, it's you,' greeted Ada with an enquiring look. 'Come in.'

'No, I won't thanks,' said Hilda. 'I'll only be a minute.'

'Please yourself.' Ada folded her arms and stood in the doorway, waiting.

'I've called because there's something I want you to know and I'd sooner you heard it from me.'

Ada's eyes lit with interest. 'Oh, yeah?' she said.

'Charlie Mollitt and I are getting married soon,' came Hilda's proud announcement.

The other woman's mouth fell open. She hadn't expected anything as juicy as this and couldn't wait to spread the word. At their age, really . . .

'Aren't you going to congratulate me?' asked Hilda.

'Well, yeah, of course,' said Ada grudgingly. 'I hope you'll be very happy.'

'Thank you. I'm sure we will.' Hilda was about to come to the main purpose of her visit. She knew that Ada was going to have an absolute field day when the news broke about Libby. Gossiping was food and drink to Ada and she would never change. 'I just want to remind you that I'll be one of the family, so please don't bad-mouth the Mollitts to me – not ever again.'

'Well, really . . .' objected the startled Ada.

'I mean it, Ada,' Hilda went on, meeting the other woman's eyes. 'If I hear that tongue of yours wagging about my new family, you'll live to regret it.'

'I've got better things to do with my time . . .'

'I'm glad about that,' said Hilda evenly, 'because I don't want to fall out with a neighbour. So, now that we understand each other, I'll say cheerio.'

'Ta-ta.'

Hilda walked down the path, knowing that the whole neighbourhood would know about her and Charlie's forthcoming nuptials by the end of the day. You didn't need to make an official announcement when you had Ada as a neighbour.

One winter Saturday evening just over two years later, there was a gathering around the television set in the Mollitts' living room. The family had expanded and now included Jess's husband, Bruce, Charlie's wife, Hilda, and Libby's son, Danny, a dark-eyed toddler, who was a year

311

and a half old. They were also joined this evening by Babs and Don, now married, and Cindy.

'There she is,' cried Jess excitedly. 'The third from the left.' She kissed the head of her nephew, who was sitting on her knee in his pyjamas, and pointed at the screen. 'Look, Danny, your mummy's on the telly.'

He squealed with delight, though he wasn't old enough to know what all the excitement was about.

'My heart's in my mouth for her,' confessed Babs. 'We know how nerve-racking live TV is, don't we, Jess?'

'Not half.'

'She seems to be doing it right, anyway,' observed Ronnie, now a smart, well-balanced, seventeen-year-old, who was proud of his twin sister, even though he would never admit to that sort of thing for fear of seeming soft.

'She wouldn't dare do otherwise with us lot watching, would she?' pointed out Todd, still a quiet, studious boy, who regularly came top of his class. 'She knows we'll murder her if she embarrasses us by messing up.'

'I'm so glad we persuaded her to audition for Burtons again,' Jess mentioned.

'Yeah,' agreed Hilda reflectively. 'She achieved her dream despite everything.'

Jess was proud of the way Libby had coped with her difficult situation. It had been extremely hard-going and there had been a good few tears and tempers along the way. But, overall, she'd been brilliant, and had surprised them all by knuckling down and getting on with things. After her condition became common knowledge in the family and she'd accepted her responsibility, she'd seemed to mature almost overnight. She'd held her head high throughout the pregnancy and introduced her son to the community with pride, refusing to allow the Ada Pickleses of this world to upset her.

Determined to provide for her little one, she'd stayed on at the factory for as long as she could before the birth and worked an evening shift after his arrival, with grandparents on hand to babysit.

It was Jess's idea for her to try again for a place in the Burton Girls, having already persuaded her to go back to dance lessons as a break from domesticity. Fortunately the rules at Burtons had become more relaxed towards the end of the decade, the issue forced by the changing attitude of women generally, and the new breed of much more outspoken Burton recruits. So the fact that Libby was an unmarried mother hadn't spoiled her chances.

She'd proved to them all that she had backbone and was prepared to live with her unfulfilled dream. But Jess saw no reason why she should waste her considerable talent because of one unfortunate lapse, especially as Hilda was happy to look after Danny while Libby was out working, with back-up support from Jess and Babs when they weren't on duty at their own jobs. After all, if Libby didn't do this while she was young her chance would be gone for ever.

She'd taken some coaxing; mostly because she was worried about leaving Danny, but also, Jess suspected, because she was afraid of failing a second time. But you only had to look at the television screen to see that her fears were unfounded and everyone in this room was delighted that her lifelong dream had come true. More than just personal achievement, she was earning a decent wage so was able to meet her financial commitments to her child.

She lived at home when she was working in London but sometimes had to go away to work, as Jess and Babs had before her. Danny was Libby's son but he was also a family child, adored by them all. When his mother wasn't around there was no shortage of people willing to stand in for her. Most girls in her position wouldn't be so fortunate, Jess knew that, and thanked God that the family had been there for Libby.

Looking back over the past two years, Jess could see that there had been many changes. She and Bruce had married and now lived in a small house near Churchfields. Bruce hadn't been able to pull out of the sale of his shop but took over another one that became vacant in the Broadway soon after and ran his menswear business from there, with Ronnie as his assistant.

Don and Babs were settled in the flat over Dean's Stores with Cindy, who would be three next spring. As for Hilda, she had already been so deeply involved with the family over a long period, she'd slipped into the role of Charlie's wife as though born for it and without ever trying to replace their mother.

Jess was recalled to the present by Bruce, who was saying, 'Seeing your sister on stage, I suppose you must wish you were there with her, eh, Jess?'

Once that would have been true but now she was happy with her life as it was, being a wife to Bruce, helping her dad in the shop and running her dance school.

'No I don't,' she told him. 'I adored every moment while I was doing it and I wouldn't have missed it for the world but I wouldn't want to go back.'

'Nor me,' added Babs, kissing the golden head of her daughter, who was sitting on her lap, and smiling at Don next to her. 'I'm very happy with my lot.'

'As long as I can keep my hand in by running my classes, I'm happy,' said Jess, squeezing Bruce's hand.

The dancers high-kicked off the stage to loud applause and Ronnie stood up. 'Right, now that I've seen my skin and blister on the telly, I'm off out with my mates to a dance.' Doughnut had been sitting at his feet and went to follow him. Ronnie got down on his haunches and stroked his

313

head gently. 'No, you can't come with me this time, boy, because dogs aren't allowed in dance halls. You stay here with the others and I'll see you later.'

'Don't be too late home, now,' warned his father, on his way to the kitchen to get them all drinks, followed by Hilda, who had made sandwiches earlier.

'I'm not a kid, Dad,' Ronnie reminded him, striding towards the door, looking smart in a fashionable suit. 'See you.'

Todd headed for the kitchen to investigate the food situation with Doughnut at his heels. The two couples sat chatting at ease with each other, earlier complications assigned to the past.

Still in reflective mood, Jess found herself looking further back. All families had trouble and heartache, and the Mollitts had had their share since Mum died. There had been crises, rows and seemingly irreconcilable differences. Each one's own personal traumas had touched the lives of them all and they had all shared the pain of losing a loved one. At times there had seemed to be no end to it.

But they'd taken the knocks and emerged from the battles as a unit, still friends – well, most of the time, anyway. There would doubtless be other dramas and new disagreements at some time in the future, as was the nature of human existence. But Jess knew that they would surmount whatever problems came because the spirit her much-loved mother had instilled into this family lived on.

CAVAN COUNTY LIBRARY

314